HOME*town*ADVANTAGE

AK LANDOW AUTHOR

COPYRIGHT

Home Town Advantage

Copyright © 2025 by Author AK Landow, LLC

All rights reserved.

No part of this book may be reproduced in any form or by any electronic or mechanical means, including information storage and retrieval systems, without written permission from the author, except for the use of brief quotations in a book review.

Published by Author AK Landow, LLC

ISBN: 978-1-962575-26-3

Edited and Proofread By: Chrisandra's Corrections

Cover Design & Illustration By: K.B. Designs

❀ Formatted with Vellum

DEDICATION

To all the amazing women in my life who support me. It doesn't come from all the obvious places. Sometimes it comes from the unexpected ones. It makes it that much more special. From the bottom of my heart, thank you.

"All you've got to do is dream… and believe.
And work your butt off to get there."
~Caitlin Clark

BEAVERS

#8 KENNEDY JEFFRIES
#11 PALMER PAYNE
#18 LAYLA LADRÓN
#22 SULLEY O'SHEA
#44 SHAY WALKER

MEET THE BEAVERS

MEET THE CAMELS

CAMELS

#6 PRESLEY LADRÓN
#19 VANCE MCCAFFREY
#30 CHAMP WILLIAMSON
#88 DAYLEN HUMBLECUT
#97 BEAU FUDD

PROLOGUE

SULLEY

"Momma, I'm about to lose reception. You know how it is up in the mountains. Hopefully this will be an easy fix, and I'll be back home before the storm gets too heavy."

Her voice is laced with a hint of paranoia, which has only gotten worse in the past few years. "Sweetie, I think this snowstorm is coming in faster than was forecasted. Turn around and come home." With a shaky tone, she adds, "Please."

She's not wrong. The snow wasn't supposed to start for another two hours, but it's coming down so hard now I can barely see out my windshield, and I'm still thirty minutes away from my destination.

I hate to disappoint her, but this is important to me. I choke back the tears as I whisper, "It's all we have left of him. I need to try."

She's silent, no doubt stifling her own emotions. It's been several years since my brother, Finn, passed, but it never gets easier.

I'm on my way to his cabin in the secluded Montana mountains, over an hour from my parents' house. This place was his baby. For a few hopeful months, we thought he left behind an actual baby. Instead, we had our hearts broken all over again.

An hour ago, we received an alert that the power in the cabin went out, and the temperature in the house was rapidly dropping. That means that the backup generator never kicked on. My father has been a heating and air conditioning repairman for thirty years. He's out on emergency calls for people who fear losing heat ahead of the supposed storm of the century. He couldn't come up here to a cabin over an hour out of town with no inhabitants. Keeping people safe is his priority. Mine is safeguarding the one thing we have left of my brother. The place where he dreamed of spending time with his family one day, only to have his dreams torn away by a roadside bombing overseas.

If the generator doesn't work and the cabin loses too much heat, the water in the pipes will freeze, causing them to split and eventually thaw and flood the place. I won't let that happen. He left the cabin to me for my future family to enjoy, and no matter what, I will make sure it's taken care of. I spent enough afterschool hours and summer days helping my father to be able to fix a few minor kinks in a generator.

My mother whispers back. "Please be safe. You're all I have left. I love you, Sulley."

"I love you too, Momma." It's silent. "Momma? Momma?"

No answer. I must have lost her. There's no reception up here. It's one of the things my brother loved the most. It was a place to unplug. To get away from the craziness and connect with people more intimately. That's the kind of guy he was. The kind who always made you feel like you had all his attention. The kind who, despite our eight-year age difference, included me in everything. He came to every basketball game of mine until the day he deployed. And when he came home to visit, we'd shoot hoops for hours. He even surprised me on my senior night in high school by showing up in the gymnasium. He was the first person to believe I'd be a basketball superstar. I know I wouldn't be a professional basketball player if it weren't for him pushing me when he was alive. Even in death, I can still hear his voice inside my head, encouraging me when I need it the most.

By the time I reach the cabin, there is over a foot of snow on the ground. Wow, this came in super-fast. I better fix the generator. I might have to ride out the storm up here, and the last thing I want is to freeze to death while doing it. Perhaps I shouldn't have come up, but I couldn't bear the thought of losing the last truly special possession of his I have.

I take in the majestic wood cabin my brother and his then-best friend, Vance McCaffrey, spent two years building. My brother was sixteen when my grandfather died and left him the land. Finn had worked construction jobs for the previous three years and used that money and skill to build this place. It was his pride and joy. Every spare second he had was spent up here working on making it everything he had dreamed of.

Finn designed this cabin. Our family has very little money. He enlisted with hopes of saving enough to enroll in college when he got out so he could study to become an architect. When he died at only twenty-six years old, he was in his final deployment.

Vance was our high school's star quarterback and the golden boy of our town. Everyone worshiped him, including me. He was my first crush before I truly knew the term crush.

He and Finn were inseparable. Even when Finn decided to enlist and Vance got a college scholarship, their friendship never waned. If anything, it grew stronger. They were like brothers, which is why I'll never truly understand why Vance did what he did.

I hadn't spoken to Vance in years, but now we play in the same city and can't seem to avoid running into each other. He's the star quarterback of the Philadelphia Camels. I play for the Philadelphia Beavers, a new professional women's basketball team.

For my first season, I rented a small apartment with a teammate as I learned about Philly, not wanting to buy anything quite yet. I went straight from college ball to the pros without a minute to catch my breath.

But I'm committed to my new team and my new city. I just bought a small walk-up brownstone. I'm very proud of that fact. While my salary as a professional athlete didn't quite pay for it, the fact that I've somehow become the face of women's basketball did. I have new endorsement offers every day. In fact, I owe a call to my agent, Tanner Montgomery, to let him know which new endorsement opportunities I'm interested in accepting.

I came home for the holidays to spend quality time with my family before embarking on the adventure of a lifetime. However, I ended up staying a few more weeks because this year's holidays were extremely difficult for my mother, and I wanted to spend a little extra time with her before I officially moved to Philly.

I pull the hood of my bulky jacket over my hat-covered head and take a huge breath. You've got this, Sulley.

I slip into my gloves before opening the car door. I'm immediately hit with a gust of ice-cold air. Holy crap, it's cold, well below freezing temperatures.

As I approach the cabin, I look down at the doormat, remembering when Finn bought it. It reads, *"Nice Underwear."* He thought it was the funniest doormat he had ever seen.

When I step inside, I realize it's nearly as cold in here as it is outside. Shit. I need to move quickly.

Making my way to the back door, I open it, step back outside, and locate the snow-covered generator. With a nasty chill running through my body, I sweep away the snow on top and pull a few of my father's tools from my bag. I'm not sure which, if any, I'll need.

I run through the list I know by heart. First, you check the fuel lines. They look good. The levers are in the proper position. Then, I open the panel and check the wiring. I don't see anything loose. Damn, I was hoping this would be a quick fix.

The snow and wind start to pick up. There's no chance of my making it home. There's no doubt in my mind now; I'll be riding out this storm up here alone. My poor mother is going to be freaking out.

I check a few more things. The only thing left I can think of is that the triggering sensor isn't calibrated properly. Sure enough, when I flick the manual override a few times, the generator kicks on. Phew.

The place will take several hours to heat up, but at least it's moving in the right direction. Hopefully the pipes will remain in good shape until then.

I should go inside and build a fire. It will help move things along and will keep me warm while I wait. There's always a pile of wood at the ready by the fireplace. That was one of my brother's steadfast rules. Always have dry wood prepared. Yep, he was a Boy Scout through and through.

After securing the tools, I head back inside and remove my shoes. I was out back for a total of seven minutes and was wearing heavy snow boots, yet my toes are practically numb. I hope no one has to be outside in this weather. I don't think they could survive more than twenty to thirty minutes.

Using my Girl Scout skills, I build a roaring fire in no time. As soon as it's good to go, I turn on the sink. The water spits a bit, but it does eventually pour out as it's supposed to. That bodes well for the pipes.

I check on a few things in the three bedrooms and the faucets in the two bathrooms. There's not much here, but everything seems to be in working order.

I'm making my way back toward the fire when suddenly the front door bursts open with a loud thud, and a snow-covered male body collapses inside and to the floor, facedown.

I run to him and find him shaking uncontrollably. Falling to my knees, I ask, "Are you okay?" I poke his body with my finger when I don't get an answer. "Sir, are you okay?"

I can hear the sound of teeth chattering. Slowly turning over, the man stutters out, "C...c...c...cold."

Once he's face up, I suck in a breath and yell out, "Vance? What are you doing here?"

"W...w...worried. Y...y...y...you..."

His eyelids flutter a few times before his eyeballs roll to the back of his head and he passes out. At least, I hope he's only passed out.

After checking his pulse and confirming he's alive, I notice he's soaking wet. His overgrown, dark brown hair is covered in ice. I look out the door and don't see his truck. How did he get here? What the hell was he doing out in this storm?

He's not wearing gloves. His fingers are white. His body is cold. I'm not a doctor, but I know he's in the early stages of hypothermia.

After closing the door, I try to shake him awake. "Vance! Vance! Wake up!"

His eyes blink open to a semi-conscious state. They're glazed over, but open.

"Can you get over to the fire? I can't carry you." The guy is six feet five inches and must weigh nearly two hundred and fifty pounds. Three hundred while soaking wet like this.

He wordlessly crawls, more like rolls, inch by slow inch, toward the fire. He's still shaking. I need to get him out of these wet clothes.

As soon as he gets close to the fire, he passes out again. At least he's in front of the heat now.

It takes me a good fifteen minutes, but I peel his wet clothes off him until he's in his boxer briefs. Fortunately, those are dry. He was only wearing a T-shirt under his jacket. Was he insane going out in this weather dressed like this?

I run around and grab as many blankets as I can find, and then lay his clothes close to the fire so they can dry. Unfortunately, there are no clothes in this cabin. Besides the few well-worn sweatshirts I kept for myself, we donated all my brother's belongings after he passed.

Vance is unconscious but still shaking. His toes and fingers are starting to turn blue and feel like icicles. The fire is warm, but the temperature in here has only risen a few degrees. I know he's in real danger.

Shit. I've never wished more that I hadn't gone to Girl Scouts because I know what I have to do.

I look up to the ceiling and offer a silent apology to my brother before removing my clothes until I'm in only a bra and panties. Sliding under the blankets with Vance, I wrap him in my arms to give him as much of my body heat as I can.

Holy crap, he feels like a block of ice. His body temperature must be dangerously low.

I hold him tight to the warmth of my body and rub my hands all over him. He's all muscle. He was always built, but never like this. Holy hell.

He starts mumbling, incoherently at first, but at some point, I can make out a few words.

"Not...think...I wanted to..."

Huh? I think he's hallucinating.

I lay there in front of the fire with my arms wrapped around him, hoping to feel the iciness of his body begin to thaw. It takes a little time, but eventually it does. In fact, it gets so warm and cozy that eventually I doze off with him.

I'M AWAKENED by lips moving over my neck and something very long and hard between my legs. Blinking my eyes open, I see Vance's piercing green ones staring at me.

I fell asleep with my arms around him, but now his surround me, and he's on top of me.

He rubs his thumb along my cheek and whispers, "Your eyes look so blue right now. You're beautiful, Sullivan Aisling."

I'd like to say I immediately push him away and kick him in the balls for daring to say that to me after all he's done. But I don't. I simply stare into the most gorgeous face ever created. The one I spent a lifetime dreaming about.

Years of fantasies are trickling through my head when Vance McCaffrey, the man I've hated for years, the man who tried to destroy my family, the man who betrayed my brother, the man who nearly derailed my career, does the worst thing possible.

He kisses me.

ONE

EIGHT MONTHS AGO ~ DRAFT DAY

VANCE

"You're sweating like a whore in church, man. Chill the fuck out. Everything will be okay." Daylen reaches into a bowl and grabs a celery stick. He's always got celery sticks around and eats them like normal people eat M&Ms or a bag of chips.

I turn on my sofa and scowl at my closest friend, Daylen Humblecut. He and I have played football together for nearly ten years on the Philly Camels. I'm the quarterback, and he's the tight end who's my go-to man in all big situations. Our personalities might be night and day, but we have an on-field chemistry that can't be manufactured. It's special.

I take in his appearance. He's even larger and taller than I am, and I'm a huge man. Despite his size, he's the biggest marshmallow on the planet. He's always happy and full of silliness. I'm the opposite, taking things too seriously and rarely seen with a smile on my face. It's only gotten worse for me through the years, especially the last five.

Daylen recently shaved his blond hair short, but it's already grown at least an inch this week. He often messes with both the hair on his head and his facial hair. In fact, he's currently sporting a bizarre mustache. "Why do you look like Rollie Fingers right now?"

Rollie Fingers was a famous baseball player in the seventies who was famous for his handlebar mustache that looked like he twisted and curled the ends with his fingers.

He throws his head back and booms out his famous house-shaking laugh. "Oh shit, that's funny. Kam called me Captain Lou Albano the other day when I still had the goatee decorated with rubber bands." Captain Lou is an old-school professional wrestler.

I can't help but chuckle. Kamryn Hart is a professional soft-ball player in Philly. She's been dating our buddy, Cheetah, for a few months. He's a professional baseball player. Kam is a riot. Besides my firecracker of a grandmother, Kam and Daylen tend to be the only people who can make me smile with regularity.

Running my fingers through my wavy, overgrown hair, I blow out a long breath and nod toward the television. "If the Beavers draft Sulley, shit is going to get weird for me."

Daylen and my agent, Tanner Montgomery, are the only two friends who know my full history. It's something I've miraculously managed to keep under wraps for years.

I gave Tanner my blessing to pursue Sulley as a client, and he's now her agent. In some small way, this is how I can keep my promise to her brother, Finn, to always look out for her. There are a lot of shady agents out there. Tanner is one of the best men I know. He'll make sure no one takes advantage of that big, innocent heart of hers.

Daylen's smile fades, and he pats my back. "I know, man.

It's not ideal, but Philly is a big city. I doubt you'll have to see her much, if at all."

Seeing my childhood best friend's little sister on a regular basis would be crazy for me on about a thousand different levels. I've known Sullivan Aisling O'Shea her entire twenty-three years, but I remember the first time I truly *saw* her.

It was also the last time I saw Finn. The last time things were good in my life.

FIVE YEARS AGO

I pull my old beat-up pickup truck, the one I still keep at my parents' house in my hometown, into the small airstrip at the Helena Airport. Finn is due to land any minute now.

Nearly eight years ago, when we were eighteen, he enlisted in the Marines. That's what most of the boys in our hometown do if they don't have a family ranch. They enlist. A few lucky ones, like me, get college scholarships to play sports, but those without a working family ranch answer the call of duty. It's an old-school town full of cowboys and blue-collar workers. No one can afford to go to college without significant financial assistance.

After I signed a big contract last year, I started funding college scholarships for the top ten students in my high school's graduating class. I wanted to encourage the kids to work hard. My annual donation is technically anonymous, but everyone knows where it comes from. I'm the only person from this town to ever make six figures, let alone the eight I'm currently being paid to throw a pigskin ball.

When we were twenty-two, Finn was up for re-enlistment. I had just signed a small rookie contract, but I offered to pay for him to go to college if he didn't re-enlist. He was too proud and declined my offer. His second and final deployment is almost over. Even if he has the money saved, this time, I'm going to insist he let me pay for him to go to college. All he ever talked about when we were kids was becoming an architect. He's been drawing *Finn's Fantastic Designs* for as long as I can remember. That's how he started signing his drawings when we were in kindergarten, and it stuck. All his designs have that at the bottom, but the cabin he designed and we built in high school was his pride and joy. The days and nights working with him to help make his dream cabin become a reality are some of my best teenage memories. Watching his drawings from a notepad turn into a home truly blew my mind. He's so talented. It's time for his dream of being a real architect to become a reality. I can't wait to be his first client.

I exit my truck as soon as I see him appear on the airplane steps. With a huge smile, I shout, "Look at Sergeant O'Shea. Fucking handsome little devil." He's six feet, one inch, which isn't small, but it's a lot smaller than me, and I've always loved giving him shit about it.

As soon as his eyes find me, I see his larger-than-life grin. It's been a long time since he's been home. Years. He looks a little worn but still has his Irish good looks with fair skin, light hair, and blue eyes.

In his uniform, holding himself with perfect posture, he makes his way to me and we hug for the first time in over two years. I do my best to hide my emotions as I slap his back. "So fucking good to see you, brother."

He squeezes me tightly. "You too, man. Thanks for the ride."

He pulls away and peeks into the back of my truck. "Where's Maddie?"

Finn had asked me to stop by his girlfriend's house to pick her up on the way here, but not to tell her why. He wanted his last-minute short visit to be a surprise for her.

Finn and Maddie have been on and off together since junior high. He wanted to get married before his first deployment, but she told him she wanted to wait until he was done with his service, which was originally supposed to be only four years. When he didn't have enough saved for college, he re-enlisted. She was angry and temporarily broke up with him, but they rekindled things when he was last home visiting and plan to get engaged when this final deployment is over in just one more month.

"Her mom said she was at work," I lie. "You mentioned you wanted it to be a surprise, so I couldn't exactly pull her away from work without explanation."

He nods in understanding as his eyes find my backseat again. "I see you got the bouquet I requested."

"I'm a good listener." I blow him a kiss. "I love being bossed around by a big, bad, sexy Marine."

He chuckles as he lifts his wrist and looks at his watch. "I need you to get me an hour away in fifty minutes. Is your slow ass up for the challenge, nineteen?" He's called me by my number for as long as I can remember.

"Let's hit it, twenty-two." And I've always called him by his. He was a talented wide receiver in high school, not quite good enough for a college scholarship, but he was my number one target from Pop Warner ball through high school. Us throwing the ball around in the backyard until it was too dark to see was the norm throughout our early childhood.

He tugs on my hair, which I wear a lot longer than I did the last time he saw me. "I hope your long locks don't slow us down. Fucking hell, you'd be crucified by the guys in my platoon."

I chuckle as we both get into the truck, and I peel out of there as fast as I can, knowing how important it is for me to get him to our final destination.

He motions toward the cowboy boots I'm wearing. "I can't imagine you have much need for those in Philadelphia."

I shrug. "You can take the cowboy out of the small town, but you can't ever take the small town out of a real cowboy." I wink. "Besides, chicks dig the cowboy vibe I bring to the big city."

He lets out his unique Finn laugh. One I haven't been able to hear in person in a long time. For some reason, it comforts me. It makes me nostalgic for my youth.

"I guess grumpy cowboys are a big hit in the city?"

I uncharacteristically allow a small upturn in my lips. "I do alright."

"Anyone special?" he asks.

"Nope. I'm having too much fun. I'm in no rush. Not like you. Maddie will be happy that you'll finally be home for good next month."

His face twists a bit.

My shoulders fall. "What am I missing?" I suck in a breath. "Don't you fucking tell me you re-enlisted for another four years."

He shakes his head. "No, nothing like that. They've asked me to stay on an extra six months to assist in training the new recruits, but don't worry, I said no. I thought about it for a hot second. The extra money would be nice, I could buy Maddie the ring I know she wants, but I'm done. It's time for me to come home. It's time for my life to begin. One more month, and then it's civilian life for me."

I'm not sure if he's trying to convince me or himself. Either way, I sense trepidation. Without hesitation, I offer, "I'll pay for the ring. Please just come home as scheduled."

He immediately stiffens. "I'm not a fucking charity case, nineteen. Don't make me say it again."

"I know. You're my best friend, and I love you. I just want you home and safe." I give a genuine smile. "Plus, I might want to build my dream house in a few years. I need my favorite architect to get his degree so he can design it."

His shoulders relax. "I appreciate the offer, but no thanks. I have only ever asked two things of you." He holds up two fingers.

I turn my head back to the road, unable to even consider what he's implying. "Yeah, yeah. I don't want to talk about it."

He's never accepted a dime from me, but we've had many conversations over the years where he's asked that if something ever happened to him, I would always look after Sulley and Maddie. He's made me promise that to him no less than a hundred times.

Fortunately, he drops the subject and looks at his watch again. "Mom said they're announcing her at exactly seventeen-fifteen...errr...five-fifteen."

I'm going over a hundred miles per hour. I nod. "We'll make it."

At five-fourteen, we pull into the parking lot of our old high school. I speed through until we reach the gymnasium entrance, where we both quickly exit the car and run inside, leaving my truck illegally parked out front.

The gym is packed to the gills with people and the press, including ESPN cameras. Stated simply, Sulley O'Shea has put our school and our hometown on the map. We had some attention when I played here, but nothing like this. She's widely considered the best high school basketball player in the nation and got a full ride to college for next year. She had her pick of any school in the country and is headed out to a college in California. Thanks to her, the high school team is undefeated and the top seed going into the state tournament next week. Tonight is their last regular-season home game. Sulley's senior night. It took a lot of string-pulling, but Finn was granted a forty-eight-hour leave of absence to be here. She has no idea. He's surprising her.

I haven't seen Sulley in a long while. I usually spend a good portion of my off-season with my family in my childhood home, but I had a few end-of-season obligations and endorsement opportunities this year. I just got home last night in time for Finn's arrival.

They're announcing her now as her parents walk arm in

arm with her onto the court. Phew, we made it just in the nick of time.

I take in Sulley's appearance. Wow, she's gotten tall. She must be around six feet. She got more of their father's height than Finn did.

We entered the building behind them, where they couldn't see us. The announcer finds Finn and me. With a huge smile on his face, he says into the microphone, "There's an extra special someone here tonight to wish Sulley well."

Sulley's head immediately begins to swivel as she scans the crowd, and when she turns her head our way, that's when it hits me for the first time. Sullivan Aisling O'Shea is now a woman. A stunningly beautiful woman. When the fuck did that happen?

I think my jaw drops. I know my mouth goes dry. Her dark hair and peaches-and-cream skin make her blue eyes shine in a way I've never noticed before. I suppose she was always Finn's cute little sister, always hanging around, always trying to keep up with the boys. But what I'm seeing now takes my breath away.

Even in her warm-up suit, I can see curves that were never there before. What is happening? Am I a perv? She's technically an adult now, but this is little Sulley. *Not so little anymore.*

Her bright blue eyes fill with tears when she finds Finn. She instantly begins sprinting in his direction and then jumps into his waiting arms, wrapping herself around him like a koala bear. I've never been more jealous of Finn than I am right now.

I shake my head. Where the hell did that come from? It's Gully Sulley, the nickname I teasingly gave her as a little girl because she'd believe anything we'd tell her. We once told her the Wicked Witch of the West was in town looking for little girls and she needed to hide. She was missing for two days. No one could find her. The police were searching everywhere.

Once he sets her down, she turns her head and smiles at me. "Hi, Vile Vance."

I chuckle at her longtime nickname for me. "Congrats, Gully Sulley."

Her smile widens. It's spectacular.

She tugs on my hair. It makes my dick twitch in my jeans. "You look like a girl."

I wink at her. "You play like one."

She crosses her arms. "Proud of it. You should be so lucky. Maybe you guys would have won it all this year if you played like a girl."

I can't help but grin at her sass. The once insecure kid is no longer that. She's a confident woman. A *sexy* confident woman.

As she turns and walks back to center court, Finn elbows me in the stomach. "Why are you smiling so much? I didn't even know you had teeth. Don't look at my sister like that. Ever."

I touch my lips. Fuck, I'm smiling like an idiot. I quickly set my trademark scowl back into place. "I just watched a real military homecoming take place. Not on some TikTok video that makes everyone cry. I can't be happy for you?"

He runs his tongue along his top teeth. "That better be all it is."

It's a good thing he doesn't know my dick is currently pushing against my zipper.

He walks out with her to join their parents. The entire gymnasium gives him a much-deserved standing ovation. I'm so happy we made it in time. He earned this day. He spent countless hours with Sulley in their driveway helping her learn how to play ball. I can't think of the O'Shea house without remembering the thudding sound of a basketball bouncing in the driveway and Finn and Sulley out there practicing.

I envy their close relationship. Finn is the closest thing I have to a sibling. My heart swells with joy as I see how happy he and Sulley are that he's home today to share in her big milestone. I'm grateful I was able to be here to witness it.

The game eventually begins. I sit with Finn and his family as we watch Sulley score fifty-three points en route to demolishing their opponent. She's a phenom. There's no doubt about it.

I also happen to notice she's wearing number nineteen, just like me. I wonder if it's a coincidence.

I remember this trip home fondly because it was probably the last time I was truly happy. The last time I didn't feel the weight of the world on my shoulders. The last time I could show my face in my hometown. The last time I saw my best friend, Finn O'Shea.

TWO

DRAFT DAY

SULLEY

The league commissioner stands at the podium on the big stage, flanked by cameras and oversized screens. I sit in the front row of the auditorium, holding hands with my parents on either side. Hundreds of people are sitting behind me, but all eyes and cameras are on me. I'm suddenly feeling relieved that I'm in a designer outfit. The first one I've ever owned. I still can't get over how many fashion designers reached out to my agent about dressing me for this day. I didn't even have to pay. I was only asked to drop her name whenever I'm being interviewed today.

I've long been projected to be the first pick in the draft, but until it happens, I can't help but be on edge. I'm finally here. In New York City for the WNBA draft. The last twenty-three years of my life play like a movie behind my eyelids. Nearly everything I've done, every sacrifice I've made, has been building toward this moment.

The middle-aged commissioner leans toward the microphone in her orange pantsuit. "With the first pick in the WNBA draft, the Philadelphia Beavers select Sullivan O'Shea, guard from the University of Montana."

It's the moment I've waited for my entire life. The one I've dreamed of since my brother gave me my first basketball at two years old. It's supposed to be the best moment of my life. I can feel my parents both squeezing my hands in happiness, but I can't help that Finn's face flashes through my mind. He should be sitting with us right now, taking it all in. I certainly wouldn't be here without him. Why do I get to realize my dream when he never got to realize his?

I silently tell him that I love him before standing to a loud sea of cheers with a huge smile on my face. I accept tearful hugs from my parents as what feels like a million flashes go off in my face, coming from all angles.

Making my way to the podium, I shake the commissioner's hand before she holds up the first-ever jersey in Philly Beavers franchise history. It's got my name and number, twenty-two, on the back.

Through high school, I was number nineteen after my child-hood crush, Vance McCaffrey, but I took my brother's number in college and plan to continue that. Nineteen is the last number on the planet I want to wear now.

The owner of the Beavers walks onto the stage to join us for a series of photos. Her name is Reagan Daulton. She's a billionaire businesswoman. She brought me to Philly recently to show me around town. Much to my surprise, I quickly learned she's very down-to-earth. In fact, she's a riot. Only in her mid-thirties with blonde-haired, blue-eyed model good looks, she's completely self-made and is probably one of the most impressive women I've ever met.

In a Beaver's pink pantsuit, she offers me a genuine smile and a big hug before holding my hand in the air for all the photographers to get their fill.

I'm immediately whisked backstage, where my new agent, Tanner Montgomery, is waiting for us. He's an attractive man in his forties with dark hair and a beard that are both a little gray.

He offers me a warm embrace. "Congrats, Sulley. It's a big day. Take it all in. Very few athletes get to live their dreams like this." He pulls back and winks at Reagan. "Better open up your checkbook. You just got yourself the biggest star on the planet."

Reagan lets out a laugh and jokes, "We'll see about that, Montgomery." She then turns to me. "We've signed a few veterans from other teams and will obviously draft a few more players today. I'm sure you're having a celebratory dinner with your family. Do you have time to meet a handful of your new teammates later tonight? Let's say nine o'clock? I'll text you the location."

I nod. "Sure. I can't wait to meet them. Thank you for the opportunity. I won't let you down."

IT'S JUST about nine when I walk into the address Reagan gave me. Much to my surprise, it's a regular New York City pub. I like that she chose this instead of a fancy place. I feel more comfortable here.

The hostess tells me that a private room has been reserved for us in the back. I take a few deep breaths to calm myself as I make my way through the restaurant.

I'm incredibly nervous for tonight. It's going to be a mix of women who I've likely never met before. I went to a college close to home. I'm moving to a new, big city, far from my hometown. I haven't had to make new friends since preschool, though I've never been one to have many female friends. It's all so overwhelming.

Reagan welcomes me and introduces me to each of the four other women sitting there. My new teammates. As a huge fan of the game, of course I know who they all are, but the only one who I've previously spoken to is Palmer Payne. She was drafted by the Beavers in the second round today. She's extremely tall and curvy, with fair skin, wavy brown hair and violet-tinted eyes always covered with glasses. She played at Texas University. They were big rivals of ours, as we were often the final two teams left standing in the NCAA Tournament.

I know from her television interviews that she's a huge introvert, so I do my best to greet her warmly. Smiling, I say, "I'm so happy you're finally on my team and I don't have to play *against* you anymore."

My words seem to put her at ease. She visibly relaxes as she fixes her glasses and nods in agreement. "I was thinking the exact same thing."

The other three women sitting at the table have been in the league for years. As a new team, the Beavers were given the opportunity to steal one player from every team in the league. Teams were allowed to protect five players from their rosters, but any other player from each team was fair game.

I first notice Shay Walker, who was previously with the LA team. She's been in the league for eight or nine years. She has mocha-colored skin, dark hair, and big brown eyes. Having a veteran power forward like her will be invaluable.

I then notice Layla Ladrón. Layla has been a guard in the league for five or six years. Her husband plays for the Philly Camels. It makes sense that she'd be picked up by the Beavers, reuniting her with her husband. She's an attractive Latina woman with brown hair and eyes. I think she recently had a baby.

Finally, I see Kennedy Jeffries, also known as the black widow of women's basketball. She was a senior in college during my freshman year. We played against her team twice. She has a reputation for having a ton of edge both on and off the court. She's beautiful, with light skin, jet black hair, and green eyes, but rarely, if ever, is she seen with a smile. For the past three years, she's played for the pro team out of New York City and has been suspended a handful of times for dirty play. I suppose it's better to have her on our team than to have to play against her. I suffered a few hard elbows from her during those games my freshman year.

After we place our drink orders, Reagan clears her throat. "Ladies, thanks for being here. I'm truly excited to have you all on the first team of this new franchise."

With a mischievous smirk, Kennedy asks, "Why did you name the team the Beavers? Are you into beavers like Shay?"

Shay rolls her eyes and gives Kennedy the middle finger. I guess there's no love lost between those two.

Without an ounce of shame, Reagan responds, "Personally, I'm more into snakes; that's why I named the softball team the Anacondas."

Reagan started a new professional softball team in Philadelphia last year, the Philly Anacondas. When I visited recently, I met a handful of the players. They were incredibly welcoming, and I hope we can become friends when I move to town.

She continues, "But if you're into beavers, then power to you. I think beavers pair nicely with anacondas, but beavers pair well together too. Whatever tickles your oyster or creams your Twinkie is fine by me."

Palmer practically chokes on her drink while the rest of us can't help but laugh. It kind of breaks the palpable tension in the room.

Reagan smiles through it all, completely unruffled by Kennedy's clear attempt to rock the boat. "As I was saying, I'm excited to have you all. I will be publicly naming the head coach tomorrow, but I trust I can confide in all of you that it's Lakshmi Ganjam."

We all perk up at that bit of news. Lakshmi Ganjam is one of the biggest names in basketball. A legend. She coached the Olympic team to a gold medal last year.

Before she leaves, Reagan tells us to have a good time and that the drinks are all on her for the night. She strongly encourages us to get to know each other as we will be teammates for the foreseeable future.

Once she's gone, Kennedy glares at me. "Well, Queen Sullivan O'Shea. We were all dragged here kicking and screaming to roll out the red carpet for you. I imagine we'll be doing that all season. How lucky for us," she says sarcastically. "What is it that the queen would like to talk about?"

My shoulders fall at her tone toward me. I was hoping for a fresh start. Not drama.

I wish I was the kind of woman who stood up for myself more often. I suppose I've become accustomed to taking it on the chin. Looking around the table with four faces staring at me, I only manage, "Umm…well…are you guys excited about moving to Philly?"

Kennedy scoffs. "Absolutely not. I fucking hate Philadelphia."

Layla raises an eyebrow. "Didn't you grow up in Philly? Isn't it your hometown?"

Kennedy's father is the famous Jett Jeffries. He was the quarterback for the Philly Camels for the back half of his career and then retired and became their coach shortly after the team drafted Vance.

Kennedy narrows her eyes. "No, Ms. Know-it-all. We moved there when I was a kid. New York is where I was born and where I consider my home. Where I intended to play for my entire career until a new team was formed so Sullivan could carry the new franchise on her shoulders with her shining star power."

Oh man, she hates me. I swallow, feeling so nervous and uncomfortable. "You can call me Sulley. All my friends and family do."

She glares at me. "Got it, *Sullivan*."

Layla shrugs. "I'd think you'd be happy to live closer to your family, Kennedy. I know I am. I was considering retirement until this opportunity presented itself. I asked my team to let me go.

Presley and I splitting time between Philly and Miami has been hard, and now we have a baby to consider."

Presley Ladrón is the placekicker for the Philly Camels. Layla has been playing for the team out of Miami. This move must be perfect for her.

Shay nods in agreement. "I respect that. I'm lucky that my girlfriend, Alyssa, works from home and can live wherever I do. It would be devastating to be apart from her for weeks or months at a time."

Kennedy rolls her eyes. "I would *never* live my life around someone else. Anyone who does so is nothing but a walking red flag." Her green eyes light up for the first time. "In fact, that might be a nice icebreaker for us. I did that once with a team."

I ask, "What would be a nice icebreaker?"

"Red flags," she answers. "Everyone shares their most random red flags when it comes to potential partners."

Layla smiles. "Ooh. I like this game. I'll go first. Men who wear chain necklaces are my biggest ick." She has a look of disgust on her face. "You just know that shit has been dangling on another woman. On her chest, on her face, maybe even in *other* places." She shivers. "Ugh. So gross."

We all laugh. I shake my head. "I suppose I never thought about where a man's necklace has been, but now I'll never unsee that."

Layla nods. "Right? What about you, Sulley? What's one of your red flags?"

"Hmm." I twist my lips. "Given that I grew up in a bit of a cowboy town, the most unattractive thing on a man for me is wearing sandals."

They all spit in laughter, and I smile as I continue, "I never saw one until I spent a little time on the West Coast. It was so… off-putting." I scrunch my face. "It's just so unmanly."

Shay nods in agreement. "A lot of men in LA wear sandals. I think lesbian red flags are different from hetero red flags. The most obvious one for me would be U-Haul lesbians."

Palmer asks, "What's that?"

"A lesbian who moves in with their partner quickly, like after just a few dates. It's a whole running joke in the lesbian community. We even have greeting cards with the term."

Kennedy's mouth drops in clear shock. "Really? I've never heard it."

Shay quips, "Because you move from man to man like I go through dildos. There's no way you've ever lived with a man."

Kennedy shakes her head. "Fuck no. I'm too young for that. The only thing I want is a good time. Nothing else, for now. My parents had a shitty marriage. It took way too long for them to get divorced. I'm out the second I see something I don't like. Plus, I went to Catholic school."

I raise an eyebrow at her. "What does Catholic school have to do with relationships?"

She bites back a smile before she answers, "Catholic school girls are like caged wild animals. We all leave for college and become hos."

Shay giggles. "Ah, Catholic school girls. Any hole but the holy hole."

Kennedy nods. "I definitely had friends like that in Catholic school." She looks at Palmer. "What about you, quiet one? What are your red flags?"

Palmer shuffles nervously. She's the kind of woman who I'm not sure has ever dated. I have no idea whether she's into men or women. She's attractive, but so shy and seemingly uncomfortable in her own skin.

She adjusts her glasses. "I don't know. I suppose I don't like short guys."

Kennedy shakes her head. "Six-foot-five guys are short for you. That's not really a red flag. Give us something else."

She chews on her bottom lip nervously. "Ummm...well...I'm not sure."

Kennedy rolls her eyes in obvious annoyance. "This isn't

hard. Something that turns you off that might not turn off others."

I stare at Kennedy, mustering all the strength I can to confront this intimidating woman. "Maybe she's uncomfortable answering. Leave her alone."

Palmer shakes her head. "No, no. I want to participate. I saw a guy do something a few weeks ago that was shocking. I...I suppose it could be considered a red flag."

We all lean toward her in anticipation.

"I saw a guy bite into a KitKat. Right across the four bars. There are natural breaks in a KitKat. Why would someone just bite into it? That's crazy." She seems totally appalled at the notion.

We all giggle. Even Kennedy smiles as she admits, "That was unexpected but perfect, Palmer. I accept your answer."

Palmer has a huge grin as she straightens her shoulders a bit. "Thank you. What about you, Kennedy?" she asks.

Kennedy pulls out her phone and swipes a few times. "I keep a running list in my notes. I have hundreds of them. Hmm. Let me find a good one." She swipes a few more times. "Ooh. This one is good. Men who know every word to the rap verse from 'Waterfalls' by TLC. The chorus is fine, but the rap verse is a huge red flag. There's no legitimate reason for a man to know that."

We all burst into hysterical laughter. I can't help but beg, "Please give us more from your list."

With a bemused expression on her face, she looks down at her phone and begins to scroll. "I seriously have over a hundred. Men who use Androids, men who take a lot of selfies, and men who call you *baby* on the first date. They are all non-starters for me. Oh, and men who love to tell me how they were four-year varsity athletes in high school. I'm like, *bitch, I was a Division One All-American athlete and am now a professional athlete, but please tell me about your junior year of high school second-team all-conference award.*" She rolls her eyes. "You ladies know who I'm talking about. Even you, Shay."

We all nod in agreement, Shay included. That's so true. *All* men love to boast about their childhood athletic prowess as if it remotely compares to ours.

We end up closing down the place as we drink, talk, and laugh for hours until the middle of the night. Even Kennedy warms up a bit. I think. It's hard to tell with her.

I've never had a mix of teammates like these women, but maybe it won't be so bad. I like that everyone is different but we have a common love for the sport of basketball and an understanding of the hard work and sacrifices made along the way. For the first time, I'm truly excited about my big move to Philly.

THREE

VANCE

Presley grunts as Beau easily helps him place the heavily weighted bar back in its slot on the bench in our team gym. Presley Ladrón, who we often all call Elvis for obvious reasons, is our placekicker. He's the smallest guy on the team, though he can probably out-squat nearly everyone. He's Latino, with brown hair, brown eyes, and olive skin. Beau Fudd, on the other hand, is massive. He's a defensive end who must be at least six feet, eight inches and over three hundred pounds. He could probably bench the weighted bar Presley was using with Presley still attached to it. He grew up in a military family and has always worn his dirty-blond hair buzzed short. He's a bit of a dichotomy. He's built like a beef-cake but happens to be highly intelligent. He's been working toward his PhD while playing ball. He believes there's a science to building muscles and is always sharing things with us to help us along.

Presley looks at both Beau and me. "Are you guys good to come out tonight? Layla was pissed at me this morning when I told her I hadn't asked you yet."

Beau and I exchange knowing glances as I quip, "She's always pissed at you, Elvis."

The two of them have a love-hate relationship. The Bickersons, as I often call them, are constantly going at each other, though it's usually in Spanish so we can't understand them. Just as quickly as it starts, it turns sexually charged. Five seconds after yelling at each other, they're practically having sex in public. They give me whiplash sometimes.

He shakes his head. "Nah. Now that we permanently live in the same place, it's so much better. I think the dual residency was wearing on us. She's only gotten truly pissed at me once this week. We were having lunch at a café. I could tell she wanted a meaty burger, but she's so uptight about dropping those last few pounds of baby weight. I told her not to worry about a salad and to get the damn burger. Unfortunately, the waiter was standing there, so Layla snapped at me for being a Neanderthal and telling her what to order in front of him. I swear, women want their hair pulled, to be choked, and your handprint on their ass, but they go feral if you try to tell them what to do in public."

I chuckle. "That's true." As I do my seated, one-arm bicep curls, I add, "I feel like you were being nice by saying that."

He nods. "I know. Honestly, I was kind of annoyed at her over-the-top reaction. She realized her mistake at some point."

"Did she apologize?" I ask.

He lets out a laugh. "Women don't apologize. When they know they were in the wrong, they crawl into bed naked to gauge your level of anger." He wiggles his eyebrows up and down. "I'll never be angry enough with her to miss out on naked time with my beautiful angel. Even after all these years together, that woman still does it for me in a big way."

I'm sure it doesn't hurt that Layla is sexy as hell. I certainly wouldn't know what it's like to be with the same person for so long. I haven't had a serious relationship in years, and obviously none as serious as Presley and Layla's.

Our recently drafted rookie, wide receiver Reece Sanders, looks like he's struggling on the bench press. I'm about to go help when Champ offers his. Champ Williamson is new to our team this year. He's a running back who was recently traded to the Camels from the Wranglers out of Dallas.

He's a black man with a blond-dyed mohawk. He's built like a prototypical running back, being a little shorter with endless muscles capped off by huge quads. Despite being new in town, he's meshed right in with our group. I like him. He garners a lot of attention from women, but I'm pretty sure he's gay. I hate that he feels the need to hide it from us, but I equally don't want to push him to reveal anything he doesn't feel comfortable sharing.

As Champ moves toward the bar to help Reece, Reece quickly places it in its place and practically jumps away from Champ. "Nah, man. Don't touch me. I'm good."

Champ's jaw tightens. "No problem. Just trying to help."

What the fuck is this kid's problem?

Our coach, Jett Jeffries, is seated in the leg press machine as he pushes out hundreds of pounds. I swear the guy is stronger than most of the defensive linemen on our team. He's a retired quarterback but was one of the best in the game in his day. I know I wouldn't be half the quarterback I am today without him as my coach.

He's in his late forties, with dark hair like mine, though it has some gray in it now. Women on social media are obsessed with him. He's like a poster child for silver foxes and daddy videos. I think songs have been written about his green eyes. And when he got divorced a few years ago, he had to get security because of all the women hounding him. Nonetheless, he remained humble. In fact, he hates it when we rib him about his sex symbol status.

He assesses the situation just as I did and approaches Reece with a murderous look on his face. "Hey, rook, respect your teammates or you'll find yourself on jockstrap washing duty faster than your last time in bed with your undoubtedly paid entertainment. Do I make myself clear?"

Reece fearfully mumbles, "Y...yes, Coach."

"Good. Now get the fuck out of here. You're done for the day. No one wants to see your ugly face anymore. Don't come back again until you learn to show a little respect to your teammates, all of whom are much better and more accomplished than you."

Reece's face falls in horror as he croaks out, "Yes, Coach," before practically sprinting out of the gym.

Coach Jeffries turns to Presley and calmly asks, "How's the baby sleeping, Elvis?" He's obviously trying to change the subject to spare Champ any lingering embarrassment.

Presley shrugs. "Meh. A few good nights here and there, but mostly nights where she won't go to sleep. We sometimes have to rock her for hours."

Coach Jeffries smirks in amusement. "Your generation is soft. When my kids wouldn't go to sleep, we'd mix NyQuil in with their formula."

Presley's mouth widens. "Seriously? You drugged your kids?"

Coach waves his hands dismissively. "Oh, please. NyQuil is nothing. I called my mother when Kennedy was a baby and we couldn't get her to sleep. She said, *give her NyQuil, and if that doesn't work, I used to give you a little chloroform.*"

Presley inhales a sharp breath. "She must have been joking."

Coach shrugs. "Honestly, I'm not sure. With her generation, you never know. I think each generation tolerates a little less than the one before it. You fuckers have fancy filtered water. When I was a kid, my mother used to make me drink straight from the metal-rusted hose that had been lying in the dirt in my backyard for twenty years."

I pinch my eyebrows together. "Why didn't you at least drink from the sink?"

He scoffs. "'Cause I wasn't allowed inside the damn house until dinnertime. I was sent out after breakfast with a brown bag full of processed bologna for lunch and told not to come home until it was dark out. I didn't have a fucking water bottle full of designer five-dollar water. I didn't have a cell phone or a watch. Sundown was my time marker. Generation X. Raised on hose water and neglect. Yet here we are, still living our lives."

I bite back my smile. Coach loves to bring up Gen X as having it rough all the time. I'm not sure if he's trying to be funny or trying to make a point. Either way, we all find it wildly amusing.

Daylen walks into the gym. I look up at him and scowl. "You're late, asshole. You were supposed to be here an hour ago." We're not in season quite yet, but we're religious about our workouts. We have to be in our profession. After our time in the gym, Daylen and I always head to the field for me to throw him some passes. Now the whole day will be off. Fucker.

Coach shakes his head. "Only one time in my life was I ever late to practice. The coach made me run laps for the first half. I've never forgotten."

Daylen pinches his eyebrows together. "Running laps? What's so memorable about that?"

Coach deadpans, "My dad was the coach. He was my ride to practice. He was the reason I was late. That's how hardcore things used to be."

Daylen chuckles as he runs his fingers through his hair, which seemingly grew several inches this week. What does this guy eat that his hair grows so ridiculously fast? He wiggles his eyebrows up and down at me. "I have a good excuse. I was busy engaging in a sportsman's double."

I raise an amused eyebrow of my own. "Is that so?"

Coach Jeffries asks, "What's a sportsman's double? Two workouts in a day?"

Daylen lets out a loud laugh. "Umm, no. It's when you do a

mother and a daughter at the same time. I was at Reading Terminal Market this morning getting my favorite fruit shake when a cougar, probably around your age, Coach, maybe a little older, was eye-fucking me. She was hot as hell."

The attention of fifty players and coaches now turns to him, and he continues, "So she asked if I had ever done two generations in the same family." His eyes move to me. "You know a sportsman's double has always been on my bucket list." I do know that. "I told her I was game, assuming the younger version looked like her mom. If so, it was going to be epic. I followed her to her apartment around the corner." He scrunches his face. "But...umm...when we walked in, she yelled out, *Mom, I brought us a snack.* The twenty-five-year *older* version of my cougar walked out, not the *younger* version I assumed I'd be getting."

We all start laughing. Beau asks, "Did you turn around and walk out?"

Daylen shrugs. "Nah. I let the ladies get their kicks. It was my community service for the day. Plus, I still got to check it off my bucket list even if it wasn't exactly as I imagined." He winks. "The cougar and the granny were left very satisfied with a fun story to tell their friends."

Our collective laughs get louder and louder.

He smiles. "I even posed for pictures. In bed."

For anyone else, this story would be appalling. For my best friend, it's the regular course of business. He's so uninhibited and carefree. I wish I had a little of him in me, but he hasn't dealt with what I have for the past five years. Some days, I can barely keep my head above water as I mourn everything I lost by making the decision I did. I won't say I regret it, I don't, but it forever changed my life.

Beau crosses his meaty arms as he stares at Daylen. "I thought we were sunbathing this afternoon."

"Sunbathing?" I ask. "What the fuck?"

Beau responds, in a completely serious tone, "I like to

sunbathe naked. Exposing your testicles to UV light increases your testosterone by over two hundred percent."

Beau is very into testosterone production and its impact on building muscles.

Coach mumbles, "You've got to be fucking kidding me. What kind of bullshit is that? You pullin' my chain, Fudd?"

Beau shakes his head. "No, sir. It's not bullspit. It's science. Look it up. UV light anywhere on the body is good for testosterone production, but especially on the testicles. It's part of my training regimen. You know I take training seriously, sir."

It's true. Beau Fudd is a training machine. It's why he's built like a tank and can easily push his way through three-hundred-and-fifty-pound linemen like they're fruit flies.

And that's how, on that particular afternoon, nearly the entire Camels football team ended up sunbathing naked on our field instead of practicing.

SULLEY

Palmer's eyes move up and down my body in our new apartment. "Wow, Sulley, you look amazing."

I study myself in the mirror and take in my appearance. I'm wearing skin-tight brown leather pants with an equally tight, sequined red tank top. Running my hands down the smooth pants, I ask, "You don't think it's too much? I've never worn anything like it."

Palmer and I moved into an apartment in Philly together. It's a short-term lease that will get us through our first season. I want to learn about this city before I decide exactly where I want to buy a place. Palmer was nervous about living on her own, so I told her we could temporarily rent an apartment together as we begin to navigate a much bigger city than either of us has ever lived in before.

She shakes her head. "Not at all. You're so pretty. I'm used to seeing you in baggy basketball uniforms without makeup. Your makeup is gorgeous too. You look like a movie star."

Kennedy walks into my bedroom and interrupts, "Thank you. I can do yours too if you want. I've never seen eyes the color of yours. They're practically purple. I could make them sparkle like you wouldn't believe."

Kennedy insisted on taking me shopping today and then equally insisted on doing my makeup. I don't know what changed from the night in New York, but she's been much nicer. Almost welcoming. I obviously haven't spent a lot of time with her yet, but I think she's the kind of person who assumes the worst in people until proven otherwise. I also think she puts up a tough exterior, but she isn't as hard as she'd like people to think. I'm guessing there's more to Kennedy Jeffries than meets the eye.

She's in a barely there black skirt with an equally tiny silver tube top. She has a beautiful body and doesn't seem afraid to show it off. Her dark hair is pulled into a stylish ponytail, and her makeup looks professionally applied, making her big green eyes pop. It almost looks like they're fake, even though I know they're not.

Layla made arrangements for us all to go out tonight with her husband, Presley, and his friends. I couldn't say no. These women are my new teammates, and I need to make friends in Philly. Layla has been beyond excited about it.

I'm praying Presley isn't friends with Vance McCaffrey. I haven't seen him since the nightmare fallout the year my brother died. I know by moving to Philly it's inevitable that I'll run into him at some point, but I don't need it in week one, and I certainly don't want to sit at a table with him all night.

Palmer fixes her glasses. "Oh, I wouldn't be comfortable like that. I wouldn't look nearly as good as you and Sulley."

I shake my head. "That's not true at all."

Before I can continue, Kennedy interjects, "You know what I

read the other day? That female psychopaths are likely to go bare-faced and not wear any makeup. Is that what I'm working with, Palmer?"

I place my hand on Kennedy's shoulder. "Leave her alone. If she's not comfortable wearing makeup, power to her. She's beautiful without it."

Kennedy shrugs. "Okay, but just know that men fall in love with what they see. Women fall in love with what they hear. That's why women wear makeup and men lie."

I can't deny that men lie. I know a quarterback who does so freely.

Kennedy sighs. "What about the outfit?" Palmer is in baggy jeans and an oversized, thin sweater. "Can we put you in something a little sexier? Aren't you looking to get laid?"

Palmer's eyes nearly pop out of her head. "Umm, no. My mission is *not* to get laid tonight."

Kennedy gives a short, hard nod. "Well, then you're good to go. Mission accomplished."

So much for Kennedy being nice.

Thirty minutes later, we're walking into a club. It's called Club Liberty and is supposed to be a Philly hot spot.

The club is beautiful. It's modern but plays homage to Philly in its touches. The sleek, dark walls are covered in photos of the city. The lights are strobing, and the music is blaring.

Layla immediately comes running toward us with a huge smile on her face. She looks stunning in a short gold dress, showing off her extremely long legs, curvy hips, and full ass. You would certainly never know she recently had a baby.

She wraps her arms around me. "I'm happy you're here. We're going to have so much fun. We don't get out much anymore, but I like to come here to let loose when we do. My mom is watching the baby tonight so we can get our freak on. Right, mi amor?"

She's a little tipsy already. I love how relaxed she is.

An adorable brown-haired man I hadn't noticed smiles from

behind her as he wraps his arms around her waist and kisses her cheek. "I love it when you get freaky. Juego encendido, hermosa." *Game on, beautiful.*

She places her hands over his and leans back into him in a familiar way. "Sulley, Palmer, Kennedy, this is my short king, my husband, Presley."

His face falls. "I'm nearly six feet tall. I'm not a short king." He then playfully bites her neck.

She giggles. "You're shorter than me. That's what you get for marrying a basketball player."

He twists his lips. "Hmm. Worth it." He looks at the three of us. "Welcome to Philly. You may be the tallest friend group ever. It's a good thing all my friends are tall too." He waves his hand in invitation. "Come. We always have a private booth upstairs with security so no one bothers us." He twists his lips. "Some women go a little feral for my teammates."

We follow him up a guarded set of steps to what appears to be a balcony overlooking the dance floor. I'm silently praying one last time that his friend group doesn't include Vance.

I see a large round booth flanked by security. Sure enough, four very famous football players are sitting there with drinks in hand.

There's one that stands out to me. He always has. He's wearing his trademark jeans with a flannel top. Every other guy is dressed more fashionably, but not Vance. I can't see his shoes, but I'd bet my next endorsement deal that he's wearing cowboy boots. His ever-present frown is firmly in place. I'm sure he's as happy to see me as I am to see him.

I can feel my heart start to beat faster, like it always has when Vance McCaffrey has been near me. I hate him with every fiber of my being, but I equally can't ever forget what it felt like the first and only time he touched my body.

FIVE YEARS AGO

Today was the worst day of my life. I watched a coffin with my brother inside be lowered into the ground. I wish I didn't look. The image will forever be burned into my mind.

I don't remember the undoubtedly beautiful eulogies, as most of them came and went in a blur, just like the rest of the day. He was loved by everyone who knew him. I only remember Vance's speech, where he talked about brotherhood. Vance's mother had complications during his delivery, and she had to have a hysterectomy. He's an only child and spoke passionately about how Finn was the sibling he never had. How much he truly loved my brother. How there is now a hole in his heart that will never go away. I know the feeling.

He looked exactly like I felt. Broken.

The house has been full of people expressing their deepest sympathies. In some ways, that makes it easier. Late at night, when it gets quiet, that's when reality truly settles in.

Finn will never walk through the front door again. I'll never hear his unique laugh again, the one that would always bring a smile to anyone around. It was like Woody Woodpecker, and I loved it. I would give anything to hear it one more time. We'll never shoot hoops by the garage in the middle of the night until my mother yells at us about the noise. He'll never see me play another game of basketball. He'll never achieve his dream of being an architect. I'll never get to see a true Finn O'Shea original come to life. He designed his cabin on a torn piece of paper and couldn't do everything he wanted because of the costs. I couldn't wait to see a true architectural masterpiece, born in his brain, come to life. I manage to crack a small smile at the notion of *Finn's Fantastic Designs*, his childhood name for his countless drawings that somehow stuck.

My parents are barely holding it together, but when Maddie walked into the funeral with a visible baby bump, my mother physically collapsed. Deep sadness set in that my brother won't know his child, but it also gave us a shining glimmer of hope that we'll still have a piece of him to hold onto. I pray this baby can keep my parents going in what I know will be dark days ahead for them.

Finn last visited for my basketball senior night three months ago. Maddie already has a decent-sized belly, but I suppose some women pop early. She's super tiny, so perhaps small women show more easily.

It's late at night, and I'm sitting in the treehouse that Finn and Vance built for me when I was six. I'm on the always-present bed of blankets, hugging my knees as I look around. Every single thing in here reminds me of him, my favorite being where he carved our initials in the support beam.

There are inspirational quotes everywhere. He drew them in here before he left for his first tour. He told me to come in here when I needed a push since he wouldn't be around anymore. Now he'll never be here for me again.

I squeeze his dog tags in a tight fist. My parents let me keep them when his belongings were returned to us from the military. A matching pair that will never again be reunited with their owner. They'll be my most precious possession. I won't ever be without them again.

It sounds like the house has finally emptied, and the bevy of indistinct voices has fallen silent. I hear the familiar creaking of the treehouse ladder and then see Vance's head appear through the opening in the floor. "Mind if I keep you company?" he asks in his deep velvety voice.

I nod before he finishes his ascent into the treehouse. He looks ridiculous in here. He's such a big man. Vance was always tall, but now he's filled out as well. He's an imposingly perfect creature.

His unique Vance scent immediately fills the small space. I'd know he was in a room before I saw him. He has always smelled exactly the same. It's not cologne or anything fake. It's Vance

McCaffrey. It's woodsy, spicy, and masculine. Too bad they can't bottle it.

He sits directly across from me with his knees bent in a similar position to mine. Our shoe-covered toes are nearly touching.

"How are you holding up, Gully Sulley?"

My eyes fill with tears as I answer honestly. "Like my heart was physically ripped out of my chest. Like there's a gaping hole that will never be filled."

He blows out a long breath as his eyes brim with unshed tears. "Me too, kiddo. Me too."

I flinch at the word *kiddo* and he notices. "Sorry, it was just an expression. I know you're not a kid anymore."

I'm used to sarcastic remarks from Vance, but his red-rimmed green eyes convey nothing but sincerity. I know he's hurting as much as I am.

I croak out, "I don't know how to do life without him, Vance. He was my biggest cheerleader. He lifted me up when I was down. He told me what I needed to hear in my moments of self-doubt. He protected me. I feel so…unsafe without him."

Vance visibly swallows as he reaches for my hand. It's the first time in my life that he's ever held my hand in a tender way. Our fingers thread together perfectly. His touch warms my soul in a way I can't describe.

He squeezes it. "I know I'll never be half the man Finn was, but if you let me try, I want to be all those things for you. I promised that if something ever happened to him, I'd always look out for you and Maddie. I intend to honor that promise."

"You two talked about him dying?" I ask.

Vance licks his dry lips. "I never wanted to, but he always brought it up. *All* the time. *Every* conversation. Protecting the two of you was the most important thing in the world to him."

I bite back my tears. "Now it's three. Do you know if Maddie told him about the baby?" I hope she did. I hope he knew he was going to be a father.

He has an indecipherable look on his face. "You'd have to ask Maddie."

Maddie hasn't spent much time at the house since we got the news of Finn's death. She's barely spoken to us. It's kind of weird. You'd think she'd want to be close to us. Perhaps she's grieving in her own way.

I nod. "I just hope she lets us be close with the baby."

We've never been particularly close to her. Frankly, I never understood what my brother saw in her. He was too good for her. I hate myself for thinking that, but it's what I've always felt deep inside, not that I've ever outwardly expressed it to anyone.

He squeezes my hand again. "You should talk to her. Don't worry about money for the baby. I'll take care of all its needs."

I squeeze his hand in return. "Thank you for always being such a good friend to him. Hopefully I'll go pro in four years, and then I'll be able to support the baby too. If you can help until then, I promise to pay you back every cent."

The corner of his mouth raises slightly. "No need. You just keep your head down and play ball. I'll take care of the rest. And if you need anything at all, please don't ever hesitate to ask."

I exhale a long breath before admitting, "He left me the cabin. I'm not sure why me and not Maddie. Maybe his will is old. Maybe it was drafted when they broke up. I was thinking I should sell it and give the money to Maddie for the baby."

Vance immediately shakes his head. "Absolutely not. We both know how much he loved that place. Do *not* sell it. I told you, Maddie will be taken care of. Don't worry about that."

I nod, knowing he's right. Finn wouldn't want me to sell it. "I'm not sure I'd have the heart to do it. When the baby comes, maybe he or she can spend time there."

Vance smiles. Something I've rarely ever seen. "I think Finn would love that."

For some reason, the image of Finn's baby in Finn's house without him there sets me off into a fit of loud, uncontrollable sobs. Vance momentarily freezes before awkwardly moving his body next to mine and holding me. "Let it out, Sulley. It's okay to cry. I'm right here. I'm not going anywhere. Ever."

I let my head fall onto his chest and cry for what feels like hours until I must pass out.

When I blink my eyes open, I'm in my bed. I have no idea how I got here. Is there any chance the past week has been a nightmare?

I can feel that I'm wearing what I wore to the wake. This is real. Finn is gone.

Could Vance have carried me? I'm not a small woman. I'm six feet tall. While my future college coach wants me to put on about twenty-five pounds of muscle before I get there, I'm not light.

I realize my head is still buried in Vance's broad chest. I look up and he's staring down at me. He whispers, "Sorry. I carried you to bed, but you asked me to stay with you. And then you fell back asleep on my arm. I didn't have the heart to wake you."

I don't remember, but I feel so safe and secure in his arms. I can't help but cup his stubbled cheek with my hand. It's coarse and rugged. He's so manly. I'm used to high school boys. I've even dated a few college boys, but Vance is no boy. He's a man. The most beautiful man I've ever seen in my life.

Maybe it's the emotions of the week and the fact that he's taking such good care of me. Maybe it's the fact that I've dreamed of having Vance in my bed countless times. Maybe I just need to feel something other than heartache. I can't help but tilt my face and bring my lips to his.

I'm not sure what I intended or what I expected, but I definitely didn't expect him to return and then deepen the kiss. His lips latch onto mine just before I feel his tongue slip into my mouth. I'm enveloped in the familiar smell of Vance, and now I know how good he tastes too. I match his intensity by sliding my tongue over his and into his mouth as I kiss him with everything I have.

Every stroke of his tongue breathes warmth back into the

coldness that's consumed me since we got news of Finn. It's everything I need to feel whole again.

His hands move under my sweater and up my bare back. The sensation of Vance McCaffrey touching me like that causes an uncontrollable moan to leave my mouth. My body suddenly feels ablaze with desire.

He pulls me as close to him as possible. I feel him harden on my stomach. Up my stomach. Wow, he's big. The satisfaction I feel at knowing I made him react this way is indescribable.

I manage to roll us until I'm situated on top of him, straddling his big body. His extreme hardness is now pushing against my soft center. I can't help but grind against it.

I wish I could tear both of our pants off our bodies to feel his bare skin on mine. My panties are soaked.

His hands now roam my back freely, but it's not enough. I want more. I need more.

I break our kiss so I can sit up. With trembling fingers, I grab onto the bottom of my sweater and remove it, tossing it to the side. His heated gaze gives me the courage needed to do the same with my bra.

His green eyes are full of lust as they slowly rake over my body. This is the first time Vance has ever stared at me this way. I've always been Finn's little sister, but that's not how he's looking at me right now. Right now, he's looking at me like I'm the only woman in the world and all he wants is to tear the rest of my clothes off my body.

That thought alone makes me shiver, but when his enormous hands cup my breasts, I just about orgasm from the sensation of being touched so intimately by my dream man.

The coarse pads of his long, wide thumbs brush over my hardened nipples. He breathes, "You. Are. Perfect. Sullivan Aisling."

My hands shake as I boldly move to unbutton his shirt, slowly revealing the sexiest body in existence. Vance's dark chest hair, something I have long ached to touch, covers a broad, muscular chest. The muscles are bigger and more defined than when we were younger. His years as a professional athlete have more than paid off.

I run my fingertips over it and then down his carved abs until they gently trace the hair running from his belly button into his pants. I want to see all of this perfect creature.

His breath catches when my fingers dip just an inch or so into the waistband of his pants. I want him like I've never wanted anyone or anything.

Unable to wait a second longer, I lean back down to fuse my mouth with his again. Our bare chests touch for the first time, and it's unlike anything I've ever felt in my life. It's a level of desire and passion I've never dreamed possible.

We kiss for minutes on end. My nipples rub along his chest, causing them to harden to a near-painful level. I circle my hips over his hardness, chasing my relief. Unfortunately, we both still have pants on. Damn clothes are getting in the way.

His fingers explore every inch of the top half of my body. His hands cover so much territory. Why are giant hands so damn hot? Why is his touch affecting me in a way I've never experienced before?

I sink my fingers into his thick hair. He's grown it out over the past year, and it may be the sexiest thing I've ever seen.

I can't help but grip and tug on it. I've never been with a man whose hair is long enough to do that, but I'm loving it. It's so hot. I can tell he's enjoying it too by the sounds he's emitting. I love that I'm turning him on as much as he is me.

He pulls my hair enough so that our kiss is broken. My lips are raw from the depth of that kiss. My neck is now exposed to him.

I shiver when his teeth graze my chin and run all the way down my neck to my breasts, where he bites one of them.

I can't help the loud, "Oh god," that comes out of my mouth. His cock jerks under me. If my panties weren't flooded before, they are now.

Suddenly, I'm ravenous to have him inside me. I begin to unbuckle his belt, desperate to peel these clothes away. Just as I'm about to go for his zipper, he grabs my wrist. "Sulley, stop."

I breathlessly ask, "Why?"

He exhales a long breath before briefly closing his eyes, as if in pain. "This isn't right. I can't do this to you."

I shake my head. "I want this. I'm not inexperienced if that's what you're worried about."

He tenderly cups his palm over my cheek. "It has nothing to do with that." He then runs his fingers through his hair in obvious frustration. The same soft hair that my hands were just in. "Fuck, I hate the thought of another man touching you, but this isn't about that. Today was a horrible day. You're emotional. You're not thinking straight. I don't want to take advantage of you."

I nervously chew on my lower lip. "I'm thinking clearly. I want this, Vance. I've always wanted this with you."

His brow furrows. "What do you mean?"

"I've had a crush on you since the day I met you. That's why I always followed you guys around. You must know that."

He shakes his head. "No, I didn't." He blows out a breath. "It wasn't until three months ago that I started seeing you as a woman. Finn noticed and warned me away. He wouldn't want me to treat you like this. I...I can't do this to him." He slides out from under me, reaches for my sweater, and hands it to me. "Put it back on. We can't do this, *especially* today."

I can't help that tears spill from my eyes as the sting of rejection settles in. He pulls me close to him. "Please don't cry. I'd never want you to do something you'd regret. It's my job to protect you now. I'll do anything and everything to live up to my promise to him."

He holds me as I again sob until I pass out. This time when I wake up, he's gone.

FOUR

CLUB LIBERTY

VANCE

I'm not surprised to see Sulley walk into the club with Layla and her new teammates, but she looks surprised to see me. Maybe it's more like disappointment flashing across her gorgeous face. The last thing I want is to cause her any more pain than I already have.

I should leave. I begin to stand, but Daylen grabs my leg and quietly says, "You're not leaving. Let's rip off the Band-Aid. It's been five years, and you're both adults. She's going to be around. Learn how to coexist."

I sit back down and look at him. "If she gets emotional, I'm taking off. I don't want to hurt her."

He nods. "Fine."

"I can't watch a woman cry over me."

He deadpans, "I'm sure it happens every time you have sex with one and they're disappointed in the outcome."

I punch him in the leg before I turn back to the group of beautiful women walking toward our table.

I take in Sulley's full appearance. Her body has filled out in the past five years. She's got curves she didn't have when I last saw her in person.

I watch her on TV all the time, but she's not in a basketball uniform now. I've never seen her dressed like this or wearing any makeup. She looks like sex on a stick. I have to adjust myself to make room for the sudden swelling of my cock. It doesn't feel so great considering the sunburn I have on my balls from our team's afternoon in the sun today. What the hell was I thinking doing that?

Daylen looks down at my lap and chuckles while I subtly flip him the bird.

The group approaches with Layla and Presley leading the charge. We're introduced to the three girls, and then Presley introduces Daylen and me, along with Beau and Champ.

I shake Kennedy and Palmer's hands. Kennedy is Coach Jeffries' daughter and looks a lot like him, but I've never met her in all these years. I don't think they have a close relationship, though he doesn't reveal much about his personal life, especially since his divorce.

I then tentatively hold my hand out for Sulley. I see her visibly swallow before cautiously taking my hand. I inhale her scent. She smells so good. So...womanly and sophisticated. It's like a bed of flowers with a hint of coconut. I remember that coconut scent from the one and only time I got to hold her in my arms, touching her, kissing her.

Fuck. Stop it.

She gives me a forced smile. "Vance, it's...umm...good to see you. It's been a while."

Kennedy narrows her eyes as they toggle between us. "Do you two know each other?"

I nod. "Sulley and I are from the same hometown."

Daylen knows we need a topic change and immediately interrupts by asking the girls for their drink orders before flagging down the waitress, telling her what everyone wants and adding several appetizers to our order.

Kennedy carefully studies him and then starts laughing. He raises an eyebrow in confusion. "What's so funny?"

She has a bemused look on her face. "We've had a few conversations about red flags and, to be honest, you check a lot of those boxes."

He twists his lips and asks, "Like what?"

She answers, "You're wearing sandals and a necklace, and your cell phone is an Android."

His jaw widens. "*Those* are red flags? They're kind of petty. I bet you're one of those chicks who has a long list of red flags on her phone. A whole folder dedicated to it."

Kennedy proudly displays her phone. "You bet I do. I think everyone should, men *and* women. It reminds us of what we do and don't want in a partner."

Daylen shrugs. "That's kind of a glass-half-empty approach to dating and life in general. I don't believe in red flags. I'm a glass-half-full kind of guy. Instead of looking for red flags, I look for green ones."

She challenges, "Tell me a green flag of yours, Mr. Perfect."

"Someone who doesn't have a list of red flags on her phone," he cheerily replies.

Kennedy rolls her eyes. "What else?"

He scratches his chin. "Hmm. Good in bed."

She lets out a laugh. "That's just a nice way of saying that being bad in bed is one of your red flags."

He winks at her. "Like I said, glass half full. And I don't get many complaints in that department, sweetheart."

She sighs. "Ugh. You're a player. Also on my red flag list. You've probably slept with hundreds of women."

He gives her a lopsided grin. "Thousands. Proud of it."

She shakes her head. "I hope you wrap it before you tap it, big guy."

He nods enthusiastically. "When I was fifteen, my father showed me a thirty-minute PowerPoint presentation on why I should use condoms." He deadpans, "It was all pictures of me."

She scowls at him. "I feel like your birth certificate is an apology from the condom factory."

He rolls his eyes at her. I don't think I've ever seen a woman annoy him as much as she's clearly bothering him. "Sugar lips, I'm so well-equipped that when I was born, I got a girth certificate."

We all chuckle at their interaction, though I can visibly see how uncomfortable Sulley is. I hate seeing her like this.

Presley leans toward Layla, "I'm the only one you've been with, right, cariño?"

She bites back a smile. "Yep, all the others were nines and tens."

The group breaks out into hysterical laughter, but Layla simply grins and leans over to kiss his cheek. That's how they are. She busts his balls, and he enjoys the attention while deeply loving her.

Daylen asks Sulley what he knows I want to ask. "Sulley, how are you adjusting to the city? I'm sure it's a huge change for you coming from Bumfuck, Montana. Though I've been there and it's a lovely town."

She nods, unaffected by his attempt at humor. "It's going well. Everyone has been super nice. We started practices. The team is already gelling well. I think we'll be competitive in year one." It's unusual for expansion teams to be competitive right away, though I suppose the Anacondas won a league title in their first year in existence.

I can't help but ask, "Where are you living?" I need to know.

Her face falls, and she mumbles, "I'm living with Palmer."

She points to the shy woman who Beau can't stop staring at. "We're just renting an apartment for this first season until we learn the city. I'm hoping to be able to buy a place in a few months."

Finn would be so proud that she's in a position to be able to buy her own house. I want to say this, but I know I've lost the right to do so. I ask, "Where's the apartment?" I want to make sure she's in a safe area. I'm suddenly worried that she's not.

"Independence Mall. It's a lively area." She cracks her first smile, albeit a small one. "I love how full of history it is. It's like high school textbooks coming to life."

That's a nice area of the city where the Liberty Bell and the Constitution Center sit. I don't live too far from there. For now.

Daylen stands. "I'll be back in a bit. I need to go point Percy at the porcelain."

Palmer pinches her eyebrows together and speaks for the first time, albeit very quietly. "What does that mean?"

I sign in annoyance. "Daylen likes to come up with random ways to say he has to use the restroom. He gets off on it."

Kennedy scoffs. "You're a pig."

Daylen chuckles. "I am. Oink, oink." He grabs my arm. "Come with me to siphon the python."

I brush his hand away. "Huh? I'm not a girl. I'm not going with you to the bathroom. If your balls are sunburned from today, I don't want to see them. Go apply some aloe vera to them like the rest of us did."

He gives me a subtle kick under the table, and I exhale a breath as I stand and follow him down the stairs. Once we're out of earshot, I ask, "What's your fucking problem, D?"

He runs his fingers through his Miracle-Gro hair in obvious frustration. "I don't like that Kennedy chick. I needed a minute to get away before I said something nasty to her, and then Coach would get pissed at me."

"She's hot. Very much your type." Not really. He likes blondes. I enjoy messing with him though.

He makes a look of disgust. "Judgmental bitches aren't my type."

"Whatever. Why the hell did you need me?" I bark.

He toggles his head back and forth. "Sulley is clearly uncomfortable around you. I thought she might need a minute too."

My shoulders fall. He's right. "I'll leave," I immediately offer.

He shakes his head. "No. I think you should pull her aside. Maybe a peace offering is in order. Elvis is excited to have Layla playing in Philly. He wants us to go to all the home games with him. He wants us to spend time with Layla and her teammates. You two need to bury the hatchet. There was such obvious tension. It's going to be awkward as fuck for everyone. You need to put a pin in it."

I nod in understanding. I don't want our friends to suffer, and he's right that Presley will be asking us to go to Beavers' games all the time. Anytime Layla's team from Miami played in Philly, Presley would buy the whole front row for us to attend the games and cheer her on. Plus, I genuinely want to watch Sulley play. I never missed a college game of hers on TV. Even if I wasn't home, I'd record it and watch it later. Getting to see her play in person under the guise of supporting Presley and Layla is appealing to me.

I notice that nearly everyone from our table has moved to the dance floor. It happens every time we're here, but I never dance. I'm not very good at it. I'd rather sit in our booth and watch from above. But Sulley is out there smiling and dancing with her teammates. I can't take my eyes off her body moving to the fast beat of the music.

Daylen places his hand on my shoulder. "At no point in the years I've heard about Finn and his little sister did you ever mention she's gorgeous and you have a major thing for her."

I snap my head at him. "I don't have a thing for her. I want to protect her. I promised him I would."

My best friend's face turns uncharacteristically serious. "It's cool, man. I've never seen you this worked up over a woman. I know what Finn meant to you. I know the sacrifices you've made to be a good friend. I'm just now realizing how much more than that *she* means to you. I want to help. Tell me what I can do."

I look toward Sulley, who's now practically dirty dancing with Kennedy. At least twenty guys are staring at them. I nod toward the girls. "Can you get me a minute alone with her?"

He lets out a little growl. He's a bit of a Neanderthal at times. "Fuck. Only for you would I voluntarily spend time alone with Kennedy. You're definitely applying aloe vera to my balls later tonight."

I elbow him before we walk over toward them and see them both hysterically laughing. Daylen asks, "What's so funny?"

Sulley lets out an adorable giggle. "A guy just came up to Kennedy and asked her if she had a man."

Kennedy smirks. "I told him I am one, and he practically sprinted in the other direction." She rubs her hands together. "Works every damn time I need to get a guy away from me."

Daylen grabs Kennedy's hand. "Dance with me, wench."

She pulls her hand away. "Fuck off, caveman. I don't like being told what to do unless I'm naked."

Daylen scrunches his face. "Eww. Thinking of you naked is gross. I want to hear more about your red flags. I aspire to incorporate every one of them into my daily routine."

Kennedy rolls her eyes. "I feel like you're the reason there are directions on shampoo bottles."

He mouths to me, "You owe me," before grabbing a screeching Kennedy by the waist and carrying her to the other side of the dance floor, leaving Sulley and me alone for the first time in half a decade.

She starts to walk away, but I grab her wrist. "Don't go."

SULLEY

"Don't go."

My eyes fill with tears as I look down at his hand wrapped around my arm. His giant hands. The ones that were—

"Give me one dance, Sulley. For old times' sake. I want to talk to you."

I look back up at him, snapping out of my daydream. Why are *his* eyes pained? Does he regret what he did?

I exhale a long breath and reluctantly nod, mostly curious as to what he could possibly have to say to me at this point.

As if on cue, the faster song ends, and a slow one begins playing.

Dear life, when I asked if this day could get any worse, it was a rhetorical question not a challenge.

He holds out his arms in invitation. I reluctantly move toward them, though I maintain a safe distance. Not safe enough to avoid his scent. He smells the same as he always has. I hate that it's comforting and feels like home. That I want to blanket myself in it so all the bad things in the world go away.

His thumb rubs across a tear I didn't realize had dropped from my eye, and he whispers, "Please don't cry, Gully Sulley. I hate it."

I lift my chin and steel my voice. "Don't call me that. Nicknames are for friends. We're *not* friends."

He pinches his lips together before nodding and tentatively placing his hands on my hips. I lightly place my fingertips on his shoulders, wanting to touch the least amount of him as possible.

His green eyes meet mine. "I know you hate me, and I understand why. Despite that, I want to try to be friends." He cracks a small, lopsided smile. "We used to be friends, Sulley. Can we get back there? Please. I think we're going to be in each other's lives.

It would be easier for all our friends if we could do so peacefully."

Pain slices through my body as I can barely manage to whisper, "I don't know that I can ever get there. We can't undo what you've done to my family."

His hopeful face falls. "Just know I care about you. I always have and I always will."

Care about me? What a joke. My jaw tightens at his hollow words. Instead of being sad, I start to get mad. "Fuck you, Vance. You don't care about anyone but yourself."

He shakes his head. "That's not true."

"It *is* true. It's all about your precious image. You don't have any regard for the people in your life. You do whatever you want with no consideration for the carnage you leave behind." I push him away. Feeling the tears building, I start to walk away but turn my head back to him and grit out, "When was the last time you saw your daughter?"

I WAKE in the morning feeling like my head might explode. I'm not hungover. I cried for hours after my interaction with Vance. My mother told me not to let him get to me, and the first time I saw him, I ended up a mess.

Kennedy and Palmer immediately took me home and let me cry in their arms. They must think I'm crazy.

I peel my eyes open. And I mean peel because I didn't remove my makeup and cried until there were no fluids left in my body. My eyelids feel like they were glued together.

I see Kennedy on one side of me and Palmer on the other, all squeezed together in my bed. I only just met these women, and yet they took such good care of me. I'm suddenly feeling very fortunate for my new friends.

Female friendships have long been a struggle for me. I grew up a tomboy, refusing to do anything considered "girlie." That didn't lend itself to many girlfriends. Then, when I was about twelve, I started getting a ton of attention for my basketball play. The girls at school hated me for that. I was on a bit of an island throughout high school. In college, my teammates didn't like the fact that all the focus and media attention were on me. Despite my always shifting our success to the team, the media only wanted to interview me. I was the one getting NIL deals left and right. I was the one who was credited with our team's success. I never asked for the attention, but it was there, and my teammates resented it.

Put simply, it's been lonely. Girl hate is something I've gotten used to. It's become what I expect, but that's not what I got last night. Just the opposite.

I feel Kennedy place her hand on my arm. I turn my head and see nothing but concern written on her face. She rubs my arm as she whispers, "Are you okay?

In a hoarse voice, I manage to croak out, "I'm sorry about last night. I'm so embarrassed."

I feel Palmer's hand on my other arm. "Don't be. We all have our moments."

Kennedy asks, "Do you want to tell us what has gone on between you and Vance McCaffrey to trigger you like that?" Her voice is laced with compassion. "I want to be supportive, but it's hard when we don't know the facts."

I let out a long breath. I owe them this for taking care of me last night. I've never talked about it with anyone but my family. It might feel good to finally let it all out. I hope I can trust these women. My gut tells me I can.

I nod. "Can we do this over coffee? I need some caffeine before we dive into my past."

Twenty minutes later, I've scrubbed my face clean and we're sitting around our kitchen table with mugs of coffee. I've popped a handful of Advil and am ready to confide in them.

I look at both of my new friends. Their eyes convey nothing but genuine concern.

I begin, "I've known Vance since I was born. He and my brother, Finn, were best friends. More than best friends. Brothers. They did everything together. Our parents are the best of friends too. I honestly have very few childhood memories that don't include the McCaffrey family. Vance and Finn were eight years older than me. I worshiped them and followed them everywhere, but they always indulged me, letting me tag along. I idolized my brother and had a massive crush on Vance. As I'm sure you can imagine, Vance was the town hero. The golden boy. Untouchable. Loved by all."

They both nod in understanding.

I continue. "When they were eighteen, my brother enlisted in the Marines in hopes of saving money to go to college for architecture." I smile at the memory. "He was designing things for as long as I can remember. Vance left to play football in college. My brother's forever girlfriend, Maddie, stayed in town to help on her parents' small ranch. I come from a town where most don't go to college. My brother wanted to get engaged before he left, but Maddie refused. I thought it was weird, but I sort of respected that she wanted to wait until his four years were done. When he reenlisted for another four years, she was livid, and they broke up. But eventually, they got back together when he was home visiting. As you know, Vance became a big star in that time period."

I take a long gulp of my coffee. "A month before his final deployment was supposed to end, Finn was granted a leave of absence to come home for a brief visit for my basketball senior night. It was then that he told us he agreed to a six-month extension. We were upset about it, but he said the military was throwing too much money his way to turn it down. That he would then be in a financial position to buy Maddie a nice engagement ring, start college, and still afford a place for them to live."

Tears fill my eyes. "Three months later, he was killed in the line of duty. He should have been home already. If he didn't agree to that extension, he'd still be alive. It was a dark time for my family, but our shining light was Maddie walking into his funeral visibly pregnant. We were so damn happy that we'd have a piece of my brother. I think it kept my parents going on the days shortly after he died, when they struggled to put one foot in front of the other. At the end of that summer, I left for college. I don't know if you remember, but I started college in California."

Palmer nods. "I remember. At the time, you were a year ahead of me."

I offer a small smile. "Right. I was only a month or so in when my mother called that Maddie was in labor. It was ten weeks too early. We were freaking out that the baby couldn't survive. I immediately got on a plane. By the time I landed, the baby was born. She was ten pounds." I hang my head. "Full term."

Palmer and Kennedy look confused. Kennedy asks, "What does that mean?"

I swallow. "It means the baby wasn't conceived when my brother visited. Prior to that, he hadn't been home in nearly two years. The baby very obviously wasn't his. She cheated on him."

Palmer gasps as she places her hand over her mouth. "Oh, how horrible for you and your family." She places her other hand over mine. "I'm so sorry for what you went through."

Kennedy has a stoic look on her face. "This story gets worse, doesn't it?"

I nod. "It does. Those few weeks were a blur. It was like we lost my brother all over again. It eventually came out that Vance fathered the little girl. My brother's best friend slept with his fiancée. Apparently, it was a drunken mistake, but that doesn't really matter. It was a shock to all. Maddie was barely remorseful. Vance bought a huge house for her and their daughter, but he never sees them. You've never heard of Vance having a daughter, right?"

Kennedy shakes her head. "No. Never."

"Right. The asshole doesn't even acknowledge his own daughter. I'm sure it's because he doesn't want the PR hit from sleeping with his best friend's girlfriend. He's kind of ostracized from our hometown now. He rarely visits his own parents. An occasional pop-in for a holiday, but that's it. He basically paid for it to go away and not tarnish his perfect all-American image."

Kennedy mumbles, "What an asshole."

I wipe my tears. I can't believe I have any left after last night.

Palmer pinches her eyebrows. "What happened to you? You never went back to California."

"I was a mess for many months. I dropped out of school and moped around the house, occasionally helping my father in his business." I shake my head. "I was a lost soul. The will to play ball had left my body. My parents were too fucked up at the time to push me to do anything. It was like three zombies coexisting."

"What changed?" Palmer asks.

"A few months later, maybe in January or February, a Marine buddy of my brother's showed up at our front door. They had already sent us his personal belongings, but apparently a letter had been entrusted to his friend, and he was instructed by my brother to deliver it in person if he passed, which is why it wasn't with his original stuff. It was a letter addressed to me." The tears start up again. "My brother knew if something happened to him, I'd lose my way. It was his final wish for me to keep playing. To achieve my dream of playing professional basketball. It was the kick in the ass I needed, but I didn't want to go back to California. It suddenly felt so far from home. I called the coach at the University of Montana. She was more than happy to have me. She had been trying to recruit me since I was ten. I enrolled the following fall and got back on track. All thanks to my brother's words from the grave. I carry that letter with me everywhere. It's in my wallet. It helps me through the tough times."

They both have tears in their eyes. Kennedy sniffles. "I

suddenly feel the need to call my little brother. We're not very close. I'm a shitty sister."

"Don't take him for granted," I plead. "You never know what could happen."

She nods. "I won't. Thanks for sharing this with us. Now I understand how you felt last night." Her face turns cold. "And now we're going to have a lot of fun fucking with golden boy Vance McCaffrey."

FIVE

VANCE

I'm at my agent, Tanner Montgomery's, house. He hosts a monthly poker game for some of his longtime local clients, the ones he considers friends. It includes Daylen and me from the Camels, and Cruz "Cheetah" Gonzales, Layton Lancaster, and Trey DePaul from the Philly Cougars. Cheetah and Trey are still playing ball, but Layton retired last year after a gruesome injury in a World Series game. He's now on the coaching staff of both the Cougars and Anacondas. His wife, Arizona Abbott, plays for the Anacondas.

Tanner has a high-end man cave in his basement and always has a ton of food and drinks for us. I consider this group among my closest friends in the world, but Tanner and Daylen are the only ones who know my full past. Tanner has worked hard through the years to keep things under wraps, per my request.

Everyone has arrived except Cheetah. He texted that he was running late.

I ask Layton, "How's the wedding planning coming?"

He already eloped with Arizona, but they're having a big

wedding for family and friends this fall after her season is over. I believe Daylen has termed it a *performative wedding*. They're doing it during our bye week so Daylen and I can be there.

He smiles widely. "It's awesome. I can't wait. She's changed my life for the better."

Layton was the biggest playboy around for years. Seeing him like this is shocking, but in a good way.

I slap him on the back. "I'm happy for you. Don't forget to text me the name of your builder."

He and Arizona are designing and building a big house in the suburbs. I want to do the same. It's time to see Finn's vision come to fruition. It's another promise I made to him.

Layton winces. "Shit. I keep forgetting." He pulls out his phone. "Sending you Collin Fitz's contact information now. He's a character, kind of goofy, but he's the best at custom mansions. And once you decide to move forward, he gets shit done quickly. He knows people in the permitting offices. It's amazing how efficiently he works."

I feel my phone vibrate, knowing his text came through. "Thanks, man." I make a mental note to call Collin first thing in the morning.

Cheetah comes rushing down the stairs. He's a blue-eyed Latino man who is widely considered one of the fastest players in baseball. "Sorry, guys. I was with Kam."

Daylen shakes his head. "I can't believe you snagged her."

Cheetah shrugs. "I'm not sure I've snagged her. Sometimes I'm not sure how much she likes me. She tolerates me because I'm so damn good in bed."

Daylen smiles broadly with a celery stick dangling from his mouth like it's a cigar. "You can tell how much a woman likes you by her feet."

"Her feet?" Cheetah questions.

Daylen nods. "Yep. If they're behind her ears, she likes you a lot."

Cheetah chuckles. "Then I guess she likes me."

Cheetah then looks at Tanner. "Were you able to get us the tickets I asked for?"

Tanner nods. "Yep. I got a bunch for the Beavers' home opener. It was a hot ticket. People are clamoring to see Sulley. My phone is ringing off the hook with offers for her."

Cheetah smirks. "'Cause she's hot."

I scowl at him. "It's because she's the best basketball player on the planet. Don't be such a sexist asshole."

He raises his eyebrow. "And she's hot. What's wrong with you?"

I shake my head. "Nothing. She's worked her ass off. She deserves your respect."

Cheetah, Layton, and Trey all stare at me, dumbfounded. Trey asks, "Do you have something going on with her already? Didn't she just move here a minute ago?"

I shake my head. "I've known her for her whole life. She's like a little sister to me." That taste of the word sister feels bitter in my mouth. While I feel protective of Sulley, I don't see her as a sister at all.

Trey smiles. "Whatever you say, loverboy." He winks. "I see what's happening here. I'm not blind. My wife writes romance novels. I see the story unfolding." He pretends like he's opening a book. "Star quarterback reined in by star basketball player, producing superstar babies for generations." He pretends to close the book. "Happily ever after. The end."

Daylen mercifully, and likely purposefully, interjects, "Speaking of being blind, I had sex with a blind woman once. She told me I have the biggest dick she's ever laid her hands on. I said, *you're pulling my leg.*"

The collective group laughs as we otherwise have a typical night of poker. We all make plans to meet at the Beavers' opening game.

I'M both nervous and excited for Sulley's home opener. They played their season opener in Miami a few days ago. I watched it on television. The players on the other team were extremely rough with Sulley. She was elbowed and shoved constantly. They don't seem to like that a rookie is getting so much media attention. I don't like what they're doing to her.

She brushed it off and scored twenty points with eleven assists and seven rebounds. An amazing rookie debut. I like how calm she is under pressure. She never lets anything or anyone get to her.

So many players in the league are giving interviews saying that Sulley is overhyped, and that she won't be as productive in the WNBA as she was in college. I don't understand why they're trying to bring her down. She's good for the league. She has a huge following. Their season opener was the most viewed WNBA game in history, and Beavers home and away games are sold out for the entire season, with people clamoring to watch her play.

Tanner purchased a ton of seats for tonight, all right on the floor, and we get to enjoy the fruits of his labor as we sit down. He's busy making his rounds, shaking hands with people. I suppose that's part of his job. He's very good at it.

I'm sitting with Daylen, Presley, Beau, and Champ. I insisted on coming early to watch warmups and to ensure we don't miss the player introductions. I need to see the first time she's announced in front of the home crowd and watch all the fans go wild for her. She's earned this moment. It's a long time in the making.

I see Layton and Arizona walk toward the seats next to us, hand in hand, with huge smiles on their faces. She's an absolute stunner with her California height, blonde hair, and blue eyes. The crowd erupts with excitement when they notice them. Layton and Arizona are the unofficial sweethearts of Philadelphia. Their love story is plastered everywhere, and they seem to relish it. They wave to their sea of fans without a care in the world. I envy how carefree they seem to be.

They're followed by Bailey Hart, Kam's identical twin sister, and then Cheetah, who's holding Kam's hand as she enters behind him. Bailey and Kam are brunette stunners. Both are sexy, though Bailey is sweet while Kam is a little crazy, making her perfect for Cheetah. Few people know this, but Tanner is in some sort of secret physical relationship with Bailey. She's much younger than him, and she nannies for his daughter in the off-season, but he's into her. *Very* into her.

Apparently, Sulley has already made friends with the players on the Anacondas. It's nice to see women's professional athletes being supportive of each other. The players on the Anacondas became overnight sensations here in Philly last season. Hopefully their star power will rub off on the Beavers, and Philly will embrace the new basketball team similarly.

Layton turns his head and looks down the row of seats toward Kam. "You were the last to arrive."

The guys on the Cougars play a game of whoever is last to arrive has to share a random, fun fact with the group. They seem to get off on it. It's kind of annoying, albeit slightly amusing at times.

Kam rolls her eyes. "I've got a good one for you. The first testicular cup was used in hockey in 1874. The first helmet was used in hockey in 1974. It took men a hundred years to value their brains as much as they value their dicks."

Daylen lets out the loudest laugh I've ever heard in my life. I swear, ten thousand people stare at him. He's wildly amused by Kamryn. Though he'd never admit it out loud, I think he secretly wishes he'd met Kam before Cheetah did.

I look across the court and nod my head at Coach Jeffries. He's sitting with his son and ex-wife. I imagine they're here to cheer for Kennedy. He nods in return.

I then notice Tanner's eight-year-old daughter, Harper, walking onto the court with his ex-wife, Fallon. Harper sprints toward Bailey and leaps into her waiting arms. I guess she loves her nanny.

Kam and Cheetah slide down, allowing Harper and Fallon to sit next to Bailey. Fallon and Bailey seem friendly. I wonder if Fallon knows Tanner is banging the nanny. Not my business.

Harper bounces from person to person until she gets to Daylen, sitting next to me, and climbs onto his giant lap. Her blue eyes look up at him. "Uncle Daylen, who's your favorite Beaver?"

I narrow my eyes at him to ensure he keeps it clean. He winks at me, aware of my thoughts. "Hmm. I think Layla Ladrón. I've known her the longest." He points to Presley. "This is her husband. That's what he's most famous for. No one would even know his name if he wasn't married to a superstar like Layla."

Harper's face lights up. "Oh, cool. Do you want to know who my favorite player is?"

Daylen pretends to think about it. "Well...if I had to guess, and it's only a guess, I'd say Sulley O'Shea."

Harper gasps. "How did you know?"

He tugs on her O'Shea jersey and gives her his goofy grin. "Just a wild guess."

Harper looks down at her jersey, which is now a bestseller, and giggles. "Oh right. Daddy says I can meet her after the game. That she's super nice."

I see the number twenty-two on her jersey. I know why she wears that number. It was Finn's. I noticed on her senior night in high school that she was number nineteen. I wondered if it had anything to do with me. But she's been twenty-two ever since. I have no doubt Finn would love that. I'm happy she made the change.

Daylen nods. "She's very nice, but Kennedy Jeffries is a meanie. Stay away from her." He makes a look of disgust. I swear I've never seen a woman get under his skin like Kennedy has.

The players are all introduced. I can't help the tears that sting my eyes when Sulley is announced to a huge standing ovation, and she points up at the sky. I know who she's thinking of in her big moment. It's the same person I think of during my big moments.

Finn is looking down with so much pride right now. Knowing I had a small hand in making this happen fills me with happiness, even if Sulley doesn't realize it.

I can't help that my hand finds the spot on my body under my left arm, close to my chest. My small testament to Finn.

The game gets underway. Their starting lineup includes all four girls from the other night, plus Shay Walker, a veteran power forward. It's cool that Sulley is a starter right away. She's that good.

The cameras find us during the first timeout, where we all happily engage in a beer chugging contest. It's not even close. A beer is like a shot to a man like Beau Fudd. He can down an entire can of beer in under two seconds. It provides entertainment for the crowd though. They seem to get a kick out of famous athletes chugging beer.

The other team is pushing the envelope on physicality with Sulley. It's pissing me off. We've been yelling at the refs all night, but the other team is barely ever called for the blatant fouls taking place.

Kennedy, on the other hand, has been pushing and shoving anyone who does anything underhanded to Sulley. Kennedy is undoubtedly the enforcer and protector. Despite her slightly off-putting personality, I find that endearing.

As the muscle of the group, Kennedy boxes out the other team and grabs rebound after rebound, feeding Sulley. I can see Coach Jeffries beaming with pride as he watches her tough, selfless play.

Palmer is getting manhandled a bit. She's the biggest player on the Beavers, and I imagine she's usually one of the biggest players in any given game, but their opponents have a few girls who have been overpowering her all night. It's flustering her.

Sulley, on the other hand, is cool as a cucumber, hitting logo three after logo three. She's unstoppable. I think every person here knows we're in the presence of true greatness. That we're witnessing the beginning of what we all know will be a historic career.

The capacity crowd is going nuts. All the Beavers' games are being nationally televised, something nearly unheard of in women's basketball. The Sulley effect, as it's being called in the media, is real. She's a bona fide superstar.

The Beavers are down two points in the final seconds. Kennedy is inbounding the ball right in front of me. She stomps on my foot. It's not the first time she's done that tonight. What's her problem?

She passes the ball to Sulley and then immediately sets a pick for her. Sulley dribbles around the pick, pulls up at least ten feet behind the three-point line, and shoots the ball. The opposing player practically tackles her when she does. It's overly violent. It's the same player who has been elbowing and pushing Sulley all night.

The shot goes in. At the same time, the crowd goes wild, but Kennedy comes barreling toward the player who fouled Sulley. The head coach runs to pull Kennedy away from the girl before she can do anything too drastic. Damn, Kennedy has a temper.

Time has expired. The Beavers win. The whole team runs to Sulley, the hero. We're all on our feet, clapping and cheering.

Daylen grins at me. "She's fucking good, man. The real deal."

I can't help but crack a smile of my own. "She sure is. She's gonna go down as the best of all time. Mark my words."

After the excitement of the victory dies down, most people begin to leave the arena, but Daylen and I stick around a little longer, as do Tanner and Harper. I know Sulley hates me, but I want to congratulate her when the media is done with her.

Harper tugs on Daylen's jeans. She loves the big oaf. "Uncle Daylen, wasn't that the best basketball game ever?"

He nods. "Sure was. Sulley was great."

She shrugs. "I liked watching Kennedy. She's tough, like a softball player." Harper holds up her little fists like she's going to fight.

As if on cue, Kennedy walks over to us with her pout firmly in place. She looks at me with pure hatred. "You should take off, asshole."

Daylen interrupts, "Hello, sugar lips. Cheery as ever. Harper, the *little girl* standing right here in earshot of you," he raises his eyebrows in warning to Kennedy, "was just saying how much she looks up to you. Maybe do a better job of acting like a role model." He glances down at Harper. "Kennedy is a good example that a little girl can be anything she wants when she grows up." He mumbles, "Despite her disposition."

Kennedy narrows her eyes at him. "Don't tell this little girl she can be anything she wants when she grows up. Then it might occur to her that she can't, which she never considered in the first place."

Daylen scowls at Kennedy before softening his face and turning his attention back to Harper. "Sweetie, let's go find your dad. Crazy is sometimes contagious. Let's get away from it before it rubs off on you." He takes her hand, and they walk away toward Tanner.

When they're out of earshot, Kennedy looks at me. "Why are you still here?"

"I want to congratulate Sulley."

She shakes her head. "Stay away from her. You're a walking trigger for her. She doesn't need that in her life right now."

I roll my eyes. "You don't know anything about our relationship."

She crosses her arms. "I know more than you think, McCaffrey. She's a superstar. Don't dim her shine."

Both our eyes move to Sulley, who appears as though she's finally giving her last interview. I'm about to walk over when an extremely tall, skinny man, likely in his twenties, walks over to her, lifts her, and twirls her around. They both smile before he kisses her on the lips. He then starts talking to the reporter, basically hijacking her interview.

My eyes widen, and I practically bark out, "Who's that?"

Kennedy smirks. "Her boyfriend."

"She's been in town for all of five minutes. She already has a boyfriend?"

"They've been together for over a year. He went to U of Montana but now plays ball in Europe. He flew in for the weekend. He surprised her last night." She winks at me. "It was quite a reunion. Palmer said she had to wear headphones to drown out the screams."

I ball my fists, and my jaw tightens. I didn't know she had a boyfriend. The thought makes my stomach turn.

Kennedy studies me carefully. "Do you have a thing for her?"

I shake my head. "No. I'm just protective, that's all. I didn't know about this guy."

She pauses briefly, clearly not believing me. "Like I said, leave her alone. You've inflicted enough damage on her."

At that, she turns and walks away.

I stand there and watch as the guy holds up his phone and pulls Sulley close to him. It seems like he's talking into the camera and recording something. Who the hell is this guy?

SIX

SULLEY

I'm in Shane's long T-shirt and my panties with messy bed hair as I walk him to my door. This weekend was a quick but nice surprise.

Shane and I started dating about a year and a half ago. His senior year and my junior year at the University of Montana. He had transferred in for his senior year after some sort of drama with his previous college program. We were the golden couple on campus, with me the star of the women's basketball team and him the star of the men's. He was always taking me to nice meals and showering me with gifts and affection. I've never been treated like that by a man, and we had a good time.

We were floating on cloud nine for those first few months, but things turned a little sour when he didn't get drafted into the NBA. He was inconsolable.

I tried to be there for him, writing off some of his comments to me that I wouldn't be as successful if I were a man and about how he could beat me in basketball. It was juvenile, but his childhood dream was shattered, so I gave him some leeway.

After a bit of a rough patch for him personally and us as a couple, he eventually accepted a spot on the roster of a team out of Italy and has been playing in the EuroLeague.

I was able to visit him once for a very quick few days, and he's been home a handful of times, but the past year has been challenging. It's not just the distance. My star has risen considerably, even more than when he was in college with me, and his doesn't look like it's going anywhere. He's usually outwardly supportive, but I can sense a little resentment in him when we talk on the phone. A few off-hand comments here and there. But he makes me happy, and I let them slide. He's comfortable and, frankly, the distance almost makes it easy. I don't have time to date and am not interested in casual encounters, so spending a few days holed up with him every few months is nice for me. I can blow off a little steam and then send him on his way.

He's a huge social media guy, always posting videos of us on TikTok and Instagram. I can't keep track of all his various accounts. I'm not much of a social media person, posting very sporadically, but I participate in his because it makes him happy. I know it drives him nuts that I have a bigger following than he does, but that's out of my control.

We get to the door, and he turns, taking me into his long arms. His hands slide up the backs of my thighs onto my panty-covered ass. Kissing my lips softly, he breathes, "I miss you already."

I smile into his mouth. "I miss you too." I run my fingers over his new crew cut. "I still can't believe your hair is so short."

"Hmm. It's hot in Italy at this time of year. The longer hair was becoming difficult. You don't think it's sexy?" he jokes.

He has dark hair. It used to be overgrown and almost identical to a certain quarterback I once had a crush on. In fact, the first time I saw Shane from behind, I thought he was Vance, even though their bodies are nothing alike. Shane is six feet, ten inches, a few inches taller than Vance. He's also much skinnier.

Vance is broad with muscles. But there was something about his hair that had me wanting more, remembering the one and only time I got to run my fingers through Vance's. A hair-tugging fetish may have been born that night.

I saw Vance at the game last night. He stirs so many emotions in me. I know I need to get used to him being in my life. He's friends with Layla's husband, and we're going to see each other. Layla has been nothing but kind and welcoming to me. In fact, all my teammates have been the same. I don't want to ruffle any feathers or be the cause of tension or drama. I've decided that crying fits like the other night are not ever going to happen again. I'm going to co-exist with Vance McCaffrey as best I can.

"No, honey, I love your haircut. It's sexy," I lie. I hate his haircut. A girl needs something to grab onto during sex. It's a little annoying that he cut it so short, given how much he knows I like running my fingers through it and pulling it.

He rubs his erection against me. I'm not sure how he's hard again. Besides my game last night, we've done nothing but have sex for two straight days. In between the rounds of sex, he filmed a ton of videos and took a bunch of photos of us. I offered to show him around Philly, but he wasn't interested. He just wanted to stay locked up with me.

"Good. Do you think you can come visit next month?" he asks hopefully.

My face falls. "Shane, I'm in season. You know I can't take time off to travel overseas."

He tilts his head back and blows out a breath. "I can't be the only one doing the work in this relationship, Sulley."

"What do you want from me, Shane? I went straight from my school season to the draft to my pro season. I've barely had a minute to breathe. And it's not cheap to fly over. I'm trying to save money to buy my first house."

He pulls away. "I know it's not cheap, but I manage. And I don't have *a million* offers for endorsements like you do."

His tone is pissing me off, but I'm not up for a fight, not right before he leaves.

I pull his shirt so we can be close again. "It's been a nice weekend. Let's not spoil it. Thank you for surprising me. I wish you didn't have to leave so quickly. You don't have any games this week. Maybe you could move your flight and stay a little longer."

He shakes his head. "Practice, babe. You know how I feel. Practice makes perfect."

I nod in agreement before he kisses me one last time, insists on a few more photos, and then leaves for the airport.

As I walk into our little kitchen, Palmer exits her bedroom on her phone. "Thanks, Mom. I promise to be safe. Love you too. Talk to you tomorrow."

She ends the call as she exhales a long breath. "My mom is intense. She thinks we live in a war zone."

I giggle as I sit at our small table. "My mom too. You should have seen her in New York City for the draft last month. She had at least seven containers of pepper spray on hand at all times. She wants me to carry a gun in my purse, which I refuse to do."

I know how to handle guns, but I'm not walking around with one.

Palmer smiles. "Yep." She pops the P. "Same here." She looks around. "Shane left?"

I nod. "Yes. Short visit. He has practice in the morning, but it was sweet of him to surprise me."

"He seems…nice."

I study her face. Palmer has zero poker face. "You don't like him?" I ask.

She shrugs. "I don't know him. You two only left your bedroom to play ball."

Embarrassment creeps up my neck. "Sorry. We had some catching up to do."

"At least he's tall." She plops down onto a chair at the kitchen table. "It's so hard for me to find men taller than me."

"Beau is taller than you," I tease. It was clear the other night that Palmer is smitten with him.

Two rosy dots form on her cheeks. "I don't think a guy like Beau Fudd would ever be interested in me. He's gorgeous. He could have any girl he wants."

"*You're* gorgeous. You just need to believe that too."

"I'm big. Men don't like big women."

I shrug. "It's about finding the right fit. All of us are in the same boat, being unusually tall. Beau is significantly bigger than you."

She has a giddy look on her face as she practically coos, "He *really* is. Did you see his quads in those jeans he was wearing?"

I nod my head. "They were hard to miss."

"They looked like they were going to burst through. I've never been around a man like him."

Wow, she's crushing hard.

"Right. How would Beau be with a small, regular-sized woman? He would crush her. He needs someone tall like you, Palmer."

She leans on her hands with a dreamy look on her face. "Do you really think so?"

"I do."

Suddenly, there's a knock at the door and a loud, familiar voice shouts, "Sex police."

Palmer and I laugh as I stand and make my way to the front door, opening it for Kennedy. Talk about surprises. Kennedy is widely considered the bitch of the league. The black widow, for her dark hair, dirty play, and less-than-sunny disposition. That's not what I've seen through our first two games. I've seen a good teammate who protects me at every turn. I've never played with anyone like her. She's like having a hockey teammate. The guy whose job it is to come in and check the opponent into the boards just to make a point.

Basketball has become a significantly more physical game in the past few years. Contact that once would have been a foul is now considered acceptable. Kennedy fights hard for every single rebound. She's constantly creating lanes for me. She's like a tank. A machine. It's a very undervalued aspect of the sport. I wouldn't be putting up the kind of numbers I have in our first two games if it weren't for her tough, unselfish play.

And her support the other night, refusing to leave my side, is something I'm unaccustomed to. I was unsure about her at first, but I officially like Kennedy Jeffries. A lot.

Opening the door, I joke, "The black widow is here."

Her face falls. "Ugh, I hate that nickname."

I shrug. "It suits you. Plus, she's a superhero. You should embrace it."

She makes a look of disgust. "Guys always want me to dress up as Black Widow. It's creepy as fuck. I've added it to my red flag list." She hands me a coffee. "I brought you guys caffeine. Shane left, right? I didn't bring him one."

I nod. "He's gone."

She walks in, and we all sit around our small kitchen table. She nods toward the half dozen vases of flowers. "Where did all those come from?"

"Reagan Daulton said a ton of fans sent them to me at the stadium. I couldn't take them all home with us, but I took a bunch, and I grabbed all the accompanying cards so I could read them. The fans here are so nice."

She rubs her hands together in excitement. "Ooh. Grab them. Let's read a few."

As I walk into our living room to locate the big bag of notes and cards, Kennedy shouts, "What are those dark red, ugly flowers? I've never seen them before."

I smile to myself, knowing exactly which ones she's talking about. I yell back, "They're called Chocolate Cosmos. They happen to be rare. Smell them. They smell like chocolate."

I can hear their chairs scrape across the floor before they mutter, "Holy shit."

I giggle as it resurfaces a few childhood memories.

We begin going through the box of notes. Most of the notes are from fans kindly wishing me well. My favorites are from little girls telling me that I'm their idol. It's very humbling to be seen that way.

There are a few weird ones, like the one person who wrote, "I bet you sweat glitter." There's one that truly gives me the creeps that reads, "I love watching you on and off the court."

But then I get to one that blows me away. It's typed on a florist's card.

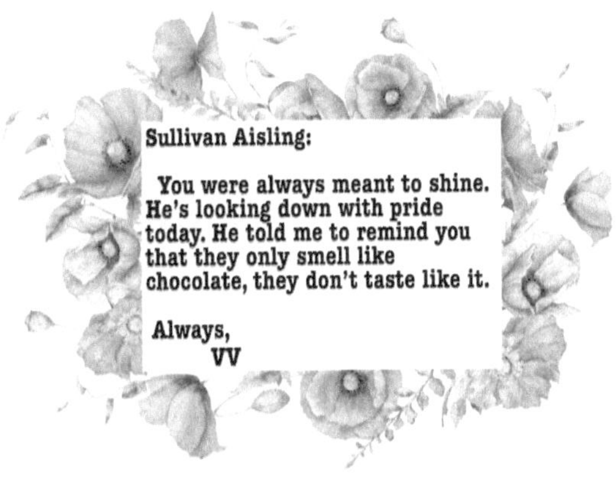

I'm not sure I realized that I had tears streaming down my face until Palmer hands me a tissue. They both look at me in question. Kennedy asks, "Who's VV?"

I wipe my eyes and blow my nose. "Vile Vance. I called him that as a kid. He and my brother would fart without regard for my presence. I'd call him Vile Vance and my brother Farty Finn. As for the flowers, Finn used to buy me Chocolate Cosmos on special occasions to remind me that it's okay to be different. Not all packaging is perfect, but it doesn't mean it isn't sweet. I was an awkward kid, skinny with bizarrely long legs and arms. Being the butt of jokes wasn't easy, but my brother and Vance always turned it into a positive. I suppose I should have realized they'd be from Vance. He and my brother once talked me into eating the flowers, promising they tasted like chocolate too." I force a small smile. "They don't. In fact, they taste disgusting."

Kennedy nods in understanding. "I guess that was nice of him." She looks like she wants to say more about the topic, but doesn't, instead asking, "Did you get Layla's text about her dinner party in a few weeks?"

I shake my head. "I haven't checked my phone this morning."

"She invited us and all the guys over for a small party at their house." She twists her lips as she looks at me. "Are you...okay with that? Are you okay seeing him? I won't go if you don't want to."

I shake my head. "I'm not going to be the girl who causes friend issues. It's fine. I'm truly sorry about my breakdown the other day. I'm over it. I promise. Everyone should feel comfortable hanging out without the risk of me losing my shit. It won't happen again. I want us to be social. Layla and Presley are married, and our friends will all be hanging out. I'll be totally fine. I'll just...ignore him."

She leans back in her chair and sips her coffee. "I swear, all of women's problems start with men. *Men*tal illness, *men*struation, *men*opause, *guy*necologist, *hist*erectomy.

Palmer and I laugh at her ridiculousness, yet I can't deny that she makes a good point.

WE'RE in the locker room after practice. Coach Lakshmi calls me into her office. When I enter, I see Reagan Daulton standing there in her fancy business suit. Even though she's never been anything but kind to me, I find her extremely intimidating. There's something about the way she carries herself that makes me feel on edge around her.

She glares at me. "Close the door and have a seat."

I do both, suddenly feeling like I'm in the principal's office, about to get into trouble.

She crosses her arms. "We've got a bit of a problem."

My shoulders fall. "What's wrong?" I'm running through anything I could have possibly done to piss off this powerful woman.

"You have an overwhelming sea of admirers. More than I anticipated. We're getting deliveries for you by the truckload, by the hour. I'm not sure how to handle the flow. Thousands of flowers, candy, stuffed animals, and bags of mail every single day. I can't imagine you want all this stuff."

I blow out a breath of relief before shaking my head. "No. Can you donate everything to a local children's hospital, or something along those lines? Everything except the Chocolate Cosmos. I'd like those if there are any more of them sent."

She smiles softly. "That's a nice idea. I'll have my assistant take care of it, though if this continues, I might have to hire someone to manage it all."

I can't fathom the fact that she might have to hire someone to deal with deliveries sent to me. It sounds crazy.

I tentatively add, "I'd like to keep the mail, though. If people make an effort to write me notes and send them, I want to try to find time to read them."

She nods. "Of course. You haven't gotten any of these deliveries to your apartment, have you?"

I shake my head. "No. Why?"

"I'm just ensuring your safety. No one should have your home address. Make sure you safeguard it. You're a bit more of a star than I've had to manage with the Anacondas, and your safety is a concern for me."

My jaw drops. "I'm not a bigger star than those girls. Arizona Abbott is everywhere." Magazines, billboards, commercials. *Everywhere.*

Reagan nods, seemingly in thought. "It's different. She's a bit older than you and only first became a household name with the team's success. People didn't know her as well during the first five or six years of her professional career. You're already a huge name. You came to us as an individual brand. Fans watched you transition into a college superstar. They feel vested in finding out whether you can do the same professionally." She rubs her lower lip with her index finger. "It can be dangerous when fans think they know you personally."

"Okay." She's got me a little scared. "What does this all mean?"

She leans her behind on the edge of Coach Lakshmi's desk and crosses her arms. "I have genuine safety concerns. Maybe I should hire a bodyguard for you."

What? I shake my head emphatically. "No way. That's completely unnecessary. Look, Mrs. Daulton—"

"Reagan," she interrupts.

"Look, Reagan, I appreciate this, but I'm trying to fit in around here. I want to blend in with my team. The absolute last thing I want is any special treatment that my teammates aren't getting. I'm trying to build bonds with them. It's going exceedingly well. Better than I could have imagined. I'm not rocking the boat by acting like a movie star with a beefy guard following me around. I don't want to be resented. It's been an issue for me in the past with teammates."

She exhales a long breath and looks at Coach Lakshmi, who nods in agreement. "They're building team chemistry and doing a good job of it. I can't argue with Sulley's logic. Of course I want her safe, but I understand where she's coming from."

Reagan is quiet for a few moments before standing. "Okay, Sulley, we'll do it your way. For now." She points at me. "If anyone, I mean any single fan, attempts to contact you or approach you at your home, I want to know. And if they do, we're going to have to make some changes. Is that clear?"

I nod. "Yes. That seems fair. I'm sure the hoopla surrounding me will die down soon."

"I need your word that you'll tell me right away."

"I promise."

I walk back out to my teammates, several of whom are sitting around laughing. "What are you all laughing about?" I ask.

Shay smirks. "Kennedy is low-key funny. I've spent the past three years hating her as an opponent, but the black widow is growing on me."

Kennedy gasps. "Me? I'm a ray of sunshine. I have a tendency to grow on people. And what I said before wasn't funny, it was true. I'm all for natural selection. Get rid of the morons. Why does a hairdryer need a label telling you not to use it in a shower? Why does an iron need a warning telling you not to iron while wearing the clothing? Let's weed out the people who would do any of that."

I giggle. "That's funny, but her list of red flags remains the most hilarious thing I've ever read."

Layla nods. "Yes, I've been thinking about those. I have a new red flag. Presley does it all the time, and it drives me nuts."

"What is it?" I ask.

She answers, "When he gives me a reasonable solution to a problem instead of babying me like I need. Drives me nuts. Just fucking massage my shoulders and agree with my insanity. Don't get all logical and rational. That's not what I need."

I let out a laugh. "I get that. You know what I realized is a red flag for me? When a guy sets his thermostat above sixty-seven degrees." I make a look of disgust. "Why are you cold? What man would be cold when it's sixty-seven degrees? It's just weird to me. Not very masculine."

Shay raises an unamused eyebrow. "Try being with small women who have no meat on their bones. They want a house at over seventy-five degrees. It's stifling."

Kennedy pulls out her phone and starts scrolling. "Ooh, I've got a good one. What about guys, I guess it goes for girls too, Shay, who have headshots when they don't have a job that requires one. Such a douchey thing to do."

We all laugh.

She keeps scrolling. "Oh, and what about guys who refer to themselves as alphas or call other guys betas? I'll be the fucking judge of that, not you."

She goes on and on with her hysterical list while we all get dressed and then go out to dinner together. I'm loving my new group of friends.

SEVEN

VANCE

"Andrew, you're on with both me and Vance."

Tanner motions for me to say hello as we sit in his office on a call with the head of marketing for Gatorade. Tanner, in his three-piece suit, is sitting at his big wooden executive desk. I'm in jeans and a T-shirt, sitting on the other side of his desk for this discussion about a big endorsement opportunity.

I mumble, "Hi, Andrew." Fuck, I hate this type of shit, but I know I need to strike while the iron is hot. I won't be this marketable and make this type of money forever. In fact, I'll be lucky to squeeze another five years out of my career.

Andrew responds, in an annoyingly cheery demeanor, "Hellooooo, Vance McCaffrey. I'm a huge fan. We're super-duper excited to work with you again. Handsome Harry has moved to another department, so I'll be your lucky liaison moving forward. And boy are you gonna be superlatively stoked for this next project we're doing together."

I roll my eyes while Tanner silently laughs and then

responds, "We haven't signed any contracts yet. Tell us what you're thinking, Andrew."

"Absolutelyeroo, bodacious buddy boy." What the fuck is wrong with this guy? "We want the two biggest stars in Philly, side by side, doing their thing. Passing the Gatorade bottle back and forth, if you will. We've got some fantabulous special effects to bridge the gap between the sports."

I suddenly get excited that maybe they want me to do this with Sulley. It would be great to spend a day shooting with her. "Who are you thinking of?" I casually ask.

"Tyrese Maxey," Andrew responds. "He's already signed, sealed, and psyched."

Tyrese Maxey is a young, rising star on Philly's men's pro basketball team.

My shoulders fall. "Oh. Out of curiosity, why wouldn't you want one of the new women pro athletes in town? The Anacondas and Beavers have become extremely popular. Philly is now truly a dual-sex sports town. You should embrace it and capitalize on that."

Tanner scratches his beard in thought. "That's a fantastic idea, Andrew. I have it on good authority that you're looking to create a special edition pink Gatorade for breast cancer awareness month this coming October. The Beavers have pink uniforms. You could shift focus. No offense to Vance getting a little long in the tooth, but you could do something along the lines of transitioning from the older, original, red Gatorade, like Vance, to the new pink Gatorade. I happen to represent Sulley O'Shea. There's no bigger female star than her right now."

Andrew makes a weird noise. Something between a hmm and an eek. It comes out like, "Hmeek."

I agree, "Yes, Sulley would be perfect. Great idea, T."

Tanner raises an eyebrow at me as he speaks into the phone. "What do you think, Andrew?"

"I think it's fantastically fantabulouso. Let me run it up the flagpole and talk to Maxey's people about the pivot from Vance to Sulley, and then I'll—"

I interrupt, "I meant Sulley and me. Not Sulley and Tyrese."

Andrew answers, "I think the basketball-to-basketball connection makes more sense. We'll find another zipperific project for you, Vancy. I'll contact you soon, Tanner."

Tanner gives me an amused look. "Sounds good. To be clear, you'll pay Sulley the same amount you were planning to pay Vance. The women in this town are revered and will be treated accordingly." He winks at me.

Andrew makes a few more weird noises before agreeing. "Talk soon, terrific Tanner. And—"

Tanner disconnects the call before Andrew can say anything else and looks at me. "Adjective Andrew is a lot to handle."

I nod in agreement. "Adjectives and fake words. I bet he was stuffed into a locker every day in high school."

Tanner chuckles. "Without a doubt. Probably still is." He places his pen down and gives me an amused look. "You just cost yourself a lot of money."

I shrug. "Whatever. I don't need it. I'd rather Sulley have the opportunity. Don't tell her it was my idea. She won't take it if she knows."

His face falls. "Things haven't thawed at all for you two?"

I shake my head. "I very clearly trigger her. It's hard to watch. I understand why, but it still hurts." I exhale a long breath. "I was there the first time she held a basketball. I watched her turn into the player she is now. You know what her brother meant to me."

He nods. "I do. Any thoughts on cluing her in on your big secret?"

"Nope. She's in a good place. I'm not rocking the boat."

"It might soften her on you, though."

"This isn't about me, it never was. Certainly not right now, when things are going so well for her. Maybe one day."

He runs his fingers over his beard, appearing annoyingly judgmental. "The truth usually has a way of coming out."

I run my tongue along my teeth. "Hmm. I think you're right about that. Does your ex-wife know you're fucking your daughter's nanny?"

He leans back in his big, leather chair and steeples his fingers. "You love to go on the offensive when you feel cornered. I wasn't trying to corner you, Vance. I'm just trying to help. As always. You're my friend. I've watched you needlessly struggle for years over everything that happened. It doesn't have to be this way. You don't have to carry the weight of the world on your shoulders. I know you're a good man. I wish you believed that too."

He stands and holds out his hand for me to shake, which I do. I sigh, feeling embarrassed by my immature behavior. "Sorry, man. I was out of line."

He waves his hand dismissively. "It doesn't bother me. And so you know, Fallon does, in fact, know about my physical relationship with Bailey. It's not as cheap and tawdry as you and the boys would like to think. I have real feelings for Bailey. Fallon only cares about Harper's well-being, and Bailey is good to Harper. There's no drama. The two of them get along well. While I didn't set out to clue Fallon in on things, it's a bit easier now that everything is out in the open. Easier when there are no secrets among the people you care about." He lifts an eyebrow pointedly. "Just consider it."

I nod before exiting his office and heading to our practice facility.

"D, BUTTONHOOK LEFT, NOT RIGHT," I yell out on the practice field. Daylen is off today. He's not running his routes properly.

That's the thing about Daylen. He *always* runs concise routes. That's how we connect so perfectly. And when the coverage is tight, we can read each other's minds and know it's time to change course. It's the magic formula we share as quarterback and tight end. You can't manufacture that. It's just there. It's why we've been such a successful duo for a decade. It's why you rarely hear one of our names without the other.

Daylen's contract was up earlier this year. He was willing to re-sign for less than he's worth. Tanner and I wouldn't let him, so he played hardball with management. We were both on pins and needles, as neither of us could ever imagine playing without the other. Coach Jeffries and I both went to management demanding that they pay Daylen the right amount. We all watched in awe as Tanner played management like a violin, with a little off-the-record help from me, until Daylen received every penny he's worth. Now my best friend is the highest-paid tight end in the sport and will finish his career in Philly with me.

Daylen jogs back toward me and places his hands on his thighs, out of breath. "Sorry, man. Jagger's boyfriend broke up with her last night. I was on the phone consoling her all night. She's a mess. Little fucking prick broke her heart."

Jagger is Daylen's much younger sister. I think she's around fifteen or sixteen now. His mother passed when he was young, and his father remarried a woman closer to our age than his. They had Jagger when Daylen was a teenager. Even though he only lived in the same house as Jagger for two years, he's fiercely protective of and extremely close to her.

I nod in understanding. "Perhaps we should drive down and have a little chat with him."

Daylen is originally from Maryland. His hometown is just

under two hours from Philly. It's not unusual for us to pop in for a meal now and then.

He smiles. "Not a bad idea, McCaffrey. Should I text Ashleigh that we're coming home for dinner tonight?"

I bite back my smile. "Doesn't she prefer you to call her *Mom*?" I happily joke.

His face falls. "She's eight years older than me. I will *never ever* call her Mom."

I chuckle. He hates it when I rib him about Ashleigh. Shrugging, I say, "But you have to admit she's a MILF."

He gives me the finger before we go on to finish practice and sit in the hot tub to soak our sore muscles for a bit. Daylen is showing me a handful of pictures he took of his Doberman, BJ. It stands for Blackjackie, since the Doberman is black. Her original name was Blackjack because it took Daylen a month to figure out it was a female dog instead of a male. His inability to recognize his dog's sex and her initials serve as endless fodder for obvious reasons.

Put mildly, he's obsessed with his dog. He even FaceTimes BJ when we're on the road so she can hear his voice.

We're looking at photos of BJ swimming in Daylen's pool when Coach Jeffries walks in. "Are you two studying the new plays I sent you?"

Daylen shakes his head. "Nope. BJ was practically doing laps in my pool last night. My princess has mad swimming skills. I'm showing Vance my bathing beauty. Do you want to see them too? I have photos from all angles."

Coach rolls his eyes. "There are roughly three total photos of me from the entire year of 1991, yet you have a hundred of your mutt from yesterday." He harrumphs. "Pft. Your generation and their photos. Always having the damn phones ready to snap away."

Daylen twists his lips. "Not true, Coach. It's more like two hundred of my *daughter*. And she's not a mutt. She's a purebred."

I chuckle as Coach sighs.

Daylen smirks at me before asking Coach, "How's Pierce?"

Coach has a seventeen-year-old son, Pierce Jeffries. He's a sweet, happy kid, often found hanging around the locker room over the past ten years. Coach is an awesome, hands-on father.

Coach smiles. "He's great. He's about to start his senior year of high school." He sighs. "It's hard to believe that in just over a year, he'll be leaving for college."

Daylen asks, "Is he planning to play football in college?" We know he's the star quarterback on his high school's team.

Coach shakes his head. "Nah. He's a nice player, but I never pushed him in that regard. Between you and me, he doesn't have the killer instinct that Kennedy has always had. And he's not half the athlete she is. It's always come naturally to her. Too bad those women's flag football leagues didn't exist when she was younger. She has a rocket of an arm. If Pierce had her arm, hand-eye coordination, and grit, it might be a different story for him."

Daylen mumbles, "I guess Pierce got the personality and Kennedy got the talent."

Coach chuckles. "Yep, she's a handful. God help the man who marries her one day. I'm just happy to have her back in town." He swallows. "Whether she's happy to be back or not."

He has a bit of a pained look on his face. I wonder what that's about, but it's not my business to ask.

He continues, "She indulges me now and then with a game of pickleball. The old fuckers at my club never see her coming. She wipes the floor with all of them," he announces with pride. "Anyway, check out the new plays. We've never had the type of running back we now have in Champ. I want the three of you to work as a unit. I've drawn up a few creative plays. Have them memorized before our next round of OTAs start."

I salute him. "Yes, Captain."

Coach looks around, appearing to make sure we're alone. "And keep an eye on Reece Sanders. Set him straight if needed. You didn't hear me order the code red, but I'm ordering the code red."

I nod, knowing exactly what he's talking about. Reece wouldn't high-five Champ at practice today. In fact, he goes out of his way to steer clear of Champ. It's unacceptable behavior.

A code red is a reference to Coach's favorite movie, *A Few Good Men*. It's a military term where platoon mates discipline each other within the group. It might be time for Reece Sanders to experience a Beau Fudd uninhibited tackle. Three hundred pounds of solid muscle crashing into his sub-two-hundred-pound body should do the trick. Or we could do something old school like putting hot sauce in his jockstrap.

After a quick stop to pick up BJ, we're in Daylen's custom Jeep Gladiator, his quarter-of-a-million-dollar gift to himself when he signed his new contract, heading down to Maryland. He texted Ashleigh that we're coming for dinner. She texted back that she'd make porterhouse steaks, Daylen's favorite food on this planet.

I shove BJ's head off my shoulder and toward the backseat. Wiping my shirt, I snap, "Stop drooling on me, you fucking big, saliva-producing oaf. D, your dog is disgusting."

Daylen scratches behind BJ's ear as she happily nuzzles into his neck. In a voice he reserves only for BJ, he coos, "Don't listen to grumpy Uncle Vance, baby girl. He hasn't gotten laid in months. His best chance at getting laid is ghost wanking."

I foolishly ask, "What's ghost wanking?"

Daylen gives me his goofy smile. "When you sit on your hand until it falls asleep and then jerk off. It feels like someone else is jerking you off."

I can't help but let out a laugh. "What the fuck? Is that a real thing?"

He smirks as he picks up a celery stick and begins to chew on it. "Sure is. Just be careful how long you sit on your throwing hand." He scrunches his face. "Actually, don't do it. Your hand and arm are too valuable. Or try it lefty?"

I shake my head. "I don't think I could jerk off lefty."

He straightens his shoulders with pride. "I can. I'm a very talented ambidextrous masturbater. Jerking off in a multitude of ways is my superpower. I even did it once with my own feet."

"Congrats, Captain Jerks-a-lot."

The song "Waterfalls" by TLC begins playing through the speakers, as it does every single time we're in his car. It's on his go-to playlist and his absolute favorite song in the world. He knows every word, including the rap verse. Who the hell knows that?

Daylen Humblecut does.

He begins dancing in his seat and happily singing along. "Don't go chasin' waterfalls..."

I shake my head. "Your obsession with that song is so fucking weird."

He gasps. "Best song ever. Anyone who says otherwise is lying to themselves. Doesn't it automatically make you smile?"

I scowl at him. "How often do you see me smile?"

He scratches his freshly shaven face. "You smile when you watch Ms. Sullivan O'Shea play ball. In fact, it's the first time I've seen your teeth in ten years of friendship. I think you're in loooooooove with her."

I shake my head. "You don't get it. Playing in the WNBA was her dream since she could walk. It meant a lot to Finn too. Seeing it come to fruition means something to me. Knowing I had some part in it is very fulfilling."

"Even if she doesn't know you had a hand in it? Maybe you should tell her."

I shrug. "Who cares about me?" Why are he and Tanner obsessed with me telling her everything? "This is about her and her dream. Wanting her to realize her dream is one of the last things he ever said to me."

His face turns serious. "I care about you. You don't have to carry the weight of the world on your shoulders. Not everyone is your responsibility to take care of. You need to do a better job taking care of Vance."

I turn my head and look out the window. "You and Tanner need to stop conspiring. At least be smart enough to use different words when you try to manipulate me. I don't want to talk about this anymore."

"Hmm."

We ride in conversational silence the rest of the time. Conversational because Daylen sings the whole damn time. "Waterfalls" plays no less than five times. I think he has it as every sixth song on his playlist.

It's early evening when we pull into his dad and Ashleigh's house. It's an upper-middle-class home within a nice subdivision. It's very cookie-cutter, with all the houses looking exactly the same, but it's still impressive. His father, Hank Humblecut, is a well-respected Federal judge and makes a comfortable living. He and Daylen are endearingly close. Aside from losing his mother, Daylen had a very American-pie upbringing.

The door opens when we pull in, and Jagger comes running out. At first, I think she's excited to see Daylen, but it's BJ she embraces. She falls to her knees as BJ licks all over Jagger's face, and she giggles in glee. It's very wholesome, though I chuckle as I notice that Jagger no longer is. She's in a short plaid skirt and a midriff-bearing, tight white T-shirt. Her blonde curls are wild, and she's got on way too much makeup for her fifteen years. And her height. She must have had a huge growth spurt since I last saw her. He better not bring her around the locker room. The guys will crucify him.

Daylen pouts. "What about me, Jag?"

She smiles as she stands and holds out her arms for him. Jagger looks more like Ashleigh but has Daylen's larger-than-life grin. They share it with their father, one of the happiest human beings I've ever met in my life.

They embrace like they haven't seen each other in years, with him twirling her around, even though I know it's only been a few weeks. Daylen goes out of his way to spend time with his little sister. She was the reason he was willing to accept way less money from the Camels to stay close by. It was Tanner and I who encouraged him to play hardball. Daylen didn't have the stomach for it, but Tanner wouldn't let him settle, and it worked.

Ashleigh comes into view in the doorway, and I have to bite back my smile. What can I say about Ashleigh Humblecut? She's a piece of work. She's an attractive forty-year-old woman but has gotten a little carried away with the fake boobs and Botox. Her body looks like she must spend a lot of time in the Pilates studio, and she more than loves showing it off. Her barely there tight red cocktail dress is kind of ridiculous for a family dinner at home in the middle of the week.

She offers a big smile and holds her arms open in invitation. "Come say hi to Mommy."

I can't help but bark out a laugh as Daylen rolls his eyes and leans down to give Ashleigh a quick hug. She reaches up and messes his hair like he's a child before squeaking out, "I'm so happy to have our baby boy home. We've missed you."

My stomach is shaking while I try to hold back my laughter. She's so ridiculous.

I give Jagger a warm hug. "It's good to see you. You've gotten so tall."

She smiles with pride. "I know. I love it. I'll be taller than Daylen one day soon."

Unlikely, but I love that she's confident in her height. I remember Sulley being so uncomfortable about it in her youth. It's such a contrast to how she holds herself now. I love the type of woman that Sulley has grown into.

Daylen's father then comes into view. He's enormous, like Daylen, with a similar, jovial personality. He's wearing suit pants with a white shirt and a loosened tie. They man hug like they might break each other.

He then holds out his hand for me, and I shake it. "Hank. Always good to see you."

He gives me a genuine smile. "You as well, Vance. I'm looking forward to a great season." He waves. "Come inside. I'm starving, and this food smells delicious. Sweet cheeks, you've outdone yourself tonight."

He pinches Ashleigh's ass, and she giggles up at her husband, who's twenty-five years her senior.

She winks at him and responds, "Yes, Daddy."

Yep, Ashleigh outwardly calls him Daddy. Daylen cringes, like he does every single time she says it. Fuck, I love spending time with the Humblecuts.

We make our way inside. It does smell good. I don't get home-cooked meals very often. It's a treat, and Ashleigh happens to be a great cook. I think culinary school was one of the twenty different schools Hank supported her through until she became pregnant with Jagger and decided to stay home with both her and Daylen.

We sit down and dig into the five-star restaurant-quality-looking steaks. Ashleigh smiles at Daylen and asks, "How are you finding your steak, baby boy?"

With a straight face, Daylen responds, "Quite easily. It's right next to the potatoes."

It takes Ashleigh a solid ten seconds to get the joke after everyone else does, but she eventually joins in on the laughter. At least I think she gets it. Fortunately for Jagger, she got her father's brains.

Daylen asks Jagger, "Are you feeling better than you were last night?"

She nods. "Oh yes. Will apologized. We're back together. He's coming by for dessert in a little bit."

Daylen's jaw tightens. "Oh good, he and I can have a little chat."

Jagger's eyes widen. "Be nice."

Daylen's lips twist. "Will do, sis. I'll be super nice to the demeaning fucker." Yep, he and I are going to have a bit of fun with this little twerp.

Ashleigh smacks Daylen's hand. "Don't curse. I brought you up better than that."

Daylen rolls his eyes before he looks his father up and down. "Dad, I thought Ashleigh had you hitting the gym with her?"

Hank does appear a little heavier than normal. He's a large man, but I don't think I've ever seen his stomach this big. It's hanging over his belt quite prominently.

Ashleigh gives him an *I told you so* look, but he smiles and says, "My beautiful wife is a great cook. I feel like I've spent my whole life trying to live healthy, constantly battling my weight. I want to enjoy myself. Keith Richards outlived Richard Simmons. What does that tell you about healthy living?"

Hmm. He does make a valid point.

Hank looks at me. "What's going on with you, Vance? Do you have a special lady in your life or are you a manwhore like my son?"

I chuckle. "No one special, but Daylen has a lot more luck with the ladies than I do."

Hanks nods in understanding. "And your parents? How are they?"

"Busy on the ranch. They let me take them on vacation a few months ago, but they don't love leaving the house in someone else's hands. It's always like pulling teeth to get them to go anywhere."

And I'm persona non grata in my hometown, so I rarely visit. When I do, I'm holed up in the house for a few days before I start to go crazy and end up leaving early to head back to Philly.

He smiles. "Well, tell *yo mama* that I say hello."

Daylen snaps his head toward Hank, and they give each

other bemused looks. Jagger whines, "Oh no, don't start this. It's so embarrassing."

Daylen and his dad have a thing of trading *yo mama* jokes back and forth. Daylen said it started as a way to make him smile after his mother passed but has continued as their fun little thing. It goes on and on until one of them laughs. It's basically a contest to get the other to laugh first.

Hank wipes his mouth with his napkin as he stares at Daylen. "Yo mama is so hot; her bone structure is giving *my* bone structure."

Ashleigh giggles and Jagger hides her face in mortification, but Daylen remains straight-faced before eventually responding, "Yo mama is so ugly; she has to roofie her vibrator."

I can't help but let out a laugh at that one, but Hank remains stoic as he thinks for a few hard beats before saying, "Yo mama is so slutty; she wanted to role play as a washing machine so she could have my dirty load inside her."

Daylen spits out in extremely loud laughter while Jagger shouts, "Ohmigod, Dad! That's disgusting!"

Hank eventually matches Daylen's laugh while Ashleigh giggles and happily watches the interaction. I'm honestly not sure if she even understands the jokes.

After an always amusing Humblecut meal, Daylen and I insist on washing the dishes until there's a knock at the door. Jagger pops out of her seat. "It's Will. I'll get it."

Daylen turns to me. "It's go time."

I nod. "Yep."

A skinny punk with too many piercings and baggy jeans sitting halfway down his non-existent ass walks into the kitchen. His shit-eating grin immediately drops when he's met with two giant football players staring at him like they want to kill him, along with a Doberman who Daylen has given the guard dog signal to.

Jagger rolls her eyes. "Ignore them, babe. They're nothing but big softies. All three of them."

Daylen lets out a low grumble from deep in his chest while I puff out mine. We're a combined five hundred plus pounds of muscle staring down at a kid who can't weigh more than a hundred and thirty pounds.

We basically spend the next hour scaring the kid shitless. I can now guarantee he won't fuck with Jagger Humblecut ever again.

This is the most fun I've had in a while.

EIGHT

SULLEY

We're almost done with practice, but I'm barely able to participate. Coach Lakshmi tells me to go see our team's physical therapist to work on the finger I jammed during our game last night. I scrunch my face in disgust. No one on the team likes the PT, Noah. He's a little handsy with us.

I'm alone in the training room with him as he manipulates my finger. I wince at some point, and his face falls. "I'm going to grab you some ice. I think you should buddy tape it for a bit so it doesn't get worse. It's not broken, just a little bruised." He moves behind me and rubs my shoulders. "You should be fine in a few days."

"She's here for her finger, not her shoulders, Noah," Kennedy declares as she walks into the room.

"I was trying to soothe her, Kennedy," he responds.

She makes a jerkoff motion with her fist. "Whatever. Make yourself useful. Grab me some ice for my ankle."

"What's wrong with your ankle?" he asks. "Do you need me to examine it?"

She gives him an exaggerated fake smile. "No. It's nothing for *you* to worry about. Do your job, med-school wannabe. Fetch. The. Ice."

He narrows his eyes at her before turning toward the ice-making machine. She gives him the finger behind his back as she sits next to me.

"What's wrong with your ankle?" I ask.

She shrugs. "Nothing. I didn't want you to be alone with him. He's a walking episode of *Dateline*."

I study her carefully. "You confuse me. You're the world's biggest bitch but you also manage to be an incredibly thoughtful person."

She mock wipes the dust off her shoulders. "You flatter me."

I smile. "I'm not sure I meant it as a compliment. At least not the first part."

"Whatever. Sometimes you just need to be a cunt. You never know who's having a good day and doesn't fucking deserve it. Noah *definitely* doesn't deserve it."

I can't help but laugh. "You're refreshingly unapologetically you."

She smirks. "I sure am. For what it's worth, I'm a bitch to those who deserve it, but I'm thoughtful to those who deserve that courtesy. It's quite simple. It's called being genuine. More people in this world should try it."

I nod, grateful that I seemingly fall into the latter category. "Do you want to ride over to Layla's tonight with Palmer and me?" I inquire.

She shakes her head. "I can't. I'm hanging out with my little brother all afternoon. We're going shopping." She picks her cuticles as she looks down nervously. "I've been kind of a shitty sister to him for the past few years. I left him to deal with my parents' divorce alone. I'm trying to make up for it. He's seventeen. He needs some girl advice, and I want to help. I guess when you're the older sibling…"

She catches herself and stops speaking. I shake my head. "You don't have to feel uncomfortable talking about your brother with me. It's okay. Don't censor yourself."

She nods in understanding as Palmer walks into the training room like she was rushing here. She removes the prescription goggles she wears while she plays. A little out of breath, she pants, "Oh good, Kennedy is with you. I didn't want you to be alone for long."

I can't help but smile at how thoughtful my new friends are. Female friends looking out for me is new. In fact, I haven't felt like someone truly has my back since Finn died. Not even Shane.

Kennedy glances at Palmer's goggles. "Why don't you just wear contacts? It's easier."

Palmer scrunches her face. "I don't like contacts." She looks down as she admits, "I feel like my goggles are my mask, hiding me from the world."

Kennedy looks at me and deadpans, "And *I* feel like everything she says is a subtle cry for help."

I shrug. "The goggles are a comfort to her. Whatever makes her comfortable. If she needs them, so be it. Who cares?"

Kennedy scoffs. "What she needs is to have a man snap her spine like a glow stick."

I let out a moan. "Ooh, that sounds good. I need that too."

"Wasn't Shane just here?" Kennedy asks.

I twist my lips. "He's not exactly snapping my spine. Things are always just okay with him. He's not *the one*."

I shock myself with that admission. While I've thought it internally, I've never outwardly expressed it to anyone. I suppose I've never had anyone with whom I felt comfortable expressing my inner thoughts until now.

Palmer sighs. "I feel like I'll never meet *the one*."

Kennedy shakes her head. "Fuck *the one*. None of us needs *the one*, especially not while we're so young. I'm not sitting on my ass waiting around. I managed to get myself off this morning and then bought myself a jar of pickles and a quad venti soy extra hot no foam light whip toffee nut latte from Starbucks. I really think I'm *the one*."

Palmer and I both laugh at Kennedy as Noah approaches us all with bags of ice. He smiles at Palmer. "I heard what you were saying. I love your goggles, and I'd love to take you out some time. Would you like to have dinner with me?"

Palmer bites her lip nervously. "Umm...no, I don't think it's such a good—"

He places his uninvited hand on her arm. "Oh, come on. It will be fun."

She flinches at his touch. "Well...I...it's just—"

Palmer is clearly uncomfortable. I'm about to say something when Kennedy smacks his hand away from Palmer and interrupts, "No is a full sentence, Noah. She gave you her answer. Slither away, slimeball. We're talking."

He narrows his eyes at her but does eventually retreat to his small wooden desk on the other side of the room. Fuck, he's creepy.

A skinny black man who looks to be in his forties walks into the room holding a big bag in one hand and a bouquet of Chocolate Cosmos in the other. He's the epitome of casual, high fashion, with black slacks and a cream knit shirt, clad with a complementary scarf and beret. And it's summer.

He gives us a warm smile before placing the bag on the table and offering me his hand like I should kiss it. In a slightly feminine voice, he practically sings, "There you are, Sullivan. Bonjour, I'm Carter Daulton's assistant, LeRond." Carter is Reagan Daulton's husband. "She asked me to deliver these to you. It's this week's fan mail and the flowers you asked her to pass along when they arrived."

"Oh, thank you." I take in the size of the bag. "Wow, there's a lot of mail this week."

"There sure is," he offers. "And you haven't seen all the flowers and other gifts, girlfriend. The kids at the hospital will have the brightest rooms in existence." He looks Palmer up and down and hands her a business card. "I would love to make you over. I think there's a Wonder Woman under there, Diana Prince."

Before waiting for a response, he swivels around and exits the room. I almost feel the need to clap for him as he goes.

I look into the bag, unable to believe how many fan letters I'm receiving. And I continue to get emotional every week when Vance sends Chocolate Cosmos. I know he's been gone at their training camp for two weeks, but I've still received my weekly deliveries to our stadium.

An hour later, Palmer and I are exiting the elevator toward our apartment when I see an oversized teddy bear sitting in front of our door. I smile, assuming it's from Shane. We had a little fight on the phone last night. He's probably apologizing.

As I open it, I realize that it's from a fan. Shit, this person knows where I live. I contemplate calling Reagan Daulton, but I don't want security, so I decide against it.

VANCE

I'm at Layla and Presley's house. They're having a dinner party. We just returned from two weeks of training ahead of our pre-season games starting. I've been to most of Sulley's home games and never miss any games on television. I enjoy watching her play. Thanks to Presley, all the Beavers' games were televised on the big screen in the clubhouse at our training facility while we were out of town. He loves to watch his wife play ball. It makes it easy to sit with him under the guise of supporting Layla when it's entirely about Sulley for me.

We've all been out a small handful of times since that first night. Sulley mostly ignores me, but at least she hasn't yelled at me and left in tears again. I've remained quiet as the collective groups interact and build a friendship. All except Daylen and Kennedy, who continue to bicker. It's an interesting dynamic; one I've never seen from him before.

Tonight, at the Ladrón house, I'm hoping Sulley will at least make eye contact with me, something she rarely does. I'll take any progress.

Everyone has now arrived except Kennedy, which I'm certainly not complaining about. She's bizarrely cold to me, but frankly, I don't care. I only care about Sulley.

Sulley initially mumbled a quick hello to me but then turned around and quietly thanked me for the steady supply of Chocolate Cosmos I've been sending to her weekly. I know it was her special thing with Finn. I'm glad she likes them. They're not easy to find or inexpensive, but it's worth it just for her to talk to me.

The doorbell rings, and Daylen walks over to open the door. His face falls when he notices it's Kennedy. He grumbles, "You're late, sea witch."

She immediately responds, "Better late than ugly."

He shakes his head. "Why do you bust my handsome, scrumptious balls so much?"

She shrugs in an unaffected manner. "Believe it or not, I don't consider your balls very often. In fact, I've never once thought of them. Why do all men think balls are important to women? They're not. They're pointless and weak. We're confused by them. They sit there uselessly bouncing between your thighs. They expand and contract at random times. It's fucking weird. When we buy vibrators, do you know what they don't have? Balls."

Daylen stares at her for several long beats until he eventually lets out a loud, booming laugh. "Fuck. That's funny."

She narrows her eyes at him and gives an exaggerated fake smile before sarcastically quipping, "Well, my goal of being your amusement for the evening is accomplished."

Kennedy has an interesting look. Attractive but in a totally different way from Sulley. She's hard compared to Sulley's softness. If I didn't know better, I'd think she lived a difficult life. Her green eyes are piercing, contrasting with her very dark hair. It's rare to see her without a ponytail, though she's always dressed impeccably. Even when casual, it's in designer clothes. Like tonight. To the naked eye, she appears to simply be in jeans and a white T-shirt. I know everything she's wearing is designer, down to the very expensive high heels she's got on. The other girls are in sneakers, regular jeans, and Beaver T-shirts. Not Kennedy.

Daylen turns and subtly makes a jerkoff motion to me. He usually dates bubbly, overly friendly, compliant, ditzy blondes. Basically, the opposite of Kennedy Jeffries.

She's behind him as they walk through the two-story foyer into the main living area. Layla and Presley have a traditional, modest home in the suburbs. It's nice, probably about twenty years old, not overly grand, and not as modern as newer homes seem to be. I like that it's homey and filled with toys and clutter. It's real.

As he walks by, Daylen whispers to me, "Did you know vibrators don't have balls?"

I chuckle. "Have you never seen one?"

He looks appalled. "Why would any woman I'm with need a vibrator?"

I shake my head. "You're a moron."

He tugs on his hair, which is now in a ponytail, and says, "It must be the blond in me."

We all head out to the back deck, which is made of the fake wood most people use. I inwardly laugh. Finn would hate this fake wood. He was adamant about using real wood to build his cabin. He couldn't afford the higher-end materials, but insisted on using real wood.

Layla and Presley hired a caterer to cook and serve the meal. They said they wanted to sit back and have fun. With our season about to begin and the Beavers in the middle of theirs, things are going to be crazy, so a relaxing evening with friends is well-deserved.

It's me, Daylen, Beau, Champ, Sulley, Kennedy, Palmer, Shay, and her wife, Alyssa. It's a beautiful, warm summer night.

They don't have a ton of land, but the backyard has a pool and is well-kept. Even though their daughter can't walk quite yet, there are lots of child safety gates, fences, and latches set up everywhere. I didn't know so many things existed. It took Daylen and me ten minutes to figure out how to open a cabinet. Apparently they're both child and man-proofed.

We're just sitting when Kennedy's phone starts pinging with a text notification. She looks down at it and lets out a laugh before silencing it. I ask, "What's so funny?"

She shakes her head. "Nothing. A guy who ghosted me months ago just reached out. They always come crawling back for more."

Daylen scoffs. "When a guy texts you after ghosting you for months, he doesn't miss you. He's just checking to see if you're still stupid."

"Takes stupid to know stupid," she quips.

I look at Layla and attempt to steer the topic of conversation away from childish comments. "Thanks for having us. I'm sure it's difficult while in season and having a baby."

She smiles in gratitude. "Our pleasure. Honestly, it's been harder than I anticipated. Especially now when we're both busy with our teams. I've finally agreed to more help. My mother-in-law is staying with us until my season is over."

"Where is she?" Sulley asks.

Layla points her finger inside. "She's upstairs. I invited her, but she was just as happy to go to bed early." She lowers her voice. "The only issue is that she keeps telling me what to do with the baby. It's driving me nuts. I'm like, *bitch, I live with the kid you raised. Trust me, you don't know everything.*"

We all laugh. I love seeing Sulley smile. It's so carefree and genuine.

I ask her, "How did your Gatorade commercial with Tyrese Maxey go?"

She pinches her eyebrows together. "How did you know about that? I had to sign a nondisclosure. They don't want anyone knowing about it until it's released."

Shit. "Oh...umm...I was in Tanner's office when the offer came in."

She slowly nods. "Oh. I can't say much, but it went well. Tyrese was a total sweetie."

I can't help the pang of jealousy that takes hold of me. He got to do a shoot with her and spend the whole day with her.

"Glad to hear it."

She tilts her head to the side as if she's remembering the day. "The marketing rep from Gatorade was weird though. I think he makes up words."

I chuckle. "That would be Andrew Furman."

She nods. "Yep. That's him. He told me I was..." She places her finger on her lip as she tries to recall the word. "Stupenderific. What is that?"

I have to bite back my smile. "I think the movie *The 40-Year-Old Virgin* was his biography."

She giggles. It's the first time she's smiled at me in years. I feel like a million dollars.

She says, "Probably. But I'm excited to see the end product. The shoot went well."

Daylen proudly announces, "I had a shoot this week."

I lift an eyebrow. No, he didn't. I was with him at training camp all week. He winks at me. "It was for a new fragrance in honor of Vance. It's called, *Leave Me the Fuh Cologne*."

A small smile finds its way to my lips, but I still manage to give him the finger. Kennedy snorts in annoyance. "Men are so immature."

Daylen happily responds, "I consider myself a work in progress. Is that a red flag for you?"

She nods at him. "Immaturity is. Women mature faster than men because we get our boobs at fourteen and men get theirs at forty-five."

Presley shakes his head. "Coach Jeffries is about that age. No man-boobs on him. Only muscles. He's jacked."

Layla bites her lips and lets out a moan. "Umm hmm. Oh god, yes. He's so fucking hot. Have you seen those videos of him on TikTok? So many daddy videos of him."

Kennedy sits there with her jaw open. "Are you all for real? You know that's my father, right? Can we not discuss his status as a social media sex symbol? I had to delete most of my accounts because of it. No matter what I tried, it kept popping up on my For You page." She scrunches her face. "Ugh. Disgusting."

The guys and I all chuckle. I feel the need to defend Coach. "For what it's worth, he hates it too."

"And yet he allows topless videos of him working out to be posted," she challenges. "He doesn't *have* to work out topless. He doesn't *have* to pose for the videos. Trust me, he loves the attention." She mumbles, "He always has."

I share a look with Daylen. We both know Coach is unaware of all of those videos.

Layla shrugs. "Sorry, Kennedy, but he's my number one hall pass. That man is fiiiiiine."

The caterer serves us all our food as Kennedy stares violently at Layla, seemingly waiting for the servers to leave before responding. Once they do, she bites back, "Aren't hall passes technically supposed to be for someone who's unachievable? You've likely met my father. He's a free agent now. I'm sure he's having a grand old time being single with the bevy of bimbos lined up at his door."

"He's not," I interrupt, again feeling defensive of Coach.

"He's very focused on your brother. He's put his own social life on hold until your brother graduates."

She mumbles something about doubting that but otherwise drops it before turning to Presley and asking, "Who's your hall pass?"

His eyes widen. "This feels like a trap."

Layla rubs his back. "It's okay, love. You can tell them who." She then turns and mouths to the rest of us. "He has no chance."

All eyes turn to Presley. He fidgets nervously. "It's...umm... Jennifer Connelly."

I shrug. "She's hot. A little older, but still hot. Nothing wrong with that."

Layla smirks. "Continue, chiquito."

He visibly swallows. "Jennifer Connelly from when she was riding—"

"The horse in *Career Opportunities*," Daylen interrupts.

Presley blows out a breath in relief. "Yes. So hot."

Daylen nods. "I think every guy jerks off to that scene. It's a rite of passage. No shame in that."

Career Opportunities was a cheesy nineties movie. It wasn't very successful, but every man in America had some sexual response to that scene of Jennifer Connelly riding a fake horse in a department store.

There's been music playing in the background, just barely loud enough to hear. Suddenly, Beau starts quietly singing, almost as if he doesn't realize he's doing so. It's the song "Call Me Maybe" by Carly Rae Jepsen. In his crazy deep voice, he sings as he wiggles in his seat.

Palmer starts giggling at the big guy knowing all the words. Before I realize it, almost everyone has joined in on the lyrics.

The whole group is smiling when the song comes to an end. Sulley looks at Beau. "I didn't expect that coming from you." She glances around with amusement. "*All* of you. What other girly songs do guys secretly like?"

Champ answers, "'Shake It Off'. Taylor Swift is my queen. I went to ten shows on her Eras Tour."

Layla nods. "Oh yes. Her show in Miami was amazing." She smirks at her husband. "Presley loves 'Wannabe'. He belted out a Spice Girls medley to me on our first date. I think it's half the reason I fell for him."

Presley nods. "Most underrated band ever. I'm still praying for a reunion tour."

Daylen bats his eyelashes. "I'm a Beyoncé kind of man." He stands and starts singing and dancing to "Single Ladies" by Beyoncé. He struts across the whole deck as he performs the choreography perfectly, as I've seen him do many times before, though usually when drunk. The man does have shockingly good rhythm, especially for a guy his size.

Everyone watches on with amusement. Kennedy stands and dances behind him, happily mimicking the moves in perfect unison. Before I know it, all the girls get up and join him in the choreography. Champ does too.

When it's over, Layla smiles at me. "What are *your* secret favorite girly songs, Vance? I have a feeling there's a man in touch with his feminine side under those jeans and cowboy boots."

I can't help the smirk that finds my face. Daylen coughs, "Anything Miley Cyrus."

Sulley lets out a loud laugh. "Vance particularly likes 'Wrecking Ball' and 'Party in the USA' by Miley." Her eyes flash with amusement. "He used to make my brother listen to all her songs when they were building a cabin together."

I'm a little afraid it's going to bring up difficult memories for her, but she's grinning from ear to ear.

My eyes find hers. "Well, you watched the damn *Hannah Montana* movie every day that summer. It was burned into my brain."

She giggles. "You used to sing 'The Climb' every time you drove into the mountains. Right when you passed the sign for the Beartooth Mountains."

I wink as I sing out the first line of the chorus, "There's always gonna be another mountain. I'm always gonna want to make it move…"

I pause briefly, and the whole crew joins in on the rest of the chorus, followed by a sea of laughter.

We end up having a nice evening. I'm so happy Sulley and I finally connected on some level, albeit a silly one.

I drove, so I barely drank, but the girls are mostly sauced. I offer to drive them home. Shay's girlfriend doesn't drink, so she has Shay and Kennedy in her car.

I'm driving Sulley and Palmer back to their apartment. They're sitting in the back, adorably giggling together. The Sulley I remember from childhood was a tomboy with very few girlfriends. I think they were all probably jealous of her. I'm happy she's found some nice friends here.

I can't help but quietly smile at their interaction. Their heads are practically glued together as they speak way too loudly but think they're whispering. I'm gathering that Palmer has a bit of a crush on Beau. He might be a little bit too much for a demure girl like Palmer, but who knows what could happen?

When I get to their apartment, I insist on walking them up since there's no doorman. When we get to the door, I see a bouquet of Chocolate Cosmos. Sulley turns to me. "Did you send them here this time?"

I shake my head. "I didn't know your address until tonight." I scratch the back of my neck. "I…umm…didn't want to be intrusive. I send them to the stadium each week."

She pinches her eyebrows together. "Who else in the world would send these? Maybe they're from Shane." She runs her lower lip through her teeth. "No, he doesn't know about these flowers."

What the fuck? Her boyfriend doesn't know her favorite flowers. I hated him plenty before, but now I hate him even more for being a selfish asshole.

She continues. "They're probably from my parents."

As soon as she opens the card, I know it's not them. Her face falls as it turns a shade of white.

She looks at Palmer. "We need to call Reagan Daulton right away."

What the hell is going on?

NINE

SULLEY

I t's early in the morning. We had such a great time at the dinner party last night, but then a scary, sobering return home. After we told Vance what was going on, he insisted on sleeping on our couch. Between the liquor and the fear, I didn't bother to put up a fight. There was something instantly comforting about having him here, and I was too shaken to consider otherwise.

I tiptoe out to the living room and see Vance fast asleep. He's on his back with one arm above his head and the other resting on his bare, shirtless stomach. The blanket is pooled at his waist.

I haven't seen his body in over five years. It's only gotten sexier and has never once failed to stir something deep inside me. I can't help but smile at the memory of the first summer he had chest hair. He was probably about fifteen, and it was way before my brother had any chest hair of his own. We constantly made fun of Vance. At the time, I thought it was gross. Now I ache to run my fingers through it again. My lips. My tongue.

Stop it.

My eyes travel from his body to his handsome face. Even in

his sleep, he looks like he's stressing over something. Does he regret his actions? Sometimes it's hard to believe he did what he did to Finn, but he's never once offered an explanation or expressed any remorse. How could he be so callous? And then there's the man who remembers my favorite flowers and sends them to me every week. The one who completely flipped out last night at the notion of me possibly being in any danger. Who refused to leave our apartment and insisted on making himself a barrier between our front door and me.

He's such a confusing man. He equally does horrible and thoughtful things.

He shifts slightly, and I can now see part of a tattoo creeping out from his left side, but his arm is still mostly covering it. I didn't know he had a tattoo. That's new since I last saw his body. I wonder what it is.

I try to get a closer look, but he begins to stir, so I scurry toward the kitchen and turn on the coffee maker. About ten minutes later, he enters the kitchen dressed. In his sexy morning voice, he grumbles, "Morning."

I offer a small, appreciative smile. "Morning. Thanks for staying."

His eyes take a very obvious fill of my legs in my tiny sleep shorts before he catches himself and nods. "Of course." He sits down across from me at the small kitchen table. "What will happen today?" he asks.

"I have a meeting in Reagan Daulton's office in an hour. She said she'd figure things out overnight and have a plan by the time I arrive. I have a feeling she's going to insist on some sort of bodyguard. I can't believe it's gotten to this point." My shoulders fall. "I just want to play ball. Knowing that a stranger not only knew my favorite flowers but left them at my front door and told me he liked the purple shirt I wore the other day…" I shiver. "It's freaky."

He gives me a compassionate look. "I know it's tough. All the other shit that comes with being a successful athlete. I've been through stuff like this before. I love the fans, and most are amazing, but you come across a crazy one now and then. I don't love my condo, but I live there because it's the most secure building in the city. I can't wait to move out of the city to have my own safe, private space."

I didn't know he was moving. "Where are you going?"

"The suburbs. I'm building a house." He opens his mouth like he wants to say more but thinks better of it.

The coffee maker signals that the pot is complete, so I stand and pull out three mugs from the cupboard. "You still take it black?" I ask with my back to him as I pour his.

"I do." He lets out a quick laugh. "I remember when you wanted to drink coffee like us but hated the taste. You would drown it in that crappy French vanilla shit."

I open the refrigerator and hold up a big bottle of my French Vanilla Coffee-Mate.

He chuckles. "Some things never change."

I snap my head toward him and can't help but blurt out, "Yet in a moment, everything does."

His small smile immediately fades, and his eyes hold mine. If I didn't know better, I'd think they were filled with unshed tears.

He stands. "I should head out."

I nod. "I think that's for the best."

I pour his coffee in a to-go cup and send him on his way.

AN HOUR LATER, I'm in Reagan Daulton's office. It's her main business office, not the one at the stadium. It's in a huge Center City skyscraper, and she's on the very top floor. Her office is bigger than any I've ever been in. She exudes power, wealth, and sophistication in a way I've never seen before. Yet somehow she also conveys sincerity and compassion. I like her. We all do.

She leans back in her chair behind her giant marble desk and blows out a long breath. "This isn't good, Sulley. We've got an obsessed fan who knows where you live. It's probably harmless, but I'm not willing to risk your well-being. People snap and become unhinged. We can't allow this to escalate any further. I know you don't want a bodyguard, but we at least need to find you an apartment with better security. I called in a few favors and can get you into a great building. It's very secure."

I chew my lip nervously. "Okay. I understand. How much is the rent? And I won't leave Palmer at our place alone now that whoever the fan is knows the address. She'll have to come with me."

She waves her hand dismissively. "Don't worry. I'll take care of your rent. It will be for both you and Palmer, of course. The only problem is that they don't have an apartment available for another month."

"Okay. Kennedy offered to house us. She has a guestroom."

She shakes her head. "No. I checked her building. I want you to have top-notch security. One that I know will keep you safe. A simple doorman isn't enough. We want security officers, codes, cards, the whole works."

"What are you proposing?" I ask.

Her blue eyes meet mine. "I considered a hotel, but—"

"Ugh, no."

"But I think it's too public. People can walk in and out at will. Vance McCaffrey called me a little while ago. I didn't realize that you two were childhood friends. He has several extra guest rooms in his condominium. He lives in a fantastic building, as I'm sure you can imagine. The best security around. He offered you and Palmer a place to live as long as you need it."

I immediately shake my head. "Absolutely not."

A small smile finds her lips. "He said you'd decline at first and to remind you that between his upcoming travel schedule and yours, you'd barely be there at the same time. I'm sorry to do this, but I need to insist. It's that or a full-time bodyguard."

I blow out a breath. I cringe at the thought of my teammates seeing me with a bodyguard. I *know* it would cause problems. I'm officially stuck between a rock and a hard place.

Sensing my hesitation, she sighs. "I know it's not ideal. I've hired a private investigator. If we can find the culprit, I'll loosen things up a bit, but for now, please do this. Your safety is everyone's main concern."

With a hefty dose of trepidation, Palmer and I move into Vance's condo that afternoon.

IT'S BEEN two weeks since we moved into Vance's supermodern, smart, voodoo condo. I swear, I've never seen anything like it. It's not what I would ever expect him to have. I hate it.

You can voice command everything in here from the music to the shower to the lights to the damn toilet seat. It's ridiculous. I can't believe Montana cowboy Vance McCaffrey lives here. Finn would laugh his ass off if he saw Vance in this place.

It's high in the sky with great views. That's the only part I like. Otherwise, it feels like a museum. I'm afraid to touch anything. It goes to show how much Vance has changed from the boy I once knew. I guess I don't know Vance McCaffrey like I thought. I suppose I already realized that.

We've barely seen him between our travel schedules and a severely ramped-up Camels' practice schedule heading into the start of their season. He's been very hospitable, and we're trying to be respectful guests. He's been thoughtful and filled the house with things he knows I like. I laughed when I saw the French Vanilla Coffee-Mate in his refrigerator when we arrived.

As kind as he is, I just want this month to come and go with as little interaction as possible. Besides a few awkward conversations in passing, I've mostly managed to steer clear of him at his condo, and when our friends hang out, I always position myself away from him and talk to other people.

I often catch him staring at me. I find myself wondering what he's thinking when he does. He looks so empty. Frequently appearing pained but otherwise a bit stoic. It's hard to read him at times.

The Camels arrive back in town today after a preseason game last night. We have a game tonight.

It's late afternoon, and I'm about to leave for the stadium when my phone rings. I see it's Shane, so accept the call. "Hey, babe."

"Oh, good, I caught you. Did you see my game tonight?" he asks.

I scrunch my face. He's going to be pissed. "Sorry. I messed up the time zones. I had a meeting with Tanner this morning. I've got this—"

"Are you fucking for real right now? I told you it was important to me. It was a big game, and my coach was finally giving me a start."

"I'm sorry, Shane." I feel terrible. "I'll watch the replay when I get home tonight from my game. Things are just a little crazy for me right now."

He audibly sighs. "It's always crazy with you, with the world revolving around you," he says with a steely voice dripping with sarcasm. "This whole relationship is about you and your needs. What about me? What about my needs?"

I sigh. "You're right. You specifically asked me to watch the game, and I fucked up. I'm truly sorry. I promise to make it up to you."

His tone softens. "How do you plan on doing that from across the Atlantic Ocean?"

"I've got an opportunity in Italy. That's what I was discussing with Tanner. When my season is over in October, I'm going to be able to come visit."

"Really?" He sounds so hopeful.

"Yes. Really."

"Ahh. I'm so fucking happy right now." He lets out a moan. "I've got the worst case of blue balls in existence."

I giggle. "Me too. Well, not balls, but you know what I mean."

"I do, beautiful." He starts breathing heavily. "How about some naked pics to tide me over?"

We've been through this *many* times before. I can't risk that, but I don't want to piss him off. "I've...umm...got to head to the stadium. Maybe when I get home."

Thirty minutes later, I'm in my locker room. As we all change into our warm-up uniforms, I turn to Kennedy. "Do you send naked pictures to men?"

If anyone does, it would be her. She's probably the most sexually uninhibited woman I've been around. When we go out, it's common for her to aggressively flirt and sometimes go home with a new, random guy. She doesn't even hide it. I admire how bold and unapologetic she is.

She shakes her head. "Fuck no. You can't trust any of them. I'm semi-famous, and you're legit famous. We have to be extra careful. Talk about the quickest way to go from a serious athlete to a two-dollar whore. Is Shane asking?"

I nod. "He's been asking for over a year. I haven't done it yet for fear of them somehow getting out."

She looks at me for several long beats. "Look, Shane seems like a nice enough guy, but unless you feel complete and total trust in a man, I wouldn't do it. Do you trust him to *never* release them, even if things go to shit?"

I'm silent, and she gives me a small smile. "I think we have our answer."

I run my fingers through my hair. "It's not that I don't trust him, I just don't think he's...he's..."

"He's not your forever. You told us he's not the one. I get it."

I shake my head. "I don't think so. I don't know. I guess I'm not sure."

"You should cut him loose so you can go out and have a good time."

"No, I don't want that. I care about him. He's...comfortable."

She twists her lips. "Ahh, the beginning of every great love story. He's…comfortable."

I scrunch my face at her repeating my words. I did use the word comfortable.

She places her hand on my shoulder. "I'm not here to tell you what to do. As your friend, I just want to support you."

I smile. "Kennedy Jeffries, are we friends?"

She bites back her smile. "Frenemies."

I let out a laugh. "Sure. Frenemies."

Her face turns a bit more serious. "Like it or not, you're a star, Sulley. I used to think you asked for it. Even basked in it. That was why I hated you."

"You hated me?" I joke. I'm more than aware she wasn't my biggest fan.

"Before I spent time with you? Yes. As I've gotten to know you, I've quickly learned that it's not the case. You don't want or ask for this attention. You're just out there hooping. But you're taking our sport to the next level. I know it's a big weight to bear, and you always do it with grace and humility. I admire you for it. Your boyfriend should too. His ego shouldn't get in the way of anything."

She gives me a knowing look. She's right about Shane. Sometimes I feel like I have to hide things from him because he'll get upset if things are going too well for me.

As for naked pictures, those are off the table.

I look up at her. "Thanks, friend."

She winks. "Anytime, frenemy."

A FEW HOURS LATER, we're in the fourth quarter of our game. The other team is being particularly physical with me tonight. I've taken a lot of elbows and hard body checking. The refs seem to be keeping their whistles in their pockets.

I do have my new bodyguard, though. Kennedy should have

been a hockey player or a defensive lineman. She's giving it right back to them tenfold.

I pop in a fadeaway jumper over the woman who's been the biggest culprit in pushing me around all night, Diane Garma. I know her well. She was a year ahead of me in college, and we played in the same conference, meaning I played against her a few times each year. She's always been overly physical with me. She was the first pick in last year's draft. I know there were a lot of comments made at the time that if I hadn't sat out that first year of college, I would have been the first pick last year instead of her. I'm sure she just has an axe to grind, but she's a little out of control right now.

Kennedy isn't having any of it. She's right in Diane's face after my shot goes in. "Five fucking years, Diane. You haven't been able to defend her for five years. Stop trying."

Diane mumbles, "Fuck you, Kennedy. Must be nice to ride her coattails."

"Better to grab onto her coattails with my hands than how you get through life on your knees." Kennedy backpedals but still manages to reach and wipe Diane's chin. "You've got a little something on you, D. Leftovers from your afternoon with the team owners? Maybe the referees too?"

I can't help but smile as I run back to get on defense. Kennedy winks at me with a small smirk on her face. Damn, I'm glad she's on *my* team.

Diane smacks Kennedy's hand away. Hard. The ref then blows his whistle, calling a foul on her.

Kennedy blows on her nails like it's all in a day's work. I notice all the Camels guys sitting courtside laughing. I think they're wildly amused by the fact that women trash-talk too, and none are better at it than Kennedy Jeffries.

The cameras love to find the guys. Beer drinking contests among Camels players at our games have become the normal courtside entertainment for everyone. I swear, Beau and Daylen make it seem like one gulp. I don't know how they do it.

It's always on ESPN at night. It's only bringing more attention to us. Attendance and television viewership are way up. Life is good.

VANCE

I've loved having Sulley living with me. I think she's starting to thaw toward me a bit. I've tried to be respectful and stay out of her way, but I also stocked my fridge with all the things I remember her liking. She noticed and was grateful.

They're only a few days away from moving into their new place, and I'm about to leave town for our last preseason game before our season officially begins.

While we've been super busy, we're both free later this afternoon, and I told her I wanted to show her something. She skeptically agreed.

This morning I'm in the film room with my team. We're watching game tape on our opponents, something we always do leading up to games.

We're reviewing our upcoming opponent's defensive coverage when Presley turns and asks me, "Have you seen the movie *Marley and Me*?"

"About the dog?"

He nods. "Yes."

"I've seen it. That's a good movie."

He agrees, "It is. We watched it recently. Layla cried like a baby when they put the dog down."

I shrug. "So? What's wrong with that?" I think I cried at the end of that movie too. It was so sad when they had to put him down.

He sighs. "She usually watches true crime documentaries on Netflix. Some deranged serial killer who has murdered thirty people; she doesn't cry over that. But a fake dog in a movie? *That* makes her cry?"

I hear Beau's deep voice from the back of the room. *"Marley and Me* is a true story."

My eyes widen as I turn to him. "It is?"

He nods. "Yep. It's based on an autobiographical novel. I read it. It was good."

Daylen and I exchange glances before he jokes, "I didn't know you knew how to read, Fudd."

Beau doesn't bother to respond to Daylen's ridiculousness. If there's one thing Beau knows how to do, it's reading. The guy went to Stanford and majored in biochemistry while dual-minoring in English literature and Greek mythology. He looks like he doesn't have a single brain cell, which most people assume, but it's just the opposite, and I have a ton of respect for him and the fact that he's continuing his studies despite the demands of our job. He's fairly quiet but is always game to hang out and certainly attracts the attention of a lot of women. I wouldn't call him a player, but I've seen him leave with women on a few occasions. Women flock to the big guy.

Beau looks at his watch. "Are we done? I have a date."

Daylen raises an eyebrow. "With who?"

Beau answers, "Whom. It's with *whom*. And it's none of your business."

Presley happily chimes in, "We have a new thing for date night. We have sex *before* we go out. This way, when we get home feeling bloated and tired, we can just go to bed."

I narrow my eyes at him. "Are you eighty? What the fuck is wrong with you? You should service your woman both before *and* after a date."

He shrugs. "Layla is usually mad at me by the end of a date. Now I definitely get laid. It's kind of genius. The other night we had sex before our date. She hurt her shoulder in her game, so when we were done, she asked me to help her put her bra back on. I couldn't do it, and she was yelling at me. I said, *Why would I know how to put a bra on? I've only ever taken them off women."* He winces. "It made for a tough night. If I hadn't already gotten laid, I wouldn't have gotten any at all. That's the genius in the pre-date sex plan. It's like I'm hedging my bets."

Daylen chuckles as he stands. "You kids have fun. I'm going to shake hands with the president." He leaves and makes his way toward the bathroom while the rest of us head out of the stadium.

As soon as I'm in my truck, I instruct Siri to call Maddie. She answers after several rings. In a voice that seems less than thrilled to be hearing from me, she says, "Hi, Vance."

"Hey, Mad. I sent some birthday gifts for Francesca with my check this month. I know they're a few weeks early, but I wanted to make sure she had them by her birthday and my season starts next week. I tend to lose time and forget things when the season starts."

She sighs. "Yep, they came this morning." She exhales a long breath. "I'm going to remove the card. I don't want her to know who they came from."

My jaw tightens. "You can always say they came from her father."

"No, Vance. Curtis is her father." She pauses. "At least the only father she's ever known. We've discussed this. You're not around for her. Curtis is. Hit and run fathering isn't what she needs. I appreciate all you do for her, but I can't have you upsetting the applecart."

I try to remain calm. "Listen, I'm thinking of coming home for at least a month or two this year whenever my season is over so I can get to know her properly. I want to spend real time with her."

She immediately responds, "No. She's at an age when she's going to start asking questions about who you are. What would I say? It was fine for you to pop in twice a year when she was younger, but not anymore. We've discussed this. She loves Curtis. He loves her. He's the biological father of her brother and sister. It's easier for them all to think they have the same father. Less confusing. Please. Leave our arrangement as is. She's thriving."

"But I want—"

Her tone escalates. "What *you* want doesn't matter," she interrupts. "You and I made this decision years ago. Curtis Huddle is the only father she knows. He's in her life every single day. I'm the decision maker. This is how it's going to be. You have no right. That's a fact."

There are so many things I want to say to Maddie, but I hold my tongue, like I always have. Curtis *fucking* Huddle, Maddie's husband, is a jobless piece of shit, happy to live on my money, but I can't deny that he's been there for Francesca, and she seems to love him. At the end of the day, I want what's best for Francesa, and if Curtis is it, then I'll stay where I've always been. In the shadows.

I NERVOUSLY DRIVE Sulley and me out of the city. She asks a million questions along the way, but I remain tight-lipped. I don't know how she's going to handle what's about to happen, but I'm dying to share this with her over anyone else, even Daylen.

We pull through the secluded, tree-lined gravel driveway until we reach a clearing. The property is currently full of cement trucks, pickup trucks, and two big trailers. Sulley pinches her eyebrows. "A construction site?"

I nod toward the fresh cement falling from the trucks. "They're laying the foundation today for my new house. I... umm...I wanted you to be here for it."

I don't know how she's going to react, but I want her here. I need her here.

She nods, thinking she understands. "Oh. Your new house. That was quick. You're moving forward?"

I nod as I grab my bag from the backseat and open the door. "Come on, I want to show you a few things."

We exit the vehicle and make our way to the main trailer. Walking inside, I see my general contractor, Collin Fitz. He's about ten years older than me. He owns a high-end construction company specializing in custom mansions. He built Cougars pitcher Quincy Abbott's mansion and is currently building Layton and Arizona's. When I showed him what I wanted, he was really excited about the project. He said it's completely different from anything in the area. I love that.

Collin, who is a decent-looking guy with hair a little longer than mine, lifts his head and smiles. "Vance! Glad you're here. We have a question about the fireplaces."

I shake my head. "The answer is wood burning. No self-respecting cowboy has a gas fireplace. Stop asking. My answer will never change. I don't care what it means for the chimneys. I don't care that it will cost me extra money. Wood fucking burning only."

He chuckles. "Fine. Can't blame a guy for asking. I'll make it work."

I nod as I point to the beautiful woman next to me. "This is my friend, Sulley."

Collin's grin widens. "Sulley O'Shea. The new sweetheart of Philly. I know who she is. I'm close with the Daultons. Carter and I have been friends since we were little kids. Reagan is my baby mama's cousin." He moves to shake Sulley's hand. "I'm Collin Fitz."

She shakes his hand. "Nice to meet you, though I'm not sure why I'm here."

I motion my head toward the architectural prints he has scattered across the office desk. "Can you give Sulley and me a minute with these? Alone."

Collin nods. "Sure thing, bud." He commands the three other workers to leave, and he follows close behind them, shutting the trailer door as he goes.

Sulley turns to me with a confused look on her face. Folding her arms across her body, she asks, "Why do we need to be alone? Why did you bring me here, Vance?"

I point toward the drawings. "Have a look. Please."

She walks over and begins studying them carefully. I see the moment it hits her. Her hand covers her mouth, and tears immediately fill her eyes. She whispers, "It's his design."

I pull out my wallet and remove the folded napkin I've carried in there for fifteen years. It's the one with Finn's initial sketch of my dream house. The one we planned on him designing for me. Like every sketch he drew, it's signed *Finn's Fantastic Designs*.

When the military sent home his belongings, they included preliminary architectural drawings for my house. He must have worked on them during his downtime. They weren't detailed yet, but they were more than halfway done. Either he didn't have time to finish them or he was waiting to learn how to do so in school. Either way, it was the best thing I've ever received in my life. A final gift from the grave.

Before the madness surrounding Maddie ensued, Finn's mother sent me the drawings, knowing I'd want them. I've been waiting for the right architect to bring his vision to life. I must have sent the drawings to fifty different companies before one small shop truly understood what I wanted. It took a few years of me arguing with them back and forth, but they finally became perfect and exactly what I know Finn imagined. And once I met Collin and saw his enthusiasm and skill, I knew he was the right one to build it. I had already purchased the land, which also took me time to find, but when I found this previously wooded plot, I knew I was home.

"I always promised I'd be his first client."

Tears now freefall from her eyes. It's quiet for several minutes as she takes in this moment. At some point, her pained, glassy blue eyes look up at me. "Why, Vance? Why did you do it? Why Maddie? You can have anyone you want. *Anyone.* You knew he loved her."

I pull my eyes from hers as I shake my head. "We're not here to talk about that. I can't change the past. Leave it in the past where it belongs."

"But you can explain it to me. Until the day I die, I'll never understand it."

I'm quiet. I have no words for her. None that I'm willing to give her right now.

She eventually turns her attention back to the drawings and quietly runs her fingers over the designs as if she's touching a part of him. I feel the same when I see them. I can only imagine what it will feel like when the house is done.

She studies every aspect of them carefully, as if committing it all to memory. It truly is special in so many ways. He would have taken the architecture world by storm. I know it.

It's not the modern monstrosity I live in now. I fucking hate my condo and all that it represents. My new house, Finn's design, is an homage to our roots. At its core, it's a cabin. It might be an eight-thousand-square-foot cabin that will look like it belongs in a luxury mountain magazine, but it's a cabin, a ranch, and it's exactly what I want. Finn knew. You can take a cowboy off the ranch, but even in a big city, he's still a cowboy and wants to live like one.

I point to some of the open land out the window. "When I retire, I want to build a stable and get horses. It's too hard with my travel schedule now, but in a few years, that's what I want."

She gives me a small smile. "You always loved to ride."

"So did you."

The O'Sheas didn't have horses of their own. I think it was a combination of finances and the fact that Finn was highly allergic to them. I took Sulley out on our ranch several times. She loved it.

She cracks a small smile. "Is Hail Mary still alive?"

She was Sulley's favorite horse.

I shake my head. "No, she's gone. Her daughter, Snap Count, is still alive though. You should ride her next time you're home. She handles like Hail Mary."

Sulley presses her lips together, remaining silent at the offer.

I hold up the bag in my hand. "I have a few of Finn's things. Will you help me put them in the foundation? I want to feel his presence in this house when it's done."

She turns her head, so our eyes meet again. "I don't know that I can. It feels like I'm betraying him."

I shake my head. "Just the opposite. You're honoring him. You know what being an architect meant to him. This is the only house he will ever design. You should be a part of it. He would want that."

"He designed his cabin. *My* cabin."

"He roughly sketched that on a high school notepad. We made things up as we went along. If you knew how off-kilter some things in that house are, you'd laugh. *This* house. *This* home. He designed it like the professional he should have become, and it will be built by actual construction profession-als. It will be Finn O'Shea's masterpiece. *Finn's Fantastic Designs* will be the official architect of record. His unique vision will be on display in every corner of this house and will live on forever. I'm naming it Finn's Farm."

She covers her mouth as she lets out a loud sob. Every instinct in my body tells me to take her into my arms, but I know she doesn't want that. I have to ball my fists because they're trembling to comfort her.

I motion my head toward the door. "Come. You'll regret it if you don't."

She wipes the tears from under her eyes and eventually nods. "Okay."

We walk toward the area where the cement is currently pouring from the truck. I pull out his away jersey from our high school team. I know Sulley has his home jersey. It's got number twenty-two on it. I give her a small smile. "I love that you share the same number as him."

She nods as she watches me toss it into the wet cement before it's quickly swallowed down.

I then throw in a few photos of us. I have copies, but I want photos of us to be buried here.

After a few more small items are thrown in, things we collected through the years, I pull the last item off my wrist. It's a small leather band. Sulley had bought them for us as holiday gifts one year. They were made from a football. She whispers, "You kept it."

I nod. "We refused to call them friendship bracelets because that was so girly."

She gives me a small smile.

I continue, "But we knew they were. He was buried with his. I thought I'd bury mine here."

I toss it in, and we both look on as it disappears to its final resting place. Tears silently roll down her cheeks. It's taking everything I have to hold mine back.

She tilts her head back and looks into the sky for a moment, as if communicating with him. Once she brings it back down, she unzips the small purse she's wearing across her chest. She reaches in, and I inhale a sharp breath at what she pulls out.

"You don't have to."

She shakes her head. "I can't explain it. I just have this strong feeling that he'd want me to."

She takes one last long look at his dog tags before pulling one of the two off the chain, kissing it, and then throwing it into the cement. She squeezes the remaining tag with white-knuckle force as she watches its partner find its final resting place.

Both her gesture and seeing it disappear cause a wave of emotion to overtake my body. A large knot forms in my throat.

I don't want her to see me like this, so I turn and quickly

make my way into a more private wooded area before eventually allowing myself to cry. My shoulders shake as it all hits me. I lean on a tree and sob in a way I haven't since the day we found out he was killed.

Why him? He was such a good, honorable man. He didn't deserve it. It's been more than five years, and the pain feels as fresh as it did the day we lost him.

After a few minutes, I feel her hand on my back. Her touch is tentative at first, but she eventually wraps her arms around my body, sinks her face into my back, and sobs with me.

I turn around and do what I've wanted to do the whole time we've been here. I take her into my arms and hold her tight as we both freely release the emotions that have been constantly weighing on us.

Holding her feels so right. It feels like home.

TEN

SULLEY

We were eliminated from the playoffs this afternoon. It was a bummer, but our team overachieved for a first-year franchise. We're still learning how to work together, and I'm truly excited about the future of this team.

I received the league's Rookie of the Year award. While it's always nice to be recognized for my efforts, I prefer team success as opposed to my individual success.

Nonetheless, making it to the playoffs was considered a victory. Reagan Daulton came into our locker room after the game to tell us how proud she is of us and how excited she is for next season.

We all plan to take a little time off and then reconvene after the holidays to start training as a unit for next summer's season. We only had a few weeks of practice as a team before this past season started. We need time to learn each other.

I'm equally excited about my new group of friends. We do everything together. Philly is starting to feel like a home, more than I thought it would.

The Camels are a few games into their season now. They're

playing well. Adding Champ to the roster has taken some of the pressure off Vance and Daylen. With defenses having to stack the line to stop Champ, Daylen is only receiving single-man coverage. He and Vance have connected on a few huge highlight-worthy plays already. They've won three of their first four games and are sitting at the top of their division.

They have a game tonight. Gatorade purchased a club box and invited me to attend as their guest. I told them I wouldn't come without my teammates. They agreed to include our whole team and even sent us all McCaffrey jerseys. Given that Vance has a partnership with Gatorade, I suppose them giving us his jersey shouldn't be unexpected.

My Gatorade commercial with Tyrese Maxey came out this week to much praise. It's very cute, with us *passing* the Gatorade bottle back and forth down the court. He's such a nice guy, and we had fun during the shoot. It was also a great payday for me. Enough for me to put a deposit on my very own house. It's a walkup brownstone, and I haven't been this excited about anything in a long time.

Reagan nearly had a coronary when I told her it wasn't in a secured building, but the initial craziness and hoopla surrounding me has died down, and I don't want a condo in some fancy building. I've hated where Palmer and I have lived for the past month. My new place has history and character. Somewhere that feels homey and comfortable for me.

I settle on the house in January. My plan is to spend a little time in Rome with Shane after my upcoming photoshoot in southern Italy, and then I'll head home for the holidays, returning to Philly after the new year to begin training with my teammates and to move into my new house.

I'm torn about wearing Vance's jersey, something I used to do religiously but haven't in more than five years. In the end, I throw it on because Gatorade sent it and something shifted between Vance and me a few weeks ago when he took me to see his house.

The devastation he still carries over Finn's death is very real. His love for my brother is very real. I hope one day he'll explain to me why he slept with Maddie, but I'm stuffing that aside for now. Frankly, I'm starting to wonder if maybe she didn't drug him or somehow otherwise manipulate him into sleeping with her. I swear I never thought he liked her. I don't think I imagined the glances he and I would share when Maddie was being selfish and whiny around Finn.

Vance not being in Francesca's life is baffling to me, but perhaps I'm missing something. I think Vance is holding onto a secret. It's just a feeling I have. It's like a big, incomplete puzzle, and I know I don't have all the pieces. Perhaps if we rekindle a bit of a friendship, he'll confide in me.

Layla has arranged for us to meet the boys at a bar after the game. She said if they win, it will happen. If they lose, it won't. With only seventeen games in the regular season, each one matters a lot, and they take losses very hard. I think there are also a lot of expectations placed on them this season.

The Anacondas just won another softball league championship. We were there cheering them on. It wasn't even close. Kam went on a home run tear in the championship series and carried the team to victory.

Arizona and Layton are getting married soon and were kind enough to invite me, but it's when I'll be in Italy. I'm sorry to miss it. I'm sure it will be a blast. She also told me that she's pregnant. I'm so excited for her. That will be one beautiful baby, considering the parents.

We're sitting in the club box as Layla is explaining that we'll go to the bar next to the stadium if they win, when Kennedy looks at her. "Wait, we're going straight from here? I thought I'd have time to go home and get ready. I only took a ho shower."

I ask, "What's a ho shower?"

She smirks. "Everything but the hair."

I can only shake my head at her.

Layla says, "We're going straight there. It's not like we're clubbing tonight. It's just drinks at a local sports bar. What's the big deal? I texted you about it this morning."

Kennedy blows out a breath. "I must have missed it. I swear, I'm such a dingbat lately. I had a date the other night with a guy I met on Tinder. He walked me to my door and asked if he could come inside. I told him we just met and asked if he could do it on my tits. He said he meant inside the house."

I giggle, but Palmer gasps. "You didn't really say that to someone you just met, did you?"

Kennedy winks. "Sure did. And he ended up coming on my tits anyway."

Palmer looks at her in awe. "I could never have sex with some random guy I met online on the first night I met him. Are you dating him now?"

Kennedy makes a look of disgust. "No. I went to his place the next night, thinking I'd be up for another round, but he has one of my red flags in his apartment, so I'm done with him."

I bite back my smile. Red flag conversations have become our norm. "What was the red flag?"

"He had," she winces, "a *futon* as his main couch." She says futon as though it's a bad word. "Hell to the no."

I let out a laugh. "I've had a futon in almost every apartment I've ever lived in."

"You just graduated from college. This guy is in his thirties. He has an established career. Unacceptable. Red flag. I turned around, left his apartment, and then blocked his number."

Palmer sits up straight and bounces a bit with excitement. "I've been thinking about your red flags, Kennedy, and I found another one of mine. A man who orders tater tots at a restaurant. It's very unmanly. I don't care for it at all."

Kennedy narrows her eyes. "All of yours surround food. Maybe you have an untapped food fetish."

I nod in agreement. "It's true. Yours do revolve around food. Maybe a man eating manly food does it for you." I growl. "Rawr. Like tearing into a big piece of steak."

Palmer bites her lip. "Oh my god, I do think that's hot. Maybe I do have a food fetish."

Layla lets out a laugh. "I think you might. I personally hate men who are rude to waiters. When they act like they're above one, it's such a turnoff. Honestly, I love how kind and generous Presley is to waitstaff. On our first date, we had the worst waitress in the history of the world. It took forever for her to take our orders, she then messed them up and was so incredibly rude to us throughout, even though we gave her no attitude. Presley never lost his cool and then left her a giant tip. When I asked him why, he said he couldn't imagine she was going to keep her job for long and would probably need the money." She clutches her heart. "I thought that was so sweet."

I nod. "It *is* sweet."

The girls then talk about men who make everything about them as being a red flag. Those who never ask questions about you. I can't help that Shane pops into my mind. He does that. All our conversations are about him. He gets short with me when I discuss what's going on in my life, almost as if my success is an insult to him. He never asks about me and how I'm doing in Philly. Shane doesn't know everything, but he knows I was struggling seeing and living with Vance. He's never once mentioned it, even when I lived with Vance. He doesn't ask about my brother. We've been dating over two anniversaries of Finn's death, and Shane has never once reached out. Vance, on the other hand, sends me a card every year on the anniversary. I know he sends one to my parents too.

As if he knew I was thinking about him, I notice him glance up at our box and stare right at me. He offers a little wave before tugging at his jersey and cracking a small smile. I look down at myself. He likes that I'm in his jersey.

I think I like it too. *A little too much.*

VANCE

Christ. My cock swells in my uniform pants at the sight of Sulley in my jersey. My mind keeps drifting to what it would be like for her to be on her knees sucking my cock wearing that same jersey.

I break eye contact and shake my head in disbelief. Focus, Vance. It's a big game against a division rival.

I shift my hips, suddenly realizing how unforgiving football pants are.

I tug on them to give myself some room and hear Daylen chuckle. "Are you at full salute from seeing the object of your affection in your jersey?"

"She's not the object of my affection," I spit in response.

"Yet you knew exactly who and what I was talking about." He smirks. "Hmm. Interesting."

"Fuck off, dickhead."

"I think it's the head of your dick that wants to fuck."

I pinch the bridge of my nose. "If you keep it up, I won't pass the ball to you today."

He winks. "I think you will, loverboy. I'm the teacher's pet." He starts subtly shaking his ass and softly singing, "My milkshake brings all the boys to the yard. And they're like, it's better than yours."

I can only blow out an exasperated breath at my crazy friend.

WE'RE at the sports bar next to the stadium. The fans party here after all games, and they love it when we make an appearance after a big win. The excitement is electric, and it's packed with wall-to-wall Camels fans excited at the great start to our season.

There's a balcony area reserved for us so we can wave at and interact with the fans without being completely hounded.

Due to Layla's WAG status, the Beavers ladies are already up on the balcony when we arrive. I think the fans are equally as excited to see them up there. I happily watch them wave and throw freebies to the crowd. It's good to see them getting so much attention. Even though their season ended, Philly has embraced them, and the future is promising.

Flanked by security, we walk up the steps of the balcony. With the fall nights getting a little chilly, Daylen is wearing a Camels green knit hat, as he often does after our games.

Kennedy takes one look at him and chirps, "Your cap looks like the Incredible Hulk's condom."

He shrugs, seemingly unaffected, as he calmly replies, "It's Bobby Brown."

She narrows her eyes at him. "What does that mean?"

He smirks. "My prerogative."

She exhales an audible breath. "The fact that jellyfish have survived for hundreds of millions of years without brains must give you so much hope."

He rolls his eyes. "Blow me, sugar lips."

She gives him a small smile. "I would, but my coach said I need to bulk up."

"Why are you so nasty?" he asks with uncharacteristic edge in his voice. "Do you stay up at night and contemplate the best ways to be a bitch?" he raises his voice at her. This woman truly gets under his skin. It's amusing to watch.

She nonchalantly shakes her head. "No, I stay up and contemplate random scenarios. Like what would happen if one conjoined twin committed a crime and had to go to jail? Do you falsely imprison the other one?"

He tilts his head to the side as he considers his words. "Holy shit. That's a good question. Do you know the answer?"

She lets out a laugh. "No, bonehead. I don't."

His lips curl in amusement. "I might research the issue."

Sick of their bizarre foreplay, I walk over to Sulley. Her face lights up as she sees me approach. "Nice game, Vile Vance."

"Nice jersey, Gully Sulley."

She bites back her smile. "I was contractually obligated to wear it. It was done under duress," she says in a teasing manner.

I nod in understanding. "Hmm. I get that for the game. Are you *still* contractually obligated to wear it *after* the game?"

Her eyes fall to the floor as she mumbles, "I guess certain habits are hard to break."

"What does that mean?" I ask.

Her eyes widen a bit, as if she's catching herself, before they raise to meet mine. "Nothing."

Before I can inquire further, Layla sloppily throws her arm around Sulley's shoulders. She's clearly a little tipsy. "What do you say, O'Shea?" Layla hiccups and giggles. "That rhymed. I'm a poet and didn't even know it."

She starts laughing hysterically at her own cheesy joke before eventually calming down and again asking, "What do you say?"

Sulley pinches her eyebrow together. "Umm, about what?"

"Vegas, silly. I was just telling you about it. At least I think I was. The guys on the team go for the first weekend of the NCAA tournament every year in March. I didn't go this past year because of the baby, but I usually go. So do most of the other WAGs."

The NCAA basketball tournament takes place over two weeks in late March into early April. It's a huge sports event, the first weekend being especially fun because there are so many games. With the possible exception of the Super Bowl, it's the biggest weekend in Vegas each year. We always go and have an absolute blast betting on games, drinking, dancing, and generally partying until we can't stand.

Sulley shakes her head. "I'm not a WAG."

Layla smiles sweetly. "But you're my friend, and I want you

there. Kennedy and Palmer already said they're in. They're not WAGs either."

Sulley looks at me, and I nod. "It's always a fun weekend. It's a bit of a team tradition. We rent two floors of suites at the Palms Casino. The more, the merrier."

She runs her lower lip through her teeth. "It's something I've always wanted to do but never could because I've always been playing ball that weekend. Hmm…why not? That sounds like fun. I've never been to Vegas. It's on my bucket list."

Layla squeals in excitement. "Yay! We're gonna have a blast. I'll book everything. The guys charter a jet, so you don't even need plane tickets. Just a few fabulous outfits for all the fun parties we'll attend," she bumps her hip with Sulley's, "and sexy bikinis for the pools. I'll email you all the logistics, but be prepared for a fantastic time, right, Vance?"

I nod. Vegas is sounding a lot better this year.

ELEVEN

SULLEY

I've had the most magical week on the Amalfi Coast of Italy. The company treated me like a queen. They put me up in a suite in a fancy hotel, gave me a huge daily allowance for food, were respectful during the photo shoots, and made sure to schedule work obligations so I had plenty of free time to explore the majestic area.

The company is an Italian athletic clothing line named Veloce. Apparently, they have a partnership with Daulton Holdings, Reagan's company, and she recommended me as the spokesperson. It is by far my biggest payday, and I'm so grateful to her for advocating for me. She has more than lived up to every promise she made before she drafted me, which included being supportive of me both on and off the court.

Veloce is trying to bill this line as both athletic and beachy. Seems like a weird combo to me, but the money can't be beat, and I got a free trip to Italy. Accepting it was a no-brainer.

My photo shoots were spectacular. I can't wait to see the pictures. The nights are a little lonely. Shane said he couldn't get away to come join me, but I don't mind wandering the old, cobblestone streets alone. I've experienced beauty on this trip that I've only seen in books before. You can't appreciate certain things unless you see them in person.

I'm sitting in a café on my last night here when I receive a text notification and look at my phone.

Vance: How did it go?

I've been here for eight days, and my boyfriend hasn't once asked me that question. In fact, he's only texted about how many days until we have sex again. I also noticed that he took a few screenshots of our FaceTime calls and posted them to social media without bothering to ask me if I minded. I know he's a bit of a social media whore, but when I'm in videos or photos of us together, I'm giving my consent. A secret screenshot doesn't have that.

This trip has given me a lot of time to consider my relationship with Shane. I think I'm going to enjoy my week with him, and then I might suggest we spend some time apart. I suppose I'll see how it goes, but I'm leaning toward ending things.

The sound of my FaceTime ringing breaks me from my thoughts. I look down and notice it's Kennedy. She may be the biggest shock of my moving to Philly. Second only to transitioning into an amicable relationship with Vance.

Kennedy has this hard exterior, but inside, I believe she's a good person. She hides it from the world, but I see it.

I accept the call and smile into the screen at my beautiful friend, who looks like she's in bed. "Hey! How are you?"

She answers, "I'm good. My brother had his last high school football game this weekend. It was cool to see him play. He was excited to have me there." She bites her lip. "Thanks for the advice. You were right."

She and I had a conversation recently about her relationship with her brother. She has some animosity toward her parents, which has resulted in her not spending much time with her little brother over the past few years. He invited her to his senior night game, and she was on the fence about attending. Given how much I cherish the memory of my brother attending mine, I encouraged her to go.

"That's great. I'm happy you went. It was the right thing to do. I'm sure your brother was happy."

"Crazy happy." She squints her eyes at the telephone screen. "What the hell are you drinking?"

I giggle. "A margarita. I know it's not very Italian, but I practically OD'd on Italian wine this week. Sometimes a girl just needs her comfort drink."

She nods. "I get it. Nothing beats a good margarita. The difference between a man and a margarita is that a margarita hits the right spot *every* time."

I let out a laugh. "Sure does."

"Is Shane with you?" she asks.

I shake my head. "He was busy this week. He ended up not coming down. I'm supposed to head up to him in two days, but our shoot is over early. I may travel up to Rome tomorrow to surprise him." I let out a breath. "I think I might end things. I'm not sure yet, but I'm thinking about it."

"Are you upset about the prospect of things being over between you two?"

I shake my head and answer honestly. "Not really."

She shrugs her shoulders. "I suppose that's very telling."

She's right. It is.

She continues. "No offense, Shane seemed like a nice guy, but he doesn't look like the best sex of your life kind of guy. He's not the multi-orgasm-inducing type. He looks…missionary to me."

I let out a laugh. "Yep, he's a little missionary." What I don't admit to her is that it's more than that. He's never once made me feel like I felt with Vance in my bed all those years ago, and all we did was kiss and touch a bit. I want someone who sets me ablaze like Vance did. Maybe even someone who pushes me out of my comfort zone. Hearing about Kennedy's sexcapades over the past few months has made me realize I've been missing out.

I admit, "I might enjoy a few days locked up with him before I end things, but my next man is going to be your multi-orgasm-inducing type."

"What's your kink?" she asks.

"I'm not sure I have one," I honestly answer.

"Everyone has a kink. Even Rapunzel wasn't satisfied until some guy pulled her hair."

I giggle.

She sighs. "I suppose we need to find you a man who helps you discover yours." She wiggles her eyebrows. "As soon as you get back to town, I'll help introduce you to new men."

"Sounds like a plan."

"Have you done any shopping?" she asks. "The stores there are amazing."

"Just a little bit. A few souvenirs," I answer.

"Ugh. Spoil yourself. If you get used to receiving nice things, you'll never accept a guy who gives you the bare minimum."

"Ooh, I like that line."

"Me too." Her face then falls serious. "I did call for a reason. Have you read the news at all today?"

I shake my head. "No, what's up?"

"Your agent, Tanner Montgomery, got into a bad car accident last night. Your softball friend, Bailey Hart, was in the car with him."

I gasp. "Oh my god. Where were they? Are they okay?"

Her face scrunches a bit. "It was on their way home from Arizona and Layton's wedding. I think he's going to be fine, but the news stations are saying that Bailey is in surgery. She… umm…may have broken her back. But it could just be rumors. I don't know anything for sure."

Tears fill my eyes. Bailey Hart was the first person to welcome me to Philly when I visited before the draft. She's been so kind to me. She comes to games all the time when they're not playing. My heart breaks for her.

"I'm going to run so I can find out how she is. Thanks for letting me know."

"Sure thing."

We hang up, and I'm not sure who to call. I imagine her sister and friends are at the hospital. I don't want to bother them.

I take a deep breath, knowing there's only one person who I can call right now. I find Vance's contact information and click on his number. He answers after only one ring. "Hey. Are you okay?" He sounds frantic.

"Yes. I just heard about the accident. What's going on?"

He exhales a long breath. "It was pretty bad. Tanner wrapped his Maserati around a pole. I'm trying not to bother them, but Cheetah has been sending updates when he can. Tanner only has a concussion. A bad one, but no permanent damage. Bailey fractured her spine. They think she'll walk again, but it's going to be a long, uphill battle. She's going to need months of therapy to get back to normal."

Tears fall from my eyes. "Holy shit. Poor Bailey. Is there anything I can do?"

"Nah. She's got her core group there, so nothing right now, but once she's out of the hospital, I think that's when she'll need support."

"Wow. Okay. Will you keep me updated? I don't want to bother them, but I want to know how she's doing."

"Of course. Champ is good friends with Bailey. He said he's going to the hospital either tonight or tomorrow morning. He'll update us afterward. I'll text you then. How are things going for you?"

I look around at my beautiful surroundings. "Great. Honestly, I feel like I'm in a real-life painting."

He chuckles. "I get that. I went to Italy once. It's...different from what you and I are used to, right?"

I find myself wondering who he went with. It's such a

romantic country. Why do I feel a pang of jealousy that he possibly experienced it with another woman? More importantly, why do I care?

"It is," I answer.

"Is Euro-trash boy with you?"

I let out a laugh. "He's from Massachusetts."

"Meh. He looks like Euro-trash to me."

I shake my head in amusement even though he can't see me. "No, he was busy. I'm heading up to him in Rome tomorrow."

He mumbles something about Shane being a douchebag for not spending time with me while here. Frankly, I don't disagree with that statement, though I'm starting to feel like Shane isn't the man I'd want sitting across from me at this charming café. Vance is. I get a vision of his sexy hair blowing in the breeze. The small smile he reserves for very few people, but I know I'm one of them. His green eyes practically burning a hole through me, the way they do sometimes when I'm in a skirt or dress.

I squeeze my eyes shut. Fuck, Sulley, this is Vance. The man who betrayed your brother on the deepest level. On the other hand, he's also the man who is making my brother's dream come true.

I'm silent, feeling a clusterfuck of emotions. "Vance, I should go."

"Oh, okay. When are you back in Philly?"

"Not until after the holidays. When I leave here, I'm heading straight home to my parents. Good luck with the rest of your season. Please text me Bailey updates when you can." I need to get off the phone.

"Thanks. Will do."

I'VE JUST EXITED the train in Rome and am in a cab on my way to Shane's apartment a day ahead of schedule. I'm going to enjoy my week with the man I've spent the past eighteen months with, and then I've decided to tell him that it's time for us to go our separate ways. I think he'll be heartbroken, but it's for the best. I'm hopeful it will be amicable, and we can remain friends.

I arrive at his nice, five-story apartment building and Tetris my big suitcase and me into the tiny elevator. I've learned that elevators in Italy are way smaller than those in the US, even in a glamorous apartment building like his. I wonder if they're like that everywhere in Europe. I've never been anywhere else.

He has moved since the one and only time I visited last year. He was in a nice apartment building then, but this one is even better. The EuroLeague must pay its players well.

I exit the elevator, wheel my bag to Shane's apartment, and knock. After a few seconds, the door is opened by a stunning Italian woman around my age. She's in only a T-shirt that comes to her mid-thigh. I'm about to look at the apartment number again, assuming I'm in the wrong spot, when I realize the T-shirt she's wearing is the same Beavers T-shirt that Shane wore to my game when he visited. I would know, I gifted it to him.

"Who is it, babe?" I hear Shane ask before the door widens, but not nearly as much as his eyes do when they find me. A shirtless Shane stutters, "S…Sulley. You're…you're umm…umm a day early."

Yep, because that's the problem here.

At least I now know for sure that my thoughts over the past few days about breaking things off with him were right on the mark. If I was on the fence, I no longer am. Not because he's a cheating asshole, but because I genuinely don't give a fuck that he's a cheating asshole. I'm standing here with a half-naked girl in my boyfriend's apartment, and the only thing running through my mind is that I don't want to be half-naked with him anymore. She can have him. I'm done with the narcissist.

The girl smiles innocently. In heavily Italian-accented English, she says, "I'm sorry. Who are you?"

Honestly, she looks nice. Like someone I would be friends with. I have no ill will toward her. I hate it when women blame other women for cheating boyfriends. It makes no sense to me. This woman doesn't owe me anything. Shane does. She clearly has no idea who I am and this sucks for her as much as it does for me. Maybe more.

Hmm. So many things I could do right now. I could yell and scream. I could turn around and walk away. Or maybe I should channel my inner Kennedy and have a little fun on my way out. Watch the weasel squirm a bit before I make my grand exit.

I offer a huge grin and hold out my hand. "I'm Sulley. Shane's cousin." I look at a visibly shocked Shane. "Silly, you forgot I was visiting, didn't you? So typical."

"Oh…umm…yes. I…forgot."

"Aren't you going to invite me in, *cuz*?"

Shane's mouth opens and closes a few times. He looks like a fish. It's almost comical. How was I ever attracted to him? I'm also realizing he's lost a lot of muscle mass since I last saw him. Clearly he hasn't been working out. He's suddenly so unattractive to me.

The woman pulls me inside and wraps me in a huge hug. "Oh my god, I'm sorry I didn't know you were coming, but I'm so excited to meet a member of my Shane's family. Please excuse the mess. Our housekeeper is off this week."

I look around. It's a massive apartment, and it's not messy at all. It's luxurious and looks like a decorator designed it. What the hell? Where does he get this kind of money? I can't imagine it's cheap to live in Rome. Maybe I'm wrong.

She continues, "I'm going on vacation with my family this week to Greece. We leave tonight. I wasn't going to go because I'd miss Shane, but he encouraged me to." She squeezes Shane's hand as she grins widely. "He's so good to my family. I'm beyond thrilled to meet a member of his. I wish I could stay and show you the beauty of Roma."

"Oh darn, I would have loved that," I lie. Deciding to prod further, I ask, "Why isn't Shane going with your family?"

She looks adoringly at him. "My man is such a hard worker.

He's got practices all week. I know how much he loves to practice. He's going to be a huge star."

Shane doesn't have practice this week. They're off. He was supposed to be with me all week, seeing the sights around Rome and then traveling to Venice for a romantic few days. What an asshole.

"Such a hard worker, my cousin. Never takes time off for a little fun," I deadpan at Shane. "That must be why you're *so* successful. He's always telling me, *practice makes perfect*," I say in a deep, mocking voice.

The truth is, Shane isn't a hard worker. He had the raw talent to play professionally in the US, but he didn't have the work ethic. Not what you need to take your game to that truly elite level. I massaged his ego when he didn't get drafted, even though I always knew the truth deep down inside. So did the teams in the US.

The woman naively smiles as she nods in agreement, not realizing I was being sarcastic.

"Well, I've clearly caught you by surprise, and I've got a little jetlag. I'm going to head over to my hotel. Cuz, do you want to help me take my suitcase downstairs?"

He looks like a deer in headlights. "Sure."

He starts to walk out, but I hold up my hand. "Put a shirt on." I scrunch my face as I point to his chest. "I don't want to see my cousin like that."

The nameless woman giggles as Shane quickly runs toward what I assume is the bedroom. I say to her, loud enough for Shane to hear, "What's your phone number? We should stay in touch."

She squeals in excitement as Shane runs out of his bedroom in the midst of pulling down a T-shirt. "No need. I'll give you her number."

"Nonsense, cuz. I'll send her some cute pics of you as a kid. What's your number?"

She happily gives it to me. I doubt I'll do anything with it. I just want to see him sweat and have him live in fear of me reaching out to his girlfriend.

He silently carries my bag as I send him down the elevator first with it. We could have squeezed in together, but I don't want to be that close to him.

When I eventually make my way down, he's waiting with a sheepish look on his face. "I'm sorry, Sulley."

"Sorry I found out, or sorry that you're a two-timing sleazeball?"

He nervously runs his hand over his freshly shaved head. "I'm just sorry. Why didn't you expose me?"

"Honestly, Shane, because I don't give a shit. If I caused a scene, it would show that I'm emotional over this, and I'm not. I mostly just feel bad for her. She's got to spend time with a lazy, self-centered, narcissistic asshole."

His lip twitches. "This isn't my fault. You never make time for me. I need a woman who wants to be there for me."

I shake my head as my anger finally begins to bubble toward the surface. "Don't gaslight me, asshole. I may have been weaker when we met, but I'm not anymore. The fact is that you're jealous and always have been. I need a man who supports my rising star, not one who's threatened by it or who tries to use my fame to promote his own."

I see him start to fill with anger. I imagine men like him don't like being called out on their crap. I've never once spoken like this to him before. Ugh, I've been such a doormat. Never again.

He practically spits out, "At least I don't live in the past."

"What's that supposed to mean?"

"Get over your brother's death. It's time. You can't get through anything without crying over him."

Before I realize what's happening, I slap his face so damn hard my hand stings from the impact.

He rubs his hand over his rapidly reddening cheek. "Good luck finding anyone willing to deal with your baggage. You run so hot and cold. You're high, then you're low. It's exhausting."

I can't believe what I'm hearing, but I won't let him know he's getting to me. I steel my face and grit out, "Enjoy your mediocrity." Waving my hand dismissively, I calmly say, "I feel bad for your girlfriend." I pick up my suitcase and turn to leave before looking back at him. "And by the way, I hate your haircut. You look like a walking penis. Makes sense since it turns out that you're nothing but a dick."

With a sense of relief and a giant smile on my face, I happily walk away from Shane. Forever.

TWELVE

VANCE

"Merry Christmas, Mom." I smile into my cellphone as my mother's face appears on the screen.

Her green eyes light up. "Merry Christmas! I miss you."

"I miss you too."

We have a game in New Orleans today. I offered to fly my parents in, but they declined. They always do.

I'm rarely off for Christmas. If I am, I fly into Montana for a quick night. Never more than that though. I've always offered to fly them to wherever I'm playing, and they've never once taken me up on it. Fortunately for me, Daylen's family is always around wherever we play, so I hang with them.

"How's New Orleans?"

"It's a fantastic city. You should have come. You've never been here."

Her face falls. "You know your father. He doesn't like to leave the ranch in anyone else's hands."

I nod. "Yep. I do. What are you up to today?"

She gives me a small smile, knowing it's the same thing they do every year. "We're heading over to the O'Shea house in a bit. Sullivan is in town. She's been here for a few weeks. Such a sweet, pretty girl. It's been a particularly hard year for Nancy, but I think having Sullivan around has helped."

"What's wrong with Nancy?" I hope Sulley's mom isn't sick or anything along those lines.

The first year after Francesca was born was tough on my parents' relationship with their best friends. Fortunately, forty years of friendship won out in the end. They've gone back to the status quo with the understanding they don't discuss Maddie, Francesca, or any of the events surrounding what happened after Francesca was born. My parents are privy to everything but have agreed to keep my secret.

She swallows. "It's now been five long years since she lost her son. I think all the things he'll never get to do hit her particularly hard this year. It never gets easier." She places her hand over her heart. "I can't imagine the pain of losing a child ever goes away. It's a never-ending nightmare. They don't get to wake up and have Finn home safe and sound."

I shake my head. "I know firsthand that the pain doesn't go away."

She nods in understanding. "I know, sweetie. Will you be with the Humblecuts today?"

"Yep. I'm leaving for brunch with them in a few minutes before we head to the stadium."

She smiles. "Tell them I said Merry Christmas."

"I will. Is Dad around?"

She looks out the window. "I don't see him. He's at the stables feeding the horses. He gave everyone the day off, so he's running around like a madman, making sure the animals are taken care of."

"What about MeeMaw?" That's what I call my grandmother who now lives with my parents.

My mother looks to the side and then whispers, "Her little habit cost us over a thousand dollars last month."

I can't help but let out a laugh. For some inexplicable

reason, my eighty-five-year-old grandmother has a paid porn addiction. I've tried to explain to her how easy it is to access free porn, but she has her favorite channels and refuses to make the change. She says the paid channels and websites are "interactive." I have no idea what that means, and I don't want to. I've never told a soul about it. I can only imagine the shit I'd get if my teammates found out.

"Send me the bill."

She shakes her head. "No, we'll cover it. You should see what she's into these days. That's one dirty old woman."

I hear my grandmother's voice shout, "Is that Vancy pants?"

I chuckle at her nickname. She makes new ones up for me constantly. I yell back, "Yes, MeeMaw. It's your favorite grandson. Merry Christmas."

Half her face appears on the screen because the two of them don't know how to manage to get both their full faces on the screen at the same time, and I've given up trying to explain it to them.

I see her lips turn up when she sees me. She shouts out, "Vance, I fartled in my sleep last night."

"Oh, Mother, stop it," my mom chastises as she playfully swats MeeMaw's arm.

I shake my head. "I'm afraid to ask. What's that?"

MeeMaw winks. In her always loud voice, she explains, "When you're startled awake by a loud fart. It's all downhill after eighty, Vancy pants. I can no longer control my bodily noises. The good thing is I can't hear it half the time anyway. That's how loud the fart was. It may have left a mark on my panties."

"Mother!" my mom screams in embarrassment.

I laugh hysterically, like I always do at MeeMaw. She's one of the handful of people who can always bring a smile to my face.

She squints at the screen. "There's the smile my handsome grandson should show more often. You never smile when I watch you on the tube. Even on the movie-screen-sized one you installed in the living room, you're always frowning."

She was having trouble seeing the old television with her vision fading, so I recently had a ridiculously oversized TV put in for her because I know she loves to watch me play.

"When you see me on television, I'm focused on my games. That's my game face."

She shakes her head. "Focus on finding a wife. I need great grandbabies before I enter the porny gates."

"The pearly gates, MeeMaw," I correct.

She winks. "Suuuuure."

I sigh. "This has been fun. I've got to run. I wanted to wish you all a Merry Christmas. Your gifts are under the tree. I'll be home for a visit whenever our season is over."

We say our goodbyes, and I head out to brunch with my favorite crazy family.

"YO MAMA IS SO FAT; I took a picture of her last Christmas and it's still printing," Hank says to an unflinching Daylen.

We've had a fun brunch. Ashleigh, Daylen's stepmom, showed up in a barely there Santa outfit, complete with a short skirt and halter top. Jagger refused to participate in a family photo unless Ashleigh covered up. I have some amount of compassion for Jagger for having Ashleigh as a mother. It can't be easy with the way she dresses, but she's otherwise an attentive, loving mother. Jagger should be thankful for that.

Jagger flipped for the Bluetooth sunglasses I got her. She's been wearing them throughout the entire meal, bopping to the music now playing into her ears from the sunglasses. I have to admit, they're super cool. I might need to get myself a pair.

Daylen narrows his eyes at his father. "Yo mama is so

stupid; when she went to a movie and it said no one under seventeen, she went home and got sixteen of her friends."

I let out a small laugh, but Hank doesn't budge. He almost always wins.

Hank stoically stares at Daylen and says, "Yo mama is so ugly; when she gives head, it qualifies as anal."

Daylen tries to hold it in, but eventually the floodgates open, and his loud laugh bellows throughout the restaurant. The *entire* restaurant.

Hank wipes the corners of his mouth with his napkin as he smiles in satisfaction. "Winner, winner."

Jagger covers her face in mortification. "I swear, Dad, just when I think it can't get any worse, you never fail to surprise me."

Hank winks at her. "Thank you."

Daylen shakes his head with a huge smile on his face. "Man, I never win. You're the McDaddy jokester. I bow to the king. I guess brunch is on me."

He moves his hand to reach for the check, but Hank slaps it away. "Nonsense. No child should pay for their parents' meals. It's an unwritten law."

Daylen chuckles. "I'm a grown man. And happen to make a very good living from simply catching a ball." He mumbles, "Even though Vance throws for shit. Thank God he has me to make him look good."

I elbow him, and his smile widens. Hank turns to me. "Don't listen to his nonsense. He's a grown man who drives a car intended for sixteen-year-old girls. I think Barbie has the same one in the movie. Speaking of cars, how do you like your new vehicle, Vance? Daylen was telling me about it. Now *that's* a manly car."

Ashleigh smiles. "What kind of car did you get? A sports car? I love those."

Daylen lets out a laugh. "Vance would *never* get a car like that. He's from Montana and thinks he's still a cowboy.

Homeboy wears cowboy boots and jeans when it's eighty-five degrees out...to the beach."

I roll my eyes at Daylen before turning to Ashleigh to politely respond, "No, it's not a sports car. It's a pickup truck. A Ford F-450 Super Duty." I crack a smile. "To answer your question, Hank, I *love* it."

Hank nods. "I was thinking of upgrading my truck too, but with gas prices and my long commute, it's hard for me to justify one as big as the F-450."

Daylen shakes his head. "You can get gas for under a dollar at Taco Bell. At least I do."

Hank lets out a loud laugh. Jagger smacks Daylen's chest as she giggles at his joke. And Ashleigh still has no idea what's going on. Basically, a typical meal with the Humblecuts.

SULLEY

I wake on Christmas morning. Not hearing any voices, I assume my parents are still sleeping, but when I quietly make my way to the kitchen to turn on the coffee machine, I see my mother in her nightgown sitting at the kitchen table, staring out the window with tears silently falling from her eyes.

"Momma?"

Her head snaps toward me, and she quickly wipes her tears away while offering me a small smile. "Good morning, sweetie. Merry Christmas."

I move toward her and take her hand in mine. "What's wrong?"

She shakes her head. "Nothing. Just missing him a little extra this morning." She motions toward the stocking with Finn's name on it. "Seeing his stocking on Christmas morning with nothing in it makes me sad."

It's not just this morning. She's been unusually sad these past few weeks since I've been home.

I sit down in a chair next to her, still holding her hand. "Did something specific happen? You've been down for weeks."

She turns her head and stares back out the window. "I ran into *her*." Maddie. We don't say her name out loud. "Francesca was with her. I was reminded of what could have been. That little girl was supposed to be ours. A little piece of Finn left here for us to love." She swallows hard. "I can't help but mourn for everything we've lost. Everything that was stolen from us. She's a pretty little girl. She looks exactly like Maddie."

Vance bought Maddie and her now husband, Curtis, a huge house a few towns over. They've had two more kids since. It's rare for my mother to see her, but I know it hurts when she does. At least this explains her melancholy demeanor of late.

"Do Jane and Michael spend much time with her?" I have no idea if Vance's parents have a relationship with Francesca.

Momma shrugs. "You know the deal. We don't discuss Maddie or Francesca. It was the only way for us all to remain friends. We were at the ranch for dinner before you came home." She wipes her eyes again and lets out a small laugh. "You should see the TV Vance just bought for them. It covers an entire wall. It's like a movie theater in there."

I pinch my eyebrows together. "Why so big?"

"MeeMaw's vision is slipping, but she loves to watch him play. His solution was to buy them a giant screen. It's ridiculously large, but MeeMaw loves it."

I smile. "That was nice of him." I lick my lips nervously. "I see him, Momma. Vance. I see him all the time."

She looks at me as she tilts her head to the side. "I didn't realize. You've never mentioned it."

I nod. "I know. I'm sorry. I didn't want to upset you. Our friends are friends. He's been very welcoming to me. Are you okay with that? With me seeing him?"

She shrugs. "Whatever makes you happy. I'd never ask you

to turn your back on Vance. While I'm not conflicted on my feelings for Maddie, I am with Vance at times. I loved him like a son for all his life. Jane and Michael are family to us. I hate what he did, but I don't hate him. I care too much about him to ever feel hatred for him."

It's quiet for a few long beats before I admit, "He's building the house. The one from Finn's sketches. The ones you sent him after Finn died."

Her eyes widen in shock.

"I've been there. It was just cement foundation at the time, but I saw the finished designs. They're perfect." I can't help but smile. "He's bringing Finn's final vision to life. He placed a few of Finn's belongings in the foundation before it dried. He said he wanted to feel his presence in the house. He's still hurting over the loss as much as we are."

Her tears start flowing again, and I squeeze her hand. "I'm gonna go see it when it's done. You should come too. It's going to be beautiful. Everything Finn imagined it to be. Vance is even naming the property after Finn. It's really important to him to make this happen."

She lets out a sob before straightening her shoulders. "I'm so sorry, Sulley. I'm ruining your Christmas."

I shake my head. "You're not. We shouldn't be afraid to talk about Finn. While we mourn for what we lost, I find it helps keep his spirit alive. I thought being around Vance would be a painful reminder of things lost, and sometimes it is, but it's mostly been a reminder of the happy times. We had so many."

She stands and smiles. "You're right. Let's get dressed and open presents. Fill this house with happy cheer. And we should get started in the kitchen before the McCaffreys arrive."

Momma and I have both Christmas Eve and Christmas Day cooking traditions. It's been our special time together for as long as I can remember.

I head up to my room and grab my phone to check it before

getting in the shower. My Beavers' team chat has seemingly been blowing up all morning with Christmas cheer.

After scrolling through all the well-wishes, I see the conversation turns.

> Palmer: I have a new red flag. Men whose favorite restaurant is Texas Roadhouse. Ugh. Gross. What man would want steak from there? Maybe I really do have a food fetish.

I giggle.

> Kennedy: LOL. I have a new one too. He uses three-in-one shampoo, conditioner, and body wash. Why so lazy?

> Layla: I went to my local gym yesterday, and there was a tool carrying around an entire gallon water jug. Is that entirely necessary? Is he trying to flex that he can drink a lot at one time? Why not a regular water bottle? There are refilling stations everywhere.

It goes on and on with all the girls happily chiming in. It's become our team thing, and it really is very funny.

After closing my team chat, I see a text from Vance.

> Vance: Merry Christmas, Gully Sulley. The house is done. I'm going to move in as soon as our season is over. I hope you'll come see it when you get back into town. He'd be so proud. I'm not going to send pics. I want you to experience it in person. Have a good day with our families. Wish them all a Merry Christmas.

> Sulley: Same to you. I'm sure it's amazing. I'm going to stay a few extra weeks. I'll reach out when I get back.

THIRTEEN

SULLEY

New Year's has come and gone. I'm anxious to get back to Philly.

The Camels were upset in the playoffs a few days ago. They lost on a Hail Mary at the end of the game. It was heartbreaking. Seeing the devastation on Vance's face was hard to watch. He thought this was their year. He played his heart out. Beau got hurt at the beginning of the game, and the defense wasn't nearly as strong without him. In the end, the defense broke down, and the Camels' season has come to an end.

I was planning to fly back tomorrow, but there's a snowstorm forecasted, and my flight was already canceled.

The temperature has dropped, and the wind has picked up, but the snow hasn't started just yet. I got a notification on my phone that the power is out at Finn's cabin and the generator hasn't kicked on.

It looks like I have a few hours before the supposed storm of the century hits. Meteorologists are warning that the snowfall will be at historic levels. I have no idea when else I'll be able to get up to the cabin and am afraid to wait. If the temperature in the house drops and the water in the pipes freezes, the place will flood when it warms up again.

My father is out making sure heaters are working everywhere. Despite my mother's protests, I decide to head up to the cabin about an hour away. I'm hoping it's a quick fix and I can turn around, getting me back home before the storm gets too bad.

I grab a handful of tools and throw them in a bag. I also throw in a box of granola bars and a few cans of soup on the off chance I need to ride out the storm up there. My Girl Scout group motto was to hope for the best but prepare for the worst.

VANCE

I look up at the sky as I help my father ensure all the animals are fed before the snow worsens. The storm hit earlier than projected and is coming in super-fast. We already have eight inches on the ground with no end in sight. And it's unusually cold, much more so than a normal storm. I don't ever remember a storm this bad. It's being called a bomb blizzard.

I got home last night. My season ended earlier than I thought it would. I was in the process of moving when I saw a bad storm was coming to my hometown. I knew my father would need me. I hopped on the first flight out of Philly, which ended up being the last one they allowed to land in Helena before they shut down the airport indefinitely.

Over the deafening sounds of the hurling wind, I yell out, "Dad, we should get back to the house."

The man is in his mid-sixties. He shouldn't be running around in this weather. The well-below-freezing temperatures are dangerous for anyone, let alone a man his age.

We make our way to the main house and walk inside. I

immediately remove my sweater, which got wet and is practically a frozen icicle, leaving me in a T-shirt and damp jeans.

MeeMaw greets me at the door and holds her hands out. "Give me that sweater, tiny Vancer. I'll throw it in the dryer."

I hand it to her as I chuckle at the new nickname. She has an endless supply of them. "Thank you."

She wiggles her eyebrows. "Thank me in a few hours. I'm making your favorite snow day meal."

I smile. "Your special chili?"

She winks and does a little dance. "I loaded up on Tums and Gas-X. Be sure to take a few. I don't want you farting while we're snowed in. You'll stink up the joint."

I can only shake my head at her while I hear my mother on the phone, saying, "Keep us updated, Nancy. I'm sure they'll be fine."

She hangs up and walks toward us with a worried look on her face.

"What's wrong, Mom?"

She turns her head toward me with concerned eyes. "Nancy is worried about Frank and Sulley. They're not home."

My eyes widen. "Where the hell are they?"

"Frank is being Frank and making sure every heater in the town is working properly. Sulley went up to the cabin. There was some sort of power issue, and she wanted to fix it before the storm came in. The snow has started, and she can't get hold of Sulley. You know there's no reception up there. Nancy is worried sick."

"Where are my keys?"

She shakes her head. "You can't drive in this Vance. Your old truck won't make it up there at this point. The roads are covered in ice."

I find my keys, grab my jacket, and head right out the door to the loud protests of my family. What if she got stuck and is freezing to death? I can't sit here and do nothing.

A little over an hour later, I see the snow-covered sign for

Beartooth Mountains. I smile thinking of my favorite Miley Cyrus song and the fact that Sulley remembered it. The sign means I'm about a mile out from the cabin.

Suddenly, my truck makes a few weird noises and then stalls out. Fuck, fuck, fuck. I try everything to get her up and running but have no luck.

Do I try to walk the last mile or try to fix my truck? If I stay and can't fix it, I could very well freeze to death out here. I make the decision to walk the last mile through what must already be nearly two feet of snow.

Forty-five excruciating minutes later, the cabin finally comes into view. I've never been this cold in my life. My clothes are wet and icy. My hair has icicles hanging from it. Actual icicles. I can't feel my fingers or toes. I think I'm minutes away from hypothermia setting in, if it hasn't already.

I see her car. At least I know she made it here in one piece.

I just need to make it to the cabin. The door approaches, but my vision begins to blur. That's when everything goes dark.

I WAKE FEELING WARM AND...TURNED on. I don't need to open my eyes to be able to smell Sulley. I've been smelling that perfume for over six months. The floral coconut mix drives me wild.

Maybe I froze to death and am now in heaven. The last thing I remember is Finn's cabin door finally being within reach. I remember I wasn't sure I could make it up the final hill. I had lost all feeling in my body at that point. I think my brain was frozen too. I know I made it up, but I remember nothing after that.

Blinking my eyes open, I realize I'm in only my boxer briefs, and Sulley's bra-and-panties-clad body is wrapped around mine. She's fast asleep. We're under a sea of blankets in front of the cabin's fireplace, which has a fire roaring and crackling. I can see the stonework around it that I fucked up, but it was too late to fix. The mortar had hardened. Finn and I had a good laugh about that and all the other imperfections in this place due to our inexperience.

I lift my head enough to notice my clothes laid out in front of the fire. She must have found me and somehow dragged me inside and gotten me undressed. I'm a big man. I'm not sure how she could have done that on her own.

I lift my head further and scan the room for someone else. The person who must have helped her. Nope, no one else is here.

She lets out a soft moan in her sleep, and my dick further hardens to a near-painful level. I look down at her body as best I can while it's pressed against me. She's so sexy. She was beautiful all those years ago when we were in her bed together, but she's filled out a bit more. She's got curves she didn't have then. So damn perfect.

I don't dare move for several minutes for fear of waking her and ending this. I simply hold her and stare at her. Her cherry red lips curve perfectly. They adorably murmur slightly in her sleep. I ache to suck them into my mouth.

Her face is relaxed too. She's not looking at me with her usual pained animosity. There are so many things I wish I could tell her.

I continue to take in the most stunning creature in existence. There's no denying how much I want her. I think I've wanted her since that last day with Finn.

Sulley stirs a bit before sleepily rolling onto her back. She manages to pull me with her. My cock presses into her warm, soft center.

Oh my god. My heart is beating a million times per minute. She must feel it with our chests pressed together.

Her eyes slowly begin to peel open. The eyes I spend every

night dreaming of. The eyes I pretend are staring up at me every time I stroke my cock.

They widen slightly when reality hits, but she doesn't push me away. She stares at me. I don't see the normal hurt in them. Maybe I'm delusional, but I think I see lust swimming in them.

The pace of her chest rising and falling increases in intensity. Her sweet, warm breath fans my face.

Unable to help myself, I touch her soft, flawless face with my fingertips. "Your eyes look so blue right now. You're beautiful, Sullivan Aisling."

With the last of my restraint gone, I bring my lips to hers. It's been nearly six years since we last kissed, but her taste is immediately familiar and comforting.

I'm not sure how she'll react. I brace my balls for the knee I'm confident will land on them but am pleasantly surprised when her tongue slips into my mouth and she runs her fingers through my hair.

That's all the signal I need. I turn into a greedy, starving man. I suck on her lips and then deepen the kiss, welcoming her taste as I devour her.

My hands roam over every inch of her warm body. At least those areas within my reach. She's just as smooth and soft as I remember her being. God, she sets me on fire.

She wraps her legs around me and grinds her hips over my hardness, letting out a series of moans that cause my cock to leak.

Every little noise is sexy. She's usually careful with her words and actions around me. But not right now. Right now, she's in the moment, feeling what I'm feeling.

I kiss and lick my way down her neck. Her coconut scent is strengthening. Her hands begin to tug on my hair like they did that night in her bedroom. I swear I've only left my hair long in hopes that she'd one day tug on it again.

I pull down the cups of her bra. I've dreamed of her rosy,

pink nipples nearly every day since the one and only time I saw them. Her tits are a little fuller now and every bit as magnificent as I remember them to be.

I tug on her taut peaks, and she pulls my hair tighter. I can't take it anymore. I move my way down and circle her left nipple with my tongue before sucking it into my mouth.

Her back arches, and she breathes out, "More."

My hand runs up the soft skin of her thigh as I move it closer and closer to her center. She relaxes her leg's grip around me, giving me access to the contact we both crave.

I ever so gently run the backs of my fingers over her panty-covered pussy. She's soaking wet.

She thrusts her hips toward my fingers, begging for more. In a husky voice I barely recognize, she whispers, "Touch me."

Maybe I really am in heaven.

I slide her panties to the side and run my fingers through her soft, swollen center. So damn slippery. She's dripping. Six years ago, she admitted her crush on me, but I assume it ended after the baby. That's not what I'm getting from her right now. I'm getting nothing but desire and a need mirroring my own.

I slide one finger inside her as I increase my suction over her nipple. Her body contracts around my finger. Pulses.

I need to taste her. Unable to wait a second longer, my lips drag down her gorgeous body. I lick, nibble, and inhale her along the way. I want to explore every inch of this perfect creature and worship her for hours.

With one set of fingers now holding her panties to the side and the other hand with two fingers now pushing into her, my tongue sweeps through her for the first time.

She lets out the loudest moan, filling the small cabin. It's almost feral. It's music to my ears.

The combination of her noises, her hair pulling, and me tasting her for the first time practically has my eyes rolling to the back of my head.

My tongue works in circles over her little, perfect bundle. I explore her and quickly learn the spots that make her moan and those that make her body contract. Her juices are covering my scruff. She's so damn responsive. It's sexy, and I'm confident I've never been this turned on by a woman in my life. I'm thrusting my hips on the blanket-covered floor below me just to get a little friction on my aching cock, though it's not quite the friction I need.

Her back arches and she yells out, "Oh god, Vance. Don't stop. Please don't stop."

Stop? I would happily spend every minute of my life doing this.

Her sounds grow louder and louder. If there were another house within a mile, I think they'd hear us. Sulley is a screamer. So fucking hot.

I can tell she's getting close. I usually like to talk a woman through it, but part of me is afraid she's in a trance right now, and if I talk, it will wake her. But she did yell my name earlier. At least she knows it's me.

I add another finger inside her, stretching her to the max. It only serves to make her moans increase in volume. Her hips elevate. She's teetering on the edge. I just need to push her over.

I lift my head slightly and mumble into her. "Come for me. Let my tongue make this pretty pussy purr."

As soon as I rewrap my lips around her clit, her body begins to tremble at a level I know is completely out of her control. She yells out before coming in a rush on my tongue and all over my fingers and face, soaking me in the best way possible.

I keep my movements going until I'm sure I've pulled every last drop out of her.

I feel like I might die if I don't get my dick inside her in the next minute. After tearing her panties down and off her legs, I release my cock from the confines of my boxer briefs.

Bringing my lips back up her body, my mouth finds hers

again. She's still whimpering from her post-orgasmic state, but she kisses me right back. In fact, she licks around my face and sucks on my lips. I guess she likes her taste nearly as much as I do.

My cock runs through her wetness, and she convulses again. She's still sensitive from her orgasm seconds ago.

She should have the chance to see my cock before I enter her. I'm big. Very big. Most women are a little frightened the first time, and I've found that allowing them to set the pace, at least at the beginning, is helpful.

I roll us until she's on top. Our lips remain sealed together while her hips gyrate over my cock with her pussy enveloping it in wet warmth.

She swivels so that my tip nears her entrance. We're almost there. I'm leaking with anticipation. Dear god, please let me sink inside this woman. I'll never ask for anything else again.

She breaks the kiss and sits up on me. She's naked except for her bra pulled down below her tits. Her hair is messy and wild. Her cheeks are flushed.

I run my hands up her body as I cup her breasts. This is how we were in her bedroom all those years ago. The same thought floats through my mind as it did then. "I've never seen anything so beautiful in my life."

She smiles dreamily but then begins to look around at our surroundings. I see the moment something changes in her eyes. It goes from lust to regret in the blink of an eye. Tears fill her eyes.

She practically leaps off me, falls to the ground, and cradles her knees to her chest, wrapping her arms around them. She starts rocking back and forth. "Oh my god. What have I done?"

I sit up and place my hand on her back. She immediately flinches and yells out, "Don't touch me!"

I pull my hand away. "What's wrong?"

Tears begin flowing from her eyes as she rocks back and forth.

"What's wrong?" she shouts. "What's wrong is that I'm making out with the man who stabbed my brother in the back in the house my brother built. I've just betrayed him on the grandest level. I'm a horrible person. A horrible sister. Oh my god."

She keeps repeating *oh my god* over and over again while rocking and crying.

I'm at a loss. I don't know what to do for her.

After pulling up my boxer briefs and throwing on a T-shirt, I grab one of the blankets and wrap it around her. I kiss her temple and whisper, "I'm sorry."

We're silent for several minutes until she eventually stops crying. She sits, staring at the fire, looking a million miles away.

Eventually, I stand and make my way to the front window. Sulley's car is completely buried. There must be three or four feet of snow out there. I've never seen anything like it. And it's still snowing.

Making my way to the kitchen, I open a few cabinets, but there's not much in here. Four cans of soup and a few other things. I see an old can of hot chocolate powder mix.

She loved it when she was a kid. Maybe that will make her feel better. I boil water and mix the hot chocolate into a mug for her.

She's still staring into the fire as I walk back toward her. Handing it to her, I again whisper, "I'm sorry."

She shakes her head. "It's my fault. I let it happen."

I sit down next to her. "We both got carried away."

She turns her head to me. "Why? Why did you do it?"

"I'm sorry. I woke up with you nearly naked in my arms. I've wanted you for so long and—"

"Not *that*, Vance. Maddie. Why her? Tell me the truth for once."

I'm silent for several long beats, letting only the silence and the crackling of the fire fill the air.

She blows out a breath of frustration before yelling, "Tell me something real, Vance. Something truthful. Anything!"

I swallow hard as I admit, "The day of Finn's funeral, I carried you from the treehouse to your room and stayed with you."

She nods. "I remember."

"When you woke up, I told you that you had asked me to stay with you and then fell asleep on my arm."

"What about that?" she asks with clear anticipation.

I nervously lick my lips. "You never woke up. You never asked me to stay. I stayed because I loved having you in my arms. I wanted you in my arms."

Her brow furrows. "I don't understand. You rejected my advances that night."

I shake my head. "It wasn't because I didn't want you." I nervously run my fingers through my hair. "Trust me, I wanted you. I stopped what was happening because you just had the worst day of your life. You were an emotional wreck. We both were. I didn't want our first time together to be associated with that horrible day."

Her face softens at my admission.

I can't help but reach out and move a piece of hair from her face. I tuck it behind her ear before rubbing my thumb over her cheek and lips. "I wanted you then, and I want you now, Sullivan Aisling."

I bring my lips within a hairsbreadth of hers, waiting for her to close the distance. But she doesn't. We just sit there and breathe the same air.

FOURTEEN

SULLEY

I let out a laugh. "It was Stacey Rosegarten, trust me."

Vance twists his lips. "Are you sure?"

"Vance, I followed you and Finn to the drive-in movie theater all the time. You were making out with Stacey when Ellen Gold dumped a bucket of water in the back of your truck. All over poor Stacey."

He scratches his head. "Ellen's fatal attraction to me was always over the top, but I thought it was Grace Dunger who she dumped water on in my truck."

We've been stuck in the cabin all afternoon and evening. After he blew my mind with the best orgasm of my life and then I lost my mind with regret, we agreed to make the most of our time stranded in this cabin without drama. We're going to be here for at least another full day. It would be pointless to make it miserable, so we're burying the heavy and keeping it light.

We did the one puzzle we found in a cabinet, we've played a few games, and we've reminisced about old times. We're now fully dressed, sipping on our soup late at night, discussing the many women who pined for Vance in his high school days and the girl drama that often ensued from him being the hottest ticket in town.

I shake my head. "Grace Dunger was the one you made out with in the stadium tunnel after your seven-touchdown performance on homecoming of your senior year."

He raises an eyebrow. "Why do you know this?"

I scrunch my face. "Because I saw it and cried my eyes out. My mother had to take me home. I was inconsolable."

His face softens. "I didn't know you were there." He tilts his head to the side. "Wait. Back up. What do you mean you followed us to the drive-in? Stalker," he jokes.

"I told you I had a little girl crush on you. You guys went to the drive-in nearly every Saturday night. Finn and Maddie were always in his car doing…things." I make a look of disgust. "You usually had a new girl each time, but you always backed into your spot, laid out blankets in the bed of your truck, and would make out the whole time with the lucky lady. I was so jealous. I always wanted to be the one with you in the back of your truck at the drive-in getting McCaffed."

He lifts an eyebrow. "What's McCaffed?"

I giggle. "My younger, innocent way of thinking about whatever you were doing to those girls under the blankets. I don't think I appreciated what must have really been going on, so I termed it, McCaffed. I was there in the darkness, all the time, thinking how lucky they were."

He pinches his lips together. "I didn't notice."

I give him a small smile. "I know. I was a little girl. Why would you notice? You had your pick of any girl in the high school."

He licks his lower lip. "If you were older, a woman, I would have picked you. Every single time."

I raise a bemused eyebrow. "Suuuuure. I heard the rumors about what Leslie Smooter let you do to her."

He chuckles. "I'm serious. Finn noticed."

"Finn noticed what?" I ask.

"The moment I stopped seeing you as a little girl. As Finn's tagalong sister. It was your senior night. My jaw was practically on the floor when you turned around. I guess I hadn't seen you in around fifteen months or so. In that time, you blossomed into a stunning woman. I was blown away. He saw it in my face and told me to stay away."

I can't help the smile that finds my face. "Really? That's kind of...sweet."

He smirks. "I had a hard-on throughout the entire game watching you play while sitting next to your parents and your brother. It was so uncomfortable."

I burst into laughter. "Not so sweet. Sweaty girls playing basketball do it for you."

He shakes his head. "No, seeing your body move so gracefully did it for me. I love watching you play. You're like a gazelle out there. You exude confidence and joy. You're always calm and collected. I haven't missed a single game since."

I pinch my eyebrows together. "What do you mean?"

"I've watched every single college and professional game. Obviously not in person, though I did quietly sneak into a few of your college games under cloak and dagger. I'd watch them on TV. Even if I couldn't catch a game live, I'd record it. I honestly haven't missed one single game."

I quickly do the math in my head. That's around two hundred and fifty games.

I shake my head in disbelief. "I can't believe you did that."

"You're a generational talent, Gully Sulley. Finn would be so proud of you."

I whisper, "I hope so."

He nods. "I know so. He was always bragging about you. Every single conversation I had with him."

Not wanting to let things get too heavy again, I stand. "I saw some toothpaste in a bathroom drawer. I'm going to finger brush my teeth before bed. I'll leave it out for you to do the same."

He smirks. "Are you saying my breath stinks?"

His breath was like the sweet nectar of heaven when it was on me. Around me. In me. But I play it cool. "Yep. That's why I call you Vile Vance. It's your stinky breath."

His face falls as he cups his hand out in front of his face and attempts to smell his own breath. I inwardly giggle that I made him feel so insecure about it as I make my way to the bathroom.

We fall asleep by the fire, under the same blanket, with our backs facing each other. In my fantasies, this night would go a little differently, but that's where they need to remain. In fantasyland.

I WAKE in the morning and don't see Vance in our makeshift bed. Turning, I see him by the window. I quietly stand and make my way toward him. I stand beside my forever crush as we both take in the beauty of the snowfall. It's white as far as the eyes can see. Every item. Every tree. They're all covered by several feet of undisturbed snow.

"It finally stopped," I quietly announce.

He nods. "Minutes ago. I've never seen so much snow in my life. I checked everywhere in and around the cabin. There's nothing resembling a shovel. We're going to have to wait until plow trucks can make their way up here."

"I…umm…guess we have at least another day and night in paradise."

He nods. "That would be my guess too."

I notice him staring at a big clearing in the woods. It used to be full of dozens of huge, beautiful oak trees.

"I sold them," I admit. "Last year. I had a big tax assessment on this place. A developer came in and offered me way above market price for the oak trees, so I sold them to him to pay off the taxes."

"They were great trees."

"They were," I agree. It doesn't need to be spoken for us both to be thinking that the tree closest to the house, the biggest and best, was where Finn and Vance carved their names as the builders of this cabin. *McShea Brothers*. That's what they called themselves. I happily included that tree with the others I sold.

After more makeshift teeth brushing and a little granola bar breakfast, we decide to play hangman. There are only so many games you can play with two people and nothing but a few crinkled receipts and a pen from my bag.

With pen and paper in hand and his legs crossed facing me, Vance says, "It's something he always said to me when we were building this place."

I lean my elbows on my knees and narrow my eyes at him. "How would I know what he said to you? I wasn't here most of the time."

He rolls his eyes. "It's a known phrase. You definitely heard him say it. Just guess the damn letters. That's how this game goes."

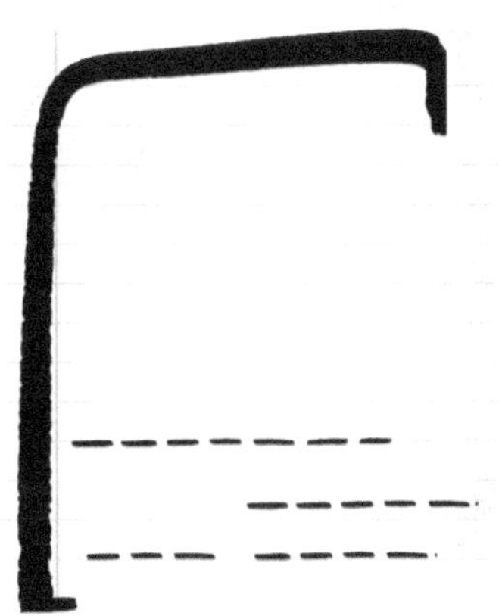

"Ugh. Fine."
"R."
"There's one R."

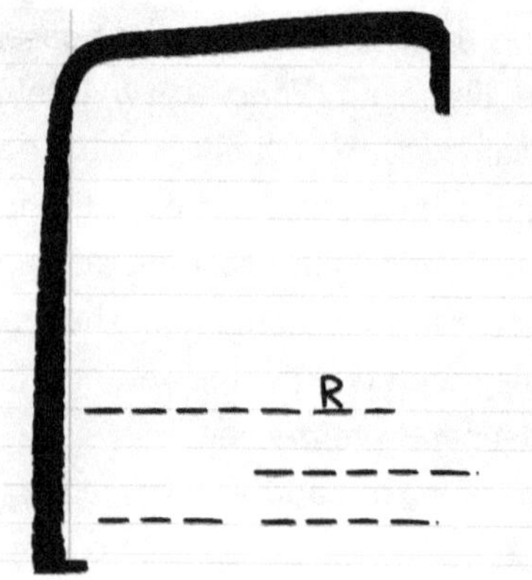

"Q."

"Who guesses Q at the beginning of a hangman game? No Q."

I stare at him, trying to get into his mind. "T."

"Two T's."

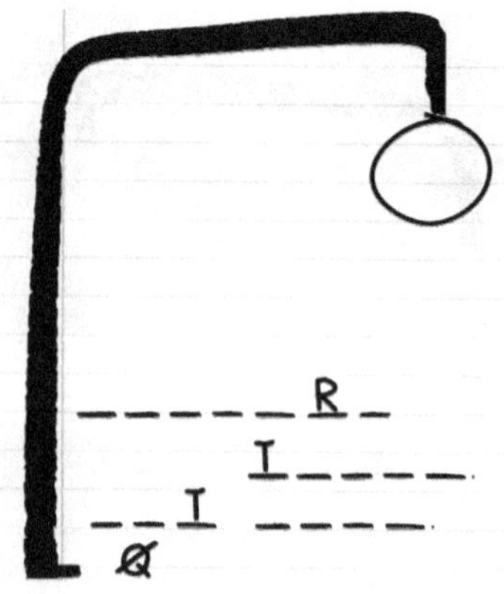

After guessing E, M, P, N, L, B, S, and C, I have a pretty good idea what it is.

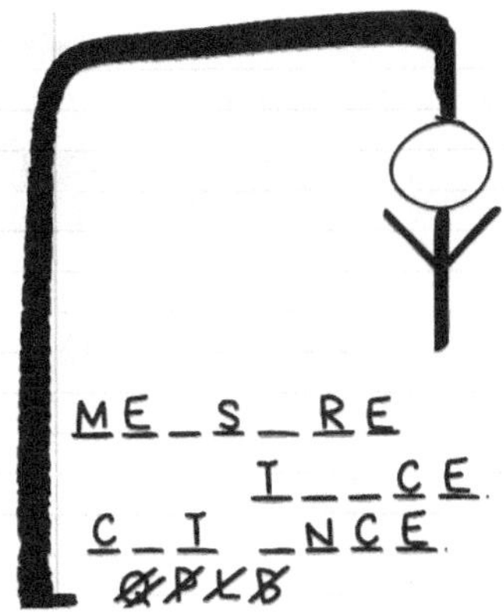

He's right. It's something Finn always said when working on the cabin, my treehouse, and all the other little projects he had going on. I smile in satisfaction. "I know it. *Measure Twice. Cut Once.*"

His ridiculously handsome face lights up. "You got it, smarty pants."

He goes about filling in the rest of the letters and hands the paper to me while he stands and goes to put water on the stove to make more hot chocolate.

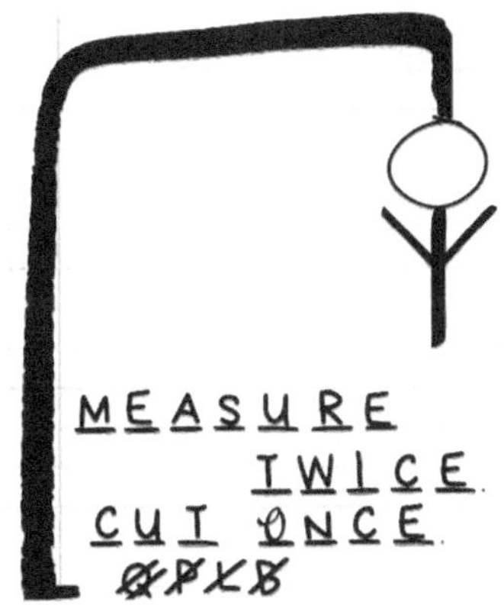

I happily stare at the phrase, letting memories flood me until one letter catches my eye. The O. It has a distinct swivel at the top. One I know I've seen before. I rack my brain as I try to remember the last time I would have seen Vance's handwriting. He did send cards every year on the anniversary of Finn's death, but he always signed his name only. There's no O in his name. Maybe the Chocolate Cosmo cards? Nope. Those messages were always printed by the florist. Why is that O so freaking familiar?

A thought occurs to me, but it can't be right. That wouldn't make any sense.

I reach for my bag and pull out my wallet. Folded in there, as always, is the letter Finn had his military friend deliver to me months after his death. The one that got me motivated to re-enroll in college and play ball again.

I study it carefully, line by line, until I find what I'm looking for. An uppercase O. It has the same exact swivel.

My eyes widen in realization.

He turns around with a smile, holding the can of hot chocolate mix. "Two or three scoops of chocolate this time?"

With a shaking hand, I hold up the letter. "F...Finn didn't write this, did he? You did."

He mumbles, "Shit," before he turns off the stove, runs over to me, and falls down to his knees in front of my seated, lifeless-feeling body. "Sulley, please don't be upset."

My eyes fill with tears. "Why would you do this? Why do you hate us?"

His face falls, and he shakes his head. "Hate? That's the exact *opposite* of why I did this." He nervously runs his fingers through his thick hair. "Fuck, Sulley, you dropped out of college. You wouldn't leave the house. You were a zombie. I did it *for* you. *For* him. He would have hated that you weren't in college. That you quit playing ball. You wouldn't have talked to me about it at that time. Your parents were zombies right along with you, not pushing you to get back to life. I did what was necessary to get you up and running again. To live your life. To reach your potential."

My mouth opens and closes several times. I'm speechless.

Completely and totally speechless. Shock isn't a big enough word for what I'm feeling right now.

Eventually, I whisper, "What about his platoon friend who delivered it? Did you hire him? Did he even know Finn?" Why can't I remember the man's name? What kind of sister am I that I can't remember his military best friend's name? The one who changed my life.

Vance nods. "Of course Eric knew Finn. They were close friends. He and I still keep in touch. I reached out to him about how much it would destroy Finn to know what you were doing with your life. We came up with the plan together. I wrote the letter since I knew you best. Eric delivered it to make sure it had the desired impact." He steels his face a bit. "And I would do it again. It worked. It got you back to school. Back playing ball. Back to the land of the living. You were always destined for greatness. It was time for you to fulfill that destiny. In the absence of your brother, we stepped in and gave you the push you needed. Even if you never talk to me again, I don't regret it. Not one little bit."

I feel like I'm having an out-of-body experience right now. It's like I'm floating above, watching the scene take place. History has just been rewritten. *My* history. I should be mad at him for deceiving me, but I can't bring myself to conjure up those feelings.

What would I be doing right now if I didn't get that letter? Would I have gone back to school? Would I have started playing ball again?

I honestly don't think I would have. He's right. I did need it. All this time, I thought it was Finn who saved me, but it wasn't him. It was Vance. My guardian angel isn't watching from above. He's standing right in front of me.

My mind suddenly flashes back to last night when I was first frantically undressing him and later nearly naked and on top of him, looking down at his flawless body. I was in a post-orgasmic haze and then had my little freakout, so things were a little cloudy, but I'm starting to remember his tattoo. It didn't hit me at the time, but it is now.

I point a shaky finger at him. "Take…take off your shirt."

"What? Why?"

"Take it off," I demand with determination in my voice.

He lifts his T-shirt over his head. "Turn to the right and lift your left arm," I further instruct.

Realization hits him, and he does as I ask.

My trembling finger finds the tattoo. It reads *McShea Brothers*. It's done similarly to the way it was carved into the tree. There's smaller wording under it that reads, *Not brothers by blood, but brothers by heart.*

Tears fill my eyes as I trace the letters over and over again with my fingertips. I must do it twenty times. Vance says nothing. He doesn't move. He simply allows me to explore his tribute to my brother and their bond.

Overcome with emotion, I lean over and softly press my lips to the tattoo before kissing my way up his body. I move my fingers and lips across his chest, stopping at his sexy chest hair like I've wanted to do for as long as I can remember.

Taking a brief pause to inhale his unique Vance scent, my lips continue their upward movement over his throat and chin until I reach his lips.

Like him, I'm on my knees as my lips brush over his. His eyelids flutter, but he doesn't otherwise move.

Our eyes meet, and we stare at each other. He's kept his promise to look out for me. He's been doing it from the shadows for six long years. I'm done fighting with myself. Even if it's only one time, I want to know what it's like to be with Vance McCaffrey, the man I've lusted after for most of my life.

I lift my sweater over my head and remove my bra. He breathes, "What are you—"

"I want you," I interrupt. After I trace his lower lip with my tongue, I whisper, "I'm not stopping it this time, and neither are you."

His massive hands cup my entire face. If I didn't know better, I'd swear his bright green eyes turn a shade darker.

I run my fingers down the hair from his belly button to where they disappear into his jeans. He quivers, actually quivers, from my touch.

After unbuckling his belt, I unbutton and unzip his jeans. My fingers brush over his boxer-brief-covered erection. His sexy Adam's apple bobs up and down as he swallows hard.

"You're sure you want this?"

I nod. "I do. More than anything."

"Stand up."

I'm a little concerned he's going to stop this, but I stand as he instructed. His fingers slip into the sides of my leggings and panties, and he slides them down my legs until nothing is left.

Vance McCaffrey is currently on his knees in front of me while I'm standing there completely naked. His eyes drink me in, practically worshiping my body. The younger Sulley is doing a happy dance right now. So is the current Sulley, but I'm doing my best to play it cool, as if this isn't the embodiment of every fantasy I've ever had in my entire life.

His lips kiss along my thighs until his face reaches my most intimate region. He takes a deep inhale. It's so unexpected and erotic that I audibly gasp.

My fingers thread through his gorgeous hair as he does nothing but take in my scent. I'm obsessed with his hair. It's soft and thick. And the best part? It belongs to Vance. *My* Vance.

He looks up at me. "I don't know what I want to do first."

I briefly look out the window before turning back to him with a small smile. "We've got all day. For now, I just want to feel you moving inside me."

In a flash, he's standing and lifting me while I instinctively wrap my legs around him. I screech at the quick, unexpected move.

His mouth finds mine and, within seconds, his tongue is in my mouth. It gets frantic very quickly. Like we're trying to swallow the other whole. He manages to add in a little suction, making it…perfect. It's full of want and passion.

I can feel his solid erection and can't help but rub myself against it while moving my hands across his broad, muscular back.

I feel us moving until he places me down on the small, cold kitchen island. It's in such contrast to my rapidly overheating skin.

Eventually he breaks the kiss and pulls down his jeans and boxer briefs. His cock springs free. My eyes nearly bug out of my head. I'm tall. I've always dated big men who I know have bigger-than-average penises. Shane was unusually big. I think it's half the reason I stayed with him as long as I did.

But Vance McCaffrey is in a league of his own. His cock is long, thick, and looks angry in the best way possible. I can see the veins pulsing. The tip is red and leaking.

He chuckles when he notices my reaction. "It will fit. I promise."

I shake my head and point to his third leg, which is currently staring at me as if to say he's about to destroy me. "No way that fucking monster is fitting inside me. You'll break me in half. How do you play football with that thing dangling between your legs?"

He lets out a loud laugh. With a bemused tone, he responds, "I suppose I find a way to make it work." He scratches his head. "It's umm…it tends to be easier if you're on top to start, but we can do this however you want. I should also probably give you at least one orgasm beforehand. It helps loosen things up a bit."

I bite back my smile. "I wanted to get to the main event, but I think I can get on board with a pre-sex orgasm." I lean back on my hands and spread my legs wide. "Do your worst, QB1."

"I'll make it quick." He winks, fucking winks, as if it takes mere seconds to bring a woman to orgasm. Cocky bastard.

I screech again as he lifts me like a bride, walking us back to our makeshift bed area in front of the fire. After setting me on my feet, he lies down on the blankets. I swear his dick makes a loud plopping noise as it falls to his stomach. It's that big and heavy.

He motions his hands for me. "Come sit on my face."

"Wait, what?"

He flicks his tongue suggestively. "Ride my fucking face. I want to be coated in your pussy until you're so wet you practically glide onto my dick."

Umm, okay. I'm into that plan.

I stand over him and then drop down to my knees on either side of his waist. I take in the man below me. Damn, he's perfection. Saliva pools in my mouth at the sight of him in all his glory. I might be able to come without—

Before I can finish the thought, he grabs my ass and pulls me until I'm hovering above his face, and then he drags me down until my pussy practically crashes to his mouth and his tongue plunges into my throbbing walls.

Oh dear god.

He momentarily removes his tongue and mumbles, "Don't think. Let loose. Anything goes. Ride me without inhibition."

Nervous adrenaline runs through my body, but I manage to grab onto his hair and do as he asked. I let everything go and just feel as I gyrate like a lap-dancing stripper over his face.

It only serves to encourage him. His tongue and fingers feel like they're everywhere. His scruff is burning me in the best way possible, and I happily rub myself all over it. I've never felt so sexually free.

Part of me wants this orgasm to come quickly, but part of me wants to take my time to enjoy the ride. I love seeing how turned on this is making him. I can smell how aroused he is.

His lips and tongue now work my clit while he slams two then three fingers inside of me. *Deep* inside of me. I've never felt anything so aggressive. I fucking love it. I'm already close to coming apart, and it's been just a few minutes.

I turn my head around and catch a glimpse of his dick. It's

twitching and leaking onto his stomach. The sheer size is so overtly masculine. Everything about him oozes brute strength. I've never considered a dick to be "hot" before but, hell, his is so…erotic.

Another shot of precum spurts from his tip, and that's it for me. I yell out his name at a volume I'm not sure I knew I was capable of. I'm surprised the cabin doesn't crumble with the magnitude of this orgasm. My body shakes and writhes. I wonder if I've suffocated him.

As my vision slowly returns, I turn my head back to his face. I gushed all over him. *All* over him.

Panting, I manage to breathe, "I'm so sorry. I don't know what happened."

He has a huge grin as his head pops up from between my legs. Maybe the biggest grin I've ever seen from the rarely smiling Vance McCaffrey. "What happened is that you got McCaffed."

I can't help but let out a laugh. I walked right into that one.

Easily sliding down his body, I lick all around his face. He lets out a moan. "Do you like the taste of your pussy on my face, baby?"

I shiver at his words. Vance McCaffrey just called me baby.

"I love how much you like your own juices. Maybe you'll lick them off my dick when we're done. Would you like that? Do you want to suck your come off my cock?"

Holy shit. Vance McCaffrey is dirty, and I'm here for it. All I can do is nod. I want that. Desperately.

Our eyes meet. His are burning with desire. I have no doubt mine are too. "Are you ready for me, Gully Sulley?"

I nod. "Give me your best, Vile Vance."

I lift up onto my knees and bring the python's head to my opening. He grabs hold of it with me. "Circle it. Ease him in slowly."

I roll my eyes. "It's not a car backing into a spot. It's a

monster dick trying to fit into an opening not made for a monster dick."

He smirks as he wiggles his eyebrows up and down. I love this playful side of him. Most people don't get to see it.

I take a few deep breaths and begin to take him. My heart is thumping so hard in my chest I wonder if he can hear it.

He grabs my hips and moves me in a circular motion, paying close attention to where our bodies are slowly joining as one. His thumb begins rubbing my clit. That's how big his hands are. He can grip my hips and rub my clit at the same time.

It takes a few minutes, but I finally get him all the way in. I'm guessing I'm now forever ruined for all other men. I'm completely still. Afraid to move. There's a new and wonderful sensation spreading all over every inch of me.

My body begins to tremble. I'm not sure if it's the fullness or the emotional magnitude of the moment. Perhaps it's both, but it's completely out of my control.

He lifts himself into a seated position and wraps his arms around me. Kissing up my neck, he whispers, "You did it, good girl. Now buckle up and enjoy the ride."

I smile as his tongue licks and then bites my nipple. I yell out from the unexpected pain, but he quickly sucks my nipple into his mouth in a soothing manner.

I grind my hips, and he groans before licking up my neck and finding my mouth. His tongue sweeps through me while his hands move to my hips again and begin to lift me up.

Just before I feel like his tip might emerge, he slams me back down. I suck in a breath. "Oh god, I can't. I can't take you."

He growls, "You can, and you will."

My head falls forward, and I bite the area between his neck and shoulder. I think his cocks swells even more when I do. Does he like a little pain with his pleasure?

I grab onto his hair and pull it harder than I ever have before. His head is forced to jerk back, and I think it's some sort of starting pistol for him. He goes feral, immediately flipping me onto my back with him still inside me.

His hips swivel a few times before he withdraws and then slams back into me. Over and over again. There are noises coming out of my mouth that I don't recognize. I have no idea what they are, and I can't seem to control them. I think I might be speaking French…and I don't know French.

His muscular body is so damn tight as it begins to slicken with perspiration. He's dominant male perfection at its finest. It's a sight I will never forget until the day I die.

"Can you feel how fucking hard you make me?"

Yeah, buddy. Feeling you isn't the problem here. I'm feeling all of you. Every long, wide, thick, veiny inch.

I continue pulling his hair. It only serves to incite him to fuck me harder and harder. A sane woman would consider releasing his hair, but Vance McCaffrey makes this particular woman insane. Insane with lust.

He bites my lower lip and stretches it as far as it can go. I then bite his back. Hard. A deep grumble erupts from his chest.

This is off the charts fucking hot. I've never been this turned on in my life. I didn't expect Vance to be like this. He's a machine. This has far exceeded every fantasy I've ever had.

My hands move down the hard planes of his back, but as soon as they reach his ass, he mumbles, "Hair. Back in my hair."

Yep, he likes his hair pulled. I wonder if that's why he's worn it long for the past six years, so women can pull it.

He lifts one of my legs over his shoulder. Just when I thought he couldn't possibly get any deeper, he does. There's no holding back now. I scream until my throat is dry as I detonate into a million tiny pieces. There are stars covering my vision. No, it's more than stars. I can see an entire galaxy.

"Ah, fuck. You're squeezing me. It's too good."

He thrusts into me three long, hard times before grunting into his own release, filling me with his warmth.

As soon as he finishes, he rolls us over so I'm on top. He

kisses me so damn softly and tenderly that it threatens to break me. It's such a contrast to the animalistic fucking we just did.

We kiss for minutes on end. It's like he can't get enough of the closeness. His softened cock remains inside me. I feel it start to slip out, but he grabs it and slides it back in. My body shivers at the intimate move.

Thinking of his dick covered in our collective releases, I'm reminded of our conversation before this started.

I pull my lips away and kiss my way down his slick body as his dick slips out again. I hate losing it, but I've got other plans. His sweat is an enhanced version of his scent, and I wish I could bottle it. Bathe in it. Drink it.

My lips are on his stomach while my hands run down over his muscular thighs. They're hard and defined. I need to take a picture so I can look at his body whenever I want. He was in a charity calendar one year early in his career. All professional football players in various states of undress. He was wearing only his uniform pants, which were tight around his thick legs. Let's just say it was February of that particular year for at least two or three years on my bedroom wall.

My fingers find their way to his cock, curling around his thick base. I lick from the base all the way up to the remaining come still oozing from his tip. It's a combination of his come and mine. I could feast on this forever.

I lick every inch of him until I'm sure he's clean. By the time I'm done, he's hard again.

My eyes meet his as he asks, "How do we taste?"

I smile with a mouth full of his cock and mumble, "So good."

"I want to taste it too."

He pulls me up as if I weigh nothing and smashes his mouth to mine. Our tongues duel for supremacy as he licks around my mouth.

Eventually we pull apart, and my head rests in the crook of his neck. I continue to inhale him as my breathing begins to normalize.

His fingers aimlessly run all over my back. "I didn't wear a condom. I'm sorry."

"Oh god. I didn't even think about that either. Are you—"

"I'm clean. It's been a while for me. And I've never not used a condom in my life."

I breathe a sigh of relief. "Me too. I have an IUD."

Even with condom use and an IUD, I got tested as soon as I got back from Italy. Who knows what that cheating bastard could have given me. I'm so glad I never gave in to his requests for no condom. I never even entertained it, yet here I am with Vance, and I didn't even think about it. I find myself wondering if it's a trust thing.

FIFTEEN

VANCE

"Run," Sulley shouts as we sprint naked from the bathroom to the safe and dry comfort of blankets in front of the fireplace, laughing the whole way.

We needed a shower after our sweaty marathon sex all afternoon, and then we ended up having sex for a fourth time in the shower. She's so hot. I can't get enough of her. I don't know that I ever will.

There are no towels in the cabin, so we had to make a run for the fire. We quickly slip our wet, naked bodies under the blankets, and I pull her into my arms.

We're both smiling from ear to ear. We have been all day.

I love holding her and looking into her blue eyes. Her naked flesh pressed to mine. This is undoubtedly the most intimate moment of my life. I wish we could stay stuck up here forever.

I run my thumb over her lips, loving that they're red and raw from my countless kisses. "You're a hot fuck, Gully Sulley."

She bursts into laughter. "Your dick should have its own zip code, Vile Vance."

I rub it against her as it begins to harden again. She lets out a groan. "Ahh. Oh my god. You're a machine. I am well and truly McCaffed for the evening."

"Wimp," I joke.

She smiles as we stare at each other. "Is it always like this for you?"

"Like what?" I ask.

She lifts an eyebrow. "So good. Life-changing good. Body lifting into orbit good."

I shake my head. "Today has undoubtedly been the best sex of my life. Anything else has not even been close."

She rolls her eyes. "Yeah, right."

"I'm serious, Sulley. It's never been like this for me. I've never cared about a woman the way I care about you."

She rubs her fingertips over my scruff. "Don't you date?"

I shrug. "Now and then. I'm not like Daylen or some of the other guys. I don't go home with random women all the time. When I have an itch, I scratch it. It's about physical needs. Nothing else. No one has ever felt like home to me."

Her face falls. "That's kind of sad."

I sigh. "I feel like I've been sad for six years."

She nods in understanding. I can tell she wants to ask more, but we agreed to shelve the heavy. She traces my lips with her fingers. "I wish you smiled more. It lights up the room."

I run my hands all over her soft, bare back. "I'll smile more if you spend time with me."

She turns her head away and exhales a long breath. "You know I can't. There's too much hurt. Too much history." She rolls and snuggles her back into my front. "Let's just enjoy our time up here before we have to go back to reality."

She doesn't need to say it out loud for me to know what

reality means. I betrayed her brother in the worst way possible. She'll never be able to move on from that.

I PEEL my eyes open to the morning sunlight and the familiar beeping sounds of a truck moving in reverse. My body is wrapped around Sulley's. Yesterday really did happen.

The front door of the cabin opens in a rush, and I have to squint with the bright light shining through. I see my father's imposing figure standing there. He breathes a sigh of relief. "Oh, thank god. The whole town has been worried about you two. Fuck, Vance, when I found your truck in the middle of the road, I nearly had a heart attack fearing the worst."

I croak out, "We had no reception. We were stuck in here."

He nods in understanding as he begins to assess the scene. His chin drops when he takes in the fact that Sulley and I are cuddled up together, obviously naked, under the blankets. Mercifully, she's still sound asleep. My body and the blankets mostly cover hers.

He immediately averts his gaze and turns toward the door. "I...umm...I'm going to clear off Sulley's car. I left Billy to work on yours, and Dutch is plowing. Why don't you two get dressed and come outside whenever you're ready?"

Billy and Dutch are young guys who work for my father on the ranch.

"Yes, sir. Give us a few minutes."

He leaves and closes the door behind him. I kiss along Sulley's neck. "Time to wake up, princess. We've been rescued. Sadly."

With her eyes still closed, she says, "I'm up. I needed to spare myself further embarrassment by pretending to be asleep." She covers her eyes with her hand. "Oh my god, everyone is going to know what we've been up to. I'll be the town whore."

I chuckle. "My dad would never in a million years say anything. The last thing anyone in this town thinks about you is that you're a whore. You're the town hero."

She turns in my arms so we're facing each other. "You were the town hero once."

I give her a small smile. "Not anymore." I shrug. "At least people have stopped throwing eggs at my parents' house. This egg crisis has been a blessing for them," I joke.

She smacks my arm playfully. "It stopped before that. It sucks that they've had to suffer. It's not their fault."

"At this point, it's the thing that hurts the most. I'm glad your parents let them back into their lives. It paved the way for everyone else in town to do the same. Your parents are good people."

She sighs while we lie in awkward silence.

I point toward the door. "We should probably get dressed. I need to help my dad."

"Okay. What are your plans?" she asks.

"I'm going to visit with them for a few more days before heading back. My move-in was cut short by the storm. I raced to get home so I could help my father with the ranch. What about you?"

She nods in understanding. "I closed on my new house. I was supposed to be there a few days ago to move my stuff, but my flight was canceled. I'm going to head back right away as long as Momma doesn't need me. My team has already started offseason workouts. And I need to go visit Bailey. I feel terrible that I haven't done so already."

I've talked to her on the phone several times, and I sent her a few goodie baskets, but I haven't seen her in person since the accident.

"The guys said she started walking. She's not fully back to normal, but she's getting stronger every day."

"Yep. I've spoken with her and the crew a few times. It's a

miracle. Why is she living at Tanner's house?" she asks. "I would have thought she'd be in some rehab facility."

I twist my lips. "I guess it's not much of a secret anymore. They've been secretly dating for a year and a half."

Her eyes widen. "What?"

"Yep. It was supposed to be casual, but I think Tanner is in love with her. In fact, I know he is."

Her face scrunches. "He's like...a dad. He's so old."

I smile. "He's not that old."

She bites her lower lip. "I guess he's attractive, but it's still weird. Wait, doesn't his ex-wife live with them too?"

"Fallon is a physical therapist. Tanner wanted her to work with Bailey so he moved her in too. He said she knows about him and Bailey and is cool with it. He spent, like, a million dollars to bring in all the therapy equipment she needed so she would rehab at his house instead of at a facility. Control freak."

She blows out a breath. "Fucking hell. It's like a soap opera. Someone should write a book about that crazy situation."

I smile. "Gemma probably will." Gemma is Trey's wife. She's a lawyer by day and a secret romance author by night.

Sulley visibly swallows. "I had a good time, Vance, but this ends here. I just...I can't be with you after everything that's happened."

I nod as sadness fills me. "I know, Sulley. I know."

We dress in relative silence as the best two days of my life come to an abrupt and painful end.

SIXTEEN

SULLEY

"The badass bitch is back," Kennedy announces happily, and quite loudly, when I enter the gymnasium. She even adds a little ass shake as the practice session comes to a halt and everyone looks my way.

I smile and do a little curtsy. "Sorry I'm late. Traffic was a bitch." For some reason, five miles took me over forty-five minutes.

She nods. "Every traffic jam starts with one dumbass doing dumb shit."

"Facts," Layla agrees. "Nothing is worse than Philly traffic."

Shay shakes her head. "Then you haven't lived in LA. It's brutal there. Why does there need to be traffic at three in the morning on a Sunday? What's happening that it's backed up? Who are all those people, and where are they going? Why is the biggest idiot always at the front?"

I let out a laugh. It's true. Traffic jams are one of the great mysteries of life.

My teammates all walk over to hug me. Each one lovingly embraces me.

I look around at them. "I've missed you guys. I feel like I've been away forever."

Palmer nods. "You have. I got back weeks ago. I need my girl here with me."

Kennedy gasps. "What about me, Palmer? You had the one and only Kennedy Jeffries." She turns to me. "Don't worry. You're back in more than enough time for the greatest day of the year. Valentine's Day."

I lift any eyebrow. "Umm…I'm now single. It's no longer a good day."

She smirks as she crosses her arms and shakes her head. "Nope. It's the unofficial meat market day at the gym. The best day to go. Roll into the gym after five or six in the evening on Valentine's Day. No attached men will be there. It's guaranteed to be only single men. It's open season. Honestly, it's my favorite day each year. It's basically a candy shop full of all your favorite treats. It's your birthday. It's Christmas morning. It's—"

"I get it," I interrupt. "I guess I never thought about it that way. That's a very positive outlook on being single."

She grins. "I ooze glass-half-full energy, don't I?"

I let out a laugh, as does everyone else. If there's one thing Kennedy doesn't do, it's ooze glass-half-full energy.

A young man I don't recognize walks up to me with a folded towel in his hand and holds it out for me. "Would you like a towel, Ms. O'Shea?"

I look at my teammates in question. We don't usually have towel boys at voluntary, unofficial team practices. Especially attractive ones in unusually tight clothing.

Kennedy shrugs. "I have an intern. This is Booster. He's been working for me for a few weeks. He gets school credit for it."

The young man corrects, "Again, it's Rooster, Ms. Jeffries."

She sighs. "You're so short. I feel like Booster is more appropriate. Roosters are loud and annoying. It's a stupid name. And why did you call her Ms. O'Shea? What if she got married recently?"

The poor kid's face drops. "Oh, I'm sorry. Is it Mrs.?"

"You can just call me Sulley." I correct.

Kennedy shakes her head. "Nope. Booster is going to show us all some respect. No first names. Queen is the most acceptable. We're all queens." She places her finger on the corner of her mouth. "Come to think of it, why are single women Ms. and married women Mrs.? Is it really anyone else's business if we're attached or not? Men are Mr. no matter what their status. So *our* relationships to men matter, but *their* relationships to us don't? Such sexist bullshit."

Shay stares at Kennedy. "Your brain will be studied for science one day."

Kennedy quips, "Says the lesbian in a wife-beater shirt. Tell me you're a lesbian without telling me you're a lesbian."

Shay smiles as she tugs on the straps of her ribbed, white tank top. "In the lesbian community, we don't call these shirts wife beaters." She winks. "We call them wife pleasers."

She blows Kennedy a kiss, and I giggle. "She's got you there, Kennedy."

Shay and Kennedy share bemused looks. They love to rib each other, but they've become good friends and respect one another. In fact, I know Kennedy hung with Shay and Alyssa a lot when I was gone.

Palmer throws her arm around me. "How are you? You know, since your breakup."

"I'm great," I answer honestly.

"Are you two done for good?"

I nod. "Absolutely. I don't read my books backward. I already know that story, and it most definitely has ended."

Kennedy nods emphatically. "Good for you. On to bigger and better, preferably at the gym on Valentine's Day. You were too good for him. I was happy you broke up. Speaking of good news, creepy Noah was fired."

That's kind of a relief. "How come?"

"Because Reagan Daulton walked into the training room and he was jerking off to our team photo."

I let out a laugh. "Oh my god. Are you for real?"

She smiles. "No, but Reagan is smart. She knows he's a creep. They're interviewing candidates now. Hopefully, they'll hire a woman as our next PT."

WE HAD A GREAT PRACTICE. It was fun to be back with my team. It was seamless. We're so much more familiar with each other than we were only six months ago. I think we're going to be awesome this year.

Kennedy has gotten even stronger, quite obviously hitting the gym hard since I last saw her. Her dedication is enviable.

I'm loving my new house. It's small, but it's homey and perfect. Most importantly, it's mine. Obviously the cabin is mine too, but it was given to me. My brownstone in Philly is the first big-ticket item I bought for myself. I'm full of pride over it.

With some gentle coaxing from Kennedy, I decided that I'm going to host a housewarming party next week. Layla loves to be the social planner, so I told her to invite whoever she wants. She gave me the name of her caterer, and I booked them. I feel so grown up.

With Layla picking the guest list, I know it will include Vance. I sort of miss him. I hate that I do, and I'd never admit it out loud, but I find myself constantly thinking about our two days together. I can't stop remembering the way he made my body feel. Every kiss and every touch are forever burned into my memory. I have a few lingering bite marks from him. I keep looking at them in the mirror, not wanting them to fade.

I'm now pulling into Tanner Montgomery's long driveway until I reach the house. It's not a house. It's a mansion. Being a sports agent must pay well.

I can't wait to see Bailey. I feel like I've been a terrible friend, but I haven't been back in Philly until now.

Before I have the chance to knock on the front door, Tanner's adorable daughter, Harper, opens it. Her face lights up, and she yells out, "It's Sulley O'Shea."

I smile. "Hi, Harper. It's good to see you again." She came to several of our games last summer.

"You remember me, Sulley O'Shea?"

"Of course. You were quite memorable given that you told me basketball was your second favorite sport. That you prefer softball. Usually, little girls tell me that basketball is their favorite sport."

Her face falls. "I'm sorry, Sulley O'Shea, but my mommy says never to lie. If it makes you feel better, you're also my second favorite basketball player." She gasps and covers her mouth.

I can't help but giggle. She may be the cutest kid I've ever seen in my life.

"May I ask who your favorite is?"

With her head down, she mumbles, "Kennedy Jeffries. I like her toughness."

I smile. "I like Kennedy too. I wouldn't be able to score as many points as I do without Kennedy rebounding and setting picks for me." Harper lifts her head, and our eyes meet. "It's okay to be honest. I like honest people in my life. In fact, Kennedy is one of the most honest people I know. It's probably what I love most about her."

A grin immediately finds her pretty face. "It is?"

"Yep. Can I come in?"

"Oh, yes. Sorry." She yells again, "Bails, Sulley O'Shea is here."

"You don't have to use my last name every time you refer to me. Sulley is fine."

She yells again, "Bails, Sulley is here. I told her softball is still my favorite sport, but it's okay because she likes honesty."

I hear Bailey laugh as she approaches. I wasn't sure what to expect, but she's walking fine. I wouldn't say it's perfect quite yet, but if I didn't know about her accident, I wouldn't know.

"That's because softball is the best sport." She holds up her arms in invitation. "Sulley, I'm so happy to see you."

I hug my friend and do my best to hold back my tears. "I'm so happy to see you too. You look amazing. You're a miracle. I'm sorry I haven't been around. I just got back into town and had to move into my new house. There were a few issues, and I couldn't get away until now."

She pulls back and offers her always sweet smile. "I've been a little busy anyway. It works well because Harper's mom and I want to challenge you and Harper to a game of basketball. I wouldn't have been able to play a few weeks ago." She makes a muscle. "I don't mean to sound like every guy you've probably dated, but I was an all-state high school basketball player."

I let out a laugh. "That's so true. They all love to brag about that." I'm reminded of Kennedy's red flags since that's one of them.

She nods. "Right? Same with baseball." In a deep voice, she says, "I once hit a home run when I was sixteen. Your fences are shorter. I'd be a stud softball player." She rolls her eyes. "Well, I hit about thirty home runs a summer, *jerk*. Off of all the best pitchers in the world, *Chad*."

Harper hangs on every word Bailey says and asks, "Who's Chad?"

Bailey and I share bemused looks before she answers, "It's a universal name for jerky guys. Like Karen for women."

Harper scrunches her face. "There's a Karen in my class. She's abhorrent."

Did this kid just use the word abhorrent? I'm about to ask when a shorter, attractive blonde woman with the same turquoise eyes as Harper, likely in her late thirties, appears. She holds out her hand. "Hi, I'm Fallon, Harper's mom and mega-Sulley O'Shea fan. You're my *number one* favorite player," she giggles before winking at Harper.

I smile as I shake her hand. "It's nice to meet you. I hear we're playing ball today. Harper and I are going to take you two to school." I fist bump Harper, and she jumps up and down excitedly.

We end up playing for an hour. Bailey and Fallon are pretty good. They both have skills and athleticism. Apparently, Fallon also used to play in high school. Harper is shockingly good for her age with great hand-eye coordination. Bailey has a few struggles, but she's doing well considering her back was broken a few months ago.

I learn Fallon is a professional physical therapist. I suppose Vance mentioned it, but I had forgotten. Before I leave, I encourage her to consider a job with the Beavers. She'd be perfect for it. The hours are great, the pay is probably more than what she makes now working at a hospital, and Harper would enjoy becoming a gym rat. Fallon said she'd consider it. I make a note to mention it to Reagan.

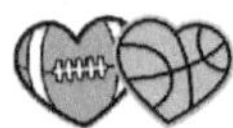

VANCE

"It's a national holiday," Daylen declares.

I roll my eyes. "No, it's not."

"Suck a Dick Sunday is a weekly holiday I celebrate. Don't yuck my yum. Please respect my religious beliefs." He bites back his goofy smile. "You have no idea how many women I've convinced that it's a real holiday."

I stare at Daylen in disbelief as he does leg presses in our team gym. From the chest press machine, I shake my head. "You're a fucking idiot, D."

He wiggles his eyebrows. "Or a genius."

I sigh and point to the large man currently on the other side of the gym lifting hundreds of pounds over his head. "Beau is a genius. I still don't understand what he was saying about weight distribution the other day at my new house."

I've been back for a few days, finishing my move into the new house. I had a moving company, but Beau and Daylen, who are bigger and stronger than the professional movers, have been extremely helpful. Beau put my entire dresser on his shoulder like it weighed ten pounds. He then put my sofa on his other shoulder and explained to us how the distribution of each lessens the effects, or some shit like that.

Beau shrugs. "I'm not a genius. I applied simple principles of mathematics and equilibrium."

Daylen nonchalantly says, "Did you know that eighty-five percent of Americans can't do basic math? It's a good thing I'm in the other twenty-five percent."

Everyone starts laughing. I can't help but smile at my friend. He's truly one of a kind.

I look over to Champ, who's doing squats at an obscene weight. "Shit, man, no wonder no one can tackle you. That's triple what I can do."

He nods. "We're going all the way this year. It's our time, McCaffrey."

I agree. We're getting older. We'll never have a better, stronger team than we'll have this upcoming season. Management added two more defensive studs so everything doesn't fall on Beau's shoulders.

I look over at Reece. "Rook, get me a towel."

He scowls. "I'm not a rookie anymore. Have one of them get you a towel, McCaffrey."

Beau is about to go set him straight when I hold up my hand for him to stop. I've got this. "You're a rook until you stop acting like a little bitch. How many passes did you drop last season?"

"Seven," he mumbles.

"How many did you catch?"

"Six."

"Right. So you're still a fucking rookie until you catch more passes than you drop, butterfingers. And if you want me to throw you the ball, get my fucking towel, you mouthy little shit. And get one for Champ too. In fact, wipe down machines for Champ today after he's done using them. You're his wiping bitch for the day."

Put simply, no one likes Reece Sanders. He's an obvious bigot, always mumbling anti-gay slurs and jokes that only he thinks are funny. The way he treats Champ makes my blood boil, but Champ never says anything and asks us to leave it be. He just takes it on the chin, never wanting to be the center of attention. Daylen, Beau, and I have discussed it. If Reece's behavior continues this year, we're going to ask management to trade or release him. He's bad news, but, at Champ's request, we're chalking up last year to immaturity. He's skating on thin ice with us right now.

He throws a towel toward Champ and brings me mine. I grab his wrist and grit out so only he can hear me, "You're a piece of shit. Learn some respect. If you can't manage it, hillbilly, we're going to have a problem. It's not a good idea to piss off the person who decides whether or not to throw you the ball. This is your last chance, Sanders. Get your act together. Grow the fuck up."

He visibly swallows as he scurries away like the rat he is. I have no faith that he will change.

Champ walks over to me and we do a little handshake followed by a bro hug. In a low voice, he quietly says, "I appreciate the support, but it only draws more unwanted attention. I've dealt with guys like him my whole life. It's not worth it."

I squeeze his hand tight and pull our bodies close so we're nearly nose to nose as I look him in the eye. "You're my teammate, which makes you my brother. I would never allow my brother to be disrespected in any way, would you?"

He shakes his head.

"Right. So you just sit there and look pretty. I'll set that prick straight. I know you put your head down, work hard, and do your job. You're not a showboat. You don't like to be the center of attention. I dig that about you. It doesn't make his treatment of you acceptable. He will treat you with respect, or I will make sure he's kicked off this team."

Champ pinches his lips together, appearing like he might get emotional. "Thanks, man. I appreciate you having my back."

I nod as we break apart and get back to our respective workouts.

Coach Jeffries walks into the gym wearing athletic clothing. His joining team workouts has become the norm, especially in the years since his divorce. I don't think it's as much about improving his body as it is about having an outlet for his sadness and frustrations. I suppose it's better than sitting at a bar.

He gives me a friendly punch to the arm. "This will finally be our year, son."

I nod. "The new guys will help."

"Yep. I pushed hard for them. You can't be expected to throw five touchdowns a game. At some point, the defense needs to make a stand. And Fudd can't play eleven positions."

Coach, who misses nothing, looks Reece's way. "You set him straight?"

"Yes, sir. It's under control."

"Good. Fucking prima donna. He should focus on catching the ball instead of the personal lives of his teammates."

"Agreed."

"You make sure Champ knows everyone has his back."

"I have. He knows."

We break apart, and he heads over to the stretching area.

I look back toward Champ. "Have you seen Bailey lately?" I went to visit her a small handful of times during our season, but I haven't been over since I returned from Montana.

He smiles. "Yes, I go over several days a week. Her recovery is remarkable. She's the strongest woman I've ever met. Google says her recovery should have taken way longer than it has. I'm so proud of her."

Coach scoffs. "Pft. Google. You know what my childhood Google was? A library. If we wanted answers, we had to go to the library and spend hours looking them up. And the lucky few had full sets of Encyclopedia Britannica in their houses. A through Z, each letter a different full book volume. You had to flip through the pages to try to find what you were looking for."

Daylen nods. "I remember having an older woman babysit me once who talked about those ancient scrolls called Encyclopedias."

Coach narrows his eyes. "Babysitters? You know who my babysitter was in the eighties? The Gen X babysitter of choice? It was my mother shouting on the way out of the house, 'Don't open the motherfucking door for anyone.'"

We all laugh. I love Coach's Gen X-isms.

My phone pings, and I pull it out of my pocket and look at the screen. It's a text from Layla to the group that there will be a housewarming party at Sulley's new house next week.

I've texted her a few times since our two perfect days together. She returned with short, one-word responses, not wanting to engage. It hurts, but what can I do? This is a situation of my own creation. I can't deny that I miss her and what we shared in that cabin.

I pull up our text string and begin to type.

> Me: Looking forward to your party. Thanks for including me.

> Sulley: It was Layla. She did the guest list.

Ouch.

Me: I miss you.

Sulley: Don't.

Me: I'm all moved in. Will you come see the house?

I see three dots pop up on the screen multiple times, indicating that she's writing, but nothing comes through, and then the dots disappear.

Me: Please. I want you to see his creation.

Sulley: Fine. When?

Me: How about tomorrow? Early evening, when the sun is setting? It's most beautiful at that time of day.

Sulley: See you then.

SEVENTEEN

SULLEY

I enter through the gate and drive down Vance's freshly paved, tree-lined, winding driveway. It's so pretty. Much different from the city. It's tucked back in the woods. If you didn't know it was here, you wouldn't know. I suppose that's the point. It affords him a lot of privacy.

I've been doing my best to avoid his texts. I give one-word responses. Until tonight, I haven't seen him since he returned to Philly. I need to keep Vance McCaffrey at arm's length. Yes, we had an amazing two days, but it's in the past, and that's where it will remain. I got to fulfill my fantasy of being with him. Now I can move on.

When he texted me about seeing the house, I wasn't sure if it was a good idea, but I do want to see the finished product. It's Finn's design. How can I not at least see it one time? It will also be a good opportunity for me to let Vance know in no uncertain terms that what happened in Montana is never happening again. It was an itch we both had. It's been officially scratched. We're done and over. I can get back to hating him for what he did to my family.

My breath catches when I reach the clearing and the house comes into view. Tears immediately fill my eyes. Before me is the biggest and most beautiful cabin I've ever seen in my life. It's hard to call it a cabin. That word cabin doesn't do it justice. It's a mountain resort. It looks like it could be an authentic luxury hotel in the Rockies. It's Finn's masterpiece. Seeing his final drawings come to life fills me with emotion. Pride isn't a big enough word for what I'm feeling right now.

The sun is setting behind it, framing it in a peach-colored hue. It almost looks photoshopped. That's how perfect it is.

There's a huge circular driveway that leaves me at what must be fourteen-foot-high oversized dark wooden double doors. The front has a magnificent wraparound porch, complete with benches and sofas. It exudes both luxury and comfort.

I exit my car and begin to walk up the small handful of steps toward the front door. Before I reach it, the door opens and Vance appears in worn jeans, an old T-shirt, and bare feet. Why are his giant bare feet so sexy?

Because every single inch of him is sexy. He's the hottest man ever created.

There's something amusing about seeing him dressed like this in front of a house that must have cost millions of dollars. At the end of the day, he's still Vance, a cowboy from a small town in Montana.

He offers me a small smile. "Thanks for coming."

"Oh, Vance, it's beautiful. Just perfect."

He nods. "Thank you. I think so too. Wait until you see the inside."

I walk in and can hardly believe what I'm seeing. It's two stories and open for as far as the eye can see, with huge, exposed wood beams and oversized round chandeliers that look like burning candles, though they're not. There are multiple fireplaces built from real stone, not the veneer you often see in homes now. They're all wood-burning, which makes me inwardly laugh since I know Collin battled him on the issue.

"Modern mountain living," he says. "That's what Collin called it. I think he was right."

I silently look around, taking it all in. Seeing my brother's vision come to fruition has me in my feels. I whisper, "He'd love it."

Vance nods as the corner of his mouth raises. "I know he would."

Looking at the beams more closely, I ask, "Are they oak? That must have cost you a fortune." Maple is more traditionally used in wood homes as it's much cheaper.

He nods. "Yep. No real cowboy would accept anything else."

I know Finn wanted to make the small cabin out of oak, but it was too pricey, and he was working within a very limited budget.

I can't help but stare at the beams. They're just so perfect. I inhale deeply. It smells like the woods and Vance. It's intoxicating.

As we walk further into the house toward the kitchen, one particular beam catches my attention. It's central and not finished like the others. It sticks out. I wonder why he chose to do that.

For some reason, I'm drawn to the anomaly. As I stand under it, I look up, and that's when I see it. The original inscription, carved into the wood. *McShea Brothers.*

My head immediately snaps toward Vance, my eyes looking at him in question.

He has a sheepish look as he shoves his hands into his front pockets. "Yes, it's *that* tree."

"When? How?"

He nervously licks his lips. "I knew about your tax liability. I also knew you would never accept money from me. I wanted something of Finn's in here but assumed you wouldn't let me have that tree on principle. It was a win-win. I had my guy offer you money for all those oak trees. This entire house is built out of the trees from the cabin property. Finn's trees in Finn's design. It's kind of fitting, don't you think?"

I'm silent. I have no words.

He runs his fingers through his hair. "Are you mad at me for not telling you? I almost did the other day when we were looking at the clearing outside the cabin, but I guess I wanted to wait for you to see it in person. How special it is."

I wordlessly shake my head. At least I do in my mind. I think I'm frozen in shock.

He walks over to me and places his big hand on my shoulder, causing a flood of warmth to run through my body. "Are you okay with it, Sulley? Please talk to me. I hate the silence. It messes with my head."

I pause for several long beats. "I…I think so."

His hand remains on me. Why does his touch affect me so damn much?

The push and pull of my emotions for this man overwhelm me. Sometimes I hate him, and sometimes I feel like I'll die if he doesn't touch every inch of my body. Right in this moment, it's the latter.

I turn my head and look at his hand on me. As if just realizing it's there, he starts to withdraw it, but I grab his wrist and bring the back of his palm to my lips for a soft kiss before softly whispering, "Thanks for making his dream come true."

We stare at each other as silence fills the air. The air between us is electric. There's no denying that.

He breathes, "Sulley."

I breathe back, "Vance."

I begin to avert my gaze from his handsome face, unable to contain my emotions, when his fingers roughly grab my chin. "Look at me."

I do.

"Talk to me. Use your words. Tell me what you want, Gully Sulley."

I swallow. I don't want to want him, but I can't help it. I do. Desperately.

My trembling fingers eventually find his belt buckle as I lose the battle within myself and admit, "You, Vile Vance. I want you."

As if I'll change my mind if I wait any longer, I frantically undo his belt and jeans, pulling them down to his ankles along with his boxer briefs.

His python pops out, standing at full, angry, mouth-watering attention.

Not able to wait a second more, I take him into my hand and drop to my knees in front of him.

He lets out a groan of pleasure. "Fuuuuck yes."

After a few long pumps, which produce a shot of pre-ejaculate, my tongue runs along his thick, long manhood. I take a deep breath, inhaling the pheromones that ooze from him. The way this man smells will forever be my undoing.

My nails scrape across his thick thighs, and goosebumps spread all over his body. He even shivers a little. I love what my touch does to him.

My tongue works him over, exploring every vein and crevice, but I haven't put that monster into my mouth yet. I'm working up the confidence.

He grabs my hair into his hands to get it out of my face, and I look up at him while he stares down at me with an intensity that makes it hard to breathe. "I've dreamed of this. You, on your knees in front of me." His eyes flash with a bit of uncharacteristic mischief. "In my dreams, you're wearing my jersey like you did at that one game, but you on your knees is my fantasy come to life. Open wide, baby. We'll take it slow at first."

Desperate to please him, I do as I'm told and open my mouth as wide as I can. With one hand still holding my hair, he strokes his cock twice with the other before slowly feeding it into my mouth. It's so domineering. I can feel my wetness dripping onto my panties.

"Relax and open your throat."

I do my best, and he pushes in until I feel his tip touch my throat…or my lungs. I'm not sure. I only know that it's so all-encompassing that I can barely breathe.

As he begins to withdraw, I seal my lips around him and suck as hard as I can. He hisses in approval.

My tongue swirls over his tip as his cock continues to slowly recede until we repeat the whole process over and over again.

I replace his hand on his base with one of mine and then the other because yes, I can fit both hands and my mouth around his cock all at the same time. I don't know whether his dick was created by an angel or a sadist, but it's something to behold. I swear it looks even bigger now than it did at the cabin. Maybe that's because it's in my face. In my mouth. Down my throat.

He continuously battles the obvious desire to tilt his head back in ecstasy, refusing to break our eye contact. It's wholly intimate. Too intimate.

His body starts to shake. His grip on my hair tightens. He's getting close. It makes me feel powerful that I'm able to drive a man like Vance mad with desire. To teeter on the edge of control. I can sense he's about to lose it.

I begin twisting motions with both hands. As soon as I do, he snaps, thrusting his cock into me like a man possessed. Deep, hard strokes. Saliva uncontrollably drips from my mouth and down my chin.

"Oh fuck," he grunts. "Fuck, fuck, fuck, Sulley. I'm coming."

I'd tell him to give it all to me, but I currently have nine inches of pure masculinity stuffed inside my mouth, practically choking me while I'm doing my best to play it cool like it's a normal everyday occurrence for a woman to deal with a man so damn big.

Vance McCaffrey losing control at my hands will forever be an image that replays in my mind, no matter what happens moving forward.

Four more long strokes and I'm blessed with the first lengthy shot of his semen. And then a second. And then a third. What the hell kind of protein does this guy consume? My mouth is full of him, but nothing has ever tasted better.

I'm still in the process of swallowing down what feels like a gallon of man milk when he pulls me up and slams our mouths together at the same time as our bodies come together. He slides his arms around me. It's warm and comfortable. Safe. It's everything I want and need.

These feelings I've been working hard since Montana to push away are popping to the surface like they were never gone. Why him? Anyone but him.

Once again, I shove all our baggage to the side and melt into the sensation of being with my dream man, knowing the pleasure he's going to bring to my body in mere minutes. The pleasure he brought to my body countless times in Montana. Pleasure only he's ever given me.

Our lips break while he tears my clothes from my body in mere seconds, as ravenous for me as I am for him. His T-shirt quickly joins the pile of our clothing on the ground.

We stand close, completely naked, as his eyes move up and down my body. His thumbs brush over my nipples. "I don't know what I want to do to you first."

I had the feeling in Montana that he was holding back a bit. I saw glimpses of his rough nature and filthy mouth, but I don't want him holding back now.

"Anything you want," I breathe. "Don't hold back."

His green eyes very clearly darken as his tongue runs across his lower lip. His eyes briefly break with mine and move toward his massive kitchen island.

My lips curl in amusement, knowing what he's thinking.

Mustering up all the confidence I can, I saunter over to the island, swaying my hips along the way. Bending over the island and sticking my ass in the air, I slowly run my hand over waist, hip, and backside before whispering, "Do your worst, big boy."

Immediately hardening again, he stalks my way. "You're about to get it good."

"Bring it. Give it all to me. Don't hold back. I want everything."

He runs his fingertips over the bones of my spine and then down the crack of my ass. I try not to flinch. I've never done anything with my back door. When I said that I wanted everything, I'm not sure I considered that it was a possibility.

But his fingers continue their path down the backs of my legs as he drops down to his knees. "I fucking love these long legs. I particularly loved when they were wrapped around my face."

Yep, I loved that too.

My body is overheating at his touch. The cold stone of the island feels soothing on my frontside.

I gasp when his hands roughly grab my ass cheeks and he spreads them apart, swiping his tongue from opening to opening. Some noise I don't recognize escapes my mouth. It's somewhere between a moan and a mewl.

"Lean all the way forward," he growls out. I do, and my nipples press against the cold stone.

His tongue plunders my channel while his fingers easily find my clit. I try not to think about where his nose must be right now.

He builds me up in no time. It doesn't take much. I'm so turned on by this whole scene.

He mumbles into me, "Your pussy is drenched for me. It's begging for my dick."

"Umm hmm."

Without warning, the warmth of his face, tongue, and fingers is gone. I feel his hands on my hips. I'm too delirious to connect the dots, so when he thrusts into me all at once, I feel like I'm being split in half. I manage to both scream and moan at the same time.

His fingers begin to dig into my hips as he pistons into me, reaching depths I know for a fact have never been reached before.

I'm screaming at a level where I know my throat will be sore. I can't control it with him. He brings it out of me.

He grits out, "Tell me you feel it. What it's like between us."

Feel it? How could I not feel what's happening to my body right now? All I can manage is, "God, yes."

That seems to further embolden him. He pushes my legs as far apart as he can, leaving me at his mercy. He's got me clawing the stone, loving the sting on my fingernails. I'm losing my mind.

He spanks my ass hard, and I can feel my juices dripping down my thighs. This man drives me insane. I can't for the life of me figure out why I'd want to deny myself this anymore.

"One day I'm gonna fuck you like this in public with my fucking fist in your loud mouth."

In public? What does that mean? We can't fuck like this in public.

Panic begins to rise to the surface. What did he mean by that? Maybe it's just part of the whole dirty talk thing he's got going on.

His body now pressed against mine and his hand around my throat brings me back to the present.

Shane once tried to choke me, but his hand pushing my windpipe was making it too hard to breathe. I freaked out and told him never again. Vance's pressure is on the sides, not directly on my windpipe. It's a choking sensation but not actually depriving me of air. Is that how it's supposed to be? This is fucking hot. I love it.

"I'm about to come, Sulley. Need you to come too, baby."

I shiver at him calling me baby. The sweet endearment is a complete contrast to the carnal way we're fucking.

His hand moves from my throat down to my clit and begins furious circles. My eyes roll back in my head as the most powerful orgasm imaginable rips through every single nerve in my body. I feel both numbness and bliss. My ears ring from the piercing sounds of my own screams. They're nearly unrecognizable to me.

"God, I love how loud you are." He pounds hard for a few seconds longer as he roars violently through his own orgasm, biting the back of my shoulder in the process. I know I'll have marks from it, and it only spurs my orgasm to last longer.

I'm lying lifelessly, completely naked, on his kitchen island. I've been here for all of twenty minutes. I'm really crushing the whole keeping him at arm's length thing.

He's draped over my back, panting heavily. Once his breathing evens out a bit more, he turns my face toward him, cups my cheek, and brings his lips to mine for a kiss. It's soft and sweet. Almost a thank you.

He whispers into my mouth, "Stay the night with me. Not because you're stuck in a snowstorm, but because you want to."

"I shou—"

Before I can decline his invitation, his lips find mine again, and I'm lost in the abyss that is Vance McCaffrey. Without any more words being spoken, and without breaking our kiss, he lifts me and carries me to his bedroom, where we repeat things all over again.

VANCE

It's morning and I'm staring at Sulley in my bed. This is how I imagined things. How it should be. Her in this house with me. Waking up together every day.

If I hadn't fucked everything up, it could be like this. I've got to try, though. I'll forever kick myself if I don't try to win her over.

We went at it again and again last night, only taking a break to refuel our depleted bodies. Naked snacks with Sulley in bed might now be my favorite pastime.

She thought about leaving after midnight but hadn't driven the Philly highways at night yet and was a little scared. I talked her into staying. On some level, I know she wanted to. I see her internal battle. I understand her struggles but desperately want her to push past them.

I pull the blankets down to reveal her naked body. She's so breathtakingly beautiful. I love it when she wraps those long legs around me.

Her pussy lips are swollen from the hours of attention they received last night. I get off on the fact that it's all because of me.

I know she's full of my come, and I love it. Once again, we didn't use a condom. I wonder if there's a chance her IUD isn't working. Nothing would make me happier than to see her stomach swollen with my baby. I harden at the thought.

Sliding down the bed, I spread her legs further and situate myself between them. I run a finger through and then into her. Her walls pulse around my finger. Still asleep, she lets out an involuntary moan. Responding in her sleep? That's so hot.

I bend my head and slowly run my tongue through her a few times. With my eyes on her face, I see the moment she wakes. She smiles and runs her fingers through my hair, giving it the tug she knows I crave from her.

Before I know it, we're going at it again. I'm insatiable for this woman. I will never get enough of her.

An hour later, we're stepping out of my shower. She glares at me. "Why are you smiling so much? It's off-putting."

I chuckle. "I love having you here. You look good in my house. I want more of it."

Her face falls. "Vance, I don't think it's a good idea."

"I think you like it but won't admit it out loud."

She blows out a breath. "I won't lie and say we don't have a strong physical connection, we do. *More* than strong. But it can't be like that between us. It can't ever go anywhere. You know why. How would I ever explain that to my friends and family?"

My jaw tics. Can't she see how much I care about her? How much I've always cared? "Give me something, Sulley." I pull her towel-covered body close to mine, rub away a few droplets of water still on her face, and look down at her. "I don't care about any of them. This is us. You and me. It's private. No one else's business."

She shakes her head. "You and me together? Everyone would make it their business. It would be plastered everywhere. There'd be nothing private about it."

She tries to move out of my hold, but I don't let her. "Vance, let me go."

"That's the problem. I don't want to let you go. What if we were to spend time together but didn't tell anyone else? We keep it between you and me."

Her eyebrows pinch together. "Like a top-secret relationship?"

I smile at her adorableness. "Sure, we can call it that."

She drags her lower lip through her teeth, and I immediately harden thinking about what those lips did to my cock last night. I see the moment she realizes it because her cheeks flush. It's the Irish heritage. Flushed cheeks are her tell. She can't hide it. I know I've got her.

Running my finger slowly under the top of her towel, I pull it until it drops to the ground. My lips find her collarbone and kiss along it, giving it a few small bites. It drives her wild. It's a definite weakness of hers.

"We could," kiss, "make love," kiss, "anytime we want," kiss, "wherever we want," kiss. I run my fingers through her center and then into her. Her grip on my arm tightens. "You could have me inside you all the time. Whenever you want it, baby."

She shivers, as she does every time I call her baby. Why is she denying herself what she so clearly wants?

I suppose I know the answer to that.

"Vance," she breathes as she leans all her weight on me. "Deeper."

"You got it, baby. As deep as you want."

EIGHTEEN

SULLEY

We're just about to finish practice. I'm in a bit of a rush to get home. Tonight is my dinner party. I'm nervous. I've never hosted anything like this. I'm grateful for Layla's help. Presley is going to stay with the baby until the sitter comes so Layla can help me get everything ready. She's going to shower and change at my house.

I dribble the ball a few times and toss an alley-oop up for Kennedy so she can attempt a dunk, but she slams it directly onto the rim and then lands hard on her ass. She groans in disappointment. "Fuck me! I'll never get to dunk. I'm too fucking short. My damn mother and her genes fucked me over."

I giggle. "You must be over six feet." She's an inch or two taller than me. "You're hardly short."

She scowls. "Not tall enough to dunk. I've worked so fucking hard on my vertical for the past three months." She points an accusatory finger at Shay. "Tongue-fu master barely has to jump and the bitch can dunk."

Shay grabs her stomach and doubles over in laughter.

"Tongue-fu master? Fucking classic, Darth Vader. I need to text Alyssa that one."

Kennedy deadpans, "Who do you think taught me the term? That's what my new bestie calls you behind your back."

"For real?" Shay asks with a proud look on her face.

Kennedy smiles and winks as Layla offers a hand to help her off the ground. She then smacks Kennedy on the ass. "You'll get it eventually. I have faith."

"At least you can reach the rim," I offer, "I can't even get up that high."

Kennedy twists her lips. "I'm not giving up. My goal is to dunk this season. I refuse to quit until it happens."

A phone alarm starts ringing, and Layla runs over to the bench and pulls out a packet of birth control pills, quickly washing one down with a gulp of bottled water.

She looks at all of us. "What? I have mommy brain right now. I swear, being a mother makes you significantly dumber. I need an alarm to remember to do everything, including taking birth control. No more bambinos for a while."

Kennedy asks, "Why doesn't Presley just wear condoms?"

Layla shrugs. "Not sure. We never even considered going back to condoms. He hates them. We haven't used them since we first started dating."

My mind goes straight to Vance and my complete and total irresponsibility. I haven't used condoms at all with him. What the hell am I thinking?

Kennedy interrupts my self-loathing. "Women can get pregnant once in nine months, but men can impregnate countless women in nine months. Shouldn't birth control be for men?"

Shay sighs. "Like I've said before, your brain will be studied one day."

Kennedy turns to her intern. "Booster, I need some ice for my ass. Go grab me some."

He nods and answers, "Yes, Queen Jeffries," before heading into the locker room.

As soon as he disappears, I ask, "Why do you make him wear sweatpants and a T-shirt that are both clearly a size too small?"

She shrugs. "Why have the women at Hooters had to wear those barely there uniforms for decades? Why do cocktail waitresses at clubs wear short skirts? Men have been doing it to women for years and years. It's my turn for payback. Revealing gray sweatpants are our Hooters tops."

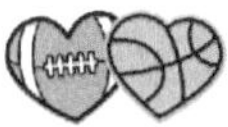

A FEW HOURS LATER, the doorbell rings, signaling my first houseguest besides Layla. I open the door to see Daylen with a celery stick poking out of his mouth. I wonder why he's always eating celery.

He kisses my cheek and hands me an unwrapped candle in a jar that reads, *I hope your neighbors aren't serial killers.*

I smile. "Thank you. Such a beautiful candle with a sweet message."

He nods. "I thought so."

Kennedy approaches my stoop right behind him. He turns when he hears her. "Did you bring a better attitude?" he asks her.

"Did you bring a better personality?" she immediately replies.

He holds out his arms like he's handing her imaginary flowers. "Roses are red, violets are blue, I have five fingers, but the middle one is for you." At that, he turns his hand and flips her the bird.

She holds her phone up to her ear. "Your village just called. They want their idiot back."

He shakes his head. "You're a fucking handful."

She shrugs. "I might be a handful, but at least my tits are too so that makes up for it."

He lets out his loud, house-shaking laugh. "I can't argue with that. Your rack is your best attribute." He wiggles his eyebrows as he stares shamelessly and obviously at her chest.

She shoves him to the side as she walks by him. "You're such a child."

"Breastfeed me then." He chuckles.

She ignores him and hands me a purple gift bag with light pink tissue paper peeking out. "Happy new house."

I smile. "You're so sweet. Thank you."

She nods toward it. "Open the gift. You can use it tonight."

Assuming it's a bottle of wine, I dip my hand into the bag only to pull out what appears to be a penis-shaped wine decanter. She smirks. "I hear things really open up in the balls."

Yep, there are two big glass balls at the bottom. "I guess we'll find out soon enough."

She giggles. "I made Booster go into the store to pick it up. You should have seen his face. God, I love having an intern. Shaming a man in the process is an added perk."

Daylen raises an eyebrow. "You have an intern?"

She nods. "I do."

"Why?"

"Because it amuses me, and I'm a busy woman. I need someone to run errands for me."

"Do you pay him?" Daylen asks.

She smirks. "Nope. That's the beauty. He gets school credit for it."

He studies her carefully. "That's actually brilliant. I need an intern."

Everyone arrives shortly thereafter, each with a gift in hand. They're all so generous and thoughtful. Beau brought me a healthy living cookbook for athletes that lists him as the author. I think there's more to Beau Fudd than meets the eye.

When Vance arrives, looking edible as always in his customary uniform of jeans, a flannel, and cowboy boots, he offers me a gift bag too. "Should I open it?" I ask.

He nods. "You can if you want."

I reach into the bag and pull out a pretty wooden picture frame. As I examine it closely, I see it's a picture of Finn and me. I remember taking it. He was eighteen and I was ten. I'm on his back at the front entrance of the cabin. It was the day they finally finished. We're both covered in paint and laughing without a care in the world.

I give him a soft smile. "I love it. Thank you."

"That was a good day."

I nod. "Sure was. I remember it clearly. I know just the spot for it."

With him on my heels, I walk through the house and place it prominently on the mantel above my fireplace. Vance smirks at me. "Is that a gas fireplace, O'Shea?"

I scrunch my face. "Yes. It's the only thing I dislike about this place, though I can't imagine finding wood would be easy in the city."

He whispers, "I'll give you as much wood as you want."

I narrow my eyes at him and mouth, "Behave."

He shakes his head and mouths back, "Never."

All I want to do is kiss that smug smile off his face. *Or sit on it.*

So…Vance McCaffrey is officially my weakness. He sexually coerced me into agreeing to a top-secret relationship. One minute I was saying no, and the next he was inside me, and I said yes. Several times. Over and over. Very loudly.

We agreed to spend time together away from any prying eyes. That is all I will ever give him. Of course, I know this is a colossal mistake, but I can't seem to help myself. I'm addicted to the sex. At least that's what I'm telling myself.

He adjusts himself in his jeans. "I can see my bite marks on your neck. Fuck, it's turning me on."

Feeling heat rush to my cheeks, I quickly fix the collar of my blouse. I thought I had it covered.

He subtly rubs his pinkie over mine. "Can I take you out on a date this week?"

I shake my head. "No. This is a top-secret relationship, remember? It's not like we can just hide away in a restaurant corner. We'll be recognized wherever we go."

He licks his lips. "If I promise we won't be seen, can I take you out? It's off the beaten path." He leans over toward my ear, and I feel his warm breath on my neck. "It will be worth your while, I assure you."

I catch a waft of his scent, and my whole body reacts. My nipples harden, and my panties dampen. Because my body is completely under his control, I'm powerless to do anything but nod in agreement.

He squeezes my hand and breathes, "Good girl."

And my panties go from damp to drenched with two simple words.

His eyes move up and down my body, landing right on my pussy. His Adam's apple bobs. "I'll take care of that when everyone leaves, unless you want me to bend you over the dining room table now."

I blow out a breath. Lord, please help me get through this night without letting him mount me in front of a full audience.

We turn and walk back toward the group, who are all sitting around with drinks in hand. I love seeing everyone chatting and having a good time in my home.

Presley holds up three fingers. "Three rules. There are only three things you need to do in order to make a woman happy. Smack her ass, tell her she's pretty, and bring her tacos."

Layla raises an eyebrow. "That ass smacking better be followed by some *long* lovin'."

He leans over and kisses her cheek. "Always, mi corazón."

Palmer looks like she's going to melt. "You two are so cute. What's the secret to a happy marriage?"

Layla smiles. "Twice a week, we go to a nice restaurant to enjoy good food, good wine, good company, and good conversation. Presley goes on Tuesdays, and I go on Fridays," she deadpans.

Presley grins widely. "Women aren't complicated. If you make a mistake, tell her you're sorry. If she makes a mistake... tell her you're sorry."

We all laugh as the caterer lets us know dinner is ready, and we sit at my new dining room table. I feel like such an adult.

They prepared a beautiful meal, but I needed to add a little touch of my own. Vance immediately notices and looks at me from across the table. "Did you give them your mother's corn casserole recipe?"

I gasp in mock shock. "My mother would disown me if I gave away a well-guarded O'Shea family secret. I made it."

He immediately reaches for the bowl. "Yum." He looks around as he scoops multiple spoonfuls onto his plate. "There's nothing better in the world than the O'Shea family corn casserole."

Without realizing our full history, Alyssa innocently asks, "Were you two tight growing up? Did you date?"

Not wanting anything heavy to mar this evening, I answer, "Vile Vance is eight years older than me. No dating. He was friends with my brother." I stick my tongue out at him. "And he would never leave our house. He was like a leech."

"Did you have a crush on him?" she asks.

The corners of Vance's mouth raise in amusement, but I simply make a look of disgust. "Yuck. Nope. There's a reason his nickname is Vile Vance. He was nothing but a smelly teenage boy."

Not even a little true. I love his smell. I always have. I'd lather myself in it if I could.

Vance chuckles. "Hmm. I seem to remember you tagging along all the time. Always wanting to be with us. I couldn't have been that smelly, Gully Sulley."

Beau asks, "What's with her nickname? I get yours, I share a locker room with you, but why Gully Sulley?"

Vance gives an amused Beau the finger before answering, "She believed anything and everything we told her. One time, we told her that lightning came from a huge camera flash in the sky, and you had to stop and smile toward the sky every time there was lightning. For, like, two years, she would smile at the sky anytime lightning struck." He chuckles. "She looked like an idiot. People thought something was wrong with her."

I scrunch my nose. "I still sort of do that. Habit." Everyone laughs. "One summer, I foolishly cut my own hair. It was terrible, and I was hysterical over it. Vance and Finn told me if I taped watermelon seeds to my forehead all summer, it would grow back faster. And I did it. Every damn day."

Vance lets out a loud laugh. "Oh my god, I forgot about that. She thought the more seeds she taped to her head, the faster her hair would grow. All freakin' summer, she had those seeds on her head. *All* over her head."

I can't help but grin at the memory. It feels nice to think about the good times. The past six years have been marred by the bad, but there really were so many good times with Vance throughout my life.

I add, "There was another summer when I was obsessed with the movie *Teen Wolf.* Finn and Vance had me convinced they were really werewolves, and I shouldn't do anything to piss them off."

Vance bites back his smile. "Right. You loved that movie, though not nearly as much as," at the same time, we both shout, "*Sixteen Candles,*" and then both break into a fit of laughter.

We're in our own world for a few seconds until I realize that everyone is staring at us open-mouthed. We are really fucking bad at this top-secret relationship thing.

I straighten up and look at Palmer. "Come on, every girl loves *Sixteen Candles.* It's an unwritten law."

I think she catches on to my deflection and nods in agreement. "Totally. I loved that movie, though I used to watch *Varsity Blues* over and over with my friends."

We then get into a whole discussion of football movies, with the guys all loving the movie *Friday Night Lights,* while all the girls unanimously prefer the *Friday Night Lights* television show to the movie as it was more about the love stories than the movie was.

After dessert, we move to sit in my living room while the caterer cleans the dining room. Daylen is showing everyone the new headshots he had taken. Kennedy and I share a bemused look, and Daylen notices. "You guys don't like my photos?"

Kennedy sighs. "It's one of my red flags."

"What is?" he asks.

"Men who have headshots taken without the need to do so."

He purses his lips. "I need them."

She raises an eyebrow. "For what?"

"My website."

"Why do you have a website? You're such a tool. I bet you drive a Subaru too."

He scowls at her. "What do you have against Subarus?"

Shay interrupts, "It's a lesbian car. No man should drive one."

Kennedy nods her head in agreement.

He twists his lips as he admits, "I had a Subaru in high school."

Everyone breaks out into hysterical laughter while Daylen starts fiddling with his phone. After a minute or two, he breathes, "Holy shit, it *is* known as a lesbian car."

The laughter only gets louder.

Palmer looks at me. "Do you mind if I take a few leftovers? Just a container or two?"

I nod my head. "Please do. There's enough food for at least a week."

She nervously tucks her hair behind her ear. "It's not for me. There's a homeless guy who lives on the sidewalk in front of my building. I feel bad for him. I was going to give it to him."

I smile. She's so sweet. "Of course. Take it all and give it to him."

Beau turns to Palmer. "Are you sure it's safe?"

She nods. "I was a little scared at first, but he's a nice guy. Despite his circumstances, he always looks happy and has something nice to say."

Beau doesn't look pleased. "Perhaps I should teach you ladies a little self-defense, just in case it's ever needed."

Kennedy lifts an eyebrow. "I'm known for being the biggest bruiser in my league. I'm not worried about the scrappy men of Philadelphia."

Daylen stands and walks over to her, wrapping his tree trunk arms around her. She scrambles. "Don't touch me, freak."

"Try to get away, Ms. Bruiser. Don't let little old scrappy me get in your way."

She thrashes and kicks her heart out, but his hold never breaks. She sighs. "Ugh, fine, but few men are fucking Godzilla like you. Now get off me. You smell like bologna."

He releases her and lifts his shirt to smell it. "I do not," he insecurely pouts.

Beau stands to his full, gigantic height. "Can I teach you ladies a few easy moves? You never know when they might come in handy."

I shrug. "Why not? Aren't we supposed to just kick you in the balls?"

He shakes his head. "Most men anticipate that." He points to the spot on his neck just under his ear. "This right here? It's an unknown weak spot. It's more unexpected if you strike this nerve. It's a pressure point, and it immediately immobilizes the nervous system. You can put a man my size to the ground in seconds. It doesn't take much force either."

Daylen shakes his head. "No way."

Beau crooks his finger. "Come here."

Daylen stands and walks to him. "Don't hurt me, big guy."

Beau rolls his eyes. "Not me. Kennedy. Come here and stand in front of Daylen."

Kennedy's face lights up. "Punching Daylen in the throat. No problem."

Beau shakes his head. "Not punching. Make a fist with your thumb on the outside, spread across your fingers." She does. "You're not going to punch with your knuckles. That takes a windup that an attacker might see coming." He points to the area where her index finger and thumb form a circle. "You're going to simply hammer chop him right on the nerve. It doesn't take that much force, but it's effective enough for you to get away."

We all sit there and practice the would-be chop on our own palms.

Daylen chuckles. "There's no way Kennedy can take me down with that."

Beau places his hand on Daylen's shoulder. "It's science. You'll go down like a bag of bricks."

"No fucking way that broom-riding, entitled princess can take me down."

Kennedy crosses her arms. "How about we make a little wager?"

He wiggles his eyebrows. "I'm intrigued. Tell me more."

"If I win, I get to pick your opening day gameday stadium arrival outfit. If you win, you can pick mine."

He nods and answers without hesitation. "Deal."

Beau points to the spot on Daylen that Kennedy needs to hit. He also clears an area in my living room so nothing breaks if the giant goes down. I have to admit, it seems unlikely that she can take a man of Daylen's size down with a chop-punch like that, but we'll see.

Daylen covers his dick with his hands and mumbles, "Just in case."

Kennedy makes the fist as Beau instructed. She narrows her eyes at Daylen. "I'm going to enjoy every minute of this. I might orgasm if you pass out."

She then gives Daylen a hard, quick chop to the side of his neck. He goes down so damn hard I'm afraid there will be a dent in my floor. He's not completely out cold, but it's like he was tasered and doesn't have full body function for at least thirty seconds.

Kennedy jumps up and down in glee at winning the bet. Beau smiles in satisfaction. I don't think I'll ever doubt the man again.

As a successful evening draws to a close, Kennedy pulls me aside. "What's going on with you and Vance?"

I act shocked. "What do you mean?"

"You're suddenly very chummy."

I shrug. "We saw each other when we were home. We see each other here. Our friends are all friends. We don't want to be the cause of drama. It's easier for everyone if we focus on the positive and not dwell on our baggage. We've called a truce."

She eyes me skeptically. I have no idea whether she believes me or not.

NINETEEN

VANCE

I pull my truck up to Sulley's house more excited about tonight than I've been about anything in a long time. I'm trying to temper down the hope that's filling me. Hope that the black cloud I've lived under for six years will be lifted.

Exiting the truck, I'm just ascending her steps when she opens her front door and emerges.

My heart stops beating.

Time stands still.

I can only stare at the goddess in front of me. She takes my breath away. The only words I can find are, "You're beautiful." It's more than beauty. It's a glow. She's an angel.

The little girl I once knew has grown into the most exquisite woman I've ever seen. I know for a fact that there's no turning back for me. No woman will ever come close to the one before me.

She's in a short summer dress with a small, unbuttoned white sweater. It's unseasonably warm, still not quite warm enough for what she's wearing, but she listened to what I asked her to wear. The dress is white with all kinds of pink, purple, and orange flowers. It's got ruffled shoulder straps, and there are little white balls on the ends. The sides are cut out, showing a bit of her toned abs. Between that and her mile-long legs, I might not make it to our destination without pulling over and having my wicked way with her.

I quickly move to kiss her, but she swerves away from my advances. "Don't. You never know if there are cameras around. Nothing out in the open. We agreed to this."

My jaw tightens as I'm slapped in the face with reality. I give a short nod. "Yes, ma'am."

Itching to touch her, I ball my hands into fists and turn to walk toward the truck, opening the passenger door for her.

Once we're both inside the truck, I reach over to take her hand in mine. She starts to pull away, but I tighten my grip. "No one can see. I need to touch you. Give me this."

She exhales a long breath. "Fine. I'm really nervous about tonight, Vance. We can't be seen out on a date. I hope you know what you're doing."

"I've got it under control. Don't worry. Thanks for wearing what I asked."

She lifts an eyebrow. "I'm not sure why a short, casual dress or skirt was necessary, but you've certainly piqued my curiosity, Vile Vance."

I run my hand up her silky-smooth thigh. "I've got plans for these legs and the heaven that sits between them. I need easy access."

She playfully shakes her head, and I laugh as I pull onto the street and head out on our long journey. We chat about nothing in particular for over an hour as the evening sky begins to turn dark. She tells me about their team practices and her excitement for their season. Her heartfelt enthusiasm is a breath of fresh air.

At some point, she announces, "I've done all the talking. You need to talk too. That's how a date works. Is this your first one?"

I roll my eyes. "No, sassy pants. It's not. I enjoy listening to you. Your passion for your sport and your new life is refreshing, Sullivan Aisling. I'm happy you've found friends. I was thinking about you as a little girl. I don't remember other girls being around very much."

She shrugs. "Female friendships have never come easily to me. I either didn't have much in common with them, or there were issues with me getting so much attention. This is the first time in my life that I feel the notion of girl power and support. I know Kennedy has a bad rep, but she's been the most welcoming and probably the biggest surprise of all. Underneath that tough exterior is an amazing, compassionate woman who's gone out of her way to be a good friend to me."

I nod. "I see it on the court. She has this protective big sister vibe with you." I run my fingers through my hair. "Off the court too. She stares daggers at me sometimes. Always has something nasty to say to me. I'm assuming she knows more about our history than anyone else?"

Sulley's face scrunches. "She does. I'm sorry. That first night I saw you, I was so triggered. I was inconsolable. Kennedy and Palmer got me out of there and held me all night as I cried. I owed them an explanation in the morning."

I feel a tightness in my chest. "I'm sorry to be the cause of your pain. I hate that."

She's silent for a bit. "Do you know how you could help?"

"How?"

"Explain it all to me. I'm convinced that I'm missing part of this story. What happened? I know I didn't imagine your disdain for Maddie for all those years. How did you go from tolerating her for Finn's sake to sleeping in the same bed? If you tell me she drugged you, I'll believe you." She whispers, "I want to believe you."

I shake my head and say, "She didn't drug me," but am otherwise quiet.

She exhales a breath in obvious frustration. "Something,

Vance. Give me something. You can open up to me." She tugs on her hair in frustration. "It's like I'm trying to put together a puzzle, but it's impossible because so many pieces are missing from the box. Why don't you have a relationship with Francesca? Tell me that."

"Maddie dictates who does and doesn't see her. Francesca thinks Curtis is her father. Maddie doesn't want her to get confused. I've asked for more time, but she won't give it to me. My hands are tied."

She shakes her head. "She can't do that to you. You have rights. You could take her to court."

I feel my body stiffen. This is not how I saw this evening going. "That would just hurt Francesca. You think Finn would want that? Francesca getting hurt and being confused? Her being dragged into court?"

Her lips twitch in anger. "What does Finn have to do with this? She's not *his* daughter. She's *yours*."

I take a deep breath before answering. "He loved Maddie. You and Maddie meant the world to him. He asked two things of me." I hold up two fingers. "They were to look after you and to look after Maddie. I take my promise seriously. It's not conditional. There's no expiration date. It was my pledge to him, and I'll see it through until the day I die," I mumble, "no matter what it costs me."

She crosses her arms. "Why did you move her two towns over? I'm sure she would have preferred to live closer to her family. She could have been closer to your parents too."

I lick my lips. I think I can answer this one honestly. "Because of your family. I told her I'd buy her whatever house she wanted, just not in our hometown. Why should your parents have to see her and Francesca every day and be reminded of what was lost? She's close enough for easy visits from her family, but not so close that it's a daily reminder for your parents. It was my one condition. She was reluctant at first but accepted it when she saw the house I bought her."

She sighs. "Does Curtis even have a job, or do they *all* live off you?"

I shrug. "Don't know. Curtis Huddle isn't my business."

I know that fucking loser doesn't have a job. They all live off me.

She purposefully bangs her head back on the headrest. "You frustrate me, Vance McCaffrey."

I reach for her hand again and pull it to my lips for a kiss. "We're here. Can we please shelve this for a bit and have a little fun?"

Our eyes meet. Her blues and my greens. I try to convey sincerity. "I just want to enjoy our night together. I planned something I think you'll like. Please. I've been looking forward to it all day." More like all week.

Her shoulders, which were practically in her ears, visibly relax, and she nods. "Okay."

I pull down a road and see it in her face when she realizes what we're doing. Her face lights up as she turns to me with excitement in her eyes. "A drive-in movie?"

I can't help my grin. "Time for you to get the full McCaffed treatment."

She giggles. "I should never have told you that word. What movie are we seeing?"

"What else? *Sixteen Candles.*"

Her face softens. "How?"

"I...umm...called the owner. He's a fan. I offered him some signed items in return for playing the movie I asked for. It took me a minute to find this place. There aren't exactly a lot of drive-ins still around, at least not near big cities."

She lifts her shoulders in excitement. "This is amazing. Thank you."

I park the car backward so we can watch from the bed of my truck. Even though it's dark out now, I grab a baseball cap from my center console just in case there are any prying eyes when we walk around the truck. Once we're in the truck bed, we'll mostly be out of sight. Between my high wheels and the high sides of the truck, no other cars will be able to see us unless they're standing on their roofs.

I pull down my cap, and she taps the bill. "Nice hat."

It's a Beavers hat.

I wink. "I've got your jersey too. A few of them. I need you to sign them sometime."

She leans her head back on the headrest and smiles goofily. "Why the smile?" I ask.

She runs her bottom lip through her teeth. "I wore your jersey to bed every night for years until…Francesca. The thought of you wearing mine does things to me."

I wiggle my eyebrows. "Glad things are stirring. It will help when I want to McCaff you in a little bit."

She rolls her eyes and moans in malcontent. "Ugh. You're *really* making me regret telling you that."

I chuckle as I exit the truck and help her into the back bed. Together we lay out all the blankets and pillows I brought and then set up the picnic dinner.

As we sit cross-legged, eating, waiting for the movie to start, she asks, "Do any of your friends know about our history?"

I nod. "Daylen and Tanner. That's it. No one else knows anything. They've known for years, though I don't think Tanner connected the dots that the famous Sulley O'Shea was Finn's sister until after he started recruiting you as a client. Once he realized the connection, he asked me if it was okay to pursue you. Frankly, I preferred it. There are a lot of sleazy agents out there. Tanner is the best of the best. You're in good hands with him."

She agrees, "He's been great. He never pushes me to do things I don't want to do. He weeds out all the offers he knows won't interest me and negotiates hard for those I do accept. Even though he's been busy with Bailey over the past few months, he's always available to me."

"Tanner is incredible. My career is in good hands with him. He always goes to bat for me. He's been wanting to grow his women's division for a while. I know championing equal pay for women in sports is important to him. He's hoping to bring on a female agent to his office. He's been looking for the right one forever."

She twists her lips. "What's the latest with him and Bailey? She lives there along with Fallon. What's their current status?"

I smile. "I don't want to betray any confidences but expect a public announcement soon."

"What does that mean?" she asks.

I point to the screen as it lights up, and the speakers blare with the familiar soundtrack of the iconic movie. "Oh look, the movie's starting."

She purses her lips. "Nice deflection. You're the king of deflection."

I let out a laugh as I put away the food and prop the pillows how I want them, against the cabin of the truck. I move to sit and spread my legs wide. Opening my arms, I motion for her. "Come here, baby. I want to hold you."

She briefly closes her eyes. "I swear to god, I just about combust every time you call me baby."

"I know. Come sit, *baby*."

She shifts to sit between my legs with her back to my front. When she leans back into me, I wrap my arms around her and sink my face into her neck. Taking a deep inhale, I practically moan, "I love the way you smell. The first time I noticed how good you smell was in your treehouse the night I carried you to bed. It was so strong. And then your bedroom and your pillows smelled the same. Like a creepy stalker, I watched you and was hard the whole time you were sleeping."

She giggles as she nuzzles her nose into the sleeve of my flannel shirt. "You smell pretty good yourself, QB1."

The movie begins, and she seems very focused. I, on the

other hand, am focused solely on her. I can't take my eyes off her legs. They go on forever. I need to touch them.

She smacks my hand as it moves up her leg and under her dress. "Watch the movie. You've got to see the setup to understand the whole plotline."

I smile into her neck. "I've seen this movie at least a hundred times. It was on the television in your house every day for no less than three straight years."

With a jovial tone, she asks, "Did you just bring me all the way out here to molest me? You could have done that at my house."

I run my nose over her cheek as I slowly remove her sweater and toss it to the side. "You said coming to the drive-in with me was a childhood dream."

She turns her head, kisses my cheek, and whispers, "It was. Thank you for making it happen."

"Plus," I add as my hand now moves uninterrupted up her dress and I nibble on her ear, "I happen to get off on a little public fornication."

The rate of her breathing increases as she spreads her legs a bit for me. "You like to be watched?"

I shake my head. "No, I like the threat of being caught in the act, not actually being seen. It's a huge high."

I can feel her swallow hard before she pants, "I've never done anything like that."

"Well then, allow me to rock your world, Sullivan Aisling."

My fingertips brush over her panty-covered pussy. Her head snaps from side to side, checking to see if anyone else is watching us. The drive-in is completely packed. There are hundreds of cars, and we're cocooned by the bustling sound of teen activity. But we're a little higher than the rest in my truck. No one can see what I'm doing to her.

It's kind of cool that drive-ins still draw people. I doubt many of the people here are our age, but who cares? I've got my hands all over my girl while we both get to fulfill fantasies.

After teasing her for a long while and watching her grow more and more frustrated, I move her panties to the side and slip a finger inside her. She gasps. I cover her mouth and whisper in her ear, "Normally, I love how loud you are, but not tonight. Unless you want an audience, I need you to try to be quiet."

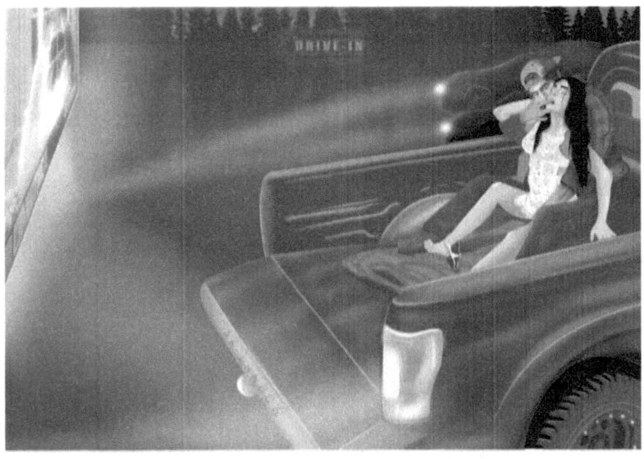

Her nails dig into my thighs as she wordlessly nods.

"Good girl."

Her whole body shivers at my touch and my words. Her pussy contracts around my finger. She's so reactive to me.

"Baby, I love when your pussy tightens at my words. It's like you won't let me go. You want to keep me inside you forever. Can you feel it too?"

She nods again as she breathes, "Vance."

"What do you need?"

She writhes in my lap, moaning, "More. I need more."

I knew she'd be into this. Licking and biting my way up and over her neck, my thumb brushes over her clit a few times. She jerks before thrusting her hips onto my fingers like she's riding them, trying to get them as deep as possible.

My free hand slips into the top of her dress and finds her nipple hard as a pebble. She's so into this. I love it.

I squeeze her nipple hard, and juices practically flow out of her while she lets out an indecipherable sound. I quickly remove my hand from her breast and cover her mouth. She's loud. *Very* loud. I can't risk anyone hearing her and finding us.

"Shh. I told you to keep quiet, bad girl."

I pull my fingers out of her and slap her pussy. Her whole body begins to shake while she moans into my hand.

Reinserting my fingers, I establish a rhythm with them inside her, my thumb moving over her clit, and my other hand now back, manipulating her nipple. She's biting her lip, trying to hold back her sounds. It appears to be a struggle for her.

When I sense she's close, I move my hand to her mouth again, knowing she won't be able to contain her scream herself. I lick along her ear and breathe, "Tell me, baby, do you want my fat cock inside that tight, greedy pussy of yours?"

Her head tilts back onto my shoulder while her entire body shudders into her orgasm. It's a good thing my hand was over her mouth because she screamed into it.

My cock is pushing violently against my zipper. I grind it against her ass throughout her orgasm, needing some small amount of relief.

Her breathing is labored while my fingers withdraw from her. I slowly run them up her body and trace her lips with them. "Do you like the way your pussy tastes?"

Her tongue slips out and runs along both her lips and my fingers before I slide them into her mouth. "Suck my fingers, baby. Suck them like you suck my cock."

She obliges and sucks them hard while twirling her tongue over the tip, exactly like she does with my dick. It drives me fucking insane.

As soon as I withdraw my fingers from her mouth, she turns her head around and seals her lips over mine for a drugging kiss. I've never been much of a kisser, but there's something so intimate and different when kissing her. It's like we're two pieces that slot perfectly together.

I can taste both her saltiness and her sweetness all at once. It's my favorite flavor in the world.

While holding our kiss, I run my hands under her dress and loop my thumbs into the sides of her panties, pushing them down until I see the damp, white lacy thong wrapped around one ankle.

That sight alone causes my cock to leak. I break our kiss and bite her lip. "I need inside you. Right fucking now."

She shifts her body forward, giving me the room to unbuckle, unbutton, and unzip my jeans. She tries to reach back and help, but it's an awkward angle. I take her hand and place her fingers on her pussy. "I'll get my dick out, you greedy girl. You keep that pretty pussy warm for me."

Another shudder works its way through her body before she does as instructed.

In a flash, my severely hardened dick is in my hand, begging to be inside her. I pull up the back of her dress. "Lift for me and sink down onto my cock. He needs you."

She places her hands on my thighs and lifts her body while moving her legs over mine. I manipulate my dick until it finds her warm, slick entrance. I slide my tip in and then grab her hips and slam her down. She lets out a loud scream. Oh shit. Someone is going to come over here thinking I'm murdering her. I both love and hate how loud she is.

I remain still inside her as I quickly swivel my head around. I don't see anyone approaching.

She always shakes uncontrollably for a few seconds as soon as I'm balls deep inside her. It's her body's way of acclimating to my size, and it drives me wild.

I have one hand over her mouth and the other now moving back up her dress, circling her clit a few times to loosen her up. "Feel good?"

She mumbles into my hand. "So good."

"Can you clench around me? I've got plans for us, and I need you to learn how to milk me."

She clenches so fucking hard that I think my dick might be permanently embedded inside her. I bite her neck. "Such an overachiever."

She lets out a giggle before doing it again. I can't help but let out a loud groan.

"Shhh," she mocks. "I don't want to have to muzzle you."

I reach into the top of her dress and pinch her nipple. Hard. Her pussy clenches again. "Are we engaged in a squeezing battle right now, Gully Sulley?"

She nods before we go back and forth a few more times, both emitting noises that are a mixture of amusement and pleasure along the way. She reaches back and threads her fingers through my hair, giving it the hard tug she knows I crave. Turning her head, her lips hover over mine. "Fuck me, Vance. Fuck me now."

"I can't bounce you without creating too much of a disturbance. The truck can't start rocking. It will draw unwanted attention. We'll need to work together to achieve maximum pleasure. Can you do that for me, baby?"

She clenches around me again. "I understand the play, QB1. Teamwork makes the dream work. Make me see stars and I'll do the same for you."

As if on cue, we both look up into the starry night. I hadn't even noticed it before. "It's a perfect night. Perfect for driving my cock into you."

"Stop talking. Just do it already."

I smile. "Do you really want me to stop talking?"

Her eyes widen. "No. Keep talking."

"You get off on it, don't you?"

She bites her lip shyly and eventually nods.

"It's okay, so do I."

I begin thrusting my hips up. I do it short and hard, not long and deep. She's going to have to clench and push down for that to happen. She does. In no time, we've established a rhythm that's quickly pushing us both to the brink.

Her hips circle while mine thrust. She pulls my hair while I run my fingers over her clit. My other hand hovers by her mouth, covering it when needed. She sucks on my fingers at times which seems to be a direct line to my dick. Her hand not in my hair is on my leg with her nails deliciously digging into my thigh, undoubtedly breaking skin, even through my jeans.

We can hear the nondescript noises of other people around us. Someone could easily climb up my truck and see what we're doing. The threat of being seen only serves to ramp things up. This is next-level. It might be the hottest sex of my life.

I can't help but bite down all over her shoulders and neck. She's going to be covered in my marks. The thought of that only spurs me on to do more.

"You're doing so good, baby. Do you like that people are close by and could see us at any moment?"

She moans out, "Y...y...yes. I can't. It's too much. Oh god, I'm coming."

"Wait for me," I instruct.

She clenches so fucking hard that my eyes roll back in my head. I truly do see stars. My spine tingles, and my balls feel like they're exploding. I have no control over my orgasm anymore. It's all under her spell.

I bite down hard on her shoulder to stifle my groan as my orgasm hits me so fucking hard that I feel light-headed. She starts to scream, but I have the wherewithal to cover her mouth again.

I shoot long, hot streams into her. It rolls on and on. Feeling her come drip down my balls drags out my orgasm that much more.

We shudder through the aftershocks of our earth-shattering orgasms. We're still panting heavily when her head plops back onto me and she buries her nose in my neck. She breathes, "Holy shit. That was intense."

I open my mouth. I want to tell her that I love her. I'm

pretty sure I have for a while, but I don't want to spoil the mood. It's not something she'll want to hear.

There are so many things I wish I could change about the past. So many regrets I have. If I had made different decisions, Sulley could be mine forever, but I know the reality. She'll never let things go and truly be mine. I need to find a way to help her get past it. Sullivan Aisling O'Shea belongs with me.

Always has, always will.

TWENTY

SULLEY

"Cheers," we all shout in unison as we clink champagne glasses. We're on a flight to Las Vegas. I've never been on a private jet before. It's the most bougie thing I've ever done in my life.

The plane is practically like a house. A nice, modern house at that. It has cream-colored leather sofas, a bar, huge recliner chairs, tables, refrigerators, bedrooms, multiple bathrooms that include showers, and nearly ten staff members catering to all our needs.

It's my friends, our Camels friends, and several other Camels and their wives. I'm doing my best to introduce myself to everyone. It's overwhelming.

Reagan had asked if her mother and stepfather could hitch a ride with us. Apparently, Reagan and her whole family are already out in Vegas for the big sports weekend. Her mother had an appointment and couldn't get out until now.

The two of them are a remarkably attractive couple, both with dark hair, and they appear to be in great shape. I assume they're in their mid to late fifties but could easily pass for being in their forties. They've been cuddling and kissing in a corner since we took off. They're so cute. I wonder if they're newlyweds.

The group is sitting around a few of the tables, having drinks now that the pilot turned off the seatbelt sign. I decide it's a good time to introduce myself to Reagan's mom and stepfather.

I approach her first. "Mrs. Knight?"

She smiles. "Call me Darian, Sulley." She points to her husband. "And call him Jackson."

I nod. "Will do. I just wanted to tell you you're more than welcome to join us." I point to the rowdy table.

"Thank you, but given the ungodly early hour in the day, we might go back to sleep. And if we start drinking now, we'll be passed out by noon."

It's super early. We wanted to get out there early enough not to miss any of the college basketball games we'll be watching on television. Layla said every sports bar in Vegas has hundreds of screens, so you don't miss any of the action.

"Makes sense." I notice their intertwined fingers. "Did you two recently get married?"

Jackson easily pulls her onto his lap and shakes his head. "Nope. It's been nearly a decade, but I still see her as my bride." He softly kisses her lips, and she stares at him lovingly while running her fingers over his scruff.

I can't help but smile widely at their interaction. They're adorable.

"Okay, I'll leave you two to sleep. If you change your mind, I think the drinking games have already begun."

I point toward my crew, who seem to be opening more bottles of booze. As I make my way back, I notice all eyes on Beau as he announces, "And that is what you call a boner shake."

Huh? "I was only gone for a minute," I interrupt. "What in the world did I miss?"

Kennedy answers, "Beau was telling us about something

called boner shakes. Apparently, he needs to drink them all the time."

Beau practically growls. "I don't like what you're insinuating, Kennedy. I drink them for the testosterone. Cholesterol is a building block for testosterone, which helps build muscle. The crazy boner is an added side effect...but I don't *need* that side effect." He crosses his arms. "I'm just fine in that department, thank you very much."

I've never seen Beau get so worked up. I can't let this go. I need more information. "What's in a boner shake, Chef Beau?" I joke, "I don't remember seeing it in your recipe book."

Layla reads from her phone. "Four eggs, a scoop of vanilla protein powder, and water. A man should shake it up and drink it at night. When he wakes in the morning, he'll supposedly have the biggest boner of his life...and all that other testosterone and muscle building crap too."

Presley scowls at her. "Did you write down the recipe?"

She nods. "You bet I did. Best boner of your life? Don't you want to at least try it? I wouldn't mind being your test subject, precioso."

He twists his lips. "Hmm. I guess we can give it a go...ya know, for science. To see if I can build more muscle from the testosterone."

Daylen shakes his head. "I don't need it. Zero problems in that department for me. I had my first orgy last night," he proudly announces as he pauses for dramatic effect while the guys hang on every word. "Okay, it was one woman, but she had multiple personalities."

They all start laughing. Kennedy shakes her head. "You're such a manwhore. Is there anyone you haven't had sex with?"

He scoffs. "God forbid I have a hobby." He stands. "This champagne is going right through me. I need to drain the main vein."

Kennedy makes a look of disgust. "Stop announcing your trips to the bathroom. It's disgusting."

With his back turned to her, he waves his hand dismissively and yells out, "Be sure to add it to your red flag list. I hope to check off every single one of them this weekend."

THE PLANE RIDE took an interesting turn when Darian and Jackson disappeared, only for us to hear them from one of the bedrooms a little while later, clearly having sex. We all got a good laugh out of that.

Limos picked us up from the airport and took us to the Palms Casino. The hotel is the biggest, most luxurious one I've ever seen. Our suites are incredible. Each has two bedrooms and a spacious living room complete with a kitchen and other amenities. I'm sharing a suite with Kennedy, Palmer, Shay, and Alyssa. We gave Shay and Alyssa one bedroom. The three of us are happy to share the other.

The hotel bars are as promised. They're huge with countless televisions showing every single basketball game. There's a ton of betting going on, but I'm not wagering my hard-earned money. I'm more than content to sit, drink, and watch the games.

I've been in basketball heaven all morning and early afternoon, not missing a single minute of any of the action.

We've enjoyed the first few games at the bar, but everyone wants to hit the pool to enjoy the beautiful weather. Apparently, the Circa Hotel in Vegas has huge television screens at its pool. I'm excited to see it.

We're changing into bathing suits, preparing to convene in the lobby in five minutes to head over to the other hotel's pool. We had all gone shopping together prior to this trip, which included us indulging in new bathing suits.

Palmer is still in her regular clothing. I look at her. "We need to go. Get changed."

Her worried eyes meet mine. "I don't think I can do this."

Kennedy and I exchange knowing glances. I thought we had dealt with this at the bathing suit store last week.

I shake my head. "Palmer, we told you, you look beautiful in that suit." She outright refused to purchase a bikini. She instead bought an elegant one-piece. It's violet, nearly the same shade as her unique eye color, and it made them shine. We were so excited when she finally decided to buy it.

Kennedy sits down next to Palmer and rubs her back. "Women are meant to have curves. You're beautiful on the inside *and* the outside. Do you know how rare that is?"

Tears fill Palmer's eyes. "It's so easy for you to say, Kennedy. You're perfect. You could be on the cover of swimsuit magazines. I just…I can't walk around next to you. I'll look like the Jolly Purple Giant."

In fairness to Palmer, Kennedy does look like a freakin' Bond girl in her gold bikini. Something about the dark hair, green eyes, and gold bikini makes for a stunning creature. Her being drop-dead gorgeous and having a flawless figure only adds to it. She's imposingly attractive.

Kennedy straightens her shoulders. "The best thing a woman can wear is confidence. Yes, I look fucking good. That's because I know I look good. You are a goddess, Palmer. I see it, Sulley sees it, and," she pauses for dramatic effect, "I'm pretty sure a certain very large, very smart gentleman also sees it. He hasn't taken his eyes off you all day. Now it's time for you to see it. To own it. Do you know how many women would kill to be as tall as you? I would. I'm jealous as hell of your height. I feel like a shrimp around you." She stands and throws her bag over her shoulder. "In fact, don't come. It makes me look better if you don't."

A small smile starts to take form on Palmer's face. She looks at me and I purse my lips. "If I were you, I'd go just to fuck with Kennedy. Make that skinny, short bitch pay."

Palmer's grin widens as she reaches into her drawer for the bathing suit. "Okay. I'll come. Give me two minutes."

I nod. "Take as long as you need."

When she disappears into the bathroom, I bow my head to Kennedy and whisper, "You're a master manipulator."

She scoffs. "Pft. I've been told that my whole life."

"You're also a closet good person."

She winks. "Don't tell anyone. I have a rep to protect."

A few minutes later, we enter the lobby with the entire crew waiting for us. Vance's eyes practically bend me over and fuck me right here. Christ, he needs to chill out and stop being so damn obvious.

Daylen lets out a loud whistle as his eyes move up and down Kennedy's body in her barely there cover, which covers exactly none of her gold bikini. "Our kids would be so good-looking. My eyes. My body. My charisma. My personality. My talent. My intelligence." He scratches his chin. "Come to think of it, you're unnecessary in this genetic equation."

We all laugh while Kennedy shakes her head. "I don't know where you got your looks from, Humblecut, but I hope you kept the receipt."

Daylen twists his lips. "Don't bite the hand that fingers you."

She makes a look of disgust. "Those hairy stubs will *never* finger me. In fact, there are three places you can stay for free this weekend. In your lane. Out of my business. And over there. Scurry away, cockroach."

Presley sighs. "If you two are done with your creepy foreplay, the party bus is here to drive us over. Everyone else is already on it."

As we walk to the bus, I notice Beau whisper something to Palmer, and she smiles. He must have complimented her. I wonder if anything is going on between them. I initially thought her crush was one-sided, but maybe I'm wrong.

"Holy. Fucking. Shit." The only words I'm capable of after seeing this hotel's outdoor setup. It's basically a pool stadium. That's the only way to describe it.

There is the largest screen in creation running the full length of the hotel, which is managing to play every single basketball game currently going on. There are multiple bars underneath the screen. There are six different long pools with seating space in between each. It's basically set up like a true stadium. I've never seen anything like it.

As was the case at our hotel bar, a man in a suit is standing there awaiting our arrival, ushering us to a private VIP area. Despite the crazy crowd, we have chairs, tables, and an entire pool dedicated to our party. This is truly how the other half lives. I won't lie; I'm enjoying the treatment. How often do you walk into a hotel room and have your entire bar and refrigerator already stocked?

I throw my arm around Layla. "You know how to throw a party, girlfriend."

She smiles. "A bunch of the WAGs helped out."

I squeeze her close. "Thanks for inviting me."

She rests her head on my shoulder. "It wouldn't be the same without you. Now let's get our drink on. It's time to par-tay."

Drinking and partying, we do. I've honestly never let this loose in my life. We've had a blast watching the games from the confines of a pool with a drink in hand. The sun has now set, but the pool party rages on. The warm Vegas temperatures make it easy to linger in the pool.

Even though Vance hasn't removed his eyes from me all day, he's mostly kept his distance. Watching him in swim trunks all afternoon has got me on edge. I'm starting to feel a little frisky. We need to find a way to spend time together. Alone.

As if reading my mind, he slips into the water and makes his way over to me. "Having a good time?"

I nod. "The best time ever. Ever, ever, ever."

He chuckles as he nods his head toward my drink. "Pace yourself. We've still got a long night ahead of us."

My mouth widens. "More partying?"

"Yep. When the games end, we'll get showered and dressed

for dinner, eat, and then hit the club scene. Vegas is a marathon, not a race. And we've got four days of this."

I set my fruity drink down on the pool lip. "You're right. I need to slow down, or I won't make it out later."

He moves a little closer to me and runs his hand up the back of my thigh until it reaches my ass, where he squeezes it hard. "I'd happily stay back with you."

I look around nervously to see if anyone is watching us. Even if they were, it's now too dark for them to see where his hand is. It looks like we're talking, which we are.

Before I know it, his fingers are under my bikini, running through me. "You're wet, naughty girl. I knew you would be. Your cheeks are flushed. I saw it from my chair. You want me inside you, don't you?"

Maybe it's the alcohol in my system. Maybe it's the fact that he looks so damn hot in his bathing suit. Maybe it's the fact that his finger just slipped into me and my legs nearly gave out. But I do want it, and I want it now. Here. Out in public.

Our night at the movie theater was the most sensual, erotic, exciting night of my life. Fulfilling a childhood fantasy and the threat of being seen at any moment? Holy shit. It was magical. I came so hard. It felt like an out-of-body experience.

And the best part, when we were done, we lay there for a long time talking and laughing. It was so easy and comfortable.

I swallow hard and answer his question about whether I want him inside me. "I do. Please. I need it."

A small smile forms on his lips as he licks them. I'm mesmerized by his tongue, thinking of all the things it's done to me over the past few weeks.

His finger pushes deep inside me. "I hope you've been working on your clenching muscles."

"I have," I offer overly enthusiastically. "Every day. All the time."

He chuckles, and I flush with embarrassment. Shit. I'm so

uncool. I've been waiting for the right opportunity for him to take me in public again, desperately wanting it to be good for him. It looks like tonight is the night to see if my new "exercises" have paid off.

Like a total nerd, I googled how to strengthen my vaginal wall. I've been doing Kegels, pelvic tilts, heel slides, squats, and bridge exercises, per my research. Every single day, I do them because I officially found my kink. Public sex. The threat of being seen floods me with excitement and a high unlike anything I've ever experienced.

He gently pushes my shoulder. "Lean over a little until I'm in. I need the angle to get inside you."

He withdraws his fingers. I hate that he did, but I know what's about to come. Me. I'm about to come.

I lean up and over the edge of the pool like I'm reaching for something. He moves behind me and slides my bikini to the side before slipping his massive cock into me.

My fingers grip the lip of the pool as my body shakes. I wonder if there will ever be a time when he enters me that my body doesn't have this involuntary reaction. He gets off on it. We've had a lot of sex in the weeks since the drive-in night. Almost every day. We're insatiable for each other. Every damn time my body reacts this way. I can't control it.

He whispers, "Okay, you can slide back now."

I lean back upright with my arms casually hanging over the side of the pool as if I'm watching the games like everyone else, with Vance simply standing behind me in the pool. While I'm sure it looks strange that he's standing so closely behind me, no one could possibly know that he's inside me. It's also dark, it's underwater, and people are either focused on their own conversation or the games taking place on the big screen. And everyone has been drinking for hours. I doubt they're noticing our slightly closer-than-normal proximity.

"Fuck, Sulley, you're so tight. And wet. Look around, baby.

Everyone is here, yet none of them know I'm inside your warm cunt right now."

He runs his hand down my stomach, hidden from view by the side of the pool, before slipping his fingers down the front and through me until they reach the place where we're now joined together. "Can you feel me?"

Can I feel him? He's all I feel. "Yes," I breathe.

"Your pussy is already so swollen. You're going to milk me now, and then later tonight, in my room, I'm going to fuck you into tomorrow."

I swallow hard. That all sounds good to me.

His fingers begin circling my clit while he casually picks up his glass and takes a sip of his drink, as if we're not having sex. "Now start clenching and milk this cock. Squeeze every ounce out of me."

I shiver at his words. His dirty talk is everything I never knew I needed. It's so contrary to his normal, quiet demeanor. I think that's what makes it so hot. It's unexpected and only for my ears.

For now.

I clench as hard as I can, and he lets out a groan. "Ahh. Fuck, fuck, fuck."

He's able to roll his hips a bit while I clench and clench. His fingers never leave my clit until we both float away into blissful paradise, all while surrounded by friends, teammates, and about two or three hundred other people, none of whom have any clue about the dirty things going on under the water.

I WAKE in the morning to the biggest case of cotton mouth in history. I need water, and I need to get back to my room before my roommates wake up. Hopefully they were too wasted to notice I wasn't with them when they got back last night. We partied our asses off until the sun came up.

We had a five-star dinner followed by hours and hours of VIP treatment at three different clubs. I barely remember coming back to the hotel, but I do remember Vance making good on his promise to fuck me into tomorrow. We went at it like animals. I think Daylen brought someone back to his room too, because we could hear a woman screaming.

In fact, now that I think about it, she and I may have had a little screaming match through the walls. I can't help but smile as the memories of it come into focus. Yep, I was drunk.

I look over at the handsome man sleeping next to me on his back. Pushing back a piece of hair from his eyes, I slide it toward his head. Even in his sleep, his brow is furrowed, and he looks stressed out. I wish he'd share things with me. I know in my gut that he's hiding something. He's keeping secrets. I think it all weighs on him.

I quietly make my way to the bathroom. After I use his toothbrush, I slip back into my dress from last night. With my heels in hand, I quietly exit his bedroom into the main living room of the suite he's sharing with Daylen. At the same time, I see Kennedy exit Daylen's room in her dress from last night with her heels in her hand.

I can't help the audible gasp that comes from my mouth. I thought they hated each other.

Her head snaps up, and she looks at me wide-eyed, immediately offering, in a low whisper, "I was trashed. I barely remember anything. Please never breathe a word of this to anyone." She makes a look of disgust. "Ugh, I can't believe I let that gorilla touch me. At least I found a bunch of condom wrappers this morning. That's a small victory."

I whisper back, "Don't you hate him?"

Her eyes narrow. "I do, but wait, are you leaving Vance's room right now? What the fuck? I thought *you* hated *him.*"

We're in a silent stare down for several seconds before I offer, "How about we agree to never talk about last night for the rest of our lives? I won't ask you questions, and you don't ask me any either."

A small smile forms on her lips before she nods. "Perfect."

Choosing to ignore the hickeys all over the tops of her breasts, I notice her left hand is bandaged. Pointing to it, I ask, "Did you get hurt?"

She shrugs. "I have no recollection." She examines it. "It looks professionally wrapped. I didn't want to wake him and ask. I'll take a look at it when we get back to the room."

"Does it hurt?"

She shakes her head. "No. It's a little achy, that's all. I probably fell. I tend to do that when I'm wasted."

I hope she's not too injured.

We exit the suite and begin our stealthy journey down the hallway toward our suite, acting like spies, fearing anyone seeing us. I take in our appearances. We're in tiny dresses with our hair a tangled mess and full raccoon eyes of smeared makeup. We look like hookers leaving the scene of a crime.

I let out a quiet laugh. "This is truly a walk of shame."

She shrugs. "I prefer to call it a just got laid parade. It sounds so much better. Classier. And at least we had sex." She scrunches her face. "If I'm being honest, it was really good...from what I remember." She points to her vagina. "I'm sore. *Really* fucking sore, but in a good way. You know what I mean, don't you?"

I stifle my giggle, finding this entire situation hilarious. "I do."

We quietly enter our suite, tiptoeing our way inside. What we see is the most unexpected sight ever. Palmer is standing in the kitchen, guzzling a water jug like she's been in the desert for a year. She's still in the dress she wore last night. Her shoes are on the kitchen counter, her makeup is smeared all over her face, and her hair looks like a small family could be living inside it.

Kennedy and I simultaneously burst into a fit of laughter.

She immediately turns to us as horror washes over her face.

She moans out, "Oh my god, I assumed you two were asleep in our room."

Kennedy and I turn our heads and look at each other before nodding in silent agreement. Kennedy looks back at Palmer. "How about we all agree to never speak of last night again for the rest of our lives?"

Palmer exhales a breath in relief before shouting, "Deal."

TWENTY-ONE

TWO MONTHS LATER

VANCE

Daylen announces to the entire weight room, "If you're doing it doggie style, you only have to last four minutes. It's twenty-eight minutes in dog years."

I let out a laugh at my ridiculous friend before one of the guys asks him, "What position makes the ugliest babies?"

He immediately responds, "Ask your mom," leaving the whole weight room in a fit of laughter.

It's been a fun few months. With both Sulley and me in our off-seasons, we've gotten to spend a lot of time together. It's always in the privacy of one of our houses, but at least I get to be with her, and I can't stop thinking about my girl. I wish I could come up with a way for her to agree to be with me for real. *Forever.*

Summer is upon us, and her new season kicks off with their home opener tomorrow night. A bunch of us are going.

The Cougars have a day game, and the Anacondas haven't started their season yet, so they'll all be there too.

I can't wait to watch the girls play again. They've been working their asses off to get ready. Hours and hours of practice time is their daily norm. They're committed to making a run this year.

I place the heavily weighted bar into the appropriate slots and sit up in time to hear Presley ask, "In *Shrek*, how does a donkey have sex with a dragon and then impregnate her? It's a plot hole."

Our weight room discussions are truly one of a kind.

Beau shakes his head. "That's not a plot hole. Donkeys don't talk either. And there are no ogres in real life except Humblecut."

Daylen gives him the finger. Beau smiles and continues, "Plot holes are more along the lines of production or writing fuckups. I don't think that's a fuckup."

I nod in agreement. "Agreed. *Shrek* is a fantasy-type movie. Donkeys and dragons having sex are part of the script, not a mistake. There's a big plot hole in the movie *The Hangover*. Vegas is the most security-conscious place on the planet, right?"

Presley nods. "Right."

"There are cameras everywhere. Security personnel are always walking around checking on things. So how can a guy be stuck on the roof of one of the biggest hotels in Vegas for days without cameras or security finding him?"

Daylen gasps. "Oh my god. You're right. It's like in *Karate Kid*. Crane kicks are illegal, as are shots to the head. Daniel should have been disqualified in the championship fight. Johnny was the real winner. That's why they had to come back thirty-five years later and give him his own show." Daylen is obsessed with the television show, *Cobra Kai*, the recent *Karate Kid* spinoff.

Beau nods enthusiastically. "Yes. Those are real plot holes.

You all want to know the biggest plot hole in both cinematic and literary history?"

Every single person stops what they're doing to listen intently. Beau Fudd is always full of useful information.

"In *Cinderella*, everything the fairy godmother turned into magic for the ball was supposed to disappear at midnight. So why didn't the glass slipper disappear too?"

You could hear a pin drop in this weight room right now. There are over forty giant football players, and every single one of them stands or sits silently in shock at this revelation.

Beau smirks. "And while we're at it, are you going to tell me that not one other woman in the entire village wore the same size shoe as Cinderella?" He tsks. "Plot hole."

Coach walks in and stops short. "Why the hell is it so quiet in here? Are you ladies trading recipes again?"

Daylen crosses his arms. "One, that was a sexist comment. You can't say shit like that anymore, Coach. Two, I just found out that my whole childhood has been a lie. The prince never should have been able to find Cinderella."

Coach rolls his eyes and shakes his head. "Get back to working out. This is the fucking weirdest team ever."

Once everyone gets back on track after the Cinderella catastrophe, Coach walks over to me. "Hey. Were you able to grab an extra ticket for the game tomorrow?"

Shit. I forgot he had asked. "It shouldn't be a problem. I'll text you later tonight when my contact is home from work."

"Okay, but just know I'm at the age where if you text me after 10:01 PM, it's most likely that I'll get back to you at around 5:47 AM."

I chuckle. "5:47 works for me, Coach."

He nods. "Good. And we're on for dinner tonight?"

"Yes, sir."

"Fantastic."

I see Reece Sanders talking to our new rookie wide receiver, Anthony Lincoln. Everyone calls him Linc. He's a good kid. He keeps his head down and works hard. He's still a little wet behind the ears, but I see a lot of potential and a bright future for him.

Coach points in their direction. "Linc is an up-and-comer."

I nod. "Agreed."

Staring at Reece, he says "Keep that fucking wolf from getting his claws into him. Rookies are impressionable. We can only roster one of them. Sanders is undoubtedly aware of that. That's the kind of guy who will sabotage another for his own benefit."

"I'm on it, Coach."

I walk over to them. "Linc, you were looking strong yesterday. I'm in the market for a new wide receiver." I look at Reece. "One with good hands. You didn't drop a single pass yesterday."

Linc's face lights up. "Thank you, sir."

I chuckle. "Vance or McCaffrey will be fine."

He smiles shyly. "Sorry. You're such a legend in this sport. It's an honor to catch the ball from a future Hall of Famer. I hope to contribute to this team in any small way that I can."

I grab his hand and bring him in for a bro hug. "I like your attitude."

After our workout, we have a team practice. Our team is looking strong. Linc is solid. He has more speed and way better hands than Reece. I'll finally have another option for the long ball besides Daylen. I have a lot of hope for this season.

After we shower, I hit the team kitchen to grab a few energy bars. I see a line of guys in front of Beau, who's working the blender. I ask Daylen, "What's going on?"

"Beau is making those boner shakes. Everyone wants to try it." He hands me a glass with a white liquid substance in it. "Here, I got you one."

He downs his glass in one giant gulp. "Hmm. Not bad. The vanilla makes it sweet." He smirks. "That's what she said."

I roll my eyes as I down my shake.

AN HOUR LATER, I'm sitting at Del Frisco's Steakhouse waiting for Coach. I scroll through Instagram on my phone while I wait. I despise all social media, but I set up the Instagram account years ago to keep an eye on Sulley and Maddie.

I smile as I look at Sulley's last post from Vegas two months ago. It's our whole big group. We had such a good time. I've never seen her so uninhibited and carefree.

I then scroll down to Maddie's most recent post, which looks like it was from today. It's a picture of Francesca on an ATV. What the fuck is Maddie thinking?

I pull up my text string with Maddie.

> Me: She's not really driving an ATV, is she?

> Maddie: She loves it.

> Me: She's five. It's too dangerous.

> Maddie: Curtis bought it for her. She's been using it all week without any problems. Leave the parenting to her actual parents.

How fucking generous of Curtis to buy that for her with my money.

> Me: I don't want her riding that death trap. They flip easily. I've seen it happen too many times to count. She's way too young for something like this.

> Maddie: I don't care what you want. Stop barking orders at me. You don't get to tell me what to do.

Infuriating bitch.

"Here's your son, Mr. Jeffries," says the hostess as she smiles and shows Coach to the table.

He narrows his eyes at her and grits out, "Do I really look old enough to be his damn father?"

The hostess withers under his glare and apologizes profusely before quickly running away.

I suppose we look like we could be related, both with dark hair and green eyes. His gray makes him look more mature, but he's in fantastic shape. He doesn't look old enough to be my father. Maybe an older brother.

I let out a laugh as he takes his seat. "Hey, Daddy." I motion toward the wine list. "I left the wine list for you. I know what a snob you are."

He reaches into his blazer pocket for his reading glasses and places them on his face before opening the wine list and carefully examining it. "Hmm," is all he has to say. Sometimes he's a man of few words.

Coach is obsessed with good wine. It's common for him to take twenty minutes to pick a bottle, especially at a fancy restaurant. I'm used to it. While I wait, I want to take out my phone so I can fucking yell and scream at Maddie, but there's nothing Coach hates more than someone who uses a cell phone at the dinner table. I'll get a long speech from him about Gen X telephone usage and how dinnertime used to be dinnertime, not a time to be on your phone. It's not worth the hassle just to tell Maddie off, especially since she won't listen to what I have to say. She never does.

For kindergarten, I wanted Francesca to go to a private school. Few kids from the public school go on to college, and I want more for her. Maddie said Francesca preferred to be with her friends. She's fucking five. Why does she have a vote?

Coach finally orders from the sommelier, who returns with the bottle quickly. Coach seems satisfied when it arrives, and, admittedly, it tastes really good. I don't know much about wine, I've always been fine with the nine-dollar variety, but I can tell this is the good stuff.

Once I have his full attention, I ask, "How's post-divorce life treating you, Coach?"

He shrugs. "Divorce sucks. I know ours wasn't the worst, but it's still hard and always painful. No one enters into a marriage planning to get divorced. She made mistakes. I made mistakes. We made mistakes. These past few years have given me a little perspective. I took her for granted. There are things I wish I had said and done differently. If you ever find the right one, Vance, don't hold back. We're cut from the same cloth, you and me. We internalize. We let things happen around us. Don't be a bystander in your life. Take the bull by the horns."

I nod. "I understand. It's good advice. Are you dating yet? It's been a long time now." Coach garners so much attention for his good looks. I'm sure he has women lined up to date him. I smirk. "Are you on any dating apps?"

He raises his eyebrow. "Vance, I still use an address book because I don't trust my phone not to lose telephone numbers in that magical cloud in the sky that holds them. Do you really think I would trust a nerd sitting behind a screen to find me the right woman?"

I let out a small laugh. Of course he thinks matches on dating apps are done by actual people.

He blows out a breath. "Would I sound too much like your generation if I told you it's complicated?"

I chuckle. "You sure would."

He smiles. "Well, it is. There's a woman I've been quietly seeing. I like her. A lot. But Pierce isn't out of the house yet, and Kennedy loves to bust my balls."

"If it makes you feel any better, Kennedy busts everyone's balls, especially Daylen's. The two of them go at it all the time."

He raises an eyebrow. "Hmm. Interesting. She's a handful,

that one. She practically lived in timeout as a kid. Let me tell you something," he points at me, "timeout does shit. You all grew up with a stupid timeout as the worst punishment imaginable. You know what my generation got? We got a belt to the ass. Marks for weeks or months to remind us of what we did wrong. Hell, I think I still have a few marks on my ass from my father's belt. I'd be jailed if I did that to my kids."

I nod. "True. Don't sweat it. Kennedy isn't all bad. You see what a selfless teammate she is. She's become super tight with Sulley, and Sulley is probably the most wonderful, morally sound person I know."

He studies me carefully. "Anything I should know about you two?"

I crack a smile. "It's complicated."

He lets out a laugh. "Of course it is. Listen, I brought you here tonight because I respect you."

"I respect you too, Coach."

He nods. "Thank you. It means a lot coming from a quality kid like you. I'm telling you something that would cost me my job. Can I trust it to stay between us?"

"Of course."

He exhales a long breath. "Management wants to win, and they want to win now, as in this year."

I shrug. That's not news. "Understandable. We all want to win."

"It's more than that, Vance." He takes a sip of his wine and swallows it down. "If we don't win it all this year, I'm out. They'll fire me."

My head starts spinning. "What? That's insane. You're the winningest coach in Camels' franchise history. You played for the Camels. You *are* the damn Philadelphia Camels. You're irreplaceable. You tell them that I won't play for any other coach. Ever."

He takes another sip. This one is a lot longer. "That means a lot to me, I hope you know that. But—"

"But what?"

"It's not just me who will be out." He has a pained expression on his face. He doesn't want to say the words out loud.

I sit back in my chair, completely flabbergasted. I feel gobsmacked. "I've given my all to this organization. Blood, sweat, tears. I've played injured. I've restructured contracts." I give him a knowing look. He's one of only a small handful of people who know I agreed to less money to make sure Daylen got to stay. Something I was assured Daylen would never find out.

"I know, son. I'm as disgusted as you are, but after six straight early exits in the playoffs, they're sick of it. It's all or nothing this year. They've laid down the gauntlet."

"I see." I shake my head in disbelief. "Why are you telling me this, especially if you're not supposed to?"

"I don't give a flying fuck about me. I've achieved everything I wanted in this sport and more. I've been working hard toward a better balance in my life. Football has cost me too much already. If this is my last year, I can live with that. It's you who I care about. You're the reason I'm still here. I know you always give it your all, but if I didn't tell you to leave every single thing on the field this year, I don't know that I could live with myself if it doesn't go our way. In football and in life, it's important to leave everything on the field. You don't want to have any regrets."

SULLEY

It's early in the morning. Our new season starts tonight. I'm so excited I can hardly contain myself. I'm in an old Camels' T-shirt that Vance left here last week. I love smelling him when we sleep apart, which isn't that often.

He had dinner with his coach last night. I told him not to

come over afterward. If he did, we'd go at it for hours, and I needed to get a good night's sleep before our first game.

I'm in my kitchen, about to brew my morning coffee, when my doorbell rings. That's odd. It's super early. Who could it be at this hour?

I open the front door and see Vance in gray sweatpants and a T-shirt. I've never once seen him in sweatpants. I examine him and realize why. He has a giant, and I mean giant, boner sticking out.

I can't help but smile as I stare at it. "Are you okay, killer? It hasn't even been twenty-four hours since we last had sex. Can't you rein that in?"

He exhales a long breath. "Beau. Fucking. Fudd. He made us all those boner shakes yesterday. I was awakened at one in the morning with the hardest, most painful boner of my life."

I burst out laughing. Leaning forward, holding my stomach, hyperventilating type of laughter.

"It's not funny. I've jerked off four times. He won't go down."

My laughter only gets louder. "This is a riot. Did he make them for everyone on the team?"

He nods. "Yes."

"Is everyone reacting like this?"

He shrugs in obvious frustration. "I don't fucking know!" His hand is practically shaking, and his brow is covered in sweat. "Please help me. I need to fuck you."

I cross my arms and raise an eyebrow. "Hmm. I'm intrigued. How many orgasms are you going to give me?"

He places his hands together in prayer. "As many as you want. I swear. I've come four times in the past five hours. I'm confident you'll be the one asking for mercy by the end."

I bite my lip. "I might be up for a little unnecessary roughness, QB1. I can't wait to check out the product of a boner shake boner."

I smile as I grab his shirt and smash my mouth to his. He

immediately lifts me, so my legs wrap around him. His hands move straight to my ass and squeeze it.

He's kissing me like he might never be able to do it again. And his big hands are moving everywhere. He's so frantic for me. He always is. I love it.

His hard length moves through my soft center. He's like a rock. I can't help but grind against the python as he manages to get me aching for him in no time.

Suddenly, the hairs on my neck raise, and I realize where we are. We're on my front stoop. I get paranoid, feeling like I'm being watched. Breaking our kiss, I look around but don't see anyone. "Let's get inside and take care of business."

"Thank fuck," he breathes.

He walks us into the house in a rush, closing the door behind him. My shirt is discarded before he takes his first full step inside, and he buries his face in my breasts.

I tap his arm. "Put me down. I need to see what I'm getting myself into. I'm not going into this experiment blind."

He places me down, and I examine him again. I do love him in his trademark jeans, but Vance McCaffrey in gray sweatpants has my nipples hardening and a throb building between my legs. The massive boner only adds to the allure. I bite back my smile while I ask, "Why no jeans?"

"Are you for real?" He points at the tent in his pants. "I couldn't fit this monster into jeans right now."

I giggle. "I'm so excited to see the product of the infamous boner shake. Drop trou, Vile Vance."

Without any hesitation, he removes his T-shirt and then his sweatpants and boxer briefs at once. I have to cover my mouth as I gasp in shock. "Oh my god! It's enormous!" It's always big, but it's…it's…angry. So fucking angry. It's red and purple. The veins look like they're moving under his skin; that's how much blood is flowing through them. His tip is oozing. What in the fuck is in those shakes?

I point at it. "No freakin' way. Keep that thing away from me.

You're going to finally split me in half this time. For real. I have to play tonight. I need to be able to both walk and run."

He whimpers as he squeezes his cock. "Please. I'll do anything. I need relief."

He looks so pathetic.

"Fine, but I'm sucking you off the first time."

A small smile forms on his lips. "Yeah…so…I'm not going to argue with that."

I giggle as I drop to my knees and inhale a deep breath. I'm going to need all the oxygen I can get.

Two hours later, we're panting as we lie naked on top of what's left of my dining room table. Yep, we broke my brand-new table. He fucked me like a man possessed. Over and over and over again. On every surface of the house, with the finale coming on my dining room table. It came crashing down with us on top. We burst into laughter, but I'm just happy neither of us got hurt. Well, I might be hurt. I haven't attempted to walk yet.

He reaches his hand over and rubs my bare stomach. Breathing heavily, he says, "I owe you a new dining room table. Totally worth every penny. Thanks for helping me. I think he's finally down."

Also breathing heavily, I respond, "He's now come seven times in seven hours. He's got to be exhausted."

Vance lets out a laugh. "That boner shake is no joke. Why do people pay for erectile dysfunction meds? All they need is a Beau Fudd boner shake."

I giggle. "Truth. Don't drink it ever again. I don't have the energy for it. What if I wasn't home?" I jokingly ask.

His face turns serious. "Then I would have gone back to my house and jerked off again. I wouldn't have gone to someone else, if that's what you're asking."

I shake my head. "It wasn't. Vance, we're not together. You're free to be with other women." I run my fingers through my tangled hair. "I guess if you're messing around with other people, just let me know so we can use condoms. I don't want to be at any risk."

He turns and cups my face. "Someone else? Sulley, there is no one else. There never will be." He licks his lips. "Don't you know how I feel about you? Can't you sense it with every kiss? Every touch? I lov—"

"Don't say it," I interrupt while sitting up abruptly. "Don't you dare say that to me, Vance McCaffrey. You know it's not like that for us and never will be. We had a deal."

The fact is, I'm falling for him too, but I don't want to be. No matter how he acts with me, he's still the man who betrayed my brother. And I know he's hiding something from me. I feel it in my bones.

He sits up and takes my hand. "Why can't it be like that for us? I know you have feelings for me too. You're lying to yourself if you say you don't feel what's happening between us. It's special. We're special."

My eyes fill with tears. "Because you lie to me. You hide things. Tell me right now. Tell me what went down with you and Maddie. I want all the details. Even the hard-to-hear ones."

His jaw tightens. For a brief moment, his lips twitch like he's going to say something real but then thinks better of it. He drops his head. "I'm sorry. I can't."

My anger rises. "Right. You won't trust me with the truth, but you ask me to trust you with my heart? To love you? Love needs action. Trust needs proof. Sorry needs change."

Tears spill over my eyes. I've been so good about not crying over Vance McCaffrey for months. I've tried to simply enjoy our casual encounters. It's all come crashing to a halt.

I shake my head, feeling the anger rising to the surface. "How dare you throw heavy shit at me on my opening day."

He sighs. "Again, I'm sorry." He winces. "You know what? I'm not sorry. I love you, Sullivan Aisling. I've loved you for a long time but feared saying anything. I was afraid you'd react exactly how you're reacting. I'm not going to be ashamed to admit it. I'm leaving it all on the field." He places his hand over his heart. "Love isn't conditional. I unconditionally love you, flaws and all. Can't you love me despite my flaws? Despite past mistakes I may have made?"

I shake my head and croak out, "It's more than a few minor flaws, and you know it. We've existed in this alternate bubble for months. One that doesn't reflect the reality of our situation. Maybe I let it get too far or allowed it to go on for too long. Maybe it's time to end things between us."

"No," he barks out as he stands and begins to angrily and silently pull on his boxer briefs and sweatpants.

"Is there a follow-up to the *no*, or has the king spoken the rule of the land?" I ask with a sharp edge in my tone.

He slides his T-shirt back over his head with a murderous look on his face as he yells, "I do *not* accept your suggestion that we end our relationship. I don't want that, and I know in my heart you don't either. We will never be over because I know we are meant to be together. I knew it six years ago and I know it now."

"Meant to be together? You can't be serious."

He straightens his shoulders and puffs out his chest. "I know for a fact that I will never love another woman the way I love you. I would marry you today if you wanted to. That's how fucking serious I am." He points at me. "We're not over. We can continue this song and dance if you want, the one where we say out loud that it's nothing but physical, but we're both just falling deeper. I'm fucking thirty-two. I know what's real and what's not. We. Are. Real."

He makes his way toward the front door but momentarily turns back to me. "I'll see you tonight at your game. I'll be the one wearing the jersey of the love of my life."

He walks out the door and slams it, leaving me speechless.

TWENTY-TWO

SULLEY

I hug Fallon Montgomery inside our locker room. "I'm so glad you changed your mind and you're officially part of the team now."

Fallon was initially hesitant to leave her job as a physical therapist at the hospital but eventually accepted Reagan's offer to work with the Beavers. She started about eight weeks ago. She's not only been our PT, helping us with various injuries and ailments, but she's also participated in team practices. She knows the sport shockingly well. So well that when one of our assistant coaches was unexpectedly ordered to bed rest last night for the remainder of her pregnancy, Fallon was asked to step in as a temporary assistant coach. It was a natural fit. We already like her, and she knows our plays and the team inside and out.

Her biggest concern in accepting the dual role was caring for Harper once she gets out of school in a few weeks, but everyone agreed that we're happy to have Harper around and on the road with us when needed.

Harper also now has a stepmom. Yep, the big announcement promised by Vance was a shocker. Bailey and Tanner got married and are expecting their first child later this year. I should say children. It's twin girls. I'm not sure Bailey would have been able to play anyway due to her back injury, but now she's definitely taking the Anacondas' season off, as she'll be in her third trimester by then.

Fallon takes a deep breath and runs her hands down her flattering white pantsuit, looking every bit the role of an assistant coach. "I hope I'm up for the challenge." She points toward my foot. "How's your ankle?"

I tweaked it in practice last week. She's been on my case about ice, elevation, and anti-inflammatories.

"It's totally fine."

She narrows her eyes at me. "Are you sure? I feel like you were limping a little when you first walked into the locker room."

That has nothing to do with my ankle. It has everything to do with Vance driving his monster python into me for two hours this morning. I had to take an hour-long bath after he left to soothe my aching body, most of which was spent crying over the state of our relationship and his unexpected declaration of love.

I don't know what to do. I both trust and don't trust him. I'm not sure how to reconcile the conflicting feelings. I trust him because I've known him since I was born and genuinely believe the man would take a bullet for me. I don't trust him because of his betrayal and secrecy over the circumstances.

The one thing I do know is I want him in my life. I hate myself for feeling that way, but I need him. If I'm being honest with myself, I know that I love him. I always have. I won't, however, admit or fully give in to those feelings until the truth comes out. And I won't wait forever. At some point, he'll have to decide if he loves me enough to come clean about whatever happened six years ago.

I haven't forgotten what Vance did for me to get me back on the court. I only wish he'd let me return the favor and be there for him with whatever burden he's carrying. I know it's all related.

I jokingly jog in place for Fallon, showing her that my ankle is fine. "Yep, I'm sure."

My phone rings and I point at it. "Excuse me."

I know who it is before I look and accept the call. The woman who has called me before every game throughout my entire career. The one who has never let me down. "Hi, Momma."

"Hey, sweet girl. Big day."

"Yep. I'm excited. Did you get the plane tickets I sent?" Because my mother doesn't trust emails, I had to print out her airline tickets and physically mail them to her.

"We did. Your dad is a little nervous, but the O'Sheas are coming to Philly," she cheerily announces.

Now that I have the house and we're in season, it was a perfect excuse for a visit. It was my holiday gift to them this year.

I grin widely. "I can't wait. I miss you so much, Momma."

"I miss you too. Have you seen much of Vance?"

I gulp. "Yes, I see him around," I reluctantly admit. "You know we share friends in common." I cringe, hoping she's not upset with me.

"How does he seem?"

That's an unexpected question. "Why?"

"Jane is worried about him."

"Oh. Maybe it has to do with," I whisper because we rarely say her name out loud in our house, "Maddie. Or even Francesca," though he won't talk about her. "Momma," I feel compelled to ask again, "do the McCaffreys spend time with Francesca? It sounds like Maddie doesn't allow Vance much time with her. I hope she gets to spend time with her grandparents."

"I assume they see her," she answers. "You know it's our unspoken agreement that we don't talk about that part of their life. They respect our pain over the situation. They even go so far as to hide all her pictures when we visit the ranch. I've never once seen one out. I wouldn't even know what she looked like if it wasn't for the occasional run-in. She doesn't have any of the McCaffreys' darker hair and skin tone in her. She's all Maddie with fair skin and light hair. And she's tiny like Maddie. She didn't get the McCaffrey height either."

Vance's whole family is tall. His father, Michael, is even taller than Vance, and Jane must be close to my height. Even though MeeMaw has shrunk throughout the years, she's still got height most women in her generation didn't have.

"Interesting. I think there's more to the story than what we know to be the truth. I can't get Vance to talk about it. Maybe you can get Jane to talk. If you want."

She audibly sighs. "I don't know, Sulley. You know it took time to get our friendship back on track. I don't think I want to rock the boat." She's silent for a brief moment. "I'm happy you're able to spend time with Vance. When you were little, Jane and I used to daydream that you two would end up together. I know that won't happen now, but I'm pleased you two have achieved some level of friendship. You share a lot of history."

My eyes fill with tears. Shit, I don't need this before a game.

"Momma, I need to get ready for my game."

"Of course. I'm sorry. Good luck. Knock 'em dead. You always do. We'll be watching. I'll see you soon."

"Love you."

"Love you too, sweet girl."

I end the call and take a few deep breaths, attempting to calm myself. I need to shift gears and get into the gameday mindset.

I'm still in my head when the locker room doors swing open with a thud, and Kennedy struts in like she owns the place. Walking into games has become a bit of a fashion show. Our gameday outfits are photographed and plastered all over social media for the world to judge. Everyone now takes time to carefully choose what they'll wear as they walk into the stadium.

Seeing Kennedy's gameday outfit immediately brings a smile to my face and lifts my spirits. She's in high-fashion jeans with stiletto heels. Her hair is styled to perfection with her always-present perfect ponytail, and her makeup is flawless. But it's her shirt that is the object of my admiration. She's wearing my college jersey. Well, it's not the actual jersey. It's a trendy, artfully torn replica of it. University of Montana, number twenty-two, with my name on it.

"Nice shirt, number eight."

She smirks. "Got to support my girl, number twenty-two. The days of the women in this league pulling you down to make themselves feel better about their mediocre play are over. There's a new queen in the sport. They'd better get used to it. The rising tide raises all ships. It's a shame they don't realize how much everyone benefits from your popularity."

The other players in the league trying to push me down doesn't bother me in the slightest. It's interesting that it bothers my teammates, and analysts love to talk about it, but I don't care at all. I'm here to do one thing. Win games for my team. Everything else is white noise.

Interviews by our opponents saying I'm all hype have become commonplace. I'm always asked to respond on camera, but I'd rather respond with good play. I won't get dragged into a mudslinging contest. It's not a good look for women. We should be supporting each other. There are plenty of seats at the table for everyone.

I'm not sure I have a bigger cheerleader than Kennedy. I'm completely overcome with gratitude for my beautiful friend.

I wrap my arms around her. "I love you, Kennedy Jeffries. You're the best friend I've ever had in my life."

She lifts her head and yells out, "Fuck, Shay, I think you turned another one."

I giggle into her neck, and I can feel her laughing too. She whispers, "If I didn't know you were fucking Vance McCaffrey, I'd think you were into me."

TWO HOURS LATER, I'm on the court warming up when I see Vance walking to his seat on the floor. Sure enough, he's wearing my Beavers jersey over his T-shirt. I'm flooded with emotion at seeing him in it.

Our eyes meet. He mouths, "Sorry."

I nod and mouth back, "Me too."

Returning my attention to our layup line, I notice Kennedy tugging at the crotch of her shorts. "Everything okay down there?" I ask.

She groans. "I had no-holds-barred sex this morning. I thought getting laid before the game would be good, but he gave me a hard pounding. I'm a little out of sorts."

I know the feeling. "Who was it with?"

She shrugs. "Some random dude I met on Tinder. I won't be swiping right for a while."

VANCE

"Oh my god, times have changed," I jokingly whine to Layton with a genuine smile.

He walks toward me to take his seat nearby with a giant grin on his face, a tiny baby strapped to his chest, and his wife sitting next to him. "I'm introducing Ryan to sports early. It's never too early to learn fundamentals."

I chuckle. "She's beautiful, man. Congratulations."

He nods as he leans down and kisses her head. "Thanks. She's the most beautiful girl in the world."

Arizona clears her throat, and Layton corrects himself. "Excuse me, I meant that she's tied with her mother for the most beautiful creature in existence."

Arizona giggles and kisses his cheek. "That's better, superstar."

My eyes meet hers. "You look great. It's hard to believe you had a baby a few weeks ago."

She blows out a breath. "Thank you. I'm trying to get back into shape in time for our season. It's no joke. Thank god I have Layton around to do the heavy lifting with Ryan. I don't know what I would do without him."

He rubs Ryan's head tenderly. "I love spending time with my best girl, cheering on Mommy. She already told me that she wants to be like her mommy when she grows up, didn't you, sweet angel?"

I inwardly laugh. Just a few years ago, Layton Lancaster would go home with a different woman nearly every night. And then Arizona Abbott entered his life, and he was a goner. From minute one, he was head over heels for her. They dealt with their share of hurdles, including his career-ending injury and the fact that Arizona is the sister of one of Layton's best friends and teammates, but I've never seen him happier, and I'm happy for him. I suppose I can't judge him for falling in love with his best friend's sister. I've gone and done the exact same thing.

Next, I see Tanner helping Bailey down the aisle. Holy shit, she popped. She wasn't showing at all during their secret wedding this past spring. She's certainly showing now. Harper is merrily bopping along behind them, bustling with excitement as always.

Then Cheetah walks in holding Kamryn's hand behind him. Layton smiles at her. "Why are you always last, Hart?"

"Because I'm the only one with a brain full of random shit, Lancaster," Kam replies. "I've got one for you today. You're going to sit here for the next ten minutes and fact-check me, but just know it's a waste of time. I'm right. I always am."

He rubs his hands together in excitement. "Give it to me."

"2013 was the first year since 1987 to have four different numbers in it."

Like she knew we would, we all sit there and run all the

years through our heads until we eventually confirm that she's correct. As always.

Daylen then meanders in. I stare at him in shock. He's wearing Kennedy's jersey over a T-shirt.

He shrugs as he passes me and plops into the seat next to mine. "Don't look at me like that. It was the only one they had in my size."

The two of them have been acting weird since Vegas. I wonder if something happened between them.

Coach strolls in and sits on the other side of Daylen. He examines Daylen's jersey, which matches his own. "Care to explain why you're wearing my daughter's jersey, Humblecut?"

"You're wearing it too, Coach."

"I'm her father."

Daylen twists his lips. "I didn't know it was hers. I bought it because it's number eight. I'm eighty-eight, but no one on the Beavers has the same number. This was the next best thing. I'm a narcissist like that."

Coach narrows his eyes at him. "You're full of shit, Humblecut."

Daylen shakes his head. "Coach, you need to relax. Maybe a little drinking and dancing would be beneficial for you. Do you want to come to a club with us after the game? Maybe you'll pick up a hottie."

Coach rolls his eyes. "A club? Do you know how old I am? I'm at an age where picking up a hottie at a club means picking up a rotisserie chicken at Costco."

Daylen lets out one of his enormous laughs. "Fuck, Coach, you're lowkey funny."

Coach sighs. "My goal in life is to amuse you, Humblecut."

Just then, Presley and Beau walk in. I narrow my eyes at Beau, and he holds up his hands in surrender. "Sorry, man. I think I messed up the formula. It was awfully strong, wasn't it?"

"Ya think?" I sarcastically reply.

Daylen nods. "I had to have sex six times before the big head would go down."

"Who with?" I ask.

He shrugs. "No one special. Just one of my regular dial-a-pussy girls."

Coach makes a look of disgust. "Dial-a-pussy? That's terrible. I feel sorry for your future father-in-law. I hope he beats you senseless...with the end of a rifle."

Daylen is uncharacteristically quiet, but the lights go out, and the player announcements start.

The game eventually gets underway. The girls are a little off at first, but they get it together after a while. Sulley finds her perimeter shot and starts sinking threes.

They're playing against the team that seems to give the most hate to Sulley. One player in particular, Diane Garma, always throws shade at Sulley in the media and then pushes her around in games. She's been talking trash to Sulley throughout the entire game.

Diane steals the ball from Layla and has a clear lane to the basket for an easy layup. Sulley hustles back and wraps her arms around Diane, taking her down for a hard but necessary foul. You'd always rather foul a player going in for an easy two points and take your chances with free throws.

Diane doesn't like it at all and starts thrashing around, but Sulley walks away with her back to Diane, avoiding an altercation. Diane begins to charge Sulley with her fist in the air. Holy shit. Is she going to punch Sulley?

Just as she's about to reach Sulley from behind, a fist comes flying into Diane's face, knocking her out cold.

TWENTY-THREE

SULLEY

I smile as Kennedy walks into practice for the first time in two weeks. "Look who it is. Ronda Rousey."

Ronda Rousey is a famous female professional fighter.

Kennedy was originally suspended for a month by the league for punching Diane Garma and knocking her unconscious. Reagan was able to negotiate the suspension down to two weeks, but Kennedy had to agree to go to some sort of anger management rehab facility. We haven't seen her in two weeks.

Kennedy was also levied with a hefty fine, but I insisted on covering that. How could I not? She protected me. I've watched the replay a thousand times. I would have been coldcocked if Kennedy hadn't stepped in.

Kennedy lets out a laugh as she holds up her fists and does a little shadow boxing dance for us. "Do you know how many offers I've gotten in the past two weeks to fight professionally? If I weren't so pretty, I'd consider it. Promoters are throwing a lot of money my way."

I giggle and sarcastically respond, "It's a shame you're so pretty."

She nods in agreement. "Yep." She points to her face. "Can't mess with the money-maker."

Kennedy's punch went viral. Black Widow memes and headlines were everywhere. I'm not surprised she's fielding offers. It's the world we live in.

Her jersey is now the best-selling one in the league, knocking me from the top spot. I couldn't possibly be happier for her.

Fallon wraps her arms around Kennedy. The two of them have gotten close. "I missed you. Are you okay?"

Kennedy hugs her back. "I'm fine. Don't make a fuss. If anyone was physically closer to Diane than I was, they would have done the same thing. That cunt was about to dole out a cheap shot to Sulley. Should I have let that happen? Fuck no. I'd do it again. Bitch had it coming for a long time. She can't face the reality that Sulley is better than her. When you fight with reality, you lose a hundred percent of the time."

I pull her close to my side. "I missed you so much. Tonight, we celebrate you getting out of basketball jail. Let's all go out for a nice dinner and then go dancing."

She grins. "Time to party." Looking over her shoulder, she yells, "Booster! Where are you? I swear, he's always slacking."

He materializes seemingly from the shadows. "I'm here, Queen Jeffries. Do you need some water? A towel?"

She shakes her head. "No, make us a dinner reservation. Somewhere nice and expensive." She winks at me. "Sulley's treating. And pick up my dry cleaning on the way home. Oh, and be sure to grab my costume for my grand return gameday entrance." She smirks. "It's a doozy."

VANCE

I'm sitting at a table by Daylen's pool with Daylen, Beau, and Champ. We're meeting the girls later at Club Liberty.

They wanted a girls-only dinner to celebrate Kennedy's return. I think Sulley is taking the team to a fancy restaurant as her thank you to Kennedy. As difficult as that woman can be sometimes, I can't deny that Kennedy will go to any lengths to protect my girl. The league may have freaked out over her violent actions, but the real world is hailing her a hero.

Daylen, who's flipping steaks at the grill, shakes his head at Beau. "If her pussy has hair, she's faithful. It's the bald ones who cheat. Grass doesn't grow on busy streets."

Beau sighs in frustration. "No way. I like them groomed. I manscape, why shouldn't they womanscape?" He looks at Champ. "Do you prefer men who manscape?"

Champ has gradually started feeling more comfortable discussing his sexuality within our small group. Never around the full team, but around us, he's begun to talk about his love life. I'm happy he feels comfortable doing so. It says a lot about the trust he has in us.

Champ scrunches his face. "Sorry, D, but I'm with Beau. You got to keep that shit clean and trim. No one wants to floss when they're giving head."

Daylen harrumphs. "Agree to disagree."

I chuckle. "The conversations we have sometimes never cease to amaze me."

BJ nuzzles her nose into Daylen's side. In his annoying BJ baby voice, he says, "Is my princess hungry?"

Bark.

"Don't worry. Daddy made you steak too. Just the way you like it."

Bark, bark.

Daylen then feeds BJ an entire steak, which she appears to gulp down all at once without bothering to chew it. He uses his BJ voice again, "Don't listen to them, pretty girl. Men like women who are au naturale, just like you."

I grit out, "That better not have been my steak."

He smiles. "No, you have the shitty cut. I save the good stuff for my babydoll."

I walk over to the grill to make sure he kept the good steaks on the grill, which he did. He smiles. "Chef Benny never buys shitty steaks." Chef Benny is Daylen's house manager and BJ's dogsitter when we're on the road. "Have I ever given you shitty steak?" he asks.

I shake my head, "Nope. You're the grill master."

He nods. "Damn straight. How are we on time?"

I look down at my phone. "Sulley texted that they'll be done with dinner in about an hour. We can head out right after we eat."

Yes, I'm anxious to see her.

He raises an eyebrow. "You're whipped. Is she finally moving the needle for you?"

I stare at my best friend and admit, "She doesn't *move* the needle. She *is* the needle."

His face breaks out into a huge smile. "I'm happy for you. You deserve this."

"Do I?"

He places his hand on my shoulder and gives me an uncharacteristically serious look. "Yes, Vance, you do. You are, without a single doubt, the best man I know. It's okay to finally let yourself be happy."

I swallow down my emotions. "She can't get past everything that happened."

"That's because she doesn't know what happened. Maybe you should clue her in on everything."

I exhale a long breath. "Now isn't the time. She's in season. I don't want to ruffle any feathers for her or the team."

He shakes his head and loudly announces, "Excuses are like assholes. Everyone has them, and they all stink."

I smirk. "Says the man who gets off on burying his face in women's asses."

He chuckles. "I meant men. Assholes are hot for women."

Champ raises his hand. "Not all men have stinky assholes."

I let out a laugh, in part because it's funny, but mostly because I'm loving that Champ has finally become comfortable enough with us to crack jokes.

WE'RE SURROUNDED by the chatter of our friends in the booth of a noisy, music-filled club, yet I can't hear anything except the rapid beating of my heart as I stare at Sulley. Her lips are painted red tonight and all I can think is that I want that lipstick on my cock.

She's engaged in conversation, smiling and laughing along with everyone else. Why can't she be like that with me in public? It hurts that she refuses to acknowledge our relationship.

I turn and look at Layla and Presley, who can't keep their hands off each other tonight. I used to be disgusted by it. Now I'm jealous. I want to be able to sit here and touch my girl too. I want her to show me the unashamed love and affection that I see Layla giving Presley right now.

I've barely seen her over the past two weeks. We had our fight, and then the whole Kennedy thing blew up, and she was busy dealing with the aftermath. Her parents visited for a few days. She didn't want me anywhere near them. Then the team had a long road trip. They only just returned.

It feels stifling when I can't spend time with her. Like I can't breathe properly.

Daylen elbows me. "Who pissed in your cornflakes? I thought you'd be happy to see her."

"Fuck off," I snap. "I'm just having a bad day," I lie.

He gives me one of his goofy smiles while he runs his hands through the hair he's once again cut. "Bad day? Do you want to hear about bad days? The airport in Vienna, Austria, has a counter solely dedicated to people who thought they were flying to Australia. Now *that's* having a bad day."

I can't help the laugh that bubbles. He always makes me smile. I mumble, "I'm not sure that's someone having a bad day or them being a moron."

He wiggles his eyebrows. "Truth." He clinks his beer bottle with mine while nodding his head toward Sulley. "You've got this, stud. Ask her to dance. Slip her the tongue. Chacha with her chesticles. Give her the hot beef injection."

I roll my eyes. "You're a buffoon."

He chuckles as he nudges me. "Go ahead. Get your groove on. Shake your booty. Bust a move. You'll be seen down there, but you won't be *seen*." He wiggles his eyebrows suggestively.

He knows I never dance. I look down at the dance floor. There are a ton of people down there. Hmm, maybe he's right. She and I could get lost in the group. This way, I could touch her. My fingers itch to do so.

I pull my phone out of my pocket and start typing.

Me: Miss me?

Her phone is on the table, so I see the moment her screen lights up. She picks it up and reads it before looking up at me. She exhales a deep breath before subtly nodding.

I type again.

Me: I miss talking to you. I miss kissing you. I miss feeling you in my arms. I miss being inside you.

God, I have zero chill when it comes to this woman. I'm so pathetic.

She looks down at her phone and closes her eyes. After several long beats, she opens them and begins typing. Her lips curl in amusement as she does.

I feel my phone vibrate and look down at it.

Sulley: What are you going to do about it?
Throw me down on this table in front of
everyone, Mr. Public Fornication? Will you lift
my skirt and do filthy things to me right here in
this club?

My girl is feeling frisky. All the blood in my body rushes south as I get a visual of doing just that. I have to adjust myself in my jeans. She notices, and her smile widens.

My eyes rake over her outfit. She's in a short skirt and tank top with those thin spaghetti strap things. I don't think she's wearing a bra. She looks edible. I can't help but lick my lips. She stares at my mouth while her cheeks redden, and she squirms in her seat.

I look down to type on my phone.

Me: Your face is red. I know you're dripping for
me, baby. Tell me, how wet are you right now?

Her phone vibrates again. She looks at it and starts typing.

Sulley: Probably about as hard as you are.

Me: Prove it.

I see her pinch her eyebrows together as she types.

Sulley: How?

Me: Touch yourself. Slip your fingers into your
tight cunt and then show me the evidence.

Her eyes widen as they meet mine again. She swivels her head around to see if anyone besides me is watching her. They aren't. They're all busy chatting away.

Her right hand disappears under the table. I lean as far

back as I can so I can try to watch what she's doing under the table. Damn, I can't see.

I lift my head back up and stare into her eyes. I know the moment she reaches her target because she shivers ever so slightly.

After a few seconds, her hand reappears, and she holds up two fingers for me to see the clear evidence of her arousal. Her fingertips are glistening. Fuuuuck. So hot.

I'm about to give her more instructions when she stares me in the eyes and brings her fingers to her mouth, slipping them inside and wrapping those red-painted lips around them. Her cheeks hollow as she sucks on them.

I'm slack-jawed right now. Hard as stone. I would kill to be the one tasting her. I would equally kill for that to be my cock inside her mouth.

I type on my phone again.

> Me: My turn. I want to taste you too. Make it happen. Get creative.

I have no idea how, but she's a smart girl. She'll figure it out.

After reading her phone, she looks around, clearly thinking of a way to oblige. Her head stops. I turn to see what she's looking at. The waitress is making her way to our table with a fresh set of drinks. She smiles as though something has occurred to her.

Her hand disappears under the table again. When the waitress arrives, she sets the tray on the table. Sulley begins helping her distribute the drinks. When she gets to my beer, Sulley runs her juice-covered fingers around the rim of my bottle several times before handing it to me.

I nod my head at her in gratitude when she hands it to me, immediately licking around the rim. I can taste her saltiness on there. I'm squeezing the bottle so hard it's a wonder it doesn't shatter in my hand.

I pull out my phone again.

> Me: Make an excuse to get up. Meet me on the dance floor in two minutes.

About a minute after Sulley leaves, I stand. Looking down at Daylen, I say, "I'm going to hit the head. I might head out after."

He's barely listening, with his attention elsewhere. I don't care where. He mumbles, "See you in the morning."

I walk down the stairs. I think I can count on one hand how many times I've been on the dance floor in all the years I've been coming here. There must be two hundred people out here, all rubbing against each other. Ugh. Disgusting. I don't know why Daylen loves being down here so much.

When I see people randomly making out, it becomes crystal clear why he likes it so much. Fucking sex maniac.

I pull my baseball cap down. It's crowded, but I'm tall and recognizable. I don't need fangirl, groupie shit right now.

How the hell am I going to find her in this massive sea of people? The thought is still trickling through my mind when I feel arms snake around my body. Delicate hands move from my chest to my abs. Normally, I'd assume it's a random woman trying to touch me, but I can smell Sulley. My body immediately reacts to her coconut scent.

I turn around and see her beautifully flushed face and lust-filled eyes. Taking in her entire outfit, I realize that not only is she in a short skirt, but she's in high boots. Her legs look even longer in those. I ache to fuck her in nothing but those boots.

I look around at all the people, none of whom notice us, lost in their own dance partners and good times. Despite the crowd size, the number of people and the darkness afford us some anonymity. The lights are strobing, making it hard to see anyone or anything.

Unable to wait a second longer, I pull her body to mine. I'm a shitty dancer, but I sway us to the beat just so we can grind against each other. It was like I couldn't breathe for two weeks, and now I finally can. She's my breath of fresh air. My oxygen. My everything.

Her hands find my hair and her tits press to my chest as she runs her tongue up my neck until she reaches my lips. She sucks on my bottom lip, and I completely lose control. Grabbing her ass, I shamelessly grind my erection through her.

She lets out a moan, and I have to kiss her. I can't wait any longer. As though it's a choreographed dance, our lips come together and our tongues push into each other's mouths. We both lose ourselves and begin fully making out. Despite my love for being intimate in public settings, I've never been this obvious, but I don't care. I need her.

My hands move around her body without any inhibition. Her fingers tug on my hair, making my cock leak in anticipation of what I know is going to happen tonight.

My knee pushes between her legs, spreading them for me, giving me the access I need. I run my hand up the front of her soft, smooth thigh. She tilts her body, encouraging my sensual path.

My fingertips ascend until they find purchase as I encounter her soaked panties. Knowing she's as turned on as I am gives me the courage to slip them to the side and run my fingers through her. She's wet and swollen. She always is for me.

If someone were paying attention to us, they'd know exactly what we're doing, but I'm finding I just don't care, and, from the looks of things, they don't either.

My fingers easily glide into her tight warmth. Her juices immediately coat my fingers. She gets as turned on by our public sex acts as I do. She was made for me.

My mouth moves to her neck, close to her ear, so she can hear me over the loud beat of the music. "Do you like my fingers fucking you in front of all these people?" I ask as I push deep inside her with two fingers.

Her grip on my hair tightens, and she tilts her head back and moans. She's swiveling her hips and pushing down to deepen the thrusts of my fingers. She's completely lost in the moment.

I look down at her. I've got one hand inside her and the other now threaded through the back of her hair. Her face is beautifully flushed, and her eyelids are fluttering. She may seem completely at my mercy right now, but the truth is clear as day: I'm the one at her mercy.

Her mouth smashes to mine again, licking, kissing, and nibbling my lips. She eventually sucks my tongue into her mouth and I just about blow my load.

When will I ever get my fill of this woman? It's never enough. I'm never fully satisfied because I always want more. I know without a doubt that I'll always feel that way.

She's riding my hand as if we're alone when we're anything but. I whisper, "Do you want to be a good girl for me?"

She whimpers as she nods.

"I want you to scream my name when you come in front of all these people. Then we're going to find somewhere for me to stick my dick in this tight pussy. When you're full of my come, I'm going to take you home and do it all over again." As I curl my fingers, I whisper, "Be a good girl and come for Daddy."

Her grip on my hair and shirt tightens, and she lets out some sort of indiscernible loud noise before letting her head fall forward and sinking her teeth into my neck. Her pussy contracts around my fingers and coats them in her come while she shakes through her orgasm.

As the last of her tremors withers away, I pull my hand

from her. She watches on with a slack jaw as I suck my fingers into my mouth. "Hmm. So fucking good, baby."

Her mouth remains wide open, and she's panting like she just ran a marathon. She releases her hold on my shirt and moves her hand down until it grips my cock before breathing, "Fuck me here. I don't care. Just do it. I feel like I'll die if I don't get you inside me."

As much as I want to put my stamp on this woman, to show everyone she's mine, to mark her as mine, I can't allow that to happen in front of all these people.

My mind is racing, trying to think of where this can happen. I'm not fucking her in a dirty bathroom, but I can't wait as long as it will take to get to one of our houses.

Suddenly remembering they serve dinner earlier in the evenings on the roof, I pull her hand into the stairwell, but we don't even make it to the steps. As soon as the heavy metal stairwell door closes and the noises of the crowd are left behind, she lifts her skirt to her waist. "Right here. Fuck me."

I pull my dick out in under two seconds, lift her legs, slide her panties to the side, and then slam her against the metal door before I thrust my dick inside her.

A FEW HOURS LATER, we're lying in her bed enjoying our post-orgasmic bliss. After the quick, hard fuck in the stairwell, I practically threw her over my shoulder and dragged her to my truck. We went to her house because it was closer, and I was about to explode all over again because I can't seem to ever get my fill of this woman.

I was able to worship every inch of her in her bed, cocooned in the delicious Sulley scent present on her pillows, blankets, and body. We lie in her now-tangled sheets, breathless and moist with perspiration. Our bodies are marked, our lips are swollen, and our souls are soothed.

The moments after we have sex have become my favorite time with her. The painful past is momentarily forgotten. We're relaxed and sated. Naked and close. We talk and laugh. It's intimate, and I crave it.

Her head is on my chest, and her fingers are lazily running through my chest hair. "Tell me something. Something you haven't shared with anyone else."

She asks that all the time. She knows I'm hiding something and won't tell her. It's almost as if revealing other truths to her makes her feel better about our past. I suppose I understand it and do my best to oblige her.

I run my fingers up and down her flawless back, loving the feel of her soft body on my rough, calloused hands. "Coach told me something in confidence. Management wants to win, and they want to win now. If we don't bring home the trophy this year, he's getting fired and I'm getting traded or released."

She lifts her head as her stunned eyes meet mine. "Are you serious?"

I nod. "Yes. He said he needed to tell me so I could make sure to leave it all on the field. As if I ever don't."

Worry covers her pretty face. "Oh, Vance, I'm so sorry. It's terrible that they're treating you this way. It's a lot of pressure on you."

I shrug. "At the end of the day, it's just football."

"You love football. You always have."

I've been thinking about everything Coach has said to me recently. I look down at her, the woman I love, and speak my truth. "Football is my job. You're my reason."

Tears immediately fill her eyes, but she remains silent.

I hold her tight as I admit, "I do love football, and I want to keep playing. I've been loyal to this organization since day one. Knowing they're willing to dump me like this has been an eye-opener. You're lucky to have the team owner you do. Reagan Daulton cares about you guys as people. I've seen it with the Cougars, and I've seen it with the Anacondas. You know she paid Layton for an additional season after his injury? She wasn't contractually obligated to do so, but said it was the right thing to do after all he's given to the organization. And she split the costs of Bailey's therapy equipment with Tanner when Bailey's insurance wouldn't cover it. That's how you inspire people to play for you, not by threatening their careers."

"What if things don't go your way?" she quietly asks.

I shrug. "I'm not sure. I'll deal with it when the time comes. If this had happened ten years ago, I'd flip out. Obviously, life has dealt me some blows that make football just a little less important. I have money and security. If football goes away, then I'll move on. It's not life or death."

She nods in understanding before whispering, "I miss him."

I pull her close. "So do I. Every minute of every single day. I hope you know that. The pain never goes away, you just learn how to live with it."

She sighs. "Sometimes I swear I hear his laugh. It was so distinct."

I can't help but crack a small smile as I think of his laugh. "It's one of the things I miss the most."

She looks up, and her sad eyes meet mine. "I won't ask you right now because I don't want to fight, I've missed you so much and don't have it in me, but one day, will you tell me everything?"

I nod. "One day. I promise." And for the first time, I think I mean it.

I'M AWAKENED by a loud banging at the front door. I look down at Sulley, still fast asleep on my chest, right where I left her. She's out cold. She's probably exhausted. It's hard to sleep properly on road trips. I crash when I get home too.

The loud banging starts up again. I don't want it to wake her. Gently placing her on the bed, I get up, slide on my jeans, and head to the front door. Opening it, I see Reagan Daulton in a black pantsuit. Does this woman ever dress casually?

She takes in my presence and state of undress. "That answers one question for me." She pinches the bridge of her nose. "God dammit, is every athlete in this town fucking each other? Where's Sulley? I've been calling her all morning and she's not answering."

"Good morning to you too," I say sarcastically. "She's still asleep. She's tired. She works her ass off for you. Can I help you with something?"

"Go wake her. It's important."

I hesitate briefly, but I know she wouldn't be here if it weren't important, so I nod at her request and then head back to the bedroom.

I lean down and kiss Sulley's neck. "Baby, wake up."

With her eyes still closed, she sleepily mumbles, "Noooo. I'm tired. Let me sleep." She reaches for my arm and tugs on it. "Get back in bed with me. I sleep better with you."

While that's extremely tempting and I'm very happy at her half-awake confession, I can't get back into bed with her. "Baby, Reagan Daulton is here."

Her eyes pop open, and she bolts upright. "Here? In my house?"

"Yes."

Her brow creases with worry. "Did she see you?"

"Yes."

She plops back down on her pillow. "Ugh. Fuck my life."

She begrudgingly gets out of bed, quickly dresses in a T-shirt and shorts, and we walk back out to see Reagan in the living room waiting.

Sulley tries to plaster a fake smile on her face, and Reagan lets out a laugh. "You look truly happy to see me."

Sulley winces. "Sorry. I'm just waking up."

Reagan looks at me. "Next time you bite her, can you do it in a less visible place on her body? She has a public image to maintain."

Sulley immediately reaches for her neck. I can't help but smirk at my handiwork: a big hickey on her neck, complete with a few teeth marks.

Sulley, cloaked in red with embarrassment, asks, "Why are you here? Is something wrong?"

Reagan crosses her arms. "Well, I was going to ask about you and Vance, but that's been answered."

Sulley pinches her eyebrows together in confusion. "Why were you going to ask?"

She holds up a large manila envelope. "I received two pictures of the two of you. One is on your front stoop. I don't know when it was taken. You're in a T-shirt, and he's kissing you. Another was at a club. His...umm...hand is visibly up your skirt."

Sulley breathes, "Shit," while she sits and pulls out the contents of the envelope. Her face falls as she studies them carefully. I can't help but look at them over her shoulder. They're kind of sexy, but I'm guessing it's not the time for me to ask to keep them.

"Who sent these?" Sulley asks. "Are they online yet?"

Reagan shakes her head. "That's the weird thing. I don't think it's a reporter or paparazzi. There was a note stating they wanted a hundred grand or they're releasing it to one of the gossip sites."

I shrug. "Who cares? Let them release it. What's the big deal if we're seeing each other?"

Sulley rolls her eyes. "You know it's a big deal to me. I don't want people knowing anything about us." She holds up the photos. "And these aren't exactly sweet, innocent photos."

I think they're sweet.

Reagan looks at me. "It's always a bigger deal for the woman. You come off like a stud, and she comes off as the whore, but that's not my main concern." She turns to Sulley and points to the photo from her stoop. "This first photo is at your house. This criminal knows where you live. You're more than aware of my concerns on this issue."

Sulley nods. "Right. I didn't think about that."

"I told you not to buy this house. You shouldn't be in a walkup. You should be in a building with security and other safeguards. I only care about your safety. Like it or not, you're famous, and while there are perks to that, there are also drawbacks. Has anyone approached you in front of the house?"

Sulley shakes her head. "No."

"Have you seen anyone suspicious?"

"No."

"Have you received any deliveries out of the ordinary?"

Sulley bites her lip as she thinks. "Hmm, I don't think so. I started getting Chocolate Cosmos every few days, but they're from you, Vance, right?"

I shake my head. "Every few days? No. I only sent them before your home opener."

Sulley's face falls. "Oh my god."

Reagan gives her a compassionate look. "I'm hiring you a bodyguard. I'm sorry, I know you're against it, but it's time."

Sulley sits on a chair and slumps in her seat. I know she doesn't want this.

"Move in with me," I blurt. "You know my house is safe. It's private and gated with a state-of-the-art security system."

Sulley looks at me with a defeated look on her face. "No. I can't do that. I'm not comfortable with it."

My jaw tightens. "You're more comfortable with a stalker? I'll protect you."

Her shoulders fall as she turns to Reagan and instructs, "Hire the guard."

TWENTY-FOUR

SULLEY

I get into the back seat of the town car waiting in front of my house. "Good morning, Keith."

My bald, beefy guard nods curtly in his always-present aviator sunglasses. "Morning, Ms. O'Shea."

I roll my eyes at his refusal to call me Sulley. He says it's unprofessional and, if there's one thing Keith is, it's professional.

It took me a few weeks, but I've gotten used to having Keith around. He's a prototypical bodyguard with huge muscles and a no-nonsense demeanor. He doesn't have much personality, but he's a nice, unintrusive guy, and I don't mind having him around as much as I thought I would. The photos and the flower thing really shook me. Keith gives me peace of mind.

At my urging, Reagan ultimately paid the blackmailer. She said it was a one-time thing. The next time it happens, she's going to the police. Having this turn into a full-blown public criminal case is the last thing I want.

It's been quiet in the months since. I don't know if the blackmailer took his payday and ran or if having Keith around is making a difference. Either way, Keith does a nice job. After several weeks of arguing, I got him to agree not to wear a suit. I feel like it's more obvious when he's in a suit, but I suppose having a giant of a man follow me everywhere I go makes it obvious anyway.

Vance doesn't care for Keith. I think he feels like it emasculates him, and he was disappointed I wouldn't consider moving in with him. Vance and Reagan came to an agreement that when I stay at his house, Keith goes home.

Vance and I have remained status quo throughout my season, and now his season is underway. I know the pressure he's feeling in his career. I'm not looking to add to it. When his season comes to an end, we will have our final come-to-Jesus moment. He either shares everything, or I'm walking away for good. I'm in love with him, and I'll be devastated if he chooses not to share, but I equally know we can't ever be more if I don't have all the facts. Part of me is terrified of the answers, but the other part knows I can't go on being kept in the dark.

My mother and I had a long talk about forgiveness when she visited. She said that, for the sake of her decades-long friendship with the McCaffreys and her own sanity, she's chosen to forgive Vance. She suggested I do the same. She even went so far as to suggest that Finn would be happy if I were to be friends with Vance. I told her nothing of our relationship, only that allowing him in my life as a friend is an internal struggle for me.

My eyes meet Keith's in the rearview mirror. "Can we pick up Kennedy today? She's having car issues. I told her we'd grab her on the way to the stadium."

He nods. "Yes, ma'am."

We make our way to Kennedy's apartment, and I text her to come down. She opens the car door and slides in. "Where's Booster?" I ask.

She makes a look of disgust. "Family vacation. I hate when employees ask for vacation time."

"He's hardly an employee. You don't even pay him."

She waves her hand dismissively. "Meh. Whatever. I had to do my own laundry this week. It sucked."

I giggle. "He does your laundry too?"

"Duh. Of course. Why else would I have an intern?"

I shake my head at her ridiculousness.

She sighs. "Too bad the guys have an away game today. I'm sure your *boyfriend* wanted to be at our championship game tonight."

The Beavers have been on fire. All our hard work has paid off. We've persevered through the playoffs, finding ourselves in the championship series. We're tied at three games apiece. Tonight will be the decisive game seven.

I cross my arms in defiance. "He's not my boyfriend."

She raises an eyebrow. "How long have you been fucking?"

"Ten months."

"Have either of you fucked anyone else in that time?"

I shake my head. "No."

"Do you want to fuck anyone else?"

I blow out a defeated breath. "No."

"He's your boyfriend."

My shoulders fall. "Until he stops hiding things from me, I refuse to call him that."

"Don't blame a clown for acting like a clown. Blame yourself for going to the circus."

I hold up my hands in question. "What does that mean?"

"He's not going to give you what you want unless you stop giving him what he wants."

I shake my head again. "No. That's not how it is with us. We're not kids. We don't play games. We have a long-shared history, both the good and the bad. He loves me. I know that. He tells me all the time."

"Do you love him?"

My eyes fill with tears. "I haven't said those words to him. I won't let myself go there until he comes clean."

"When will that be?" she pushes.

"When his season is over. He knows the time is coming when this conversation has to happen, but I'll wait until his season is over."

"That could be four months away. How many times have you pushed this off?"

I'm quiet. She doesn't know about the pressure he's under, and I would certainly never betray his confidences. I refuse to add to his stress in the middle of such an important season for his career.

She shakes her head in obvious disappointment. "The answer is that you've pushed this off too many times. You need to do this once and for all. You're only falling deeper in love with him."

She's not wrong, but the simple fact is that I miss him when we're not together.

Tears fall from my eyes, and she takes my hand. "What do you want, Sulley?"

"The truth," I answer without hesitation.

"What are you afraid of?"

I sink back into my seat. "Same answer."

She reaches for a tissue and tenderly wipes the tears sitting under my eyes. "I guess we'll deal with that fucked up statement tomorrow. Today we have a championship to win." She intertwines her fingers with mine. "Are you ready to make history?"

I wipe away my tears and smile. "Sure am."

She smirks. "Isn't it fitting that we're going to do so against Diane Garma?"

I roll my eyes. "Behave. We don't need you fouling out. We can't win this without you."

She looks my gameday outfit up and down, taking in my khaki-colored overcoat on the cold fall day. "Why do you look like Inspector Gadget?"

I let out a laugh. "I guess I'm not as fashionable as you. You look like a pimp-cowgirl."

She smiles as she takes in her oversized cow-patterned fur

coat with a matching cowboy hat, a short denim skirt, and cowboy boots. "Because I'm going to ride that bitch like a rodeo queen. Being from Montana, I thought you'd like this outfit."

I lean my head back on the seat and smile. "Nothing will ever beat the Black Widow costume you wore on the first game back after your suspension. It was iconic."

After that, Kennedy's gameday outfits became a huge social media thing. She's had several endorsement offers to dress her for games and has been basking in them. I'm happy my friend is getting the much-deserved attention.

With a bemused look on her face, she says, "It *was* iconic, but not as iconic as what I made Daylen wear for his first game of the season after losing our bet."

VANCE

Coach's worried eyes meet mine. "The second half just started. The Beavers are down by nine."

I nod at him as we quickly board the airplane in Los Angeles. We just won our fifth game of the season. We're undefeated. Unfortunately, the final game in the Beavers' championship series is tonight. We were hoping they could close it out a few days ago when we were able to be at their game, but they lost game six and are now in a decisive game seven. We're on the other side of the country. Fortunately, Coach arranged for the game to be played on the televisions of our team plane. I know he's disappointed he can't be there.

He and I are sitting in the front row together, watching the second half begin. I have to double-take the stat line on the screen. Both Kennedy and Palmer already have over twenty rebounds each. That's nearly unheard of. They're the clear workhorses of this game, no doubt. Unfortunately, Sulley is having a slightly off night. She only had seven points in the first half. It's not horrible, but she usually has more than that. Fortunately, Layla and Kennedy are both doing most of the scoring to keep them in the game. They'll need Sulley to heat up if they're going to win this. To win a big game, your stars need to step up.

I notice Kennedy only has two fouls. That's good for her, considering she leads the league in games fouled out. She's otherwise been locked in since her suspension and is having a great season.

Forty-five minutes later, there's an entire plane of football players and staff on their feet, screaming at the television. Every single person is into the game. It's been a seesaw back-and-forth offensive explosion in the second half. Sulley got hot and has been popping threes nearly every time they go down the court. But Diane Garma has been matching her shot for shot. This game will be an instant classic. It's great for the league.

Coach is going out of his mind in a way I've never seen from him, even at our games. It's fun to see him so animated like this.

We're now down one with seven seconds left in the game. The team is crowded around Coach Ganjam, and she's on her knee with a clipboard, drawing up the final play. I notice her look up at Fallon Montgomery and then smile and nod.

I'm sure the play is designed around getting Sulley the ball. She's the star of the team. You always want the ball in the hands of your biggest star in the biggest moments.

The whistle blows, and Shay inbounds the ball to Sulley at halfcourt. Palmer sets a screen to get her open, but Diane Garma slides away from the screen and stays tight to Sulley.

I see Sulley nod her head at Kennedy, who does a spin move to swivel away from her defender. She heads straight toward the basket. Sulley tosses up the ball, but it's not a shot. It's intended as an alley-oop pass.

The clock shows just under two seconds. Kennedy jumps

in the air, grabs the ball, and dunks it just as time expires, hanging on the rim, swinging for added effect. Everyone on the plane explodes in excitement. We're jumping up and down. The captain has to get on the loudspeaker and ask everyone to calm themselves, fearing we'll take the plane down.

The hometown fans look like they're going crazy on television. There's a dogpile on top of Kennedy. It's amazing to watch.

I see Coach sobbing in the corner. I bro hug him. "She was fucking awesome."

He nods as he hugs me back. "She was. I'm so proud of her. She's worked her whole life for this moment."

As soon as the craziness dies down, I pull up my text chain with Sulley to congratulate her. I doubt she'll see it for a few hours, but I want it there whenever she picks up her phone.

My eyes immediately find our text string from late last night when I was alone in my hotel room.

> Me: Good luck tomorrow. You've got this. Wish I was there to see the game in person.

> Sulley: Am I lame if I admit I miss you and hate when you're out of town?

I can't help but smile like a lunatic. We've gotten close in the past few months. Given the severe invasion of privacy she suffered, she hasn't wanted to go out as much, so we spend most nights in my house or hers.

> Me: I miss you too, baby.

> Sulley: What do you miss? Be specific.

> Me: I miss the curve where your waist fans out and meets your hip. It's soft and feminine. I run my fingers over it when you sleep.

She doesn't respond for a while. Did I creep her out?

As I'm overthinking it, a photo appears of that part of her body. It's so hot.

> Me: Perfection, just like your long legs. I love when they're wrapped around my face.

Seconds later, another photo appears. I can't see her face, but it's her from the waist down in her small sleep shorts. Her long, shapely legs take up the whole screen. God, I love those legs.

With the swelling of my cock, I slide my hand into my boxer briefs and give myself a few long tugs.

> Me: I'm touching myself while I look at your perfect body.

Sulley: With Daylen in the room? Weird.

> Me: You're a riot. I wouldn't cuddle with him, so now he's next door, undoubtedly cuddling with Champ. I'm all alone and free to jerk off to your gorgeous photos.

Sulley: Show me.

I've never in my life sent a dick pic to a woman, but I couldn't possibly pull my boxer briefs down any faster. Snapping a pic of my hardened, oozing cock, I send it to her.

Sulley: You are carved from the Gods, QB1.
Now I'm touching myself too.

> Me: Show me.

I get a photo of her hand down her shorts, but I can't see anything else.

> Me: Sullivan, show me that pretty pink pussy of yours. I want to see it glistening, weeping for me. I want to see your juices on your fingers. After you send the photo, I want you to stick your fingers in your mouth and tell me what you taste like.

I know her body. Right now, her nipples have hardened, and her cheeks are flushed. My dirty words always do it to her.

It takes a hot minute, but I get the photo I wanted. Her legs are spread wide and her fingers hover above her pussy, covered in the evidence of her arousal. It's dirty, sexy, erotic, and perfect. I can almost taste it in my mouth.

My strokes on my cock become ferocious as I stare at the image before me. I grab the lotion next to me to help myself along.

> Me: Tell me what it tastes like.

> Sulley: Like she misses you.

> Me: What do you miss?

> Sulley: The python making me lose my mind.

> Me: Tomorrow, when we celebrate, I'll fuck you into a coma. For now, baby, I need you to come for me. Yell my name so loud I can hear it across the country.

> Sulley: Come with me.

Me: I am. My hand doesn't feel as good as your tight, slick pussy, but I'm using your lotion so I can smell you. That's right, I took a bottle from your bathroom so I can smell your coconut scent when I'm not with you. I use it to stroke my cock all the time. I want your smell around me.

She doesn't respond for a minute or two. I assume that means she's enjoying herself.

A text finally arrives.

Sulley: I came.

I can't help but smile. That was quick.

Me: Show me your face.

I receive a picture of her orgasm-flushed face. Her red lips are parted and swollen. Her eyes are closed, and there's a satisfied smile on her face. It's my favorite image in the world, and it sends me right over the edge as I shoot hot ropes of come all over my stomach.

Me: Fuck, that did it for me. I came too.

Sulley: Show me.

And I do.

I LOOK at my phone when we land. It's after three in the morning. I'm sure the girls were out late celebrating but are home now. I know it's late, but I just want my girl. I need her.

I get in my truck and head straight to Sulley's house. I

notice the night security guard in his car out front, but I only wave from afar because I'm in a rush to see her. Keith is with her during the daytime. While it drives me nuts that she chose to have him over living with me, I don't mind someone watching over her, and Keith keeps things very professional.

Using my key to get in, I walk straight to the bedroom door. She's fast asleep in a McCaffrey jersey. It's a style that we used to wear during my first two years in the league. She must have held onto that jersey for the past ten years. It makes me happy to know that even when she hated me, she didn't throw it away.

I lean on the doorframe and stare at her soft features. I love her so much it hurts. Why can't things be different? Why can't they be easy? Will I ever stop paying for past decisions and be able to move forward as a happy man with a normal life?

She stirs and her eyes peel open before she croaks out, "Hey, handsome."

"Hey, beautiful. I missed you."

She gives me a sleepy smile. "You saw me three days ago."

"Three days too long."

"You talked me into sending pictures of me orgasming last night." She throws her arms over her eyes. "I still can't believe I did that."

"Best photos I've ever received in my life, but I prefer to catch the live show."

A sleepy smile finds her face.

"Congratulations," I offer. "What a great game."

"You saw it?"

"Of course. We almost took down the plane when Kennedy made that shot at the end."

Her smile widens. "It was her first dunk ever. Wasn't it awesome?"

The happiness she has for Kennedy being the hero is radiating from her.

"It was."

"I saw your drive to win your game," she says. "You were amazing. That wasn't the play called, was it?"

I chuckle at her knowledge of our plays. "Nope, Daylen was covered. Champ was my second look. He broke a few tackles and muscled his way into the endzone."

"It was a good win." She stretches as she yawns. "I'm tired. Come to bed. I missed your body on mine."

"I'm sorry I woke you, but I need to be inside you. Is that okay?"

She pulls away the blankets and spreads her bare legs, revealing that she's not wearing any panties. "I thought I might see you tonight. You're wearing far too many clothes, QB1."

At lightning speed, I remove all of them, happily leaving them in a pile on the floor as I slip into her bed, right between her legs where I belong.

I momentarily squeeze my eyes shut as I admit, "I dream of you wearing my jersey like you are right now. You have on that red lipstick and those fuck-me boots you wear sometimes. In my fantasy you're on your knees, begging for my cock down your throat." I thrust my hips against her so she can feel how hard she makes me. "As much as I want to fuck you in this jersey, I need you naked. I want to feel your soft skin."

She wordlessly raises her arms, and I lift my jersey off her, leaving her naked and vulnerable. I lay there and stare at her. She stares right back at me. Every decision I've ever made in my life starts running through my head as I silently pray she can love me back in spite of them.

She places her hand on my chest and whispers, "What's wrong? I can feel your heart beating so fast."

"It tends to do that when you're around. It belongs to you."

Her head tilts to the side as she cups my cheek, "Vance, we—"

I don't want her to tell me we're not like that. I just can't hear it right now, so I silence her by moving my lips to hers, loving the sense of calm I feel when we connect, especially after being apart for a few days. I mumble into them, "Just let me love you."

I slowly enter her, and her body shakes the entire time as she arches her back and lets out a moan. I will never tire of her body's reaction to welcoming mine.

Once the tremors subside, she threads her fingers through my hair and whispers, "Are you okay?"

"I am now."

TWENTY-FIVE

SULLEY

I'm awakened by my phone ringing. I look at my clock. It's after eleven. We slept in. I suppose that's not surprising given the hour and his mood when he arrived. It was like he couldn't get enough of me. His thirst was never fully quenched, and we went at it over and over again. There wasn't an inch of my body that he didn't worship.

Love oozed from every single pore in his body. I could physically feel it. The lines are getting so damn blurry I'm not sure I can see them anymore. I'm carrying so much guilt for letting things get this far. Am I officially past the point of no return?

I know the answer. If I lost him, I'd be shattered. Broken into a million little pieces, never to be made whole again. Something has to give, and I'm praying it's not my heart.

Grabbing my phone, I see that it's my mother. I'm hesitant to answer it with Vance beside me, but something is telling me that I should. I spoke with her last night after the big win. She wouldn't call again this morning unless it was important.

I accept the call and quietly answer, "Hi, Momma. Is everything okay?"

"No, Sulley, it's not." She sounds hysterical and frantic. "Do you know where Vance is? Jane has been trying to get in touch with him all morning. He's not answering his phone."

"I'm…umm…I'm not sure. What's wrong?"

"Francesca has been in a terrible accident. She was airlifted to Helena Memorial. Can you help us get in touch with him? It's urgent."

I swallow at what I know needs to be done. "Of course. He's…he's right here. I'll wake him."

She's silent, but I can't worry about that right now.

I shake his arm. "Vance, wake up."

His eyes blink open, and he smiles. In his crackly morning voice, he says, "Hey, sexy. You up for another round?"

I cover his mouth before this gets any worse. "My mother is on the phone." His eyes widen. "Stay calm. Francesca has been injured. Your mother has been trying to get in touch with you. You should call her right away."

He bolts his head up and reaches for his phone. After pressing the screen a few times, the phone is to his ear. "Mom, what happened?"

He stands, walks into my bathroom, and closes the door behind him. I can no longer hear what he's saying. He doesn't want me to.

"Momma, he's talking to Jane now."

"Thank god." She's quiet for a moment. "Sulley, are you two…together?"

"No," I immediately respond, but then it sort of feels like a lie. "Well…I'm not sure," I correct. "We spend time together. A little more than I let on. He wants more, but I don't know that I can ever give it to him, considering everything that's happened."

I hear Vance screaming, "Listen, you selfish bitch. I'm coming."

What the hell? He would *never* talk to his mother like that.

He yells, "No, Maddie. Too bad. I told you this would happen. How could you be so irresponsible?"

Oh, Maddie. That makes more sense. He sounds mad. *Really* mad.

My mother starts talking, but I cut her off. "Momma, let me run. I need to help him. I'll call you later."

"Oh, okay. Pray for Francesca."

"I will."

Vance walks out of the bathroom looking stressed.

"What's happening?" I ask.

He aggressively pulls on his boxer briefs like he's angry with them. "I told that dumb bitch not to let her ride the ATV, but she wouldn't listen. She *never* fucking listens." Fear fills his eyes. "It flipped, and her abdomen was impaled by the brake. She's about to head into surgery. I need to get there."

I slip out of bed. "Of course. I'll go with you." I'm not sure why, but I feel the need to be there for him.

His eyes meet mine. "It's going to get ugly, Sulley. Maddie and I don't exactly see eye to eye…on anything."

I walk over to him and wrap my arms around his body. "Well then, you'll need someone in your corner. Tell me what I can do to help."

He relaxes his body into mine as he returns my embrace. "Thanks. Flights. I'm not sure how to handle that. I need to get there. Today. As soon as possible. Maybe we should check flights from Newark or Baltimore."

It's well known there's only one flight from Philadelphia to Helena each day, and it's in the morning, meaning we missed it. Newark, New Jersey, and Baltimore, Maryland, are both less than two hours away. Each has an airport, but I have a different idea.

Two hours later, we're taking off. I called Reagan about using her private jet, and she agreed without hesitation.

I've never seen Vance so stressed, and he's always stressed. Maddie stopped taking his calls, so he doesn't have any updates on the surgery. He spoke with his parents, and they agreed to head to the hospital.

His fingers are intertwined with mine. His pained face turns to me. "I don't know what's going to happen or what's going to be said. I just want to warn you. Things are…bad between Maddie and me. And if something happens to Francesca…" His voice trails off as emotions overcome him.

"She's going to be fine," I try to reassure him. After a few long beats, I can't help but ask, "How bad?"

His tear-filled eyes meet mine. "We both know the kind of woman Maddie is. She hasn't changed since we were kids. She was self-centered then, and she's self-centered now. She'll make this about her when the only thing that matters is Francesca."

"That's her daughter in surgery. She must be reeling."

He briefly closes his eyes. "Whatever is said today, just know I love you."

"What's going to be said?"

He exhales a long breath and leans his head back on the chair. "Who knows what will come out of her mouth?"

FOUR HOURS LATER, we land in Helena. I see my parents there waiting at the landing strip.

Vance blows out a breath, almost in relief. "I'm so glad they're here. I didn't even think about how we were getting to the hospital."

We approach their car, where he opens the door for me and pokes his head inside. "Thank you for coming, Frank. I really appreciate it."

Dad nods. "Your parents didn't want to leave the hospital. We offered. She's still in surgery. We don't know anything yet."

We ride the short distance to the hospital in relative silence. I don't think my parents have been around Vance in over six years. It's awkward, but I sense no tension from them. Even though my mother said she had forgiven him, I thought they would still carry anger toward him, but they seem more concerned about Francesca than being in the car with the man who betrayed my brother.

I don't know if my mother said anything to my father about Vance being in my bed this morning. I doubt it, but I can't look her in the eyes just yet.

Less than fifteen minutes later, the four of us run into the hospital. Vance goes directly to the front desk and spits out, "Francesa McCaffrey. Where can I find her?"

The woman looks at her computer, types away, and then glances back up at him. "There's no one here by that name."

His jaw tightens. "Huddle. Francesca Huddle."

She types again and looks up. "Yes, I see her. And you are?"

"Her father."

The woman pinches her eyebrows together. "Are you Curtis Huddle?"

"No, I'm Vance McCaffrey."

She smiles innocently. "Oh, like the quarterback." Her eyes suddenly widen in realization. "Oh. Well…I'm sorry, but Curtis Huddle is listed as her father. We can't give out any information unless you're a family member."

"Check her fucking birth certificate," Vance yells.

She shakes her head. "I don't have access to that. I'm afraid I can't give you any information. I'm sorry, sir."

Vance is about to explode in anger. I grab his arm and smile at the unhelpful woman. "Where's the surgical waiting room? Surely you can tell us that."

She nods. "Third floor."

"Thank you."

The four of us make our way to the third floor. As soon as we exit the elevator, I see Maddie and Curtis sitting at one end of the waiting area. She's in tears. I have a flood of emotions upon seeing her. It's been a long time since I've laid eyes on Maddie Wells. Her parents are also with her. I haven't seen them since Finn's funeral. This feels like a time warp. An unwelcome one.

On the complete opposite side of the waiting room are the

McCaffreys. They stand as we approach. Vance's mother runs to hug him. "I'm so glad you're here."

He nods before pulling back and asking, "Do we know anything yet?"

She shakes her head. "No. The nurse just came out and said the doctor was finishing the surgery and would be out in a few minutes to update us. Your timing is perfect."

We sit there waiting. Vance and Maddie don't exchange so much as a glance, let alone any words. It's so weird. I don't know what to make of it. Their daughter is in surgery. Surely they can come together for Francesca's sake.

And Maddie's parents and the McCaffreys don't exchange any type of communication, acting like strangers. They're the grandparents of this innocent little girl. Haven't they found common ground at birthday parties and other life events? What is happening?

Eventually, the doctor walks out in full surgical scrubs. She removes her mask with a somber look on her face. Speaking only to Maddie, she says, "It was touch and go for a bit. The brake punctured her kidney. We tried everything, but it couldn't be saved. She lost a kidney."

Maddie lets out an audible sob while Curtis holds her as tears of his own trickle down his cheeks.

The doctor continues, "She can live a totally normal life with one kidney. The problem is that she's lost a lot of blood and needs a transfusion. We used every bit that we have on hand, but she still needs more. Maddie, we have your blood type on record. You're not a match. Curtis, you must be. We'll need your blood. Let's get you hooked up. Time is of the essence."

Without thinking, and in light of the silence, I blurt out, "Curtis isn't her biological father."

The doctor's eyebrows pinch in confusion, and she looks to Maddie for confirmation. Maddie nods. "She's right. He's not."

The doctor asks, "Ooookay. Who's her biological father?"

It's silent again. Now it's Jane McCaffrey's turn to let out a sob. I'm so confused. Why isn't everyone pointing at Vance?

In the wake of not one single person answering, I do. Nodding my head toward Vance, I say, "He is."

Vance's shoulders fall. In a low, sad voice, he admits, "I'm not. I've never wished more that I was than in this moment, but I'm not." He turns to my family and whispers, "I'm so sorry."

I exchange glances with my mother. She looks as flabbergasted as I feel. The McCaffreys don't appear surprised in the least. They knew.

The doctor looks around in confusion. "Who is the biological father?"

For a brief moment, I wonder if it's Finn. I can see in my parents' hopeful faces that they do too. I know it's not logical, the timeline doesn't work, but I can't help that I wish for it. If we could have one piece of him left in this universe, we'd happily take it.

Maddie crosses her arms. With a fair amount of shame in her voice, she says, "I don't know his name. I never did. He was a stranger. He doesn't even know about Francesa. I wasn't able to track him down."

I audibly gasp. My mother faints. Dad and I catch her just before she hits the ground. It feels like mayhem ensues. There are a million voices talking and shouting, but I can't hear any of them. I feel like I'm floating above this bizarre scene, questioning everything I've thought to be true for the past six years.

At some point, the doctor lets out a loud whistle, and everyone goes silent. "Folks, I appreciate that emotions are high, but we have a little girl with O-positive blood in desperate need of a transfusion to survive. Does anyone here have either O-positive or O-negative blood? She can take either. We've completely drained our supply of both. She needs it to survive. Right away."

My father raises his hand. "I have O-negative. Take mine."

The doctor nods and motions for my father to follow her. He

kisses my cheek before he goes and instructs, "Look after your mother."

I'm wordless. Unable to answer. Unable to move a single part of my body. I sit on the chair with my mother's head in my lap as she's sprawled across four chairs. She's stirring a little, but I don't know if she's awake yet. I can't seem to comprehend anything. I think I'm in shock.

Vance answers for me. "I'll take care of them, Frank. Go. They'll be fine. Thank you for doing this."

I hear Vance talking to the hospital staff about finding some juice for my mother. He returns a few minutes later with juice in hand.

Vance and a hospital worker help my mother sit up. I guess she's awake. Jane assists her as she manages to drink most of the bottle of orange juice and comes back to life. I still can't seem to move an inch or utter a word.

Vance sits in the chair next to mine and then pulls me to sit across his lap. He takes my face in his hands. "Sulley, are you okay? You look pale."

I swear I try to talk, but no words come out of my mouth. He presses his forehead to mine. "You're scaring me." He softly kisses my lips. "Come back to me, baby."

It must be the word *baby* that snaps me out of my stupor. I say the only things that come to mind "Why? Why did you lie? I don't understand. All this time. We thought...we were wrong." My voice escalates. "Why, Vance? Why?" I'm getting hysterical.

His thumbs gently rub over my face, wiping away tears I didn't realize had fallen. "I'll tell you everything, I promise. Can we please just get through this? Once I know Francesca will be okay, we'll sit down and talk. All of us."

I want to yell and thrash. Haven't I waited long enough for the truth? But I don't. There's still a little girl whose life is on the line, and that's more important than my need for answers.

I nod, still in so much shock over what's happened.

He pulls my head to the crook of his neck and caresses me over and over while kissing my head.

I don't know how long we sit there. I just know that the hand of his arm around me moves up and down my hip and thigh, and his other hand continues to caress my head and face while his lips pepper them with kisses. It's not friendly. It's intimate, and he doesn't seem to care that we have an audience in the room.

I eventually turn my head, realizing I need to check on my mother, but she and Jane are sitting there watching my interaction with Vance with huge, hopeful smiles on their faces.

After about thirty more minutes, my father reemerges with a bandage on his arm and hands full of crackers and a bottle of orange juice.

He, too, takes in my proximity to Vance and his hands moving uninhibited all over my body. Vance is completely unaware that we're garnering attention, lost in another universe right now. It outwardly appears as though he's providing me comfort when, in reality, I think he needs to hold me for his own benefit, so I let it happen. I'll answer the inevitable bevy of questions I'll be getting later.

The doctor walks back through the doors a little while later to say that Francesca's body is accepting the blood, and it's looking good. How ironic that Francesca now has O'Shea blood flowing through her body.

The doctor offers for Maddie and Curtis to see Francesca in the recovery room.

Maddie takes a deep breath before walking over toward our group. She first looks at my father. "Thank you, Frank. I'll never be able to repay the kindness you've shown my daughter."

My father nods. "She's an innocent little girl. Any decent person would have done the same."

Maddie turns her attention to Vance. "Do you want to come back with us?"

"I do," he answers.

Maddie looks like she's been through the ringer. I'm sure she has. Her pretty face is marred by hours of crying. Her eyes are red, and there are bags under them. She's suffering. I can see it. I'm sure Vance can too.

When he stands, he looks like he wants to say more but fortunately thinks better of it. At the end of the day, she's a mother scared shitless for her daughter.

Recognizing his demeanor, she holds up her hands. "I know. You don't need to say it. You were right. She never should have been on that thing. It certainly won't happen again."

I'm not sure why it surprises me that they would talk about everyday things like that, but it does. I often have a hard time imagining Vance and Maddie interacting, mostly because he never cared for her when she was with Finn. I'm not sure I ever once saw him have a conversation with her.

When he disappears with Curtis and Maddie, I'm immediately accosted by Jane and my mother. Neither can contain her grin.

I roll my eyes. "Will you two gossips cut it out. You both practically have hearts in your eyes."

They giggle before my mother happily announces to both of our parents that she woke me up this morning with her call and Vance was with me. The insinuation is more than clear. My poor father is covering his ears while Michael McCaffrey chuckles.

I sigh. "Yes, we've been spending time together. It's casual. Stop making it more than it is."

My mother grins. "For how long?"

I bite my lip. It really has been a long time.

"Since the snowstorm," Michael announces.

I cross my arms and scowl at him. "Thanks, Michael."

He smirks. "You're welcome, sweetie."

Jane grabs my mother's hand. "We're going to share grandbabies, and they're going to be gorgeous."

My mother shrieks in glee.

I pinch the bridge of my nose. For fuck's sake. Now they've got us having babies.

TWENTY-SIX

VANCE

I look at Francesca's peacefully sleeping face. It's been a long time since I've seen her in person. Maddie has completely blocked my access and there wasn't a damn thing I could do about it. If I took her to court, all Maddie had to do was ask for a paternity test, which she's threatened to do hundreds of times when I tried to push for visitation or offer any input into her life decisions. Daylen thinks I should leverage my child support payments to get what I want, but I would never do that to Francesca.

Tears fill my eyes as I take in her soft features. I hate that she's suffered, and I'm thankful she's asleep and not currently feeling pain. I'm sure she's got a long road to recovery ahead of her.

As I sit, I can see the color coming back into her face. It's amazing how quickly and visibly the transfusion is working.

"We're keeping her sedated a little longer. She'll be asleep through the night," the doctor interrupts us from behind. "We want her to get a good night's sleep so her body can heal. You all should head out and get some rest yourselves."

Maddie shakes her head. "I'm not leaving her. I'll sleep in the chair." She points to the extremely small, uncomfortable-looking chair in the corner. "Curtis, please get home to the kids. Vance, you can come back in the morning if you want."

I want to stay too. I want to sleep in the tiny, uncomfortable chair and watch over her. I want to say a million things to Maddie, like that she's a fucking idiot for allowing a five-year-old to drive a motorized vehicle. But I don't. I'm sure it's been a traumatic day for her. We'll talk tomorrow.

I kiss Francesca's forehead and then chat with the doctor in the hallway about her recovery needs and tell him to give her the best of the best and bill me for it. She seems confused, likely due to the revelation that I'm not her father, but acquiesces nonetheless.

My parents invite everyone over to their house so we can all chat about what's happened. Apparently, MeeMaw is at the house cooking her famous chili for everyone, anticipating a hungry crew and food being her love language.

I'm finally ready to unburden myself by telling Sulley and her parents the whole story. The truth.

Nearly an hour later, we somberly and silently walk into my parents' house to the loud sounds of a woman moaning in ecstasy. My mom runs toward the living room and yells out, "Mother, turn off the television. Right now!"

MeeMaw doesn't hear her, and before Mom has the chance to turn it off, we all see what MeeMaw is watching. Porn. Not just regular, run-of-the-mill porn. Double penetration porn. Two men and one woman. The woman is happily taking it in both the front and back entrances. Sulley spits in laughter. My father and Frank share bemused looks. Mom is mortified.

She scrambles for the remote control, fumbling with it. Somehow, she manages to turn up the volume, making the moans that much louder. Despite the situation, I can't help but smile. Leave it to MeeMaw to add some levity to a tough day.

Mom finally finds the right button and powers it off.

MeeMaw turns to her with a scowl. "We were just getting to the good part."

I bite back my smile. "I think they were already at the good part, MeeMaw."

She shrugs. "The guy in the rear door is my favorite actor. I watch him all the time. I'm a member of his fan club on Facebook. You should see what he can do with his tongue. He looks just like your grandfather did at that age. Not as well hung, but otherwise very similar." She has a wistful look on her face. "Boy, did he love it when I'd give him a no-denture adventure."

"Mother!" my mom shouts. She pinches the bridge of her nose while she grits out, "We need to have a serious conversation with the O'Sheas. I think it's your nap time. Why don't you head to your room? I can smell the chili cooking. I'll keep stirring it and wake you when the timer goes off."

MeeMaw takes in the situation, realizing something serious is going on. She's no dummy. I doubt my parents told her exactly what was happening, they don't like to upset her, but she's still sharp as a tack. She looks at me and winks. "Sullivan is so beautiful, isn't she, Fancy Vancy?"

I nod. "The most beautiful woman in the world. Next to you, MeeMaw."

She smiles and winks again as she makes her way to her bedroom.

My mother invites everyone to sit in the living room, which they do. All eyes are immediately on me, undoubtedly anxiously awaiting an explanation.

I look at my parents, and they both give me a nod of encouragement. They may not visit often enough, and they may not agree with all my decisions, but never for one minute have I ever felt anything other than wholehearted support from them.

I blow out a long breath before beginning. "Before we start,

Nancy and Frank, I need you to know that I'm in love with your daughter. I see no reason to pretend otherwise anymore."

Nancy and my mother squeal in delight. Sulley grits her teeth. "You're skating on thin ice with me, McCaffrey. I want what I've been wanting for a long time. The truth. Why have you been lying to everyone for over six years? I don't understand. Start talking. Now."

I shake my head. "I haven't lied to *everyone*. My parents knew." I turn to the O'Sheas. "Frank and Nancy, please don't be upset with them. They've been respecting my wishes in keeping this secret. They love you two, and your friendship means everything to them."

Nancy takes my mother's hand in hers and kisses it. I know they'll be fine. It's Sulley I'm worried about.

Sulley's face falls. "Your parents were treated so poorly by the people in this town. How could you let that happen to them? They didn't deserve it."

Dad waves his hand dismissively. "I don't care what people think of me. My son did an honorable thing, and I support him completely."

"Thanks, Dad." I lick my lips nervously before finally saying the words out loud, words that have been on the tip of my tongue to tell her so many times this year. "I have never— nor would I ever in a million years—touched Maddie Wells. To my dying day, I will *never* understand what Finn saw in her." I open my mouth but stop myself from elaborating further on my deep disdain for Maddie. "I don't need to stand here and bash her. I'm pretty sure no one here has any amount of love for her."

There's a collective mumbling about that being the truth.

I continue, "Finn and I had a lot of conversations about his mortality. He was steadfast that if something happened to him, I was to take care of Sulley and Maddie. It consumed him. He mentioned it to me no less than a hundred times during the eight years of his service. In every single conversation we had, he drove that point home. That's what I've been doing. Honoring his final wishes to take care of his girls."

Sulley shakes her head. "You paying for Maddie and Francesca's entire life feels extreme, Vance. I'm sure if he knew she cheated on him, that she was pregnant with another man's—"

"He knew," I interrupt.

Three sets of shocked O'Shea blue eyes stare at me as all of them immediately fill with tears. Sulley whispers, "He knew?"

I nod. "He knew."

SIX AND A HALF YEARS AGO

Finn and I sit in my truck as I drive him back to the airport. He's been acting strange today. Distracted. Something happened between him and Maddie last night. He went to see her right after Sulley's basketball game. Maybe they finally broke up. I hope so. He'd be better off without her. Word around town is that she's been partying hard. I have no doubt she's cheating on him. Trashy women like her always do.

When I stopped by to pick her up on the way to the airport, it was clear her mother had no idea where she was. Knowing she wasn't at work, I was able to read between the lines.

I turn to him. "I hate that your visit was so short, but at least you'll be home for good in a month."

His jaw tightens. "I accepted the extra six-month deployment this morning. I need the money."

"What?" I scream. "No. Absolutely not. Come home. You said you had saved enough for college. That was the deal. You were in the military to make enough money for college. You have it. Time to get out while you're still intact."

He takes a few deep breaths before blurting out, "Maddie's pregnant."

I think all the blood drains from my body. No, no, no. Now he's stuck with that piece of shit.

It takes a few seconds before it registers. He hasn't been home in nearly two years. The baby isn't his.

"Whose is it?" I ask.

"Mine."

I scoff. "I didn't ace high school biology like you, but I know enough to know that baby isn't yours."

He swallows hard. "She doesn't know who the father is. She was smashed. It was a one-night stand. She regretted it—"

"Oh, come on, man. Bull fucking shit. This is your chance to break free from her. She's never been good enough for you. Now you can be rid of the trashy bitch."

I don't see his fist coming before it's too late. It connects with my jaw so fucking hard I wonder if it's dislocated.

I slam on my brakes and pull over before I crash the car. My jaw is throbbing. I look at him. "What the fuck, man?"

"Don't you ever call her that. She's the love of my life. My future wife. The mother of my children."

I manipulate my jaw. It hurts like hell. "Why? She fucked another man. She's having his baby. Time to cut ties."

He shakes his head. "You don't get it. You've never loved a woman before. She made a mistake. People make mistakes. I'm sure my being gone all this time has been hard on her. I'm adding the extra six months to help pay for the baby's needs. I've thought long and hard about it. I love Maddie, and the baby is an extension of her. This child will be raised as mine. We're getting married as soon as I get back."

I stare at him in disbelief. "You don't have to do this."

"It's the right thing to do."

"Right for her. Not right for you. Please come home. Move on from her. Go to college. Get your degree. Do what you were meant to do in this world."

He exhales a long breath. "It's not your life, Vance. And," he hesitates briefly, "I think college is now off the table for me. It was one thing when it was just going to be Maddie and me, but now there will be a baby. I need to work."

I start to reply, but he holds up his hands. "Don't you dare fucking offer to pay. It's insulting." He holds up two fingers, the same two fingers I've come to hate. "Two things, nineteen, I only ask two things of you." He pauses briefly and then slowly adds a third. "Make it three now. Promise me, Vance, if I don't make it back, you make sure the three of them are always taken care of. Whatever it takes. Whatever your feelings are for Maddie, you take care of business for me. Man to man, this is all I need from you."

I stare at him. He's out of his mind.

I have no words for him as I turn my eyes back to the road and begin driving again so he doesn't miss his flight. My head is pounding from the force of the punch. The little shit hits hard.

Eventually, I mumble, "You're a fucking idiot."

He stares out the passenger window, looking a million miles away. "Maybe."

"Definitely."

He's leaving. I can't let him go with us fighting, so I try to lighten the mood. "I barely felt that punch. You hit like a girl."

The corners of his mouth turn up as he reaches over and flicks the back of my hair. "At least I don't look like one."

I chuckle as we try to engage in normal chitchat for the rest of the ride despite the black cloud hanging over us.

I hug him hard at the airport. "See you in seven months."

He nods as he hugs me just as hard. "Take care of them, Vance. Please."

PRESENT

"Those are the last words he ever said to me in person. It was as if he knew what was coming. He was gone three months later. I did a lot of soul searching in the months after his death. I naively hoped the baby would come late, and you wouldn't know it wasn't his. You all were so excited about having a piece of him left. I didn't want to take it away from you. But when the baby came, you realized the truth of the situation. It was only a matter of time before the whole town knew the baby wasn't Finn's. Maddie would be vilified. Exiled. Cheating on a war hero? It doesn't get much worse. He wouldn't have wanted that. Whether I agreed with him or not, she was the love of his life. He was fiercely protective of her."

A tearful Sulley finishes my thought. "So you made yourself the villain in this story. All for him."

I nod. "Taking care of her and that baby was his dying wish. How could I not?"

She and Nancy are sobbing. So is my mother, even though she already knew the story. Frank has tears streaming down his face too. He stands and holds out his hand to me. When I take it, he steels his face and says, "You, Vance McCaffrey, are the most honorable man I know. Thank you for being such a loyal friend to my son. I'm sorry for the things I said to you when everything went down all those years ago." He turns to my parents. "I'm sorry for allowing people to treat you the way they did that first year. I should have done more. I should have stepped in earlier. I'm ashamed of my actions."

My father shakes his head. "You were a grieving father, Frank. I never once faulted you for any of it."

Frank pinches his lips together, still overcome with emotion.

I stare at Sulley. I feel like the weight of the world has been lifted from my shoulders. Like everything that was standing in our way is gone. This barrier between us no longer exists. Can she feel it too?

I watch for her reaction. Eventually, she stands. Unable to look me in the eyes, she croaks out, "I'm sorry, I need to leave," before she practically sprints out the front door.

Nancy stands to go after her, but I hold up my hand. "I've got this."

TWENTY-SEVEN

SULLEY

I'm finding it hard to breathe. My head starts spinning after everything I've heard today. I stand and mutter, "I'm sorry, I need to leave."

Turning around, I run out the front door, gulping down the fresh air as soon as I do. I place my hands on my knees. The world feels off its axis right now. Up is down. Left is right. Nothing makes sense. Everything is blurry.

Suddenly, Vance's hand is on my back. "Are you okay?"

I shake my head. "No, I'm not. Take me somewhere. Anywhere but here."

He helps me into his old truck, and we take off. All I can think of is that if Maddie hadn't gotten knocked up by a stranger, my brother wouldn't have extended his tour, and he would still be alive. I've never hated her more than I do right now.

I'm so consumed with my hatred for her that it feels like only a few seconds later that we're pulling into my family's driveway.

After helping me out of the car, he takes my hand and pulls me toward the backyard. I'm on autopilot, trusting him to guide my body. Before I know it, we're climbing the ladder into my treehouse.

A sense of calm washes over me as I ascend into it. I take in the familiar scent. It's the fall trees, the aged wood of the treehouse, and the mustiness of the blankets that have been out here a little too long. It's home.

We sit, positioned just as we were the night of Finn's funeral. Facing each other with bent knees and toes touching.

"What's going through your mind, Gully Sulley?"

I take a few long, deep breaths. "I don't think I appreciated the depths you were willing to go to in order to honor Finn's last wishes." I look him in the eyes. "Is that what we are, Vance? Another obligation you feel to my brother?"

He reaches for my hand just like he did that night, intertwining his fingers through mine. It was the first intimate touch we ever shared, and I never forgot it.

"You know we're so much more than that." He pauses briefly as a small smile finds his face. "I remember reaching for your hand the last time we were in here. So many years ago. It's hard to believe that much time has passed. It was the moment I realized there was something more between us. It freaked me out a little. I didn't want to feel that way about you. I kind of felt like a perv."

I sigh. "Maybe we're just old friends who went through the same horrible event, clinging to each other as a safety net. A comfort."

He shakes his head. "We're so much more than childhood friends with a shared trauma. We both know that."

Tears freefall from my eyes. "Why didn't you tell me?"

He shrugs. "For some reason, it felt like a betrayal. I wanted to. I planned to. Eventually."

I whisper-cry, "I can't believe he knew. Is this why you didn't push for custody and take her to court?"

He nods. "Yes. All she ever had to do was demand a paternity test, and then I'd be erased from Francesca's life. I don't know who her biological father is. Trust me, I searched, but Finn was prepared to raise her as his own, so I was too. Maddie takes my checks and shuts me out. She's got me by the balls."

I breathe heavily, gasping for air. "I don't want that for you. It's not right. She needs to give you something." I squeeze my eyes shut. "God, I hate her so much right now," I cry. "He'd be alive if it wasn't for her."

He nods as pain stretches over his face. "I know. It's hard not to hate her. I try not to because she's Francesca's mother, but I fail every single day. I get physically sick at the sight of her and the sound of her voice. I'm sorry you have to relive this nightmare. I've been trying my best to avoid that for you."

Tears stream down my cheeks like a faucet. "You're not the one who should be sorry. If it's permission you're seeking to cut her off, or at least threaten it, you certainly have it from me."

He shakes his head. "I won't do that. Ever. It would only hurt Francesca. You think Finn would want that?"

Vance is such a good man. I've spent all these years thinking just the opposite. This is such a mindfuck.

Tears begin spilling from his eyes, and his shoulders shake. I can't help but move closer so I can hold him.

I've been so caught up in my own feelings over what's happened today that I haven't taken the time to consider his. How this lie has negatively impacted his entire life.

He struggles with his words as he whisper-croaks, "I should have paid for everything. If I did, he'd still be here. He'd be alive today."

And then he starts sobbing. Sobbing in a way I've never seen from him, not even that day at the construction site.

I hold him close to me, pulling his head to my chest. "Let it all out."

I give him the time he needs to cry for everything that has gone on and how it's impacted him. I think it's seven years of emotions finally pouring out of him. He needs this.

Once he begins to calm down, he looks up at me with embarrassment written all over his face. "I'm sorry. I don't know where that came from."

"It came from years and years of carrying this burden, a burden that wasn't really yours to bear. I know my brother. He wouldn't have wanted you to suffer like you have. And I know for a fact he wouldn't have accepted a dime from you. Ever."

"I wish I had tried harder." He takes a few deep, calming breaths, "Fuck, it feels good to get all this off my chest. I'm not sure I realized how much I needed to."

I lean over and softly kiss his lips. "I'm glad you did." I continue to hold him, running my hands up and down his body in a soothing manner. "What now? With Maddie."

He sighs. "I'm not sure. She's so difficult. I need to do what's best for Francesca. But I have no idea what that is. The team gave me emergency family leave. I'm going to stay for another day or two. We can't remain in this antagonistic state. I want to figure something out with her. I've been trying for a long time, but Maddie isn't easy. It's always been her way or the highway."

I squeeze his hand. "I understand that you need this time with them. I'm going to head back to Philly. I need to get out of here. Clear my head. Plus, I have a few team obligations I can't get out of."

His eyes study my face. "What about us? Where are we?"

I lick my lips nervously. "Can you give me a minute to take this all in? I spent more than six years hating you, and the past ten months hating myself for feeling the way I do about you. Suddenly, in the blink of an eye, history has been rewritten. I need time to process it all."

His shoulders fall. He's disappointed, but my brain is too foggy to make any decisions about my future right now.

I rest my head on his shoulder. "Can I ask you something?"

"Always."

"Why were none of you surprised to see MeeMaw watching porn? Hardcore porn."

I can feel him shaking again, but in laughter this time. "She has a bit of an…addiction. It's an expensive addiction."

"Expensive? There's so much free porn out there."

He sighs. "I've tried to explain that to her, but she insists there are advantages to paid porn."

I giggle. "You've had porn conversations with your grandmother."

He lets out a laugh. "Yep. My poor mother. She deals with it all the time."

VANCE

Sulley left. I have no idea where we stand. She said to reach out when I get back so we can talk more. I miss her already, but right now my head is spinning over how to handle things with Maddie now that everything is out in the open.

It's very early in the morning, and the door to my bedroom opens. My mother pokes her head in and whispers, "You up?"

I whisper back, "Yes."

She smiles and walks in wearing her pink robe with two mugs of coffee in hand. I have flashes of my youth. I was always an early riser. My father wakes up super early to deal with the ranch and his employees. He would wake her on his way out. She and I would then sit and drink our morning coffee together and talk until it was time for me to go to school. It's always been our special time together.

Mom is still a beautiful woman. We share our hair and eye color. She's aged a bit in the past few years, likely thanks to me, but she's effortlessly beautiful, inside and out.

I sit up in my bed and accept the coffee, black, just like she knows I like it. "Thank you."

She nods and sits on the end of the bed, giving me a small

smile. "I can't believe you've been seeing little Sulley O'Shea all this time."

I raise an eyebrow. "She's not so little anymore."

Her smile widens. "I know." She clutches her chest. "And you're in love with her." It's said as a statement, not a question.

I nod. "Very much."

"How does she feel? I know she had a giant crush on you as a little girl."

I run my fingers through my hair. "Am I the only one who didn't realize that?"

She giggles. "She was so young. Why would you have noticed? You certainly never lacked for female attention."

I roll my eyes, and her laughter deepens.

"I think she loves me, but she's never uttered the words to me. She's been fighting her feelings for obvious reasons, but I believe they're there. There's something...magical that happens when we're together. I can't explain it. I breathe better when she's around me. She's a natural extension of me. She feels as much a part of my body as my legs and arms."

Tears fill her eyes, and she reaches over to squeeze my hand. "Oh, Vance, I'm not sure I ever saw you as romantic, but wow. That's the most beautiful thing I've ever heard. You deserve all the happiness in the world. You've more than earned it."

"Yesterday was intense. Sulley is still absorbing it all."

She nods. "I'm glad it's finally all out in the open. As much as I hated keeping secrets, I mostly hated how it negatively impacted your life. The shine in your eyes dimmed when everything happened. And right now, this morning, I see them shining again."

I swallow. "I'm still confused."

"About?"

"Maddie. Francesca. All of it. I don't know the right answer. I just want to do the right thing. I want to do right by him. Telling the O'Sheas everything doesn't change that."

"Vance, you don't owe him your life or your happiness. He died, and it was tragic, but a piece of you died that day too. Do you think Finn would want that for you?"

I shake my head. I know he wouldn't.

She rubs my hand. "I think it's time for you to find the right balance. You can honor the spirit of his final wishes without it negatively impacting your life so drastically."

"How?" I ask. "How do I ever find common ground with the woman who's responsible for his death? If she didn't cheat on him, he'd still be alive. I don't see a way forward with Maddie."

She gives me a knowing smile as she rubs my arm. "I have a few ideas. I think you're finally ready to hear them. It starts with forgiveness."

TWO HOURS LATER, I walk into the hospital and then into Francesca's room. Francesca is still asleep, and Maddie's curled up in a tiny ball on the chair. Good thing she's small. I don't think my leg would have fit on that chair, let alone my whole body.

I walk over to Maddie and look at her sleeping form. I think I prefer her sleeping. She doesn't talk.

I study her face. I guess most men would consider her to be attractive. She never did anything for me, but Finn was always enamored with her, as were many guys in our hometown.

My mother said a lot of stuff to me this morning that made sense. I'm not truly a parent, so I suppose I didn't understand some things Maddie said and did. Mom gave me a little perspective. I know Maddie and I need to talk. It's time. We can't go on the way we have been.

Her eyes slowly blink open, and she croaks out, "Hey."

"Good morning. I can stay with her if you want to go home and shower. Maybe deal with your other kids?"

She shakes her head. "No, Curtis can manage them. I won't leave Francesca. She woke once during the night in terrible pain, scared shitless. They had to give her another sedative. I hate her being on all these drugs. If she wakes again and I'm not here, she'll freak out. I refuse to leave her."

I nod in understanding. "You're a good mom, Maddie."

She lifts an eyebrow. "I must be delusional from sleep deprivation. Did you just compliment me?"

I twist my lips. "I guess I've been a little hard on you. I'm sorry."

She blinks a few times. "Are you on drugs too?"

I chuckle. "No."

"Can you say that all again into my good ear?" She reaches for her phone. "Wait, I want to get it on video."

I smirk as I roll my eyes at her dramatics. "Can we talk?"

She sits up and stretches her back and arms as she yawns. "Of course. I don't want to fight, though. I don't have it in me right now." She slouches, almost in defeat. "I'm exhausted. Physically and emotionally. You were right about the ATV. Curtis is getting rid of it today. I made a mistake. She was excited, and I was happy to see her happy. Never again."

"I'm not here to fight. I come in peace. I promise."

She tucks her hair nervously behind her ear and says, "Oookay," as she eyes me skeptically.

I pull up a chair and sit so we can talk eye to eye. "I've been thinking about how things are with us. It's not good for anyone. You. Me. Francesca. I want to make some changes."

"Like what?"

"I want a real role in her life."

She starts to talk, but I hold up my hands. "Let me finish. I know I'm not her father. I know I'm not here for her like a father should be. I won't accept all the blame for that, you've blocked my access, but I accept the blame for how I talk to you. I also understand why you want her to have a consistent father figure. You're right about that. All I want is what's best for her. I'd like you to introduce me to her as an uncle. When I'm in town, I want to see her. I want to be able to talk to her on the phone, dote on her, and send her gifts like uncles often do."

She appears to digest what I'm saying. At least it's not an automatic no.

I continue, "I'm not going to write checks anymore. What I'm going to do is set up a trust fund for her. College will be paid for. Dance classes, sports teams, prom dresses, clothing, anything she needs, you can draw from the trust. The O'Sheas will be the trustees. Finn was prepared to raise Francesca as his own. They know that now. They know *everything*. I'd like you to consider giving them access to her if they want it. I'm not demanding it, but I'm asking you to consider it."

She nods. "I've never blocked them from seeing her."

"I know. They didn't have all the facts then. They do now. I realize what this means for your luxurious lifestyle—"

Her eyes fill with tears, and she holds up her hand. "Stop." She exhales a long breath. "I know what you think of me. What you've always thought of me. Not a single day goes by that I don't have to live with the burden of knowing my actions in some way caused him to die. It obviously wasn't intentional, but I'm not ignorant to it. I'm a human being, Vance. I have a heart. It eats at me, but I put one foot in front of the other for my children. I don't control the past, so I focus on the future. I won't lie to you, at the beginning, I was happy to take and use your money to live high on the hog. I've never had money, and it was nice not to worry about it for the first time in my life. I know you don't think we work. Curtis works. He might not make the kind of money you do, few people do, but he makes an honest living. And I've been slowly taking college classes online. When my youngest goes to school, I plan to get a job. For the past two years, I've set aside most of the money you sent in an account for Francesca's future. I suppose it's a less fancy trust-type thing. What you're proposing sounds more than reasonable to me."

If you told me the apocalypse was coming tomorrow, I'd be less surprised than I am by these revelations. Perhaps I've been seeing her wrong, like my mother suggested. Perhaps I've hated her for so long that I couldn't see past certain things. She's clearly grown up. I think it's time for me to do the same.

I take her hand in mine. "I owe you an apology. I've vilified you for a long time. I was wrong. I'm admitting I was wrong. You made a youthful mistake. We all do. I certainly made my share."

Her shoulders begin to shake with soft sobs. "Despite everything that's happened, I can't view it as a mistake. It gave me my daughter. She's my everything. Do you know how conflicted it all makes me feel? If I hadn't gotten pregnant, he'd be alive. But I refuse to regret it because she's my heart and soul."

I never appreciated the level of her torment. She's been hurting as much as I have. She feels guilt, just like me.

"I guess we both need to forgive each other *and* ourselves."

She wordlessly nods as she reaches for tissues and tries to wipe away her tears and runny nose.

I take a deep breath, a few of them, before saying, "If you want to file to change her birth certificate to name Curtis as her legal father, I won't fight you on it. He's her father in all the ways that matter. He's earned it."

She sucks in a breath as hopeful eyes find mine. "Really?"

I nod. "Really."

Just then, we hear Francesca's little voice. "Momma."

Maddie jumps out of the chair, runs to her bedside, and takes her hand. "Yes, angel, Momma's here."

"Where am I? Why can't I move? What are all these machines? Where's Daddy?"

Her voice is so sweet. She speaks in full sentences now. I'm realizing I've never heard her talk like this. She was babbling the last time I was with her.

"You had an accident, but you're going to be fine. You're going to have to stay in bed for a few more days, but you'll be as good as new soon. I promise."

Francesca's curious, big, brown eyes find mine. "Who's that man, Momma?"

Maddie turns and looks at me. She gives me a small smile. "That's your Uncle Vance."

TWENTY-EIGHT

SULLEY

"I'd rather adjust my life to your absence than adjust my boundaries to your disrespect. That's what I told him," Layla says as she brushes a piece of lint off her skirt. "It was empowering after two years of a rollercoaster relationship. It finally set me free from him and his toxicity. Like this weight was lifted from my shoulders. The next month, I met Presley. I might give him shit, but he makes me feel loved and respected. Always. Every minute of every day. Sometimes it takes the right one to come along to truly show you how wrong the last guy was."

Kennedy, Palmer, Layla, Shay, and I are at a television studio in New York City, about to be interviewed on a popular late-night talk show about our big championship win. They asked to interview only me, but I refused. We compromised on the starting lineup appearing together.

We're sitting in the green room chatting before we're called out onto the stage in front of a live studio audience. Layla was telling us about her last boyfriend before she met Presley. He sounds like a real asshole.

Her last sentence resonates with me. It reminds me of Shane. I always knew on some level he was the wrong one, but having Vance back in my life has shown me just how wrong Shane was for me. Vance celebrates my achievements like a partner should. My successes are his successes. He loves me wholeheartedly and wants nothing but the best for me at all times. I never have to censor myself around him. I miss him the second we're apart. That's one of the biggest differences in my relationship with him and Shane. I was happy to be with Shane when he was around, but equally happy when we were apart.

I wonder what Shane is doing now. I saw he's no longer playing in the EuroLeague. I'm not surprised.

Kennedy nods. "There's no bigger red flag than a guy who disrespects you." Mischief plays in her eyes. "And guys who shout *Kobe* when they take a basketball shot. So annoying."

I giggle. "True. Speaking of red flags, I think I found another new red flag recently. Guys who wear ankle socks at the gym." I scrunch my face. "It's kind of girlie."

Layla smiles. "It is. The aforementioned disrespectful asshole also had a giant state flag hanging in his bedroom." She purses her lips. "Gross. I should have known then. Total red flag, pun intended."

Kennedy snorts in laughter. "That's a good one. You can tell a lot about a man from his bedroom. What about the guys who don't even have a bed frame? Just a mattress. Are they still in a frat house? Total fuckboy move to not bother with a frame."

Palmer bites her lip nervously. "I've got another food red flag. When a man sticks more than an inch or so of a banana in his mouth, it gives me the ick. Is he trying to prove he can deep throat it? I don't want to see that. It's not impressive."

We all burst into hysterical laughter. In between hard laughs, I manage to sputter, "You *definitely* have a food fetish."

Palmer bites back her smile. "I think you're right." Shrugging, she unashamedly says, "A girl wants what she wants."

My mind drifts back to Vance. I left Montana two days ago,

telling him I needed a little time and space to think about us. He lied to me for years, but I suppose he had a good reason. Does that make the lying okay?

I look at the collective group. "What about things that some might see as red flags, but you're not sure it's a red flag for you?"

Kennedy sucks in an excited breath. "Ooh. Like possessiveness? I lowkey love a possessive man. Not irrationally possessive, but *she's mine, don't fucking touch her* is a sexy vibe for me."

Palmer nods. "And bossy. I think I'm into bossy, authoritative men."

I narrow my eyes at Palmer. "Where did that come from?"

She fidgets nervously and looks down. "Nowhere. It just… sounds hot. Someone telling you what they want and when they want it. I think I'd be into that."

"Is that what you meant?" Shay asks me.

I shake my head. "Not exactly. No one likes a liar, but what if they think they had a good reason for lying to you?"

"Like what?" Layla asks.

Before I can answer, the production assistant opens the door. "It's time, ladies."

Ten minutes later, we're seated on a couch being interviewed by a famous late-night host in front of a live studio audience.

He looks at me. "Sulley, you were a little cold in the first half of that final game but then came out on fire in the second half and carried your team to victory. What changed for you at halftime?"

I give him a small smile. "I didn't carry my team anywhere. Everyone contributed to our victory in that final game. Going hot and cold is part of the sport. That's why it's not a one-person sport, and that's what makes these ladies such great teammates. When one of us is down, another picks up the slack. I had a terrible first half, but these amazing women kept us in the game. Look at Kennedy and Palmer's rebound numbers. How often do two players on the same team get that many rebounds? If anything, *that* kept us in the game. *That* carried us to victory. And how about Kennedy's dunk to seal the deal?"

He turns to Kennedy. "Is it true it was your first dunk ever? Even in practices?"

She smiles broadly. "It was. I've been working on it. I appreciate that our coaches had enough confidence in me to call my number in the big moment, and that Sulley saw it through. She made a great pass and gave me the best opportunity for success."

I nod. "I never had a doubt. No one works harder than Kennedy Jeffries."

He gives us a knowing look. "It must be in the genes. Your father has always been known as a hard worker. Judging by all the love he gets on social media, he looks like he's still working hard…on those biceps." He looks at the crowd with a giant smile plastered on his face. "Am I right, ladies?"

The audience laughs, and some women scream in delight. Kennedy doesn't flinch, though I see her lip twitch a bit. Before she says something she'll regret, I interrupt, "I think Kennedy stands on her own, out of her father's shadow." I turn to the audience. "Don't you all agree that this amazing athlete should be celebrated for her accomplishments, not her father's?"

Everyone starts cheering and clapping. Crisis averted.

I think the host gets the clue that she doesn't want to talk about her father and doesn't push any further.

He turns his attention to Layla. "You're married to Presley Ladrón, right?"

Layla winks. "For now. As long as he's a good boy."

He chuckles. "I've seen a few members of the Camels at your games. Any other love connections between the Camels and the Beavers?"

Layla shakes her head and lies. "Nope. Just me."

I sigh, hating that she had to lie. I hope Vance didn't see that. He'll be so hurt.

The host eyes us all skeptically while we remain tight-lipped. What is he getting at?

He continues, "They always show the guys engaging in beer drinking contests at your games. How about you ladies show them how it's done?"

The audience starts clapping again while a big cart full of beer cans is brought out. We then have a beer drinking contest. Palmer wipes the floor with all of us, but we have a blast along the way.

A FEW HOURS LATER, I'm almost home. Keith has dropped everyone but Kennedy and me at their respective homes. As soon as the last person exits the car, Kennedy asks, "What was with the lying question? Was that about Vance?"

She doesn't know anything about Montana, not even that I went. I was gone for less than twenty-four hours, but Kennedy knows everything else. I've confided in her and see no reason to stop now. She's become a sounding board for me. It's nice to have a girlfriend to talk to about this stuff. It used to be my mother, but she's a little jaded when it comes to Vance. I'm very clear on where she stands. My other close friends on the team know something is going on with us, but I've shared very few details with anyone but Kennedy.

I exhale a long breath. "I found out that Vance never slept with my brother's girlfriend. It was all a lie."

Her jaw drops. "What? What about his daughter?"

"She's not his biological child."

She shakes her head. "I don't understand. Why would he say the child is his when he never even slept with her?"

I take a few minutes and explain it all to her. She's as in shock as I was when I found out. "Wow," she breathes, "I can't believe he did all that. What are you going to do?"

"I told him I needed time to process everything and think."

She takes my hand in hers. "Babe, you're in love with him. Any fool can see that. And he's equally in love with you. The one thing holding you back no longer exists. What's there to think about?"

I'm silent, but Keith feels the need to interject in my personal life for the first time in all the months he's been with me. "He loves you, Ms. O'Shea. He checks in with me at least two or three times a day when he's not with you to make sure you're okay."

"Thanks for the input into my love life, Keith," I say sarcastically.

"Anytime, Ms. O'Shea. You two remind me of my relationship with my wife."

"I didn't know you were married, Keith. Didn't you once tell me we should keep things professional?" I joke with him. At the beginning, I tried to pry information from him, and he remained tight-lipped, saying it wasn't professional for us to engage in a personal relationship or to exchange any personal information.

I see him crack a smile in the rearview mirror. "I'm a sucker for love. I've been happily married for forty years, ma'am. I know what true love looks like. You and Mr. McCaffrey have what it takes."

Kennedy raises an eyebrow. "If Dr. Love is done, I was going to say I tried to hate Vance, I really did, but he's…likeable. I understand you needed to get your head on straight, but—"

"But what?"

She shakes her head. "I can't believe I'm going to say this; I must be hormonal. You know I'm not a romantic, and I think you're way too young to settle down, but you guys have this amazing story. It's like a romance novel. You had a childhood crush on him, and he had no idea. Then he had one on you, and you had no idea. Tragedy struck, and he did this incredibly self-less thing to honor your brother's dying wishes, completely at his own expense. He's head over heels for you. Even before I knew, I knew. You can see it in the way he looks at you." She licks her lips. "Let me ask you something. Do you ever see yourself loving or caring for anyone as much as you love and care about him?"

I shake my head and easily answer, "No. Never."

"What's holding you back?"

"I'm not sure." I think for a few seconds longer, trying to articulate what's been running through my head. "I wish he felt like he could have told me. Maybe it's a trust thing."

"I get that, but his intentions were never ill-conceived. He tried to do right by everyone in your family, including you. He's basically been an angel on your shoulder throughout your entire adult life. If not for him helping you along, think about where you'd be right now."

She's not wrong. "I know. You're right. I think I was in shock, but I want to be with him. I can't not be with him. I...I love him."

She squeezes my hand. "I know you do. You should go get your man. Tell him how you feel and then never let go." She shakes her head. "Fucking hell, what's wrong with me? When did I turn into a romantic?"

I let out a laugh before I lean my head back on the headrest. "I'm also concerned with us going public. We're both well-known. The press will hound us. That's a lot of pressure. What if it goes sideways? It will be in the public eye."

She nods. "I get that. Maybe you can keep things private. For a little longer. You won't know unless you try. You owe it to yourself to try. Go to him. When does he get back?"

"Tonight."

"Honestly, Sulley, I think you should do something special for him. He's sacrificed a lot and laid it all on the line for you. Go suck his dick when he gets off the plane. Something like that."

I giggle. "And who says you aren't a romantic?" I ask sarcastically.

"I heard that," yells Keith from the front seat.

I roll my eyes. "Keith, didn't you once tell me to pretend you weren't here and to go about my business?"

"Now I'm invested in this relationship, ma'am."

Kennedy and I start laughing. Who knew Mr. Stiff was a softie at heart?

In a much lower voice, she says, "That whole drive-in scene thing he did for you was hot as fuck. Fulfilling your fantasy?" She fans her face. "So hot. Does he have any fantasies he's mentioned to you? You should fulfill them like he did for you."

A smile finds my face as I answer, "Yes, he has," while an idea starts to take shape in my mind.

TWENTY-NINE

VANCE

I climb into Daylen's Jeep to an unexpected huge lick across the face from BJ. I shove her toward the backseat. "Ugh. Why did you have to bring the beast?"

In his stupid baby voice, Daylen answers, "BJ was excited to see Uncle Vance." He rubs behind her ear. "Weren't you, baby girl?"

Bark.

"You know what my new red flag is, D?"

He smirks. "What?"

"People who think their pets are human. People who think their pets understand English."

He gasps. "I *know* my princess speaks English. BJ, sing for Uncle Vance." He yells, "*TLC,*" as though it's a command.

The fucking dog starts belting out and singing. It's a sound I've never heard an animal make before. I think she's actually singing. And then he starts singing "Waterfalls" along with her. It's like a duet. What the hell is going on here?

I stare at the two of them. "Fucking Sonny and Cher living their best life."

Daylen lets out a loud laugh. "Damn, I should have named her Cher."

The two-day emergency family leave that the Camels gave me has come to an end. I had to get back tonight in time for practice tomorrow morning. Daylen insisted on picking me up from the airport.

"Thanks for getting me. You didn't have to. I could have Ubered home."

He waves his hand dismissively. "Nah. I wasn't busy. I want to hear about everything anyway. It must have been nuts. Like a soap opera. I can practically hear the *dah, dah, dah* music."

By the time I'm finished telling him the story, he has a giant smile on his face. "Why are you so fucking happy, D?"

He continues his goofy grin. "Because you've allowed yourself to live in quicksand for seven years, and now you're finally out." He throws his hands in the air and shouts, "Halleluiah!"

"What does that mean? Quicksand?"

"It means every time you moved, you got deeper and deeper into shit. There's been no escaping it for you. You've been stuck and miserable for too many years. I love you like a brother. Even though you won't cuddle with me on road trips, I know you love me too. If something happened to me, I would never in a million years want you to live your life the way you have been. *Guaranteed* Finn wouldn't have wanted that either. It's time for Vance to prioritize Vance for once. Stop punishing yourself for living. You don't have to feel guilty that you get to live your dream while he doesn't." He sits up straight. "As your official best friend successor, I hereby command you to only do things that make you happy moving forward. Hakuna Matata."

As soon as he says Hakuna Matata, BJ starts singing again. And Daylen sings the words to the song along with her.

I stare at him in disbelief. He shrugs. "What? BJ's favorite movie is *Lion King*. She watches it all the time when I'm not home."

"Do you know that your dog isn't human?"

He stares at me and yells, "Hakuna Matata," and the fucking dog starts singing again.

THIRTY MINUTES LATER, I'm about to walk into my house. My plan is to drop my stuff, get what I need for tomorrow, and then go to Sulley's and lay it all on the line. I had so many things I wanted to say in the treehouse, but I wasn't sure she was in the headspace to hear them, and then I got so emotional and cried like a baby. She ended up having to take care of me when all I really wanted to do was to take care of her.

I walk through my front door, and I'm not prepared for what I see. Sulley is sitting on the small table in the center of the foyer, waiting for me. She's wearing my jersey with nothing else on but those leather boots I like and red-painted lips.

She stares at me as she leans back on her hands and slowly spreads her legs enough for me to see that she's not wearing any panties. I blink my eyes a few times to make sure I'm not dreaming this.

She smiles sexily before running her tongue along her lower lip and breathing, "Welcome home, lover."

Every ounce of blood in my body rushes to my cock. Her eyes move down to the obvious bulge in my jeans, and her smile widens.

She pushes herself off the table and walks toward me like the tempting, seductive goddess she is until she's standing right in front of me.

"Sulley, I—"

"Shh." She places her fingers over my lips, quieting me.

"No more talking. No more secrets. No more drama." She stands on her toes and runs her tongue along my lower lip while gripping my painfully hard cock through my jeans, giving it a firm squeeze. "You're always the one taking care of everyone. It's my turn to take care of my man."

My man. No words coming from her lips have ever sounded better.

She turns around and rubs her body over mine, including her ass over my cock. Reaching for my hands, she places them on her body and runs them up and under the jersey until they're on her bare breasts.

I grab onto them and sink my nose into her neck, whispering, "I love you."

She turns around and wraps her arms around my neck. Her vibrant blue eyes meet mine. They're filled with lust. Is it too much to hope that they're filled with love too?

I open my mouth to speak, but she places her finger over my lips again. "Shh. Remember the rules."

She moves her fingers down and begins to unbutton my shirt, peppering soft kisses down my chest and abs along the way until she's on her knees in front of me.

She stares me in the eyes again while she unbuckles my belt. This is my fantasy. She's giving me my fantasy.

My pants and boxer briefs are down around my ankles in seconds. Her fingernails make a slow trail up my thighs. Fuck, I love when she does that. I can feel goosebumps spreading all over my skin.

My cock is now in her hand, her fingers gloriously wrapped around me. With the other hand, she reaches for my phone, sitting in the pocket of my jeans on the floor.

Handing it to me, she says, "I want you to have this memory. I trust you."

I swallow down the lump in my throat. She has no idea what that means to me.

I turn on the video and point the camera at her. She smiles

into it as she slides her pink tongue out and laps the moisture pooling at my tip.

"Hmm, so good, QB1."

She begins to pump my shaft with her hand while her tongue explores me, licking along my veins, savoring every second of it, putting on a bit of a show for the camera.

With her eyes still focused on the phone, she wraps those red-painted lips around my tip and then slowly feeds my entire cock into her mouth until the head reaches her throat. She gags a little but refuses to pull it out. I know I will watch that part of the video over and over again. Who wouldn't love the sight of the woman they love gagging on their cock?

She establishes an otherworldly rhythm with her hands, mouth, and tongue. My free hand winds into her hair, and I begin thrusting into her. I'm finding it hard to maintain enough control to hold up the camera, but I don't want to miss a moment of this.

"Are you getting off while you suck my cock, baby?" I ask. "Is your pussy soaked for me?"

She nods and makes some indiscernible noises.

"Show me. Stick your fingers inside your cunt until they're covered. Then show me and give me a taste."

Without breaking stride, she reaches one hand down until it disappears under the jersey. *My* jersey. Sulley is wearing my jersey, sucking my cock, and touching herself to show me how much she's getting off on it. This. Is. Perfection. She. Is. Mine.

Her eyes flutter when they find purchase. This whole scene is pushing me to the edge at warp speed.

She pulls her glistening fingers out and holds them up for my inspection. I immediately grab her hand and suck them into my mouth. Her taste instantly pushes me to the edge.

"Fuck, baby, I'm about to come."

Her mouth pulls off my cock with a loud popping noise. In a husky voice I didn't know she was capable of, she asks, "Do you want to come in my mouth or on my tits?"

I'm speechless. Where did that come from? I'm usually the one talking dirty, not her. And it was filthy.

Without an answer from me, who still can't form words, she removes the jersey, lies back on the floor, and pushes her tits together. "Fuck them and then come on them. Paint them white."

Her rosy nipples are hard and pointing at me, inviting me. Without another thought, I kick off my jeans and boxer briefs and then drop down until my knees are bracketing her ribs.

The phone falls, but I don't care anymore. I prop myself up and slide my cock between her full tits, thrusting in and out without a care in the world other than chasing my orgasm.

This is solely about me. I don't know that I've had a sexual moment in a very long time that was only about me and my needs. Hell, I'm not sure I've had *any* moment only about me in years, sexual or not. This is what she's giving me. Just when I thought I couldn't love her any more than I do.

It builds and builds until I can't take it anymore. Every nerve ending in my body feels like it's on fire. I roar, and I mean roar, into my release, as long, thick, hot coats of my ejaculate cover her tits and chest.

Once emptied, I pull up to rest on my knees between her legs and look at my masterpiece. She reaches for my phone and hands it to me. "You won't want to miss this."

I aim it at her while she runs her index finger over her semen-covered chest and slips it provocatively into her mouth, lapping it with her tongue and then closing her red lips around it. "Hmm, so good." She then scoops a handful of it, spreads her legs wide, and rubs it through her pussy. "Have a taste."

Without any hesitation, I toss the phone to the side and dive headfirst in her pussy, dying to taste the combination of her and me. She laughs at my enthusiasm, but I don't care. She's always up for anything I suggest, but she's never been in control and never been this dirty. It's such a turn-on. My cock is already hardening again.

I slide my tongue up and down her slit, licking up every last drop of our combined fluids. She grabs onto my hair as she arches her back and moans out, "More. I'm so on edge. Give me more. I need it. I need you."

I think it's the first time she's ever uttered the words that she needs me. It lights me on fire as I run a finger down her folds and plunge it into her.

"You're dripping for me, baby. Does sucking my dick make you wet? Or is it me fucking your tits? Or is it when you lick my come off your nipples?"

Her eyes roll back in her head. She's so close already.

I latch my lips to her clit and suck hard, all while curling my finger inside her, stroking her inner walls in the places I know drive her crazy.

It's mere seconds before she detonates into a body-shaking orgasm. She screams so loud, I wonder if Daylen can hear it a few miles away on his ride home.

When she begins to calm down, I crawl up her body and thrust directly inside her hard and to the hilt. She yells out as another orgasm immediately wrings from her body. She has no control of the shaking going on as she convulses through the orgasm and a long series of aftershocks.

She thrashes around. Her nails scrape all over my body. She's completely lost in the pleasure.

I watch her slack-jawed because I've never seen anything so erotic and sexy in my life. She's always been responsive to me, but she's in a different stratosphere right now, and I have the best seat in the house to watch it happen.

Tears leak from her eyes, not in sadness, but in pleasure and joy. It's beautiful. She's beautiful. I'm so in love with her.

The fog begins to lift, and I see her pupils return to their normal size. I still haven't moved inside her.

Her fingers thread through my hair, and her eyes meet mine. They're full of so much emotion. I have no doubt mine mirror hers. "I love you too, Vance McCaffrey. It's always been you. It will only ever be you." She brushes her lips over mine. "Make love to me."

My heart swells to a size I didn't know possible. It's like nothing and no one else in this world matters anymore other than the woman under me. The woman I want to spend the rest of my life with.

I'm suddenly very aware of our surroundings. We're on the floor of my foyer, ten feet from the front door. My shirt is open, but I'm still wearing it. She's in boots but has nothing else on her body. It's not the right scene for this. She deserves more. I deserve more. *We* deserve more.

I wrap her legs around me and stand, carrying her to my bedroom, losing my shirt along the way.

Falling onto the bed, I start to pull out so I can stand, but she wraps her legs around me tightly. "No. Don't pull out. It feels too good. I don't want to lose the connection of our bodies."

"I was going to remove your boots for you."

She gives me a playful smile. "You don't like them anymore?"

I thrust a little deeper, and she lets out a moan. "Does it feel like I don't like your boots?"

She bites her lower lip as she shakes her head. Threading her fingers through my hair again, she gives it a hard tug and tightens her legs around me. "Leave them. Make me see stars, QB1."

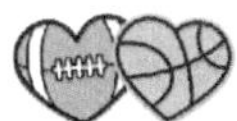

WE LAY in bed in the aftermath of the most meaningful sex of my life. We were so in sync. I didn't know where I ended and she began. It felt like my heart had the orgasm right along with the rest of my body. Both our eyes were full of tears as words of love and forever were whispered.

We're both on our backs, a little out of breath and full of

every emotion. I ask, "Can I talk now?"

She giggles as she nuzzles into me and kisses my shoulder. "I like you better when you just shut up and look pretty, but I suppose you can speak."

I reach over and pinch her nipple. She squeals as she laughs at her own joke.

Turning to my side and cupping her face, I say the words I've been wanting to say to her. "When two people are meant to be together, it doesn't matter how long it takes or how insurmountable the obstacles seem. Fate will always bring them together. I guess it was meant to take this long for us to get here, but we're finally here. There's nothing standing in our way anymore. I love you, Sullivan Aisling. I've been trying to tell you that for months. You didn't want to hear it. Yes, we have a shared past, but it only makes our bond stronger. Deeper. I wholeheartedly believe if Finn were here now, he'd be happy about this." I crack a small smile. "He'd probably kick me in the balls first for some of the things I do to you, but then he'd be happy. Because no one could possibly love any woman as much as I love you. Finn, being the protective big brother he was, would want you to be with a man who feels about you the way I do. If you'll let me, I promise to love you hard and furious for the rest of our lives. I want our forever to start now."

She swallows and fights back the tears pooling in her eyes. Running her fingertips over my scruff, she says, "That was beautiful."

"I saw it in a fortune cookie once."

She smiles.

My face turns more serious. "I meant every word."

She nods. "I know you did."

I continue, "I've been thinking about our treehouse talk of having a shared trauma. We both allow all the happy moments in our lives to have a tinge of sadness because we feel guilty that we get to be happy while he doesn't."

She tearfully nods. "It's true."

"We need to stop that. He wouldn't want that for either of us. We deserve to be happy, and I want us to be happy together."

Her blue eyes meet mine. "I want that too." She bites her lower lip nervously. "I have a proposal for you."

I smirk. "A top-secret proposal?"

Mischief finds her eyes. "Sort of. I'm concerned about the public attention our relationship would draw."

I feel myself deflating. Not this again. "Who cares?"

"I do," she says, "but not for the reasons you think. I want you to focus on your season. I don't want our relationship to be the reason you and your team are distracted. Most of our friends know. I don't care about them knowing, but I want to keep it out of the public eye until you win the Super Bowl. After that, we can freely be together however you want."

The corner of my mouth raises in amusement. "What if I don't win?"

She shrugs. "Then find yourself a new girl. I'm only in this for the glory."

I pinch her nipple again, and she shrieks.

I sigh. "I'm sick of being a secret. I'm sick of all the secrets." Even though I still have one. "I don't want any more lies in my life. I want the world to know you're mine. You were always mine, and you'll always be mine."

She turns to face me. "I've put my trust in you. Now I need you to put your trust in me. You lied to me because you knew it was best for me and my career, and you were right. This is what *I* know is best for *you*. It's my time to protect you. I need you to trust that I'm looking out for you just like you did for me. We're not telling the world quite yet. Can you trust me to look out for you like you do for everyone else in your life?"

I wordlessly nod even though I hate that she won't love me publicly. I'm completely under her spell. She could probably ask me anything, and I'd say yes.

In a jovial tone, I ask, "What if I ask you to marry me the second my season is over?"

Her face turns serious as she whispers, "I'll say yes."

"You will?"

She nods as the corners of her mouth turn up. "But only if you win the Super Bowl, so you better get to work."

SULLEY

I wake to a warm, long, wet, smelly tongue licking across my face. What the hell?

I blink my eyes open and see Daylen's giant dog, BJ, standing over me as she bends and licks my face again.

Then I hear Daylen's loud voice from downstairs, "Did you get naked when you stepped in the door, McCaffrey? If you keep masturbating, you'll go blind." There's a loud crashing noise, and then he yells, "Oh no, I can't see anything." And then he starts laughing hysterically at his own joke.

I hear his heavy footsteps coming up the stairs. It sounds like an elephant trampling through the house.

Even though I'm shielded by blankets, I'm very obviously naked. I'd like to run to the bathroom, out of sight, but I have over a hundred pounds of slobbering dog on top of me, pinning me to the bed.

Daylen's voice is getting closer. "I hope you didn't spend all night jerking off to her pic...oh, hello, Sullivan O'Shea." A huge smile finds his goofy face. "How lovely to see you here... naked...in Vance's bed. Does he cuddle with you? Because he won't cuddle with me when we share a room on road trips. He knows how much I like to be the little spoon."

I giggle, and Vance shoves the dog. "I can't believe you brought this menace to my house."

Daylen gasps. "She wanted to sing good morning to Uncle

Vance. She thought she needed to cheer you up, but apparently, Sulley has *beaten* her to it. Literally."

I let out a laugh. "Are you telling me your dog can sing?"

Vance moans. "Oh god, don't get Simon and Garfunkel going."

I hear Daylen chuckle before he yells, "*TLC!*"

BJ starts singing. She's belting out an unknown tune like she owns the joint, all from the end of Vance's bed. And then Daylen joins her. He holds out his arms, and she jumps off the bed and onto her hind legs. With her paws in his hands, they dance together as though they've done it a thousand times before.

I look at Vance in a bit of shock, and he shakes his head. "Don't get me started on the insanity of their relationship."

Daylen rolls his eyes. "I didn't know Sulley was here. You're lucky BJ likes you, *Sullivan*. She hates all women. *All* of them... except my sister."

"Why?" I ask.

"Because she thinks they're her competition for my love and affection." He then rubs behind her ear, and in a weird baby voice says, "But no one could ever pull me away from my beautiful, perfect baby girl."

Vance snorts in annoyance, and Daylen looks at me. "I honestly can't bring women to my house. She gets bizarrely territorial." He mumbles, "That and I don't want them to know where I live."

Vance sits up in bed and scowls at Daylen. "You and your mutt need to leave. Now."

Daylen covers BJ's ears. "Stop calling her a mutt. She gets very upset when Uncle Vance is mean to her."

I'm wildly amused by this conversation until I get a notification on my phone that someone is at my front door. It's not the doorbell; it's the motion sensor. I had it installed when Reagan grew concerned for my safety and Keith came into the picture.

Vance notices the screen. "Is that a delivery?"

Examining it carefully, I answer, "I think it's flowers." I zoom in on the screen and look up at him again with a smile. "Chocolate Cosmos."

His eyes widen. "Not from me."

I quickly zoom in further and realize exactly who is delivering flowers to my house.

THIRTY

SULLEY

Kennedy shakes her head. "All this time, and it's been creepy Noah stalking you? Why am I not surprised?"

We're sitting in a club box at the Camels game. It's Reagan Daulton's box, and she offered me access to it for every remaining home game. I think she bought it as her way of looking out for me, knowing I'd be at their games for the rest of the season and not wanting me out in the open crowd.

I sigh. "The police aren't doing anything about it. All they can prove is that he left flowers on my doorstep. It's hardly a crime."

"What about the photos taken of you and Vance?"

I shake my head. "They didn't find anything when they searched his laptop, and they didn't find any money when they reviewed his bank accounts. I was granted a temporary restraining order because he stole my address from company records, but he hasn't otherwise technically committed a crime. He's out there roaming free, and I'm freaked out by it. The thought of him knowing where I live and coming to my house gives me the chills."

Layla blows out a breath. "Wow. That's crazy. The only people who come to my house are Amazon delivery men." A small smile forms on her lips. "Oh wait, I had a solicitor come the other day. He asked for donations to an old-age home. I offered him my mother-in-law."

I let out a laugh, appreciating her attempt to lighten the conversation. I'm sick of talking about this, and Layla knows it. The second the heavy stuff for Vance and me went away, this happened, and I've been tied up with lawyers and the police for the past two weeks. When will life slow down? When can I feel comfortable walking around without a bodyguard always lurking in the shadows? When can Vance and I be together without worrying about other things?

The worst part is that, because no photos were found in Noah's possession and there's no evidence the hush money went to him, we still don't know if he's the one who took those intrusive photos of Vance and me. Though unlikely, the possibility exists that there's a second person out there stalking me.

I'm trying to shake all thoughts of having a stalker, but it's made it so that I hate being at my own house. Maybe Reagan was right and I should have lived somewhere a little more secure. I haven't slept at my house since I found Noah there. I've been at Vance's every night he's been home. He's my safe place. I sleep better with him. He had a road trip last week, and I slept at Kennedy's because I didn't want to be alone.

The game is about to begin. It will be a welcome distraction. Number nineteen emerges from the tunnel, and my heart pitter-patters like it always has when I see him in his uniform. From the time I was a little girl until now, it's never wavered.

He looks up this way. Our eyes meet, and he taps his heart a few times. Things are totally different between us since the big reveal in Montana. We're in love. It's real and it's beautiful. The guilt has been lifted. I'm free to be with him, and he's free to be with me.

He hates that I won't go public with our relationship yet, but

I think it's best. Their team is undefeated. He needs to focus on football, not dealing with paparazzi, media stories, and speculation about us.

VANCE

After a fifteen-yard slant pass to Champ, he's tackled inbounds. I quickly make my way to the line and spike the ball with ten seconds left on the game clock, not wanting to burn our last timeout. We're down three points and only four or five yards away from Presley's field goal range. A field goal would tie the game and send it to overtime.

Quickly running over to Coach, I ask, "What do you want to do?"

He furiously runs his eyes over his laminated play card before they raise to meet mine. "Are you feeling feverish?"

I crack a smile. "Always."

He nods. "Don't force it. Wishbone formation with the slant option. They'll think we're running the ball and going for the three."

"Yes, sir."

I start to walk away, but he grabs my jersey and pulls me back to him. "Only if you're certain it's there. I don't want to let this one get away from us. I'd rather take our chances in overtime."

"I know. I got it."

I run back to the huddle and let the guys know the plan. We're stacking the backfield, setting the decoy. They assume Champ is going to run the ball with the protection of our fullbacks. In reality, I'm looking downfield for the longball and the win. If it's not there, Champ will break from his man and head to the sideline for a quick pass to secure us being in field goal range.

I step under center and stomp my foot to set Daylen in motion. Hopefully the other team will assume he's blocking for Champ, meaning he'll only have single-man coverage.

I yell *hike* and everyone moves to do their job. As soon as the safety realizes it's not a run play, he sprints across the field to double-team Daylen. Reece is the only receiver in man-to-man coverage, but I have no faith in him, not with the game on the line. I go for my third option, the safe play, and throw the ball to Champ, who catches it, putting us just within Presley's range.

I'm stewing over this turn of events. If Linc were available, I would have thrown him the ball. Just before the season started, Reece "accidentally" dropped a twenty-five-pound barbell on Linc's foot. The poor kid broke two toes. He wanted to tape them and play, but our trainers wouldn't clear him until he's fully healed. He should be ready to go in the next few weeks, but not quite yet.

Champ is tackled inbounds, so I quickly burn our last timeout with two seconds left on the clock. When I run over to the sidelines, Daylen shoves my chest. "Let her rip next time. I would have fucking caught it. I had a step on my guy."

My jaw tightens as I shove him back. "The free safety was sliding over. It was too risky. My call. I made the right one."

He shakes his head. He doesn't agree. That's the thing about being the quarterback. You're the decision maker, and those decisions are made in split seconds.

He mumbles, "You would have thrown that ball ten years ago."

I sigh. "And it would have been knocked down or intercepted, and we would have lost the game right then and there. Better to be safe and go for the tie. We'll win it in overtime."

He lightly punches my shoulder and mumbles, "You're right."

To an outsider, it would look like Daylen and I were fighting. We weren't. We're competitors. Emotions run high in big situations. When the game is over, this disagreement will be forgotten. In fact, it already is.

We stand on the sidelines as Presley lines up to take the kick. It's a long field goal, but Presley nails it through the uprights as time expires to tie the game.

We head into overtime, but the other team wins the coin toss and scores a touchdown on their first drive. I never even get the chance to touch the ball in overtime. It's our first loss of the season. A tough one at that.

My teammates head into the locker room with their heads down, but I sit on the bench replaying the last play in regulation over and over again. Should I have thrown long and gone for broke? I played it safe, and all we have to show for it is a loss. Daylen was right. In my youth, I would have gone for it. If we're going to go all the way this year, I need to have faith in my teammates, especially a veteran like Daylen. I need to take a few more calculated risks to get us to the next level.

Eventually, I head into the tunnel toward the locker room, still feeling conflicted over my decision making and distraught over the loss. As I enter the tunnel, I see her standing there, leaning her back against the wall, wearing my jersey. An immediate sense of calm filters through me.

She pushes herself off the wall when she sees me. "Are you okay?" she asks with concern written all over her face.

I approach her, wrap my arms around her, and breathe her in. "I'm better now."

She looks around, undoubtedly making sure there are no prying eyes. I wish I could love my girl out in the open. More importantly, I wish she'd love me out in the open. It pisses me off that we have to be careful, but this is what I agreed to, and I have no interest in rocking the boat. Things have been too good lately between us. It's like we've achieved a whole other level of intimacy. Finally having her completely trust me means everything to me.

Her hands grab either side of my face, so I'm forced to look at her. "It was the right decision. The safety was moving over. Daylen wasn't open. You can't force it."

"Daylen doesn't agree."

"That's why he's not QB1. You're the field general, not him. This is *your* team, Vance, not his. The outcome isn't what you wanted, but you made the right choice in that moment. You gave your team the best chance to win the game. It's a shame they didn't, but they wouldn't have even gotten to overtime if you didn't get them there."

I've never had someone in my corner like this. Obviously my parents always are, but they're never here. I'm not sure I realized just how much I've needed this until now.

I rest my forehead on hers. "I love you."

She rubs her nose over mine. "I love you too."

My lips brush over hers. "I need you."

She smiles into my mouth. "You have me."

I do have her. Finally. And it's more important to me than any game.

After a little make-out session, she has a huge grin on her face. I narrow my eyes at her. "Why are you so happy? We lost."

She can't contain her growing smile. "I just got to fulfill another fantasy. Making out with you in your uniform in a stadium tunnel. The younger me is doing cartwheels right now." She scrunches her nose. "But the younger me didn't consider the fact that you had been sweating for four hours. Vile Vance has a whole new meaning now."

Suddenly feeling self-conscious, I subtly attempt to smell myself, and she giggles. "Got you." She sticks out her pink tongue and slowly licks up my neck. "Yum. I love the smell and taste of your sweat. Such a turn-on."

I go from partial chub to full mast in mere seconds. Adjusting myself, I grit out, "Shit, don't make me hard in these pants."

She lets out a loud laugh as her eyes drink me in. "Hmm, I think I like how tight those pants are."

At first, I make her stay with me until it goes down, but then I realize it won't go down if she's here, so I make her leave. She tells me Keith is driving her to her house to grab some clothes, and then she'll meet me at mine. I want to ask her to just move in with me, but it's been a crazy few weeks, and I know she wants to wait until the season is over before we talk about the future. I've dropped a few comments here and there, but I know we're unfortunately in a holding pattern for now.

As soon as I walk into the locker room, Reece Sanders is in my face. "Why didn't you throw me the fucking ball? I was open. This loss is on you and your ego."

I stare down at him. "Because I had no faith you would catch it. If it wasn't for injuries, you wouldn't have been in the game. You'd be on the bench where you belong."

He grits out, "Hmm, McCaffrey. You do love to throw the ball to Williamson. Something going on between you two that the rest of us should know about? Has he brought you over to the dark side?"

I start to charge toward him, but Daylen steps between us and shoves Reece. "Go take a shower, Sanders. Cool off. In fact, sing while you're in there. Give us a *soap* opera."

Reece's whole face snarls. "You think you're so funny, Humblecut. You're nothing but a joke. You know what, I've got a joke for you. What did one gay condom say to the other gay condom?"

"Watch yourself," I grit out.

He stares at me. "Let's get shitfaced."

I lift my fist, but Champ jumps in between all of us and holds up his hands at me. "Don't. Your hand is too valuable to this team. He's not worth it."

I want to tell him that enough is enough; he shouldn't have to be subjected to this abuse, but before I have the chance,

Champ swivels around and delivers a right hook to Reece's nose. Reece never sees it coming and goes down hard. It immediately starts spurting blood. It's definitely broken.

He begins screaming ignorant obscenities at Champ.

The coaching staff comes running out of their office. Theoretically, Champ should get suspended for this. Physically assaulting another teammate is against the terms of all our contracts and grounds for immediate suspension without pay.

Coach Jeffries takes in the whole situation. His eyes toggle between me, Daylen, Champ, and Reece until they eventually land solely on Reece, whose face and jersey are now covered in blood. "Sanders, you're off the team. Empty your locker and get your ass out of my locker room."

"But, Coach, *he* hit *me*."

Coach's lip twitches. "You had it coming. You've had it coming for a long time. And my best guess is that no one in this locker room will remember it that way. In fact, I'm pretty sure you swung first and Champ was defending himself. Isn't that right, McCaffrey?" He looks at me.

I nod. "Yes, sir. Sanders threw the first punch. Williamson was defending himself. He can't help that Sanders is a pussy and can't hit for shit."

Reece starts to plead his case, but Coach holds up his hands. "I don't want to hear it. I'm going to give you the courtesy of officially stating that you were released for roster room purposes, but if you breathe a word of Champ hitting you outside this locker room, I'll make sure you're blackballed in this league. No team will touch you. Ever. If you value salvaging your career, just walk the fuck away. Right now. Take some time to evaluate your behavior. You're still young. Make the necessary changes. You'll regret it if you don't. You've burned this bridge, but there are plenty of teams in this league who could use your talents. Don't be a fool."

Reece withers under Coach's lethal stare.

Coach doesn't have to tell the rest of the team to keep this quiet. It's automatically understood. Every single player will have Champ's back.

We all watch on as Reece Sanders slithers away from this team for the last time.

I'M WALKING to my truck when I see a familiar manila envelope sitting on my windshield. Shit, I don't need this right now.

For the past few weeks, I've had manila envelopes full of photos of Sulley and me appear with a demand for payment. Not wanting to upset the applecart, I paid the first time, but I haven't paid the past few. Enough is enough. I know Sulley doesn't want photos of us being made public, but how many times am I supposed to pay this guy off?

I haven't told Sulley about it. At first, it was because they were making a championship run and I didn't want this messing with her head. But in the weeks since, I didn't tell her because she's been so on edge about the restraining order with Noah. I was hoping they'd find photos in Noah's possession and this would go away, but they never found anything to suggest he's the culprit.

Reagan Daulton and the police are aware of everything. Just not Sulley. We collectively agreed it wasn't best for her.

I open the envelope, but it's not the normal photos of her and me. It's a note that reads, "*Check your phone, QB1.*"

I dig through my gym bag for my phone, not having looked at it since before the game. I need to call Keith to make sure he's with Sulley. When I pull it out, there's a text from an unknown number. It's a series of photos from inside Sulley's house with a message.

Unknown: You should have paid. Don't worry,
I'll collect from her.

THIRTY-ONE

SULLEY

I'm in my bedroom, packing a bag for Vance's house, when I look around and take in my surroundings. This place doesn't feel like home anymore. Once the sanctity of it was violated, I stopped loving it, only feeling safe at Vance's. Maybe I should pack a bigger suitcase and make things more permanent. I know he wouldn't mind. In fact, I think he'd prefer it that way.

I grab my larger suitcase from the storage area and begin to pack it when the doorbell rings. It's probably Keith wondering what's taking so long. I told him I'd be five minutes, and it's been much longer. He has a key but never uses it. He says it's for emergencies only. Such a stickler for the rules.

Without bothering to look through the peephole, I open the door and am shocked by what I see. "Shane? What are you doing here?"

He smiles. "Miss me?"

I shake my head and answer honestly. "Not really." I haven't given him a second thought other than to think how much happier I am with Vance.

His face falls. "Can I come in? I'd love to catch up. For old time's sake."

Fuck, I don't want to catch up, but I also don't want to be rude. We shared a year and a half together. I suppose I can give him a few minutes.

Keith appears seemingly out of nowhere. "Is everything okay, Ms. O'Shea?"

I hold up my hand. "It's fine, Keith. Thanks. He's an old friend. I might be a little longer than I mentioned. Do you mind waiting?"

He nods. "No problem, ma'am."

I motion for Shane to come inside, and he does. Closing the front door behind him, he asks, "What's with the muscle?"

"I have a few…overzealous fans. He keeps an eye on me."

"Wow. You're on the rise, just like you always wanted. That's some big-time shit." He says it with the same derogatory tone he always used when it came to my success. What did I ever see in this guy?

Yep, sometimes it takes the right guy to come along to see just how wrong the last guy was. Shane doesn't deserve to be mentioned in the same sentence as Vance.

We walk through the house to the living room area. "Can I get you a drink?" I politely offer.

He nods as he looks around. "Sure."

I walk into the kitchen, grab a glass, and pour him some iced tea. When I walk back into the living room, he's not there. I yell out, "Shane?"

He emerges from the bedroom hallway area, tucking his phone into his pocket. "I'm here. Just checking out your pad. It's really nice."

It's weird that he felt like he could just walk around my house at will. A bit of a chill works its way through my body, but I ignore it, just wanting to get through the next few minutes and get to my man's house.

I hand him his drink, and he smiles as he takes it and sits in a chair. "Thanks."

I sit on the couch across from him. "No problem." I point toward his hair. "I see you grew it out again."

He nods. "Yep. I know you always preferred it longer. My girlfriend, the one in Rome, preferred it shorter."

That mystery is solved. Now I know why he cut it when he knew I liked it longer.

"Not to be rude, Shane, but what are you doing here? We didn't exactly end on good terms, if you remember."

He presses his lips into a straight line. "I remember. I'm sorry things ended as they did. I didn't mean to hurt you."

I shrug, acting unaffected. "Honestly? You didn't. I was planning to call things off with you. Things weren't right with us for a while. We both knew that."

His jaw tics, but he otherwise remains silent. Why is he here?

In the absence of a response, I ask, "How are things going for you? Are you still living in Rome?" I know he's no longer on the team, but I don't let on.

He shakes his head. "No, that team wasn't right for me. They didn't appreciate my talent."

It takes every ounce of restraint I have not to roll my eyes. Teams don't appreciate entitled assholes who don't work hard. If every team you've ever been on or wanted to be on doesn't appreciate your talent, perhaps it's time to look inward.

No need for me to kick him while he's down. I reply, "Sorry to hear that. What have you been up to?"

He shrugs. "I've had to get a little creative. My parents told me it was time to get a real job, but I know I'm destined for greatness. I just need someone to give me a break. If only I were given the opportunities you were handed on a silver platter. You had it so easy."

This guy is delusional. I need to get him out of here.

"Is there something you need from me, Shane? I was on my way out when you got here. I'm in a bit of a rush."

"I saw your suitcase in your bedroom. Going out of town?"

Enough is enough. "That's not really your business. What is it you want from me? If you're not going to tell me, then I'd like for you to leave. Like I said, I'm on my way out. Keith is waiting for me. He's right outside," I add, suddenly feeling uneasy.

He scratches his head. "Hmm, where to start. Thanks to you, my girlfriend left me. She recognized you and did a bit of research after you left. She realized you weren't my cousin."

I shrug, not feeling a single ounce of guilt. "I didn't post us on social media, you did. And starting a relationship with a lie isn't exactly an ingredient for success."

He runs his tongue over his top teeth. "Lying, huh? Like you're lying to the world?"

"I don't know what you're talking about."

"Fucking Vance McCaffrey. How cliché," he snarls.

"Who I choose to spend time with is none of your business."

And then it hits me. How does he know? "What makes you think I'm seeing Vance?" I ask.

"It's not exactly like you've been hiding it. I've seen his hand up your skirt in clubs, restaurants, and parks. I never got that side of you, *Gully Sulley.*"

All the air escapes my lungs as things come into focus. I stand, feeling extremely unsafe. Mustering as much courage as I can, I point toward the door. "You need to leave. Now."

He shakes his head. "I don't think so. You owe me. It's time to pay."

VANCE

I race to Sulley's house, running through every red light and stop sign along the way. She's not answering her phone, and neither is Keith.

I punch my steering wheel. Where the fuck is he? I'm scared out of my mind.

The police are on their way, but I'll get there first at this point.

Our entire lives together run through my head like a movie. Tears stream down my cheeks as I fear what could be happening to her right now.

I make every promise to God. Please just let her be okay.

Pulling up to her house, I leave my truck in the middle of the street with the engine running and the door open, practically jumping out with it still moving. I see Keith's car, but it doesn't look like he's in it. I can't worry about that right now.

As I'm sprinting up her steps, Sulley comes bursting through the front door. Her tear-filled, scared eyes find me, and relief washes over her as she yells my name and falls into my arms.

I hold her tight. "Are you okay? Is someone in there?"

She starts crying. "It was Shane. He's the one taking photos of us. He's the blackmailer."

"Eurotrash guy?"

She nods and cries, "Yes."

"Where is he?"

"Lying half-conscious on my living room floor. I used Beau's neck chop move on him, and he went down. I ran out as soon as he did."

"Where the fuck is Keith?" I shout.

"I don't know," she cry-yells. "I came out here looking for him."

"Does Shane have any weapons?"

She shakes her head. "No, I don't think so. None I saw. He just wanted money in exchange for silence."

I turn and see Keith leisurely walking down the street with a cup of coffee, looking like he doesn't have a care in the world. His eyes widen when he notices her hysterical in my arms. Dropping his coffee, he comes running toward us. "What happened?"

"Where were you?" I bark.

"She...she was inside with a friend," he stutters. "She wasn't alone and said she'd be a bit, so I figured I had time to grab a cup of coffee. Like when you're around."

"Where's your phone?" I scream.

He pats his pockets and at least has the dignity to look ashamed. "I must have left it in my car."

If Sulley didn't need my arms around her, I think I'd strangle him.

I grit out, "I'm taking her to my truck. The police will be here any second." I point inside the house. "Don't let that asshole out of your sight until they get here."

With a shaken Sulley tucked into my side, I take her to my truck while we wait for the police.

THIRTY-TWO

SULLEY

My eyes search the countertop until I find what I'm looking for at the other end. "Momma, can you please pass me the butter?"

She smiles as she hands it to me while we seamlessly work to prepare Christmas Eve dinner next to each other. "Wow, Sulley, your kitchen is a dream."

I look around at what was once Vance's kitchen but is now our kitchen. I didn't want to live at my house anymore after everything that happened. I was thinking about moving in with him before the Shane incident, but his invading my home sealed the deal. And the fact is, I want to live with Vance. He's my home, and now we live together in the house designed by my brother. Every small detail of this house makes me happy, from the brilliant design to the perfect man I sleep beside every night. Our relationship is in full bloom, and there's no turning back for either of us.

As it turns out, Shane was in a mountain of debt. He'd been living well beyond his means for some time, which explains many of his spending habits. For years, he spent money like he was going to hit it big playing professionally one day, and when he didn't, he scrambled. According to the police, he first tried to capitalize on my fame. When his affiliation with me didn't provide him with enough money, he found a wealthy Italian girlfriend. When she realized what a slime he is, he got involved in a point shaving gambling incident and was permanently banned from the EuroLeague.

After that, he realized he was in real trouble and completely lost himself. Reagan's initial payoff didn't make a dent in his debt. Apparently, Vance paid him once too, but he needed more, and when Vance wouldn't pay him again, he thought he could get it from me, assuming there was a reason I didn't want my relationship with Vance to be made public. He was also shopping the story to various media outlets, trying to drive up the price. His plan was to take money from me and then sell the story anyway.

Initially, I was annoyed at Vance for keeping it from me, but he was protecting me. Again. Despite that, I wholeheartedly trust him and know he'll go to any lengths to ensure my happiness and safety.

With the case being public record, we ultimately decided to go public with our relationship. We issued a statement that we were childhood friends who recently reconnected, and love bloomed. We didn't disclose details about my brother or Francesca. The media hounded us for a few weeks. We let them get their photos of us, and now they've mostly moved on. There are still plenty of photographers hanging around when we go out, but we try not to let it bother us. And, honestly, it's made our little public sex fetish that much more of a challenge. I won't let Shane's photos deter us from exploring our needs. It's been fun, and crazy hot, to find ways to be physical without being seen.

I feel big, comforting hands wrap around me from behind. Vance's warm breath fans across my neck. "This kitchen isn't a dream, Nancy. Life with your daughter is."

I smile as I turn my head and inhale my sexy man. Jane and my mother practically coo in delight as they happily watch our interaction.

I whisper in his ear, "I think if we had sex right here, they'd grab popcorn and cheer us on."

I can feel him laugh as he whispers back, "I think that's taking our public sex thing a little far, but I'm game if you are."

I giggle as he moves next to me and asks me what ingredient I need next. "Nope, QB1. You know the corn casserole is a secret O'Shea family recipe. My lips are sealed."

My mother playfully smacks me with a tea towel. "Vance is family. Perhaps tomorrow morning might be a great time to make it official," she not-so-subtly hints.

It's Christmas Eve. The Camels have a home game tomorrow afternoon. We were miraculously able to talk both our families into visiting for Christmas this year. I know they're all hoping for a Christmas morning engagement, but that's not happening.

I hear Jane suddenly yell, "Mother! That's enough brandy in the eggnog."

MeeMaw smiles innocently. "No problem, honey," but when Jane turns back around, MeeMaw pours the rest of the bottle into the bowl and winks at me. I never realized what a deviant that woman is while I was growing up.

My mother asks, "What's with all the plastic by the door over there?" She points to the disaster that's been driving me nuts for the past few weeks. I was hoping they'd be done by now, but they're not. The contractor said to stay away from it over the holidays, and they'll be back in January to finish it.

"It's Vance's mancave. His contractor has been working on it for weeks. He won't let me see it. He said it's boys only in there."

I suppose he's been a bachelor for thirty-two years and needs a space in the house to call his own. I still think it's weird that he won't let me see it, but I'll take a peek when it's done. Collin has told me no less than a hundred times that it's unsafe down there while construction is happening.

The doorbell rings, and Vance smirks. "That must be the Humblecuts. I'll get the door. Prepare for madness."

VANCE

I look around my dining room table and realize it's full of all the people I love in the world. I've never been happier in my entire life. The future looks bright for the first time in a long time.

This is the first Christmas I've ever hosted. I've never once gotten my parents to fly to me for the holiday.

Sulley grabs my hand under the table and whispers, "Are you okay?"

I lean over and kiss her cheek. "More than okay. I love you, Gully Sulley."

"I love you too, Vile Vance."

MeeMaw is a little tipsy tonight. I'm not sure what she put in the eggnog, but she's been downing it by the gallon. She looks at Daylen. "Your sisters are very pretty."

He chuckles. "I know what you're doing, you old hag. Ashleigh is my dad's wife, not my sister."

MeeMaw giggles, and Mom shakes her head in disapproval. "I'm so sorry for my mother, Hank. I think she spiked the eggnog with her heavy hand."

Hank releases a loud laugh as he kisses Ashleigh's cheek. "It happens all the time, Jane. I can't help that my bride hasn't aged a day since I met her."

I think surgery has a lot to do with it, but I'll keep that to myself.

I turn to Jagger. "How's school going? Are you starting to think about college?"

She nods. "Yes. I've had some interest from college coaches to play softball. I'm trying to decide if that's an avenue I want to pursue."

Sulley playfully narrows her eyes at her. "Why not basketball? You have the height for it."

Jagger shrugs. "I'm better at softball. And I like being outdoors."

Sulley nods. "I get it. I'm friends with a few of the players on the Anacondas. They'll be at the game tomorrow. I can introduce you."

Jagger's eyes widen. "That would be amazing. Thank you."

We have a nice meal. Everyone gets along well. The Humblecuts are on their best behavior until dessert, when Sulley says, "Momma, this pie came out perfectly."

Hank's head snaps toward Daylen. "Did she just say *mama?*"

Daylen slowly nods his head. "I believe she did."

Oh Christ, here we go.

Jagger moans. "Ahh. Please, no. Not tonight." She turns to my family and the O'Sheas, explaining and apologizing in advance for this little game that Hank and Daylen like to play.

Daylen looks at Hank with a straight face. "Yo mama is so dumb, it takes her two hours to watch *60 Minutes.*"

There are a few low laughs at the table, but Hank doesn't blink.

Hank replies, "Yo mama is so dumb, she tried to climb Mountain Dew."

I let out a loud laugh, but Daylen doesn't even crack a smile.

MeeMaw scoffs. "Oh, please. You two think yo mama jokes are funny?" She shakes her head in disapproval. "Yo mama jokes are so old and have been done by way too many people," a sly smile finds her face, "just like yo mama."

The whole table erupts in laughter. Daylen falls to his knees and bows to MeeMaw. "You are the master. I worship at the altar of my queen."

MeeMaw bats her eyelashes. "You're not even the first man to say that to me today."

My mom covers her eyes in mortification as she shouts, "Mother!"

AFTER DESSERT, Daylen and I are cleaning the dishes. He looks at me. "You ready for tomorrow?"

I nod. "Yep. Big game." If we win, we lock up the top seed for the playoffs, meaning every game will be a home game until the Super Bowl. It's a huge advantage in football. Having your hometown crowd cheering for you is invaluable. Playing on the field you play on all year is everything.

He motions his head toward Frank, who's standing alone at my fireplace. He's staring at the Christmas stocking with Finn's name on it. "Go talk to him. I've got this."

"You sure?"

He nods. "We're almost done with these dishes. Go ahead."

"Thanks, man." He knows I planned to talk to Frank tonight.

I walk over and hand Frank a glass of bourbon. I have a very small one for myself since we have a game tomorrow, but I set another full glass on the mantel just above Finn's stocking.

Frank holds up the glass. "Thank you for this, and thank you for hosting us."

I clink glasses with his. "My pleasure. I need to talk to you. When my season's over, I want to ask Sulley to spend her life with me. I'd like your blessing."

His attention turns to the glass sitting on the mantel. "Is that for Finn?"

I nod. "Yes, sir. I thought he should be here for this conversation too."

Tears fill his eyes as he takes a long sip. "Her mother and

yours were hoping an engagement would happen tomorrow morning."

A small smile finds my lips. "Sulley said she won't agree to marry me unless I win a Super Bowl first."

He chuckles. "That sounds like my girl. How do you plan to propose?"

"Privately. I'd happily propose in front of the world, but she's fiercely protective of our privacy. When my season is over, I think I'll take her on a nice vacation and do it there, away from any prying eyes."

He takes another sip and then holds out his hand for me to shake. "I certainly couldn't ask for a better man to look after my daughter. I know Finn would feel the same."

I shake his hand in return. "I don't know. He warned me away from her."

We both smile, but he pulls me a little closer, so we're nearly nose to nose. "You were always brothers, but this will make it official." His eyes lift as they take in the scene of our two families happily interacting before they meet mine again. "He's looking down with a giant grin on his face. I promise you that, son."

I WAKE in the morning to Sulley doing that thing she does with her tongue on the tip of my dick, also known as the greatest sensation in existence. Opening my eyes, I look down at her. With a mouthful of my cock, she mumbles, "Mwy Chrms."

I chuckle. "Merry Christmas to you too. It's starting off *extremely* well."

She smiles as her hand joins her mouth, stroking me until I can't take it anymore, and I growl, "Get on your back. I need to fuck you."

She allows my dick to slip from her mouth with a plop as

she crawls up my body and rubs her pussy over my cock before bringing my tip to her entrance. "No way. You need to save your energy for the game. I'll be calling all the plays this morning, QB1."

At that, she slides down onto me. I watch in continued awe as her body convulses while taking mine. Her lips are parted, her cheeks are flushed, and her nipples look like they could cut glass. She's so fucking hot, and this is the woman I get to wake up to every day for the rest of my life. How did I get so lucky?

After she makes good on her promise to fuck me, she practically bounces out of bed to get dressed. I lie there and watch her. Her enthusiasm is contagious.

She looks at me wide-eyed. "Get up, lazy. It's Christmas morning. You have to leave for the stadium soon. I want to give you your gift." She pinches her eyebrows together. "What's wrong?"

I shake my head. "Nothing. It's just been a really long time since I had a truly happy Christmas morning. Thank you."

Her face falls as she walks over to the bed and rubs my arm. "I hate how much you've suffered. No more of that ever again. Okay?"

I nod as I take her hand in mine and kiss it. "Okay. Make sure everyone is together. I'm going to make a quick call. I'll be out in a few minutes."

"Ah right," she happily says. "Tell her I said Merry Christmas."

As soon as I'm dressed, I pull out my phone and click on the FaceTime app. It starts ringing, and Maddie answers immediately. She's smiling. "Good timing. She's been begging for an hour, and we were about to give in."

As she turns the phone, I hear her yell out, "Francesca, look who called."

I see Francesca's face as she jumps up and down. She gives me a huge grin. "Hi, Uncle Vance. Is it time to open my gift?"

I chuckle. "Hey, pumpkin. Merry Christmas. It's time."

She looks just above the phone. "Now can I have it, Momma? You said to wait for his call."

"Yes, sweetie," Maddie replies.

I see Curtis pull the new pink bicycle, *with training wheels and no motor*, out from their garage and into their living room. Francesca starts screaming with excitement. "This is the one I saw in the bike store. The one you said was too expensive, Momma."

I hear Maddie say, "Uncle Vance wanted to buy it for you."

Francesca brings her face right up to the phone. "Thank you! I love it!"

"I'm glad." I study her carefully. "Did you lose a tooth?"

She nods enthusiastically. "Yes. I just lost my first tooth two days ago. I'm the first in my class to lose one," she announces with pride. "Did you get my present?"

"Yep, your drawings are hanging on my refrigerator. I love them."

"Momma hangs my drawings on our refrigerator too."

"I understand why. You're very talented."

She grins adorably. "Momma said we're going to watch your game today. Wave to me on the television, Uncle Vance."

"I promise to do that. Have a great Christmas."

"You too, Uncle Vance."

The call ends, and I can't help the smile on my face. She's so cute. The past two months have gone well. Maddie and I have never gotten along better. I FaceTime with Francesca once a week. We've been building a real relationship for the first time in her life.

It took Sulley time, but she joined my last call. Francesca called her Aunt Sulley, and I thought Sulley would freak out, but she didn't. She's taking it all in stride.

I walk out to the living room, and both our families are sitting there happily chatting, enjoying their morning coffee.

Sulley looks at me. "Did she flip for the bike?"

I nod. "She certainly did."

Sulley appears nearly as excited as Francesca did as she walks over to me with a huge, flat gift. It looks like it could be a big picture frame.

I excitedly tear it open and am shocked by what I see. I look up at Sulley. "I've never seen this photo before."

She smiles. "I don't remember taking it. My mom found it in a box a few weeks ago, and I had it blown up."

It's a photo of me, Finn, and Sulley. It's the day we carved McShea Brothers into the tree. The day we started the cabin. We're right in front of the tree. She's on his shoulders. I think Finn and I were about sixteen, which would have made Sulley eight.

As I look closer, I realize Finn and I are looking at the camera, smiling, but Sulley is looking at me. Staring at me.

She realizes the moment I see it. "Even back then, I loved you, Vance. It's always been you. It will only ever be you."

I wrap my arms around her and bring my lips to hers and whisper, "I love it, and I love you."

MeeMaw hits my leg. "You should propose right now. It feels like the right moment."

Sulley and I smile into each other's mouths, and Sulley shakes her head. "Nope. Not until he wins the whole thing. Championship or bust, QB1. We'll see how much you really want it."

"No pressure," I sigh.

She laughs, and it's music to my ears.

I take her hand. "Come with me. It's time for your gift." I can't believe I pulled this off.

We walk toward the plastic that I know has been driving Sulley nuts. The space was done a week ago, but I had to make it outwardly look like the construction was still going on so she wouldn't go down there.

I tear it all away, and we walk down the stairs. "Just what I always wanted, a mancave," she says sarcastically.

I smack her ass. "Quiet woman, or I'll tie you up and leave you down here."

"Hmm, what will you do with me once I'm tied up?"

She's giggling at her own joke when we reach the bottom of the stairs. She gasps and then breathes, "Oh my god."

It's a full-length basketball court. There are photos covering the walls. They all revolve around basketball. Several are of her and Finn practicing together, and the rest are of her throughout the years up through their team championship photo this year. Nancy sent me some of the memorabilia she hung onto, which is now sitting on shelves in plastic casing. Some of her most important trophies, like her college basketball Player of the Year trophy and her WNBA Rookie of the Year trophy, are also sitting on shelves.

I point to the one open area. "I have a feeling there will be a lot more accolades coming. I left space for them."

She looks around with tears in her eyes. "What about your mancave? I thought you needed your own private space away from me."

I shake my head. "The last thing in the world I want is space away from you. I want you in my space all the time."

She wraps her arms around me and kisses my lips. "This is incredible. Thank you."

"You're welcome."

She toggles her head around the room. "I need to take it all in."

She walks over to the wall and starts carefully examining all the photos. As I knew she would, she looks closer to a frame that I know is unfamiliar to her. It's a sketch. A drawing of this very court signed *Finn's Fantastic Designs*. She turns to me with confusion written all over her face.

SIX YEARS AGO

I'm sitting in my condo in Philly with a nearly empty bottle of whiskey. I look in the mirror. My eyes look like I haven't slept in weeks. I don't think I have. I'm not sure I've slept in months. Not since he died.

Francesa was born two weeks ago. She was a huge baby. Everyone knew right away that she wasn't Finn's, and when the O'Sheas confronted Maddie, she confirmed it. The look of heartbreak on all three of their faces will forever haunt me. They thought they were going to have a piece of him, only to lose him all over again.

When I arrived at the hospital, my father begged me not to do it. How could I not? It was what Finn would have wanted. I owed him that much. I made a promise to him, one that I intend to live up to, no matter what it costs me.

I nearly vomited as the words left my mouth, telling them the baby was mine. The lie tasted so bitter that I wasn't sure they would believe it, but they did.

Frank punched me in the stomach. Nancy slapped me across the face. I welcomed the pain. But it was Sulley's face that devastated me the most. She hates me. She will forever hate me.

I sit down and look at the box Nancy sent me a few months ago. It's some of his belongings she thought I'd want. I haven't been able to muster up the courage to look through them, but I will now. Maybe there's something I can send them to lessen the pain. As if anything could.

I open the box and see a handful of photos of him and me. I'll cherish those forever. There's a jersey and a few other items from our youth. The box is otherwise full of rolled-up paper. What is all this?

As soon as I unroll the biggest one, I realize what it is. It's the house he was going to design for me. They're unfinished sketches, but it's very clearly what he and I had discussed I would want in a house. The bottom is signed, *Finn's Fantastic Designs.*

They're perfect. One day, I'm going to have the designs finished and build this house.

As I study them more carefully, I notice that the basement is unfinished. Besides a few measurements, there's nothing there. I guess he didn't get to it before he died. I wonder what he planned for that area. I guess I'll never know.

I flip through more sketches. One is of the cabin. It's an addition he planned to make there as his family grew. Family? Now he'll never have a wife or kids.

I squeeze my eyes shut as more tears fall. I feel like I lost him all over again. That's probably because I've lost the O'Sheas too. They've always been a second family to me, and now they're gone. No more shared family dinners. No more Christmases celebrated together.

I flip through more sketches until a folder catches my eye. It's titled *Basement Options.* Ah, this must be for that open space.

The first drawing is a traditional basement. The second is a game room. The third is a bowling alley. I smile. He loved to bowl. Most boring sport ever. We argued about that all the time. I'm convinced he did this one to fuck with me.

It's the fourth drawing that stands out. I pull it out and study it carefully. It's a basketball court. I wonder why he'd think I'd consider a basketball court in my house. I don't play.

THIRTY-THREE

SUPER BOWL SUNDAY

SULLEY

I wake in my hotel suite to a knock on the door. Quickly throwing on my robe over my pajamas, I make my way toward the door. Looking through the peephole, I see Vance standing there. What is he doing at my room? He's not supposed to have any contact outside of the team today. It's his big day.

I open the door in a rush and see him holding three dozen Chocolate Cosmos. Smiling, he says, "Happy Valentine's Day, beautiful."

Yep, the Super Bowl is on Valentine's Day this year.

I quickly pull him inside and check the hallway to make sure no one else is around. I close the door before he's noticed by anyone else. "You could get benched if someone sees you."

He rolls his eyes. "It took every ounce of restraint I had not to sneak in here last night and sink my face and cock into your pussy. If management wants me to play well, they should have encouraged *that*."

I bite my lower lip, feeling a flush crawl up my neck at his words, as I admit, "I wouldn't have minded it. After what you did to me behind the stage at the press conference, I was good to go, but we can't do this today."

My body tingles as I remember what his hands were doing to me under my dress with hundreds of reporters only a few feet away.

He places the flowers on the table, stands over me, and runs his index finger over my lower lip. "Are you telling me that you don't want me, baby?"

I swallow and croak out, "Nope."

He backs me to the wall and pins my wrists above my head with one of his big hands. With the other, he unfastens my robe. Running his finger gently over the swell of my breasts, he asks, "How about now?"

My breathing becomes labored. A throb starts to form between my legs. I can't spit out the lie, so I shake my head.

His finger makes a slow path between my breasts, down my stomach, and into my sleep shorts, over my panties. He cups my pussy but doesn't slip his finger into my panties like I'm suddenly gagging for. The pressure and heat of his hand feel like they're penetrating me. Lust coils throughout my entire body.

His lips move within a hairsbreadth of mine. I can smell his minty breath while also being cocooned in his unique Vance scent. The one that has never failed to make my heart race.

"What about now?" he commands. "I don't need to be in the lobby for another thirty minutes. Can you think of anything we could do in that timeframe?"

My body writhes, but I still manage to breathe, "N…no."

"Your panties are soaked, baby. I'm going to take them with me today and smell you during the game." His grip on my pussy tightens a drop and I'm a goner. I can't resist this man. His words and touch always get me.

I can feel him smile when I bring my lips to his before he deepens the kiss. I can't help but moan when his tongue meets mine. It's so sensual. I can feel it everywhere. God, I've missed him this week. He had to stay with the team and was subject to all kinds of fraternization rules. A few stolen moments with kisses and touches are all we've been able to manage. I'm like a ticking time bomb waiting to go off.

He makes quick work of my robe, pajamas, and panties. Before I know it, I'm naked and he's walking me backward toward the bedroom.

In a flash, I'm on my back, his mouth is around my nipple, and his fingers are inside me. In and out. I'm beyond sensitive, so starved for the love of my life.

He mumbles around my nipple, "I've missed you."

"Vance," I pant, "get the python inside me. Right now."

And he does.

WITH KEITH and a few extra bodyguards in tow, I make my way into the back VIP entrance of SoFi Stadium in Los Angeles, where I'm escorted to the private suite Vance and Daylen purchased for an ungodly sum of money. I can't get over what Super Bowl tickets cost, especially suites.

Trips to the Super Bowl don't come every year. This is the first of their career. They wanted to go all out for the big day, so that meant shelling out millions of dollars to secure a private suite for friends and family to enjoy the game. My parents, the McCaffreys, and the Humblecuts are already in there when I arrive. They're all happily eating, drinking, and engaged in conversation.

Seconds later, Kennedy comes waddling through the door looking murderous.

I bite back my smile. "You look good."

She narrows her eyes at me. "I look like a fucking beached whale. Ugh."

"You're eight months pregnant. You're supposed to look like this." Yep, Kennedy's pregnant, but that's a whole other story.

She exhales a long breath. "Don't remind me. Eleven people touched my belly on the way in. *Eleven*," she emphasizes. "It's super weird that strangers feel as though they have the full liberty to touch a pregnant woman's belly. Fuck that. It's a violation. Though I guess I'd rather they touch my belly than my hand."

"Why?" I ask.

"You know I've become a germophobe in my pregnancy. Think about people's hands. Just about every hand you've ever touched has had a dick in it. Let that thought marinate for a few minutes."

I spit in laughter but then consider it. "Wow, that's sort of true. I'll never not think of that when I shake someone's hand."

She nods. "Right?" She looks around and focuses her attention on all the roses and heart candies used to decorate the suite. "And it's Valentine's Day," she whines in a defeated tone. "I should be at a gym, scoping out the single guys. You know it's my favorite day to do that."

I look at her tummy, which has truly popped in the past two months. "I don't think you would have gotten much action."

She looks down at her belly. "Little fucking cockblocker. That's what I'm naming it. First name, Cock. Last name, Blocker."

I giggle. "It has a nice ring to it."

She smiles before looking me up and down. "Your outfit is fire. I wish I could fit into something like that."

I had calls from at least a hundred designers wanting to dress me for this game. It was ridiculous. The last thing I was interested in was high fashion. It's a football game. When a newer designer came up with something that incorporated Vance's jersey into it, I couldn't say no. And I like that me wearing it will put that new designer on the map. I'd rather help the underdog.

"I love it too."

"You should wear it in Vegas next month. I'm so bummed I won't get to go again this year. Last year was a blast."

"I can't believe it's been nearly a year since we were there." I pout. "It won't be the same without you this time."

She sighs. "I suppose." She looks around the suite. "Is Maddie here yet? I'm dying to meet this woman."

I shake my head. "They didn't end up coming. Francesca got the flu, but they created a signal for him to give her on camera. She's still the talk of the town after he mentioned her by name in his post-game interview on Christmas Day."

Vance's shoutout to Francesca after their big Christmas Day victory seemingly turned her into a star in their town. She was adorably over the moon about it. He sent signed McCaffrey jerseys to her entire class, much to the delight of every one of them. She's so proud that her uncle is a huge star.

No matter what he has going on, he doesn't miss their weekly call. I join most of those calls now. Vance has accepted her as an extension of Finn, so I've decided to put my animosity toward Maddie aside and do the same for the sake of Francesca, Vance, and Finn. I have to admit, she's a breath of fresh air. She's such a joyful, happy kid. We're going to visit her in a few weeks, and I'm going to do my best not to strangle Maddie.

"Bummer." She rubs her belly. "Let's get the show on the road. I don't want to go into labor during the fucking Super Bowl." She looks down at her belly and speaks to it. "Though your crazy daddy thinks it would be hysterical if I do."

VANCE

We're at the edge of the tunnel, about to be announced onto the field on the sport's biggest stage. I feel like I've been waiting for this moment my whole life. I'm so glad it didn't happen before. It needed to be now, when everything in my

life is finally falling into place. When I don't feel any outside pressure or stress. I get to soak it all in.

I stand with Daylen as we both find the suite containing our families. I can see everyone looking on with excitement written all over their faces.

He elbows me and asks, "You know what I realized this morning?"

"What?"

"That before women, life is like a penis. It's soft, simple, straight, and relaxed. Then a woman comes along and makes it hard."

I chuckle. "You're quite the philosopher."

He nods. "I know, right?"

I shake my head as Sulley's face pops into my mind. "Not me. Just the opposite. She makes everything easier."

With his eyes on the suite, he notices Sulley waving at me. I smile and wave back at my beautiful girl. He sighs, "When are you putting a ring on that?"

"We leave for Bora Bora next week. I've got a whole romantic thing on the beach planned out with the hotel's event coordinator. I want it to be special for her."

"What about you?"

"If it were up to me, it would already be a done deal. I'd fucking do it right here and now."

"Are you going to get on one knee?" he asks.

"Of course."

"Do you know why men get down on one knee to propose to women?"

I shrug. "I don't know. I assume it has something to do with begging?"

He shakes his head. "Nope. Think about where your head is. You're not proposing to the *woman*, you're proposing to her—"

I smack his arm. "Cut it out. You're going to ruin it for me. Fucking pervert," I mumble.

He lets out one of his big laughs.

After a bit more bizarre chitchat with my best friend, we're announced onto the field. It's surreal to be here. I want to take it all in. I don't know if I'll ever be here again.

AFTER BURNING OUR LAST TIMEOUT, the other team's offense sets up for a big third-down play. They're on our thirty-yard line. If they get a first down, they'll be able to run out the clock and secure their three-point victory. If they don't, they'll kick a field goal, giving them a six-point lead, and we'll get the ball back with less than a minute to drive the full length of the field. Either way, the odds aren't in our favor.

It's been a back-and-forth battle for the entire game. One team is going to run out of time, and it looks like it will be us. I'm trying not to lose faith, but it's hard to see the seconds of the clock tick down as if in slow motion. I can only watch from the sidelines, and there's nothing I can do about it.

They're most likely going to hand it off to the running back, wanting to burn more time off the clock. I silently pray for a miracle.

Fortunately for me, that miracle comes in the form of Beau Fudd. He breaks through the offensive line, seemingly untouched, and just as the quarterback is about to hand the ball off, Beau wraps his arms around him, taking him down. More importantly, the ball squirts loose.

Every single player on the field dives on top of it, undoubtedly fighting for that ball. There are twenty-two men currently piled on it. I have no idea who has the ball, but our entire bench is jumping up and down at the possibility it could be us. I can only imagine the fight going on at the bottom of that pile right now, but there's no one I want fighting for us more than Beau Fudd.

"Come on, Beau. Come on, Beau," I quietly whisper-plead to myself and the football gods.

The refs begin peeling the players away, one at a time. Every single person in this stadium, over seventy thousand people, is on their feet waiting for the outcome.

I can't see what's going on with all the players now circled around the fumble, but as we get to the final two, I see our guys jumping up and down in excitement before the head referee points his arm, indicating that it's Camels' ball. Our entire team and all our fans begin cheering wildly.

Coach grabs me by the facemask and brings his face to mine. "This is your time, McCaffrey." His green eyes bore into mine. "This is how legends are made. How heroes are born. Go be the hero and cement your legacy."

I nod as he releases my facemask, and I trot out onto the field, trying to temper my nerves. The ball is on our forty-yard line. We need about twenty to twenty-five yards to reasonably give Presley a chance to tie the game and send it into overtime, though the more yards we get, the more helpful it is to him. We need sixty yards for the touchdown, which would win the game in regulation.

A two-minute offense, which we call fourth quarter fever, consists of a series of smaller passing plays up the sideline aimed at gradually moving the ball up the field while giving the receiver an opportunity to step out of bounds, stopping the clock. The clock is our worst enemy right now, with only forty-four seconds remaining and no timeouts left.

Our plays are designed to give me a lot of options between our wide receivers, Daylen, and Champ, all running crossing routes. It's my job to find the most open man. It's fairly complicated, but my downfield vision and ability to find the open man have long been considered a strength.

Our opponent will give up the middle of the field, knowing we need to throw the ball toward the sidelines. They happily allow short passes up the middle, which will only serve to eat up the clock.

The ball is snapped, and I drop back in the pocket. I quickly check my first two options, but they're covered. Fuck, everyone is covered. Daylen changes course and runs through the middle of the field. I throw a fifteen-yard dime to him, and he catches the ball, dragging the defender an extra six yards along the way before he's brought down.

It gets us close to Presley's outer field goal range, but it didn't stop the clock. I wave my arm frantically to rush everyone to the line before I quickly spike the ball, stopping the clock with twenty-one seconds remaining.

After huddling my team to call the play, I stand under center. I see the other team stacking the line. They're blitzing me so I don't have time to find my second and third options. I call a quick audible, yelling, "Ricky right, Lucy left." It means that Champ will shorten his route to the right sideline, and Linc will shorten his to the left. Instead of running his route, Daylen will now stay back and block for me.

The ball is hiked. I can sense a defender coming up my blindside, but Daylen blocks him, giving me time to throw a quick pass to Linc, who steps out of bounds for a nine-yard gain, one short of the first down we needed.

There are now eleven seconds on the clock. It's third and one. The smart thing to do is to run the same play we just ran. Get a couple more yards for Presley and then step out of bounds with a few seconds remaining on the clock. If the pass is incomplete, the clock also stops, and Presley can go for the tie from where we are now.

The crowd is so loud. It's hard for me to hear the plays coming into the earpieces in my helmet. I cup my hands over my ears to listen for the play and can hardly believe my ears when it comes in. I turn my head to Coach. He nods. For over a decade, this man has always had faith in me. I refuse to let him down.

It's similar to the play we ran all those months ago, where I have both a long and short field option. Champ will not be in the backfield this time. They know we're not running the ball. The other difference is that this is the fucking Super Bowl. If we go for the long ball and miss, time will likely expire, and we'll lose. The season will be over, as might be my career and Coach's.

I quickly give the team the play. Daylen mouths, "Just throw it to me."

He's going to be triple-teamed. Throwing to Champ is the safer play.

I set Linc in motion to the right to draw the safeties away from Daylen and Champ.

I yell out hike and drop back in the pocket. Both Daylen and Linc are double-covered. One of their linemen comes charging at me, but I spin and scramble out of the pocket to my left side.

Every moment of football in my life comes flooding into my mind. Every backyard play with Finn when we were kids, where we'd act like we were in this very moment. I'd roll out, pretending I was being chased, he'd run all the way across the backyard, I'd throw the ball as far as I could, he'd catch it, and we'd jump around like crazy, acting like we won the Super Bowl.

I'm brought back to the present. Champ has a step on his man. It's now or never.

I turn my body and pump fake to Champ. One of the men covering Daylen bites, so I plant my feet and let the ball sail high into the evening sky.

I'm immediately knocked to the ground by one of their linemen, but I roll so I can see what happens in the end zone. It's like a movie, with the ball flying through the starry sky in slow motion. It's a perfect spiral on a collision course with both Daylen and his one remaining defender. It's going to be a matter of who wants it more.

I look up at the clock. Time has expired. We will either win or lose this game right now. A tie and overtime are no longer an option.

Thousands of flashes go off. I hold my breath as both men jump up high for the ball. Both get their hands on it, but Daylen gets the edge, grabbing the ball and dragging his toes inbounds before falling out of the back of the end zone and landing on the ground.

I look to the back judge, the referee in the end zone. He holds up his arms in the air, indicating a touchdown.

The entire stadium erupts in excitement. It's pandemonium. Nearly everyone rushes to the end zone while one of my offensive linemen helps me up. Daylen, being Daylen, does a little airplane move, running away from the team before he stops and does a whole dance routine.

I laugh at his antics as I make my way to him and jump onto him, as does everyone else on the team.

THE LAST TWENTY minutes have been madness. There are people everywhere. Green confetti blankets the field. Every player, coach, and reporter has been all over me. Television cameras are shoved in my face. My head is spinning. All I really want is my family and Sulley. I'm sure they're being escorted down to the field now.

I see my parents first. I hug them and they tell me how proud they are of me. And then I see my girl, hanging back, giving me my moment with my parents.

Our eyes meet, and she cracks a small smile. I just had the biggest moment of my professional life, and all I can think is that it wouldn't have meant anything if she weren't here with me.

She looks sexy as sin. She's in some version of my jersey that I've never seen before. It's like someone took several of my jerseys and created a sexier, more fashionable version of them. Designers were clamoring to dress her for this game, knowing she'd be on camera all the time. She's wearing high boots in Camels' green. She's so hot.

I begin to approach her. I'm aware of hundreds of flashes going off, but I don't care.

As she gets closer, I hear her say, "Nice throw, nineteen."

I crack a smile. "Thanks, twenty-two."

It's not lost on me that this was how Finn and I communicated, and she's never once before called me by my number. I know he's here in spirit, relishing this moment as much as I am.

My arms immediately wrap around her, and my lips find hers. I can't begin to count how many flashes go off.

"I'm so proud of you," she whispers into my mouth before our lips break apart.

I smile down at her. "I'm proud of me too."

She shrugs her shoulders and exhales a long breath. "I guess I owe you."

I pinch my eyebrows together. "What do you mean?"

The corners of her sexy red lips rise in amusement. "I told you I'd marry you if and when you won a Super Bowl." She drops down to one knee and takes my hand in hers. "A promise is a promise."

If I thought thousands of flashes were going off before, I was wrong. Now it feels like a million, but I pay them no attention.

I smile as I mumble, "This is supposed to be my role."

She looks up at me with all the love in the world. "I told you, I only marry champions. How about we both walk away with rings tonight?"

EPILOGUE

EIGHT YEARS LATER

SULLEY

I see Vance and Finn approach our stables on top of SoFi, Vance's horse. They're both in jeans, flannel shirts, cowboy hats, and cowboy boots because Finn wants to be just like his daddy all the time. Vance's big arms keep Finn's little body safe as he's seated in front of Vance with a huge smile on his adorable face.

Finneas O'Shea McCaffrey was born nearly five years ago. We never discussed what his name would be. We both just knew. Boy or girl, Finneas or Finnley, it was always going to be Finn.

Two years later, our daughter arrived. Hazel O'Shea McCaffrey was named after MeeMaw, who passed just before Hazel was born.

I was fortunate in my ability to get pregnant exactly when we planned it, always between my seasons. I never had to miss a single game. Because I have the best husband on the planet, I still don't have to miss a single game.

After a then-toddler Finn saw his father win his second Super Bowl, Vance decided it was time to retire. He helps coach at a local high school when he can, manages a real estate portfolio, and runs the Finn O'Shea Foundation, which helps families who have lost a loved one in the line of duty with both their emotional and financial needs.

I'm holding an anxious Hazel as our boys approach. She's reaching for Vance, ready for her turn on SoFi.

Vance's eyes meet mine, and my heart does a somersault, just like it always has when I see him. He tips his hat as his eyes move up and down my body. "Howdy, ma'am. You're looking rather edible today."

"What are you gonna do about it, QB1?"

He licks his luscious lips. "We've got a long plane ride in the morning. I'm sure I'll think of something."

I can feel my body flush with thoughts of what I know will happen on that plane tomorrow.

We're leaving in the morning for Montana. Since Vance retired, we spend most of November and all of December at the cabin, which we've added to. Apparently, Finn left plans for an addition, and we've seen them through. The kids spend a few days with each of our parents, giving us our own time at the cabin, and then we spend time there as a family, completely unplugged from society. I know we won't be able to spend as much time there when Finn and Hazel enter real school, but I want to take advantage of it while I can. Once I retire, we'll spend our summers there, but I'm not ready to hang up my high-tops quite yet. No matter what, we'll always find time to spend up there. It's too special not to.

Francesca usually spends a week with us too. She's a teenager now, but she and Vance have maintained a special relationship I know he cherishes.

I trade kids with Vance and instruct Finn to go clean SoFi's stall in the stables. He happily obliges, loving anything that has to do with the horses. We have two of them. For now. Finn has been begging for his own, and we might get him one this year for his birthday.

Shortly after we got married, we had the stables built on our property along with a fenced-in area for the horses to graze. We have a worker who tends to it all, but we want the kids to learn some responsibility. We told Finn he wouldn't get a horse until he proved he could take care of one. He's out there every day working hard, making his case.

Vance and Hazel take off into the woods for her short ride. I smile as I hear her giggling from a hundred feet away.

My FaceTime rings, and I look down at it. I immediately accept my best friend's call. "Hey, babe."

Kennedy smiles into the screen. "Hi. Are you flying out today?"

I shake my head. "No. Tomorrow."

"Ahh. I mixed days. They're all the same when you're on a Caribbean island. Every day is piña colada day."

I smile. "How's the big, blended family trip?"

"Great. It's like crazy on steroids. We're taking up half of this place. The weather has been beautiful, and they have a kids' camp. We're free to get our drink and freak on all day."

I giggle. "Sounds perfect for you."

She wiggles her eyebrows. "It is. I wanted to catch you before you left." She makes a look of disgust. "I hate when you go to Montana. It's like a third-world country without any reception."

"That's my favorite part of it."

I suddenly hear a loud, grinding noise. "What's that?" I ask.

She leans forward, and the noise turns off. "Sorry. I was making a Beau Fudd boner shake. I'm feeling extra frisky today. I need a good pounding…and I love fucking with him."

I let out a laugh. "Don't break anything…or anyone."

She winks. "We'll see." She leans in and whispers, "I left out a super tight bathing suit for him to wear today." She lets out a laugh. "Just wait until the boner shake I'm secretly slipping into his morning smoothie kicks in. There will be nowhere to hide that thing."

I smile as I shake my head. "Always causing trouble."

She nods. "Hell yes. Anyway, have a good time. I'll see you at our January practices and workouts. Love you."

"Love you too."

VANCE

I suck Sulley's nipple into my mouth while she rides me without any inhibition. This is my favorite way to wake up. I can't help but stare at my beautiful wife, so thankful for her and the life we have. It's perfect, just like her.

We're up at the cabin. The kids have been at their grandparents' all week, but they're coming back today, and we're celebrating Thanksgiving up here. We renovated the kitchen along with the addition so Sulley and her mom can keep up their holiday cooking traditions. Something my mother has happily joined.

I'm particularly looking forward to this year. We have a special surprise for our families.

"Oh god, so good," she yells as she pulls on my hair.

I miss my kids, but when they're gone, Sulley can be her loud self. I love it.

I grab her hips and grind her back and forth over me. "Bounce on this cock, baby. You own it. Come all over it. I want to feel your juices everywhere and then watch you lick them off me."

Her eyelids flutter as she gives up control to me, trusting that I'll give her exactly what she needs.

And I do. Within a minute or two, she comes violently and loudly. She's so sexy.

I slow things down and let her bask in her post-orgasmic

bliss. After a few moments, I breathe into her mouth, "I don't want you to move. Milk me."

Her lips meet mine as she clenches the way she knows I need over and over, bringing me to orgasm in no time.

"WHERE ARE WE GOING?" my father asks for the tenth time as we all hike through the new path in the woods behind our cabin.

I've got Hazel on my shoulders, and Finn is bouncing up and down, knowing what's coming. He's so damn cute. I might sound like an egomaniac, but I love having a mini-me. He looks like me and acts like me, though fortunately, he got Sulley's brains. I might have two Super Bowl rings, but being a father is by far my greatest achievement in life. My friends like to make fun of me and call me a stay-at-home dad, but I love every second of being there for my kids. It's the only way Sulley could continue to do what she does on the basketball court. She has peace of mind knowing I'm with them when she can't be. She's the best mom in the world, and I can't wait to continue to grow our family.

Frank scoops up Finn into his arms. "Did you know that your namesake loved telling me all his secrets? In fact, I've got a chocolate bar back at the cabin that's all yours if you tell me where we're going."

Finn giggles. "Nope. Daddy said you'd offer me candy, Grandpa. He's letting me do something special if I keep the secret."

I fist bump him. "Good man."

He smiles with pride before looking at my father-in-law again and asking, "What does edible mean, Grandpa?"

Frank looks down at him. "Something that's good to eat, why?"

Finn twists his face in obvious confusion. "Daddy told Mommy that she's edible."

I snort out a laugh while Sulley immediately grabs Finn and covers his mouth. "Shh. Stand, be quiet, and look pretty, just like your Daddy is supposed to."

Our mothers giggle, and I can't help but smile at my wife, who is most definitely not smiling right now.

We hit the clearing, and two new cabins come into view. Mom looks at me. "What's this?"

Sulley nods at Finn. "You can tell them now. Unzip your jacket pocket."

Finn unzips his pocket and pulls out two keys, handing one to my mom and one to Nancy. "Mommy and Daddy made you cabins so you can be near us when we visit."

Dad pinches his eyebrows together. "What do you mean they made us cabins?"

I smile. "We had them built for you. One for each family. All Finn O'Shea designs. Finn junior, that is." I wink at Finn. "Right, buddy?"

Finn nods enthusiastically. "Mommy and Daddy let me help. I drawed the cabins." He pulls his drawings out of his other pocket and unfolds them. "I drawed them, and then Mommy and Daddy's friend built cabins just like my drawings. Except they couldn't find purple wood like in my pictures. Besides that, they're the exact same."

Maybe not *exactly* the same, but as close as we could have reasonably done. Finn has some talent when it comes to drawing and being imaginative, but he's not even five yet. He did come to every meeting with the architects and engineers. He was fascinated by the process. I hope he becomes an architect like his uncle should have been.

Mom looks at us with eyes full of emotion. "You didn't need to do this."

I shake my head. "I'd like for you guys to spend more time up here with us when we're in town, or even when we're not, but you need your own space, and we plan to grow our family. We won't have the extra room for long."

Nancy gasps. "Are you pregnant again?"

Sulley holds up her hands. "Calm down. I'm not pregnant, but we'd like to start trying again next year."

Mom and Nancy grin like fools at each other. They live for the grandkids. They visit much more often since Finn and Hazel were born.

We walk up toward the cabin, where they all take notice of the giant oak tree sitting between the houses. I had the rest of the trees around the cabins cleared and then recycled to be used to build the cabins, but I left this tree. The inscription reads, *Finn's Fantastic Designs.*

THE END

To enjoy an extended epilogue, a glimpse into Sulley and Vance's wedding day:

ACKNOWLEDGMENTS

To Sulley and Vance: My post-Extra Innings series hangover was real, but… then I fell madly in love with you two. Way to kick off the new series (and make my cry ugly tears)!

To the Queen, TL Swan: This amazing journey would never have begun if not for you and your selfless decision to help hundreds of women. You are a shining example of the girl power quotes I place in each dedication. This crazy and unexpected new path in my life has brought me so much happiness. I owe it all to you. Please know that I try every single day to pay it forward.

To Lakshmi, Thorunn, Mindy, and Brittany: You're my daily sounding boards. You are my beta bitches and "porn friends." Your constant advice, counsel, guidance, and therapy keep me sane. Thank you for being such *good girls* and supporting me.

To Jade Dollston, Carolina Jax, and L.A. Ferro: You are my bookish besties. Our daily texts are my lifeline. I love the support we have for each other.

To The B!tch Squad Members: Thank you for supporting me in every new avenue. Knowing my characters mean so much to you keeps me going on those hard days. There's not a single second that I don't appreciate everything you do.

To Chrisandra and K.B. Designs: **Chrisandra**: Thank you for making me feel illiterate. That's what makes you such a great editor. Thank you for GIFs indicating that you want to unalive me for using italics on song names. **Kristin**: Thank you for helping this artistically challenged woman who doesn't know what she wants but does. You know what I mean.

To My Family: I truly feel bad for you. An immature mother and wife can't be easy. To my daughters, thank you for tolerating me (ish). Thank you for telling everyone you know that your mom writes sex books. I appreciate that by the time you were each six, you were more mature than me. To my handsome husband, thank you for your blind support. You never question my sanity, which can't be easy. But let's face it, you do reap the benefits of the fact that I write sex scenes all day long.

ABOUT THE AUTHOR

AK Landow lives in the USA with her husband. Her three daughters have grown into the type of magnificent women she writes about. AK enjoys spending time with her family, reading, writing, drinking copious amounts of vodka, and laughing. She's thrilled to have this crazy avenue to channel her perverted, age-inappropriate sense of humor. She is also of the belief that Beth Dutton is the greatest fictional character ever created.

AKLandowAuthor.com

ALSO BY AK LANDOW

City of Sisterly Love Series

Knight: Book 1 Darian and Jackson

Dr. Harley: Book 2 Harley and Brody

Cass: Book 3 Cassandra and Trevor

Daulton: Book 4 Reagan and Carter

About Last Knight: Book 5 Melissa and Declan

Love Always, Scott: Prequel Novella Darian and Scott

Quiet Knight: Novella Jess and Hayden

Belles of Broad Street Series

Conflicting Ventures: Book 1 Skylar and Lance

Indecent Ventures: Book 2 Jade and Collin

Unexpected Ventures: Book 3 Beth and Dominic

Enchanted Ventures: Book 4 Amanda and Beckett

Extra Innings Series

Double Play: Arizona and Layton

CurveBall: Ripley and Quincy

Payoff Pitch: Bailey and Tanner

Off Season: Kamryn and Cheetah

Faking the Book Boyfriend: Gemma and Trey (Published as part of
the Book Boyfriend Builders collaboration)

Fourth Quarter Fever Series

Home Town Advantage: Sulley and Vance

Competitive Advantage: Kennedy and Daylen

Overtime Advantage: Fallon and Jett

Grand Advantage: Palmer and Beau

Signed Books: aklandowauthor.com